1001 Dark Nights
Compilation 15

1001 Dark Nights
Compilation 15

Four Novellas
By
Larissa Ione
Lexi Blake
Rebecca Zanetti
and
J. Kenner

1001 Dark Nights

EVIL EYE
CONCEPTS

1001 Dark Nights: Bundle 15
ISBN 978-1-948050-47-0

Razr: A Demonica Underworld Novella
By Larissa Ione
Copyright 2017 Larissa Ione

Arranged: A Masters and Mercenaries Novella
By Lexi Blake
Copyright 2017 DLZ Entertainment, LLC

Tangled: A Dark Protectors—Reese Family Novella
By Rebecca Zanetti
ISBN: 978-1-945920-13-4

Hold Me: A Stark International Novella
By J. Kenner
Copyright 2017 Julie Kenner

Foreword: Copyright 2014 M. J. Rose

Published by Evil Eye Concepts, Incorporated

Sign up for the 1001 Dark Nights Newsletter
and be entered to win a Tiffany Key necklace.

There's a contest every month!

Go to www.1001DarkNights.com to subscribe.

As a bonus, all subscribers will receive a free copy of
Discovery Bundle Three
Featuring stories by
Sidney Bristol, Darcy Burke, T. Gephart
Stacey Kennedy, Adriana Locke
JB Salsbury, and Erika Wilde

Table of Contents

One Thousand and One Dark Nights

Once upon a time, in the future…

*I was a student fascinated with stories and learning.
I studied philosophy, poetry, history, the occult, and
the art and science of love and magic. I had a vast
library at my father's home and collected thousands
of volumes of fantastic tales.*

*I learned all about ancient races and bygone
times. About myths and legends and dreams of all
people through the millennium. And the more I read
the stronger my imagination grew until I discovered
that I was able to travel into the stories... to actually
become part of them.*

*I wish I could say that I listened to my teacher
and respected my gift, as I ought to have. If I had, I
would not be telling you this tale now.
But I was foolhardy and confused, showing off
with bravery.*

*One afternoon, curious about the myth of the
Arabian Nights, I traveled back to ancient Persia to
see for myself if it was true that every day Shahryar
(Persian: □□□□□, "king") married a new virgin, and then
sent yesterday's wife to be beheaded. It was written
and I had read, that by the time he met Scheherazade,
the vizier's daughter, he'd killed one thousand
women.*

Something went wrong with my efforts. I arrived in the midst of the story and somehow exchanged places with Scheherazade — a phenomena that had never occurred before and that still to this day, I cannot explain.

Now I am trapped in that ancient past. I have taken on Scheherazade's life and the only way I can protect myself and stay alive is to do what she did to protect herself and stay alive.

Every night the King calls for me and listens as I spin tales. And when the evening ends and dawn breaks, I stop at a point that leaves him breathless and yearning for more. And so the King spares my life for one more day, so that he might hear the rest of my dark tale.

As soon as I finish a story... I begin a new one... like the one that you, dear reader, have before you now.

Razr
A Demonica Underworld Novella
By Larissa Ione

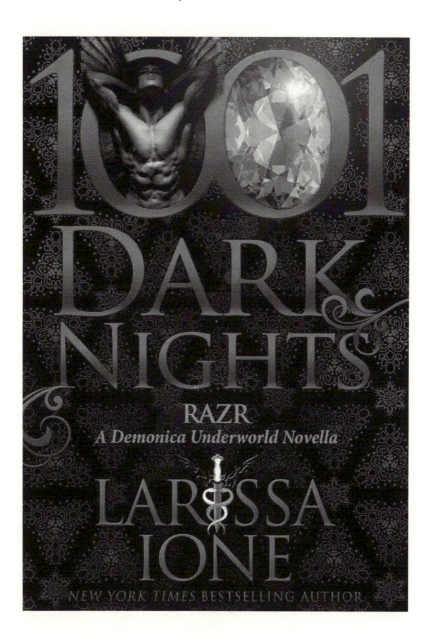

Acknowledgments from the Author

I just want to send a million thank-you's to the entire Evil Eye team. You are like family to me, and I love you dearly! I can't wait to see you all next time!

And to my readers, I just want to thank you for sticking with me on this journey. I promise you, it's just getting started and there is a LOT more to come...

Glossary

Faeway—Mystical "hotspots" in the human realm that elves can use to travel to and from their home realm.

Fallen Angel--Believed to be evil by most humans, fallen angels can be grouped into two categories: True Fallen and Unfallen. Unfallen angels have been cast from Heaven and are earthbound, living a life in which they are neither truly good nor truly evil. In this state, they can, rarely, earn their way back into Heaven. Or they can choose to enter Sheoul, the demon realm, in order to complete their fall and become True Fallens.

Harrowgate--Vertical portals, invisible to humans, used to travel between locations on Earth and Sheoul. A very few beings can summon their own personal Harrowgates.

Inner Sanctum—A realm within Sheoul-gra that consists of five Rings, each housing the souls of demons categorized by their level of evil as defined by the Ufelskala. The Inner Sanctum is run by the fallen angel Hades and his staff of wardens, all fallen angels. Access to the Inner Sanctum is strictly limited, as the demons imprisoned within can take advantage of any outside object or living person in order to escape.

Memitim—Sired exclusively by Azagoth, Memitim are earthbound angels assigned to protect important humans called Primori. Memitim remain earthbound until they complete their duties, at which time they Ascend, earning their wings and entry into Heaven.

Primori—Humans and demons whose lives are fated to affect the world in some crucial way.

Sheoul--Demon realm some call Hell. Located on its own plane deep in the bowels of the Earth, accessible to most only by Harrowgates and hellmouths.

Sheoul-gra--A realm that exists independently of Sheoul, it is overseen by Azagoth, also known as the Grim Reaper. Within Sheoul-gra is the Inner Sanctum, where demon souls go to be kept in torturous limbo until they can be reborn.

Ufelskala—A scoring system for demons, based on their degree of evil. All supernatural creatures and evil humans can be categorized into the five Tiers, with the Fifth Tier comprising of the worst of the wicked.

Chapter One

Inside the confines of his boss's office, demons swirled in the air all around Razr. The screaming, tortured souls begged for mercy or shouted obscenities and threats.

Razr tapped the ring on his right index finger against his thigh as Azagoth, an ancient being also known as the Grim Reaper, sent tiny bursts of power at each one, making them screech in agony.

Azagoth was playing with them, toying with them the way a cat would a mouse. His plush office, deep inside the underworld realm known as Sheoul-gra, had turned into a grim playground of pain.

Pain was something Razr could deal with. Subservience was not, and after hundreds of years spent as an elite battle angel, being sentenced to serve Azagoth was humiliating as shit. But it was Razr's own fault, and ultimately, he was lucky. After all, he'd been kicked out of Heaven, but he hadn't lost his wings.

No, his angelic wings and their fate would be determined by whether or not he could repair the damage he'd done a century ago.

So, yeah. Hanging out with Azagoth and his band of freaky minions wasn't exactly a great gig, but it could be worse. Still, as he stood across from Azagoth, who looked especially Grim Reaper-y in a black hooded robe, his green eyes glowing from the shadows, Razr didn't see how it could be worse at this particular moment.

Azagoth flicked his hand in dismissal, and a wave of *griminions* swarmed into the room like ants, their own miniature black robes dragging on the floor, their faces hidden by cowls. They gathered the demon souls and scurried away, disappearing into a tunnel in the wall to whatever hellhole they belonged in. When Azagoth turned his attention to Razr, the chill that settled on Razr's skin quickly penetrated all the way to his bones.

"I want to know why you wear a damned burlap sack and flip-flops every damned day. You have access to anything you want, but the only times you aren't dressed like a medieval monk are when you leave Sheoul-gra." Azagoth cocked his head and intensified his focus, leaving Razr feeling like a germ under a microscope. "Is the clothing part of your punishment?"

Razr started. He'd been living in Sheoul-gra and working in Azagoth's employ for over a year now, and this was the first time his boss had asked him anything that wasn't work-related.

"Yes," Razr said, but it was a simple answer to a complex issue.

"Your situation is unique. You aren't fallen, but you aren't a Heavenly angel, either. You aren't even Unfallen," Azagoth said, referring to the in-between state of an angel who had lost his wings but who hadn't entered Sheoul, the demon realm, to complete his fall from grace. He glided over to the wet bar and splashed rum into two glasses. "Heaven created a new designation of angel just for you."

"Yeah," Razr drawled. "Ain't I special." Except he wasn't. There was another who had shared his status, his former lover Darlah, presumed dead after failing to return from a mission.

A mission that was now Razr's alone.

Azagoth handed him one of the glasses, and Razr struggled to hide his surprise. And suspicion. The other male rarely acknowledged his existence, let alone treated him like an equal. "For some reason, you *are* special."

This was really getting weird. Azagoth had never shown any interest in him, but honestly, Razr was shocked that the guy didn't know more about Razr's story. He'd figured Heaven would have given Azagoth the full scoop, but apparently not.

"What I can't figure out," Azagoth continued, "is why you haven't managed to take care of your business and get back into Heaven."

Unable to remain still under this bizarre scrutiny, Razr swirled the rum around in his glass. "It's not like you give me a lot of free time."

"So it's my fault?" Azagoth's voice was smooth as velvet and just dark enough to raise the hair on Razr's head. One didn't just accuse the Grim Reaper of stalling shit. Not if they liked wearing their skin.

"Not at all," Razr replied carefully, because his skin was pretty useful right where it was. "It's just that I have limited resources in Sheoul-gra. I need more time in the human and demon realms."

Instead, he was stuck training Azagoth's army of Memitim and the Unfallen refugees who had taken sanctuary here. Although, in truth, if Razr *had* to work for Azagoth, schooling angels on battle tactics wasn't the suckiest thing he could do. It was a challenge he enjoyed, given that angels were notoriously hard to get to work together, and his specialty was teamwork.

He'd just rather be training angels in Heaven than in Hell.

The door to the office opened, and Zhubaal, Azagoth's right-hand man and Razr's direct superior, escorted a broad-shouldered male who smelled of sunshine inside. The angel, a big bastard in a plain brown hooded robe who went by the code name of Jim Bob, strode past Azagoth and stopped in front of Razr, which was odd, considering the angel tended to keep conversation limited to Azagoth.

Which probably meant he wasn't being straight with his fellow angels about his business here. Razr had never met the guy in Heaven, so he had no idea of Jim Bob's real name or what his game was, but if Razr was ever reinstated as a full angel, he'd have to do some investigating.

"What happened to your head?"

Razr jammed his fingers through his short, dark hair. "What, you liked the bald look better?"

"Yes. Also, this is for you." He held out a thick gold business card embossed with silver letters that spelled out "The Wardens."

"What is it?"

"It's where you'll find what you're looking for."

Razr stopped breathing even as his heart revved from a sudden injection of hope-fueled adrenaline. He stared at the silver letters as if they were a lifeline and he was drowning. "Are...are you sure?"

"I have it on good authority."

Razr's hand shook so hard he nearly dropped the card. This was it. The way to repair some, if not all, of the damage he and his teammates caused when they'd lost three of Heaven's most valuable weapons, the Gems of Enoch, and got their human custodians killed. One gem, the Terra Amethyst, had been recovered, but two remained: Darlah's Fire Garnet and Razr's Ice Diamond.

Finding either or both would return Razr to full angel status and erase the stain on his reputation...and his soul.

Azagoth, clearly knowing what Razr was thinking, nodded. "Go," he said. "Take as much time as you need."

Razr sucked in a stunned breath, but really, he shouldn't be all that shocked. Azagoth might have a reputation for cruelty, but he was generous with those who were loyal to him. Razr was about to thank him when the angel wing glyph on the back of his hand, usually invisible, began to glow. Fuck. It had been less than twenty-four hours since the last time. He usually got thirty-six, give or take a couple of hours, to recover. Although once he'd gone barely eight. The random nature of this particular angelic punishment was a pain in the ass.

"That was shitty timing." Azagoth, the King of Demon Souls and Understatements, pulled a well-worn cat-o'-nines out of his desk drawer. Because, of course, one must always be prepared for spur-of-the-moment torture. He held up the weapon with way too much enthusiasm. "Mine or yours?"

Razr's personal flogger was in his pocket, and he swore he felt it burning through his robes. "Yours," he muttered, figuring it was always better to get someone else's stuff bloody.

Azagoth held the cat out to Jim Bob. "Want the honor?"

Razr bit back a groan as the angel took the weapon and stroked it like an old lover. "It's been a long time."

"Really?" Razr said. "Because you seem like the type who gets off on torture." It was a stupid thing to say to someone who was far more powerful and who was about to turn Razr's back into hamburger, but he'd never been known for his tact.

Jim Bob, who rarely even smiled, laughed. Clearly, the guy's sense of humor circled the gallows. Razr would respect that if he weren't the one swinging at the end of the rope. "Will you stand or kneel?"

"Well," he drawled as he dropped his robe so he was standing naked in front of Azagoth, Jim Bob, and Zhubaal, "I figure I'll start on my feet and end on my knees. That's usually how it goes."

Jim Bob made a "turn-around" gesture, and after taking a deep, steadying breath, Razr assumed the position, bracing himself against the wall with his palms. "How many?"

"Six," Azagoth said before Razr could answer. "I don't know why."

"I do." Jim Bob's soft reply hung in the air and reeled through Razr's mind. How did Jim Bob know? Sure, everyone in Heaven probably knew about Razr's screw-up with the Gems of Enoch, but few were privy to the specifics of his punishment. The guy must be well connected in Heaven, which only added to the mystery of his dealings with Azagoth.

The whistle of the nine leather straps, each tipped by sharp bone spurs singing through the air, interrupted Razr's thoughts. Pain exploded across his shoulder blades and forced a grunt from him. But not a scream. He never screamed.

The second blow was worse, the third so intense that he sagged to his knees. Usually he could stay on his feet until the fifth strike, but Jim Bob was strong, and he wasn't holding back. That was the thing about floggings in the angel and demon worlds versus the human one; Razr could take hundreds of lashings from a human. Hell, he could take thousands and not die.

But when someone with superior strength and mystical capabilities was wielding the whip, the damage increased by a factor of *holy shit*.

The fourth blow knocked the breath from his lungs, and the fifth made him see stars.

The sixth, placed low on his hips, knocked him onto the cold floor, sprawled in a pool of his own blood.

Maybe this was the last time. *Please let this be the last time*, he thought, just before he passed out.

Chapter Two

"Ma'am, pardon my French, but you're full of shit. There are no fucking deposits here. No Taaffeite has ever been found in Madagascar. This is a waste of time and a waste of a fuckton of money. I don't care about your credentials. Like I said, you're full of shit."

Jedda Brighton resisted the urge to punch the man in his unshaven, saggy face the way she'd been wanting to do for the last two weeks. Two weeks of putting up with the mining engineer's alcohol-fueled crude talk and casual sexism, which he blew off as her being an oversensitive snowflake when she called him on it. Two weeks of watching him treat the local diggers like slaves. Two weeks of listening to him bitch about his "whore of an ex-wife" and "outrageous" child support. He was the type of asshole who, if a woman turned down his advances, would accuse her of being a lesbian.

Because sure, didn't all women love an overweight, abusive slob who looked and smelled like a walking hangover and who thought he was God's gift to women? If not for his considerable wealth, no woman would put up with him, and he either didn't know that, or he didn't care, which made him either stupid, or scum, or both.

Jedda was going to go with both. Hell, she wouldn't put up with him for even this job if it weren't for the fact that she needed him to dig for gems she couldn't otherwise reach on her own.

"First of all," she said in her snootiest voice, "I'm fluent in a dozen languages, including French, and what you just said wasn't even close. Second, I'm the best damned gemologist *and* mineralogist in the world, and if I say there's a bloody fortune in

Taaffeite here, you can rest assured that there is." She smiled sweetly. "And after you find it, you can shove it up your ass."

He waggled sandy brows that glistened with sweat from the oppressive heat in this godforsaken jungle. "How about you do it for me?"

Sweet Satie One-Eye, he was disgusting, and even Satie, an elf hero of lore who had fought giant demonic maggots, would agree. This guy was a whisky dick personified. Adjusting her hard hat, Jedda stepped around him and headed inside the mine. "You really don't want to taunt me."

"Taunt...or tempt?"

Ugh. Gross. In the last two weeks, had this idiot not figured out that she didn't play well with others? Especially not *human* others? She supposed she should at least be grateful he wasn't aware that she wasn't human, but then, maybe if he knew she was an immortal being he'd leave her alone.

She might have to reveal her secret just to freak him out.

He followed her down the relatively cool shaft, past workers who were busy extracting gemstones that, while less valuable than Taaffeite, would still net Tom's mining company a nice profit. But he still played the injured party, insisting that this venture was a waste of time and resources.

She knew better. As a gem elf, she could sense minerals that gave off energy undetectable to humans, energy that she survived on. Enchanted stones, gems that had been blessed or cursed or used in powerful rituals, were the most life-enhancing, especially when absorbed into a gem elf's body, but there was always a risk involved when using them, as she knew very well.

Her boots crunched down on uneven ground, but she kept her footing, her enhanced reflexes and night vision giving her a distinct advantage over humans and most demons. Tom followed her much more slowly, cursing now and then, muttering his displeasure at being bested by a woman. She had no doubt he was generally capable in situations like this as long as he kept to a safe human pace, but his macho attitude wouldn't let him lag behind, and he had no idea she was genetically suited for this exact situation.

She laughed when she heard him trip and fall. "You okay?" she called back. "I can slow down if you need me to."

"I'm fine," he barked, and she laughed again at his volley of obscenities. What an asshole.

She kept going, reaching out with her senses as she navigated the dark tunnels. She could feel the elemental vibrations change as she passed each new mineral, some of them leaving no more impression on her than common gravel, others whispering to her like potential lovers. But none of them possessed the special signature of the Taaffeite. Still, she was close. She couldn't quite feel the deposit yet, but she could smell it, a faint anise and berry tang in the musty earth that made her mouth water. Every gemstone had its own unique scent, some spicy, some sweet, and Taafeite was a delectable combination of both.

What felt like a cool breeze tickled her skin from an unexplored tunnel on the right. It was narrow, with jagged stones jutting from the sides like a giant cheese grater. Carefully, she went to her hands and knees and started to crawl.

"Hold up there, sweetheart," Tom called out. "My men haven't reinforced this yet, and I'm not about to—"

"Shut up!" She paused, inhaled, tasting the sharp bite of beryllium and aluminum on the back of her tongue. "It's here," she breathed excitedly.

Giddy with anticipation, she turned up the intensity of the light on her helmet, and there, just ahead in a space big enough to stand, was a glint of violet peeking out of the boring gray and brown stone all around it.

Grinning, she scrambled the remaining distance in the crawlspace, and when she stood, she marveled at the sight of a thick vein of one of the rarest gemstones in the world. There was another vein near the ceiling, and she could sense more deep in the walls. She doubted there was more than about seven hundred carats' worth of Taaffeite here, but at around three to four thousand dollars per carat on the human market and double that on the demon one, the stones would net a respectable haul. And because it was so rare, adding even a hundred carats to the market would increase the value and the demand since right now few knew about it, and those who did were collectors.

Very carefully, she plucked a chisel from her gear belt and dug a jagged hunk of stone from the surrounding rock. Under the light from her helmet, the purple gem glittered, even with all the rough material coating it. Its aura glowed with stunning intensity, something the obnoxious human crawling toward her wouldn't be able to see.

She closed her fist around the gem and inhaled, letting its vibrations absorb into her body. Power pounded through her, making her flesh throb and her blood surge. This was a natural stone, untouched by anyone, so its energy was pure, neutral, and unenhanced. It would give her added strength and stamina, but it wouldn't add or subtract from any of her special abilities.

It was, in the simplest of terms, life.

Tom emerged from the tunnel like a grumpy bear awakened from hibernation. "What are you doing?" As he stood, dirt cascaded off him in a choking cloud of dust.

She opened her fist. The gem was gone, the earth and rock that had surrounded it nothing but crumbs in her palm. "I'm admiring my find," she said, letting the remains fall to the floor of the cave.

As he studied a vein of Taaffeite, she dug another, about the size of her thumb, from a crevice nearby.

"Nice work, honey," he said, talking directly at her breasts. "I'm impressed. Everyone said you're the best. Should have listened."

"Yes, you should have." She turned toward the tunnel to escape this cretin, and as she did, he slapped her on the ass. Instant, searing rage welled in her chest, and fuck it, she was done with his shit. Her anger destroyed the tight control she kept on herself, and suddenly the cave lit up with the soft, iridescent glow emanating from her skin. She knew her eyes, normally ice blue, were glowing as well, still blue, but more intense.

"What the fuck?" Tom leaped backward in fear, but the fear turned to terror when she smiled and held up the gem she'd just dug out of the earth.

"Remember what I said you could do with the Taaffeite when we found it?"

Later, she wondered if the other miners heard his shouts for help. She also wondered how long it had taken for that stone to dislodge itself from his ass—and if he'd sifted through his shit to find it.

Chapter Three

Razr had always liked Scotland. The weather was moody, the landscape could almost be described as arrogant, and the people were tough as shit. Liking the place was a crazy contradiction for him, because he both envied the humans who lived here and was thankful he didn't *have* to live here. Nice place to visit, and all that.

Today's visit, however, wasn't about seeing the sights, drinking the whisky, or eating haggis. Just twenty-four hours after Jim Bob gave him the gold card, Razr was taking back what was his and restoring his dignity and reputation.

Since he'd lost his ability to flash from place to place when his wings were bound, he'd taken a Harrowgate, a transportation system used by demons to travel around the human and demon realms, to the outskirts of a walled village populated by dhampires. Few knew of the existence of the half-vampire, half-werewolf beings, and even fewer knew about their Scottish villages. Humans were especially clueless; their eyes might see the towns and the people, but their primitive minds wouldn't register any of it, and wards placed around the properties would repel humans on a subconscious level.

His boots left deep prints in the soggy earth and fog dampened his jeans and formed tiny droplets on his jacket as he walked toward the village's walled east entrance. He could smell the recent rain and taste the ocean salt in the air, but he didn't let any of that distract him from the fact that he felt more than one set of eyes keeping track of him. Dhampires were cautious folk, secretive to the point of paranoia, as vicious as vampires and as unpredictable as werewolves. They'd gotten the best and worst of both species, and only a fool would let their guard down around them.

Just inside the village wall he was met by thatch-roofed houses and a burly female with short-cropped dark hair, razor-sharp fangs, and a crossbow slung over her shoulder. An unusual ripple of energy surrounded her, unusual in that while dhampires were certainly a formidable species, they weren't generally associated with special gifts. This dhampire, however, looked like she kicked ass with special abilities on a daily basis, and maybe bragged about it.

As a battle angel, he could appreciate that.

She propped her fists on her hips and blocked his path. He *didn't* appreciate that. "State yer business, yer species, and yer name," she said in a thick Scottish accent. "And make it quick. I don't have all day." She snapped her fingers in a show of impatience.

Man, he wished he still had angel status and more powers than the few weak defensive skills he'd been left with, because no one spoke to angels with so much disrespect. So instead of a display of power and wings, he decided to mess with her.

"Maybe I'm a human traveler named George who just wants to stop for a meal."

"Ye came through the Harrowgate, so ye aren't human or ye'd be dead, ye lyin' ballbag." She crossed her arms over her chest and leaned in. "I'll ask one more time. Who are ye, and—"

"My name is Razr," he ground out, extending the gold card Jim Bob had given him. "I'm a fallen angel, and I'd appreciate it if you got out of my face."

She sniffed and wrinkled her nose. "Ye don't smell like a fallen angel."

That was because this lyin' ballbag wasn't one. "What do fallen angels smell like?"

"Shit."

Ah. "Well, I'm newly fallen. Maybe I have to earn my stench."

Unamused, she snatched the card away and frowned down at it. "Why do ye want to see them?"

Did she think he was born yesterday? Or even a century ago? "I'm sure those who wish to see a secretive group of people don't tell you why they're here."

"No, they don't. But what they don't say is as important as what they do."

"And what am I not saying?"

She smiled, her lips peeling back from those wicked-looking fangs. "That ye're seeking something. And it's important. Which means ye need to be nice to me or ye won't get it."

Damn, he hated inferior beings on power trips. "Fine," he sighed. "You're a...sturdy female with big muscles and a voice so deep and breathy that Darth Vader would be jealous. Is that nice enough?"

She laughed, breaking the ice. "Come on." She led him down a cobblestone street lined with small houses and quaint shops, and then onto a dirt path through a thick copse of trees. He followed her until they came to a clearing, in the middle of which a stone tower stood. As they approached, a big male and a petite female exited.

A wave of power rolled off them, the same as the female who'd brought him here. And then he knew. These were the Wardens, the Triad, three dhampires chosen by fate or blood or some mystical crap to guard the most priceless things in the world. And they were in possession of his gemstone.

The male, his dark hair swinging around his shoulders, spoke first. "I'm Galen. You've already met Rhona." He gestured to the petite, fire-haired female who hung back but who radiated more power than the other two combined. "That is Isla. State your business."

"You people aren't real friendly, are you?" They stared, and he resisted the urge to taunt them more. As an angel, he was used to the stick-up-the-ass types, and he knew they often had short fuses, and he didn't want to fuck this up. "I'm here because I believe you're in possession of something that belongs to me." He held out his hand so they could see his ring. The ice-blue diamond glittered in the hazy sunlight that managed to punch through the gray sheet of clouds above. "It's this stone's larger mate."

Isla started to reach for it but pulled back at the last second. "May I?"

"You can touch the ring, but I can't remove it." No, the only way this particular piece of jewelry could come off his finger was if he was dead or his finger was severed.

She smoothed her finger over the stone. "Yes," she murmured.

"We do have its mate."

Excitement shot through him. Excitement, and a whole lot of hope. He'd been waiting decades for this moment. *Get ready, Heaven, because I'm coming home*. "Then I can have it?"

The three Wardens glanced at each other, and then, in a coordinated move, they formed a circle around him, each about ten feet away. Beneath him the ground began to glow with an eerie green light and the ice-blue gemstone he'd been hunting for a century appeared before him out of thin air.

It was as beautiful as he remembered, its oval shape and smooth, polished surface reflecting light and unpredictable angles onto the grass.

"You can hold it," Galen said, "but it cannot leave this circle."

Too relieved and enthralled to question Galen's words, Razr reached for the apple-sized diamond. The moment he came into contact with it, a sense of comfort washed over him. Comfort and joy and vindication. He wished he could have punished the evil bastards who had stolen it and the two other Gems of Enoch and murdered their hosts, but there would be time to hunt them down later. Right now he had to take his prize to his superiors and get his wings and powers unbound. After that, he could bond the gem to another human host and then finally, *finally*, he'd have access to its powers again.

But wait... Had Galen said the stone couldn't leave the circle?

Dropping his hand, he rounded on the Warden. "This diamond belongs to me. I have the right to take it."

Isla laughed, and he swore she'd just gotten taller. No, she *had* gotten taller. She now stood half a head above Galen who, at around six-five, was as tall as Razr. "We are bound by laws you can't even begin to understand, *fallen*." The emphasis she'd put on "fallen" made him wonder if she meant it as an insult...or if she knew he was lying. "You might be the original owner, but we made the storage contract with the one who gave it into our care. It is not our place to hand it over to you."

Son of a bitch. He ground his molars in frustration. His stolen property was right in front of him. His waking nightmare was within inches of being over. And these museum guards were going to keep it from happening. For the millionth time, he wished he had the full use of his powers. He couldn't even channel the gem's powers without a host to amplify its energy.

But he did have friends. Friends in very low places...and friends in very high places. If he took his case to the angelic court, they could grant him an army of angels to help him reclaim his property—which was really Heaven's property. These dhampires wouldn't stand a chance.

"I can come back with a hundred angels," he warned. "A thousand. You can't keep what is rightfully mine."

Galen barked out a laugh. "A million. It wouldn't matter. As Isla said, we're bound by laws beyond your ken. The things we store are beyond your reach. But you are welcome to try. We haven't seen much battle recently."

"Or ye could stop being a fucking dobber and find the current owner yer own damned self," Rhona suggested. "Everything ye need to know is at the tip of yer fingers."

Could it be so easy? Hastily, he palmed the diamond and closed his eyes. In a flash of light, an image popped into his mind. A female. A stunning female with long silver-blue hair and eyes the color of the stone in his hand. Her pale skin was flawless and brilliant, as if she'd walked through a cloud of diamond dust. More information came at him like a data download, and within seconds he knew where she worked and where she lived.

Smiling, he opened his eyes. And then he casually tried to pocket his diamond and walk away. The Wardens even let him.

Probably because the moment he stepped outside the glowing circle, the stone melted away and he was struck by a bolt of lightning.

Still, electrocution and third-degree burns aside, it had been a pretty good day.

Chapter Four

It turned out that Jedda Brighton had some damned impressive credentials in the fields of gemology and mineralogy. According to Razr's cursory research on the wealthy recluse, she'd gone to the best schools, she owned her own business in the form of an outlandishly upscale London jewelry store that dealt exclusively in rare and exotic gemstones, and she was world-renowned for her uncanny ability to locate pockets of valuable minerals deep in the earth.

All of that information was public knowledge. What wasn't public knowledge—at least, human public knowledge—was that her jewelry store was a front for the underworld dealing of cursed and enchanted gems.

Which meant that she was, almost certainly, a demon.

Maybe even one of the very demons responsible for the Enoch gems' loss.

A deep growl rumbled in his chest as he made his way across the floor of the building where he expected to find his target. Mozart filled the air, lending a bizarre normalcy to the attending crowd of assorted demons, werewolves, vampires, and even a few humans who reeked of evil or greed. The massive castle, high in the mountains of Austria, was apparently the setting for this year's annual Underworld Sorcery Event, at which Jedda had been advertised as a guest speaker.

Razr had missed her presentation, but he'd arrived in time for the awards dinner. People were mingling, their hands and claws full of appetizers and cocktails, or in a few cases, mugs of blood. The stone in his ring vibrated in warning at the close proximity of the demons, but thankfully it wasn't glowing. He'd gotten one of

Azagoth's sons, Hawkyn, a Memitim skilled in alchemy, to temporarily change the properties of the surface of the diamond in order to conceal the color and the glow. He didn't want to take any chances that Jedda would recognize that the gemstone in his ring had been cut from the one she'd left with the Wardens.

The vibration grew stronger, becoming more of a pulse than a constant buzz. Odd. It only did that in the presence of its mate. Did it somehow recognize Jedda as the current owner of the larger stone? Had she...bonded with it?

Damn, he hoped not. If she had, the stone would need to be purified in the blood of a dying angel, which meant waiting like some kind of Heavenly vulture for a fellow angel to die.

Shit.

He swiped a glass of sparkling wine off a passing server's tray and cursed this stupid event. He hated parties. He especially hated demon parties. And this one was crawling with the suckers.

Suck it up, cupcake. You are, perhaps, only mere minutes away from being reinstated as a full-fledged battle angel.

Fresh enthusiasm sent a shiver of anticipation through him, even as his ring pulsed more feverishly. He looked around, seeking the source, and there, in the corner near the punch bowl, was Jedda.

And damn...she was...extraordinary. His breath clogged his throat as he took her in, because although he had known the greatest beauties to ever have existed both in the Heavenly realm and the human one, she was unique.

At least a foot shorter than he was and dressed in a stunning sapphire sheath that blurred the line between business-chic and cocktail dress, she was peering into her own glass of pink bubbly, her long, silver-blue hair framing a delicate face. As in the picture he'd seen of her in his mind and in her shop he'd visited before coming here, creamy skin glittered almost imperceptibly, and when she looked up, eyes that matched her hair glowed like twin gems.

Amazing.

She was a demon for sure, but what kind? He'd never seen anything like her.

He'd just started toward her when a hand came down on his shoulder from behind. Instinct kicked in, and he spun around, prepared to defend himself from whatever malevolent scumbag was trying to accost him. Instead, he found himself staring into a familiar face. A familiar *dead* face.

"Lexi? Is that...you?"

The pretty lion shapeshifter grinned and did a little twirl in her strapless red evening gown. "It's me," she said in her sing-songy Irish lilt. "In the flesh. Again."

Again was right. "I thought you died." He looked her up and down as if to reassure himself that she wasn't a ghost. He hadn't known her well, had only met her because her shifter pride had helped him follow a dead-end lead about his Enoch gem a while back. "I was told you'd been killed in a dance club explosion or something."

"Yeah," she sighed. "Thirst blew up and sort of dismembered me. But it turns out I have nine lives. And not because I'm a cat." She shrugged, her long brunette curls bouncing around her bare shoulders. "Evil witch, ancient curse, you know the drill."

"Sure, sure," he said absently, his gaze locking on Jedda again. Excitement surged through him now that his prey was nearby. "Excuse me," he said. "I need to see someone before I go." He gave her a brief hug. "It was good seeing you. Glad you're alive."

"Me too." She clanked her glass against his. "Enjoy your evening."

He moved toward Jedda, his pulse inexplicably growing faster as he neared her. He'd been in the presence of blindingly gorgeous females with unimaginable power in his centuries of life, and none of them had affected him like this. No, this was different, a mix of attraction and anticipation he would almost compare to battle lust.

The thought made him slow his approach, his mind tripping over the implications of that. Was he hoping she was one of the demons responsible for the theft of his property and the deaths of his friends, in which case he'd kill her, or was he hoping she wasn't involved? And which was worse? Oh, he had no problems with killing demons—it was what he'd been bred for. But it seemed like such a shame to slaughter someone so unique. Or so attractive.

Idiot. You never drooled over demons when you were a full-fledged angel.

No, he hadn't. There had been a clear separation of class and species back then. But ever since he'd had his wings bound and his powers muted and had been tossed in Sheoul-gra to serve Azagoth, he'd relaxed his standards. Not intentionally, but he had to admit that living life on the other side of the tracks had given him new perspective.

He just wasn't sure if that was a good thing or a bad one.

Jedda looked up as he stopped in front of her. Up close, she was even more beautiful, with full, pouty lips made to stir up some wicked male fantasies. Her fine, perfect features made her seem delicate, fragile, even, but something told him she was stronger than she looked. Which made him wonder how that strength would play in bed.

Down, boy. Get what you want and get back to Heaven and females suited to your status. And species. "Hello, Ms. Brighton. I'm Razr."

Cocking her head slightly, she gave him a long, assessing once-over before saying with just a hint of an English accent, "Razr? That's not a common human name, is it?"

Either she couldn't sense his species or she was testing him. Either way, he didn't see any reason to lie. "It's my fallen angel name. A take on my given name. Razriel."

"Ah." She gave him another long, measuring look, taking in the expensive suit Azagoth had given him for the event, and he wondered what she was thinking. "Until tonight, I'd never met a fallen angel, and now I've met two, including you."

"Tonight? Is the other one here?"

She nodded. "Shrike, the event organizer. He owns this place."

Well, that was mildly alarming. Fallen angels reveled in power and status, which meant that this shindig had probably been arranged for a purpose. An evil purpose.

"Huh," he said casually. "Never met him."

"I hadn't either until I agreed to speak at the conference. He seems...very intense." She paused to wave at someone near the grand piano. "Are all fallen angels like that?"

"There's a saying in Heaven," he said lightly. "Angels keep their humor in their wings."

"So when they get cut off..."

"So does their humor." He shrugged. "Of course, fallen angels do grow wings eventually."

"But their sense of humor doesn't grow back?"

"Oh, it does," he said, thinking of Azagoth and his pitch-black sense of humor. "You just don't want to be on the funny side of it."

She reached up and toyed with the multicolored choker around her slender neck, the dozens of rings on her fingers glinting in the light from the chandelier overhead. There were even little gemstones decorating her nails. She must be wearing a freaking fortune in jewels.

"Well, what about you?" she asked. "You seem to be a little less on the intense side."

He narrowed his eyes in mock suspicion, figuring that flirting might help get him what he wanted. Plus, as he'd already established, she was hot—for a demon. Especially for a demon. "Is 'intense' code for 'asshole'?"

She laughed, a delicate sound that was almost...musical. What kind of demon was she? A succubus, maybe? That would explain why he was picturing her tangled in bedsheets and why his cock was throbbing against the fabric of his pants.

"I say we change the subject." Still smiling, she took a sip of her drink. "So what brings you to the conference? Did you catch any of the panels?"

Panels? He could only imagine the topics at a place like this. *Plague Spells 101: The Pros and Cons of Magically-Enhanced Viruses. Warlocks and Witches and Sorcerers, Oh, My! Human Sacrifice: Yea or Nay?*

"No," he said, clearing his throat. "I just arrived, actually. I came to see you. Glad I tracked you down." Instantly, she lost the impish smile, and he cursed his mistake at making himself sound like an obsessed nut job.

"Tracked me down?" Even the temperature of her voice dropped a couple of frosty degrees.

"Not like a stalker or anything," he said hastily and in a bid to come off as charming. Not creepy.

He hoped.

"I went by your shop, but your staff told me you were giving a presentation tonight at a conference in Austria. Took it from there with research, and here I am." He put on his best chagrined face. "Not creepy at all."

She must have agreed, because there was a slight thaw in her eyes. "This is a very...exclusive...gathering, Mr. Razr. How did you arrange an invitation? Especially at the last minute?"

"I'm a fallen angel," he explained with a hint of fallen angel-like imperiousness. "I get what I want." Hadn't hurt that Azagoth let Razr do a little name-dropping, either. No one wanted to piss off the being who would eventually be in charge of their soul.

"Really." Her voice, now completely ice-free, went low, a caress that stroked him just under the skin. "Intriguing." She gave him a coy look as she lifted her glass to her mouth. "So why did you go to so much trouble to track me down?"

"I'm looking for a very special gemstone, and I hear you're the best at locating rare and precious stones."

"I am," she said with an arrogance he had to admire. "But why is this such an emergency that it couldn't wait until office hours tomorrow?"

"No emergency." He shifted closer to her, testing his boundaries. "It's just that I saw your picture at your shop and decided I didn't want to wait to meet you."

Her ruby lips curved in amusement. "Flattering. But you're avoiding the real question."

Lowering his voice to a conspiratorial whisper, he dipped his head closer to hers. "The room has ears." Most likely, anyway. Plus, he wanted to get her alone in case things got...complicated. She didn't reply, instead sipping at her drink as she eyed their surroundings. "I'm sorry... Did I say something wrong?"

"No." She stroked the stem of her glass, her jewel-encrusted fingernails reflecting the hall's flickering light in sparkly little bursts. "I'm just trying to decide if I should tell you to make an appointment or if I should suggest we go somewhere more private to talk."

Those nails. He was mesmerized, and his mind kept thinking about what they'd look like—and feel like—in places much more intimate than the stem of a champagne flute. Was she doing that on purpose? His dick sure thought so, and it tapped against the fly of his pants, begging for the same attention.

It was a damned good thing he'd buttoned his jacket.

"I vote for private," he said, his voice humiliatingly hoarse.

He'd come over to seduce her, but she was clearly the one who held the cards in this game.

Succubus, for sure.

She made him sweat for a few seconds before finally nodding toward one of the exits. "I saw a balcony out that way." She started toward it, but a flash of light drew his attention, and he reached out to grab her elbow. "Wait."

"What is it?"

His gut churned as he checked out the next flash of light. Then the next and the next. Shit. Not good. He pulled her close and whispered into her ear. "Let's get out of here. Away from this conference."

"Aren't you naughty?"

"Yeah. Naughty. Let's go."

"But dinner is—"

He took her glass from her and placed both his and hers on a tray, his alarm growing as robed Ramreel demons with halberds began to station themselves around the room, the clop of their hooves ringing out over the sound of the guests and the music.

"Forget dinner."

"Look, I was invited for a reason," she snapped, clearly annoyed by his manhandling. "It would be rude to leave now."

He nonchalantly shifted his gaze to the four corners of the room, starting at the northern side. "See the glowing symbols painted on the walls?" At her nod, he continued. "Those symbolize sacrifice. Sacrifice to Lothar."

She frowned. "Who is Lothar?"

"How can you not know who Lothar is?" he asked, incredulous. Lothar was listed as one of the most famous scumbags in the first chapter of Demons For Dummies. "Didn't your demon parents teach you about the hundreds of patron fiends you can worship? You aren't limited to Satan, you know."

Her haughty sniff announced her irritation. "My parents didn't fill our heads with ridiculous fables—"

"They're not all fables. Definitely not this one." He tightened his grip on her arm and made a beeline for the exit. "Lothar is known as the Prince of Riches. A sacrifice to him gets you everything you want, and since you are one of the guests of honor..." He trailed off, letting her finish the thought. At her sharp inhale, he knew she'd pieced it together.

"I'm either part of the plan to get the riches...or I'm a sacrifice."

"Exactly."

"Well then," she said crisply, "I don't see why I need to hang around." Clever, how she made it sound like leaving had been her idea.

"That's what I've been trying to tell you," he ground out.

They'd nearly made it to the main doorway when a big blond male blocked their escape route. The dark energy emanating from him marked him as a fallen angel, which meant this could only be Shrike, the fallen angel who'd put this whole thing together.

"Leaving so soon?" His smile, showing way too many teeth and far too much of his gums, was as greasy as his slicked-back hair.

Razr was about to tell the guy to fuck off when Jedda offered an apologetic smile. "I have a family matter to attend to, Mr. Shrike," she said, inching closer to Razr. "And Razr kindly offered to escort me home."

Razr had to give her points for diplomacy, but Shrike didn't bite. "Unfortunately, I can't let you do that," he said. "The festivities are about to start, and I haven't had a chance to speak to you about my proposal."

"Yes, well, this is a bit of an emergency." Jedda adjusted her sparkly shoulder bag with an impatient tug. "Why don't we set up an appointment at my office for sometime this week?"

The smile on Shrike's face turned predatory, and Razr cursed inwardly. This was about to go south, and the bitch of it was that with Razr's angelic abilities bound, Shrike was a fuckton more powerful than Razr. Any negotiations would be all about Razr's ability to bluff his way through shit.

"As I said," Shrike practically purred, "the festivities are about to begin."

Suddenly, the lights shut off, leaving the space lit only by the flickering flames from the candles and torch sconces on the walls.

Yeah. *Real* south.

Speculative murmurs rose up, and unholy excitement charged the air.

"I don't like this," Jedda whispered, and Razr experienced the oddest desire to comfort her. To protect her. And not just because she was in possession of his gem. Heck, she might be responsible for stealing it and killing the humans who had been protecting it.

If so, he'd deal with it. But right now his only goal was to keep her safe.

And to get out of this alive.

Chapter Five

Jedda had been in a lot of uncomfortable and downright dangerous situations before, but something about this one made the others, even the battles, seem tame.

Shrike wasn't your average Big Evil. He was Bigger Evil with an attitude. She had no idea what fallen angels were capable of, but it was probably safe to assume that they could make most demons look like kittens.

Razr, on the other hand... She wasn't sure what to think about him. He was smoking hot, for sure. She'd always been a sucker for dark hair and dark eyes, and she'd bet her life-stone that beneath his exquisitely tailored suit was the body of an athlete. He probably had amazing wings, too.

But there was also a familiarity between them that didn't make sense. She would have remembered meeting him, and yet she swore she felt a connection, as if their pulses were synced. And if that was true, then his pulse was pounding as hard as hers as she watched a bunch of blunt-snouted, horned dudes with wicked blades on the ends of long poles advance toward the center of the room. She thought the weapons were called halberds, but she supposed their name wasn't important. The fact that they could cleave a body in half was.

Razr moved close, and while Jedda was capable of taking care of herself in most circumstances, she had to admit to being grateful that he was, at least for now, her ally.

"Shrike," Razr growled. "What's going on—"

He broke off as, in a single, coordinated move, the halberd guys swung their blades so suddenly and so fast that she didn't have time to scream before a dozen heads plunked to the floor. Their owners' decapitated bodies collapsed next to them with wet, obscene thuds.

"Lexi!" A roar of rage tore from Razr's throat as a female in a crimson evening gown hit the tile, blood spurting from her headless neck.

Nausea and horror rolled through Jedda, and she stumbled backward as the shock wore off the crowd. Some people screamed, some cried, but most laughed.

Razr launched in a blur of fury. His fist slammed into Shrike's jaw, knocking him into a wall. Before Shrike could recover, Razr had Shrike by the throat and pinned, their faces nose to nose. "You killed her! What the fuck?"

"This *is* a demon dinner party," Shrike growled through bloodied lips. "What did you expect?" He smiled, one Jedda assumed was intended to be comforting but only came off as terrifying. "Besides, wasn't Lexi cursed with a bunch of lives and deaths? She'll pop up again somewhere." His eyes lit up with a malevolent crimson light, and little bursts of lightning sizzled at the tips of his fingers as he raised his hand toward the back of Razr's head. "But you won't."

"No!" Jedda shouted. "Don't do it, Shrike. He's with me, and if you kill him, I swear that whatever 'proposal' you have for me is going to die with him. I will *never* work with you."

Shrike snorted, but he dropped his hand to his side again. "I think you will. But I'll let him live. For now."

The crowd began to chant a bunch of mumbo-jumbo Jedda didn't recognize, but she did understand one word: Lothar. Her gut churned again.

"Fuck you." Razr shoved Shrike hard enough to make his skull crack against the wall. "Let us leave, you piece of shit. The ceremony is over."

One of Shrike's hooded goons spotted his boss's predicament and headed their way, the edge of his blade dripping with blood. Jedda forced her wobbly legs to move closer to Razr so she could tap him on the shoulder and impress upon him the urgency of their situation. Shrike might have shelved his homicidal urges for the moment, but he seemed like the kind of psycho who could change his mind in an instant. "Hey, maybe you should back off a little…"

"You really have no choice but to release me." Shrike's deceptively calm voice wigged Jedda out. In her experience, hotheads were far better to deal with than people whose emotions ran cold. Both could be dangerous, but hotheads were more predictable and easier to manipulate. Shrike didn't strike her as either of those things. He gestured toward a closed door nearby. "Why don't we go someplace quieter to talk?"

Razr hesitated. He was going to refuse and get them both killed, wasn't he? Man, she'd been sealed inside collapsed diamond mines and had never felt this trapped. Finally, just as she was counting the number of goons between her and the nearest door, Razr cursed and backed off. What he didn't do was stop glaring daggers at the other fallen angel. Not even while Shrike led them to a grand library full of literary classics, modern fiction, and a sprinkling of demonic tomes.

Seething at Shrike's trickery and betrayal, and still hopped up on an adrenaline dump, she rounded on the bastard as soon as the door closed. "What is it you want, Mr. Shrike? And why didn't you simply make an appointment instead of inviting me here for this...this...spectacle?"

She looked over at Razr, who stood a couple of feet away, his fists clenched at his sides and his dark eyes smoldering. Hatred practically seeped from his pores, and she swore she could feel it in a wave of acid heat washing over her skin.

Shrike walked around the desk and sank into the leather chair behind it. He gestured for both her and Razr to take seats in the two chairs across from him. She accepted, but Razr shot the other fallen angel the bird and remained standing, his gaze sharp, his stance deceptively relaxed. Jedda got the impression that inside he was coiled like a snake and ready to strike.

Shrike shot Razr an annoyed glance but then focused on Jedda. "I invited you here because the things I'm going to ask you for aren't going to be easy to find. Hence, the sacrifice. It's important that its energy envelops you."

Evil bastard. Jedda didn't have a whole lot of room to lecture anyone on the subject of ethics, but she'd never tricked anyone into attending a murder-themed dinner party.

No, but you've killed too.

Dammit, no she hadn't. Not intentionally.

But she'd benefited from the death, hadn't she?

Shoving her errant thoughts back into the deepest recesses of her mind where they belonged, she looked Shrike in his steel-gray eyes. "I don't appreciate the deception," she said in her brisk business voice, the one she used when dealing with deplorable people like Tom from the Taaffeite mine. "And I definitely don't appreciate being enveloped in some strange spell. So I don't think I'll be doing business with you." She started to stand, but lightning fast, his big hand clamped around her wrist.

A snarl rang out, freezing her in her seat more effectively than Shrike's grip ever could.

"*Release her.*" Razr's eyes glittered with the threat of violence. It made her wonder what fallen angels were capable of. And it was a little bit of a turn-on.

Shrike grinned, a smile so cold she shivered. "As long as she promises to hear me out."

Shit. She didn't want to hear another word from this bin of burning rubbish, but she also didn't have a death wish, nor did she want to see Razr flopping around on the floor next to his head.

"Of course," she agreed with forced calm, hoping to alleviate the tension and get this meeting over with. "I suppose it can't hurt."

"Good." Shrike released her, and she resisted the urge to rub her wrist, where her skin burned as if his fingers had been sticks of fire. "Now, here's the deal. What I want will be a challenge, but I know you'll come through for me."

"Just tell me what it is, and I'll tell you if I think it's possible."

For some reason, he looked amused, and she didn't like that one bit. "You are, of course, familiar with the famous crystal skulls of Mesoamerica."

She couldn't stop herself from rolling her eyes. Not only was every one of them almost certainly fake, but if he wanted one he could easily hire any competent dealer in antiquities. He didn't need her for that. "Of course. But—"

"Are you also familiar with the crystal devil's horns?"

She sucked in a startled breath. The existence of the crystal devil's horns wasn't common knowledge. Even most of those who were familiar with the legends didn't believe they existed.

"I'm sorry," Razr said, "but what the fuck is a crystal devil's horn?"

Shrike sat back, the smug look on his face so obnoxious she wanted to slap it off. "Not long after the first crystal skulls came onto the scene, a human archaeologist digging in Mexico discovered a curved crystal horn, much like a ram's horn. It was perfectly seamless, with no flaws."

Jedda leaned forward eagerly, unable to contain her excitement. She loved mysteries that surrounded the elements of the earth. "It was found deep inside a cave full of human skeletons, and it was reportedly hot to the touch. The man who found it went insane shortly afterward, and the horn was lost to the ages. But then, in 1938, Adolf Hitler sent a team to the same cave in search of more treasures. They found another horn, and they assumed that it, along with the first one, belonged to a crystal skull. But no skull that matched the horns was ever found."

Shrike shook his head. "A skull was found." He dug into his desk drawer and pulled out a black and white photo of what she could only describe as a crystal skull. A crystal *demon* skull.

"That's incredible," she murmured. "All the other skulls are human, or at least primate in nature. But this looks like something you'd find in a demon graveyard." Its long, pointed chin and sharp teeth gave it a monstrous profile, and two perfectly round indentions at the temples appeared to be the perfect resting places for horns.

Razr strode over and pulled the photo to the edge of the desk. "Where is it now?"

"According to my sources, Satan himself owns it." At Razr's snort, Shrike took insult, his mouth tightening in a grim line. "You have something to add?"

"No," Razr said, the odd note in his voice making Jedda suspect he knew something pertinent to this conversation. "It's just that Satan hasn't been seen in a while."

Shrike tapped his long fingers on the desktop. "So you believe the rumors that he's been usurped?"

Usurped? Jedda hadn't heard that. But then, she'd never, not in her hundred and forty years of life, been interested in the politics of the Heavenly, human, or demonic realms unless they affected her directly. Heck, she was barely interested in her own species' politics.

At Razr's casual shrug, she sighed. "Look, I don't know what you want me to do about this. You'd be better off hiring someone who locates antiquities. I'm a gemologist. I specialize in finding gems that are still rough in the earth or that have been enhanced with supernatural abilities."

"Don't toy with me, sweetheart. I know you deal in all gems. And the devil's horn is one of the most precious."

Shit. How could she get out of this without revealing the truth—that certain types of crystal were beyond her ability to sense? Not only that, but quartz crystal, like that associated with the skulls and the horns, might as well be her kryptonite? She'd learned that in the most embarrassing way imaginable.

"Mr. Shrike, only two horns are believed to exist. I'm not sure I can find either one of them." She cleared her throat. "And I'm certain that I won't find them if you call me sweetheart again."

He laughed, but she'd expected no less. "I have faith in you. But I'm not finished." He braced his forearms on the desk and leaned forward. "There's something else I want."

Of course there was.

"Have you heard of the Gems of Enoch?"

Her heart stopped. Just...stopped. Her chest tightened, her breath burned, and her stomach dropped to her feet. Beneath her skin, she felt her panic response rise up, and she had to force herself to calm the hell down.

And was it her imagination or did she see Razr tense up out of the corner of her eye? Had to be her imagination. Unless he sensed the sudden, cold terror inside her?

She hid her anxiety behind a forced laugh. "Mr. Shrike. Surely you don't believe that silly legend."

"It's no legend." Shrike's brows slammed down in annoyance. "Three gemstones made of angel blood and tears. Each was rumored to possess different powers, and each was placed in an angel's care. These gemstones, when activated together, formed powerful magic. But around a century ago, three extraordinarily powerful demons defeated the angels and stole the gems."

He was right about the stones, but he'd gotten the story wrong. Very wrong. "I'm sorry," she said, "but I'm not wasting my time on a silly goose chase."

"It's true," Razr chimed in, not helping her at all. "At least, the existence of the stones is reality." He wandered around the library, his gaze seeming to take in everything at once, and Jedda got the feeling he was committing every tome and every artifact on display to memory. "Shrike fucked up the story though."

"Really." Shrike glared. "Maybe you could tell me where I went wrong and how you know this?"

"The exploits of the angels who used the gems in battle are well-recorded in Heaven's Akashic Library, and I like to read." Razr ran his hand over a pile of books on the table near the window. "According to several accounts, demons didn't defeat the angels. Demons murdered the humans who were the custodians of the gems."

Well, that was a little closer to the truth, she supposed. But only one human had been killed, and the guilt weighed on her like a two-ton boulder.

Shrike gave a skeptical snort. "Why would angels need human custodians?"

"Because the power contained in the stones needs a conduit." Jedda immediately cursed her loose lips. "At least, that's according to the legends," she added quickly.

Storm clouds gathered in Shrike's eyes and his fingernails dug into the desktop. "It appears that my source hasn't been entirely forthcoming with information," he ground out, and man, she wouldn't want to be that source. Then, just as quickly as the storm came in, it passed, and Shrike looked between Razr and Jedda. "If humans hold the gemstones, how do the angels draw on the power?"

"I don't know," Razr replied as he flipped through a book about carnivorous vegetation in the demon realm. "I didn't get that far in my reading."

Jedda knew the answer to Shrike's question, but she didn't feel like sharing. Hell, she didn't feel like *remembering* that the angels wore special jewelry made from their corresponding gemstone. The angel who had murdered Jedda's sister had worn an amethyst charm around his neck that matched the stone Manda possessed.

"This," Ebel said as he rubbed his finger across his

necklace's pendant, "*allows me to tap into the power of the gem I know is in your possession.*"

He looked at Jedda, Manda, and Reina in turn, his icy gaze sending a tingle of dread skittering up Jedda's spine. He'd caught them in the house they'd shared, a sprawling seventeenth century French manor that had belonged to their deceased parents.

"*Where is it? Where are all three of them?*" *He moved toward Manda as she cowered in the corner, his booted foot coming down in the puddles of blood and gems spilled all over the floor.* "*I sense mine. You reek of it. I want it back.*"

"*She can't give it to you!*" *Reina screamed.* "*It's impossible.*"

He grinned, and around his neck, the amethyst charm glowed. Suddenly, his hand flew out, and a gash, larger than the others he'd inflicted, split Manda's skin from her shoulder to her elbow. She shrieked in pain as blood streamed down her arm and pooled on the floor. Gems formed in the blood, some no larger than a karat in size, while others, like the duck-egg sized enchanted lapis they'd stolen from a vampire a couple of decades before were more impressive.

Which was bad. The larger the stones that formed outside her body, the more damage was being done to the inside of her body.

"*Do you want to understand the full power of the gems?*" *he asked silkily, and no, Jedda really did not. She and her sisters had each claimed a stone and absorbed its considerable energy. That energy had given them abilities they hadn't possessed before, but they'd been aware that the power of the gems wouldn't be fully unlocked without their mates, and now it looked like they were going to find out how powerful those things were.*

Screams blasted through Jedda's brain, screams that belonged to her sisters, herself...no, wait...

She blinked, realizing she'd been lost in the past, when right here in the present people were screaming from beyond the door. Shrike was grinning.

"More sacrifices," he purred, the ecstasy in his voice almost as disturbing as what was happening in the other room. "Lothar is demanding. And with every scream, his will is seeping into you."

Horror left her struggling to breathe. "What...what do you mean?"

"I mean that every day that passes without you bringing me what I desire will cause more and more misery for you. Don't worry, it won't kill you. But before the month is out, you'll wish it would."

Razr tossed the book onto the pile on the table and spun around. "You sick fuck." He twisted the ring on his finger as if trying to find something to do with his hands that wouldn't involve strangling the bastard sitting across from them.

Jedda voted for the strangling.

Shrike's eyebrows climbed up his forehead. "You're a fallen fucking angel." He sneered. "An Unfallen, I suspect, but you still fucked up enough to get kicked out of Heaven. So don't tell me you've never killed anyone."

Razr's voice went low and ominous, and the hair on Jedda's neck stood up. "As an angel I killed thousands of fiends like you. Some of them even deserved it."

"So will Jedda," Shrike said, "if she doesn't bring me what I want." He speared her with a look that promised agony on a grand scale. "And you will update me daily on your progress, or I'll send my men to deal with you."

Son of a bitch. This was why she was in business for herself. Why she refused to work for anyone except on her own terms. She didn't like being controlled or tied to anyone, and what Shrike was doing both tied her to him and controlled her choices for the next month, at the very least.

Fury scorched her throat with every word. "So you brought me here under false pretenses in order to force me to do your bidding?"

"This wasn't entirely a ruse." Shrike steepled his hands on his desk, his countenance so laid back that she got the impression he fucked people over a lot. And got off on it. "I do sponsor a legitimate annual sorcery conference. You can Google it."

She had, which was why she'd felt comfortable attending. "I'm so going to destroy you on Yelp," she snapped.

Razr laughed, but it abruptly cut off as he glanced down at the back of his hand, where the raised outline of what looked like a wing was glowing with an eerie crimson light. Had it been there earlier? She didn't think so.

"Well, well," Shrike murmured. "An *Azdai* glyph."

Razr's gaze snapped up to meet Shrike's. "What do you know about *Azdai* glyphs?"

"I know more than I should." Shrike's expression softened, even as his voice grew bitter, leaving Jedda more confused than ever.

"I need to go." Razr made a "come with" gesture to Jedda and started toward the exit, but Shrike shook his head and the clank of a heavy lock sliding into place rattled the door.

"We aren't finished here."

Razr wheeled around with a hiss. "If you know anything about *Azdai* glyphs, you know I have to."

"I know you need someone to deliver your punishment." Shrike came smoothly to his feet. "I'll do the honors." He held out his hand. "I owe you for the right hook and the cracked skull."

"Go to hell."

"Once again, I'll point out that you have no choice. This castle is on lockdown and I just decided to keep it that way until you agree."

"What is going on?" Jedda demanded. "I don't understand any of this."

Razr explained, but his gaze remained locked with Shrike's, a battle of wills that she had a feeling wasn't going to end well.

"Azdai was an angel before humans even knew what angels were. Before the rebellion that got Satan thrown out of Heaven." Razr sucked air between his teeth as if he was in pain, but Jedda had no idea what could be hurting him. "Azdai hurt humans in the way human children sometimes pull the wings off flies. He was curious and cruel, and he had to be punished. Fallen angels didn't exist yet, so Heaven came up with this glyph and the punishment that goes with it." He held up his hand, where the feather-shaped glyph burned bright crimson, so angry she flinched. "When it lights up, it means that it's time to experience punishment. If the punishment doesn't take place immediately, we suffer until some asshole angel shows up to inflict the punishment tenfold." He reached into his jacket pocket and pulled out the most beautiful ivory-handled cat-o'-nine tails she'd ever seen. Even the little bone spurs on the ends of the leather strands had been polished to gleaming perfection. "And we can't inflict the punishment ourselves." He unfolded the compact handle and locked it into place, and then he passed the torture device to Shrike. Jedda's stomach turned over at the realization that the cat was about to be used. "We earn extra credit when the punisher is merciless."

"Extra credit?" she asked, feeling utterly sick.

"We can go longer between beatings."

She put her hand over her belly, but it didn't quell the nausea. "That's...barbaric."

"You'll get no argument from me," Razr said as he removed his jacket and shirt. As she suspected, he was as fit as an athlete, his well-muscled broad chest tapering to a narrow waist and abs she'd bet would make diamonds seem soft in comparison.

"Wait." She leaped to her feet and tried to reason with Shrike. "Don't do this," she pleaded. "I'll do whatever you want. I'll do my best to find the items you want—"

"You're already going to do that," Shrike said.

She looked over at Razr, who was now removing the various weapons strapped around his hips and looking at her like she was crazy for wanting to help him. She kind of felt that way, she supposed. This was none of her business. Heck, she didn't know why he was even in the office in the first place except that, oh, right, he'd tried to save her from the Dinner Party From Hell and had gotten caught up in the trap Shrike had set for her. So, yeah, this was all her fault, and she didn't want to see Razr hurt.

"What can I do?"

Razr flung his clothes and half a dozen blades onto a chair. "You can make sure this asshole doesn't fuck with me when I pass out."

With that, he reached out and grabbed the wall.

Chapter Six

This sucked. Usually Razr's punishment came from Azagoth or Hades, although Zhubaal had filled in a couple of times. Z didn't like it, not like Azagoth and Hades, who both seemed to enjoy doling out a little torture, even among friends, but sometimes things couldn't be helped.

"Please," Jedda whispered as Shrike's heavy steps crossed the room. "Surely this can wait—"

"It can't," Shrike said, his eyes glowing with that unholy crimson light again. "Even now, he's feeling pressure build inside. His skin is burning. His blood feels like lava. Every minute without punishment increases the agony. Isn't that right, Razr?"

Unfortunately, yes. "How the fuck do you know?"

Shrike stroked his finger over the cat-o'-nine's smooth handle, and how fucked up was it that Razr actually experienced jealousy? He hated the cat. But it was *his*, and he despised the fact that this fallen angel fuckwad was caressing it.

Yeah, fucked up.

Shrike's voice was soft, almost...tender. "Does it matter how I know?"

Not really, but Razr guessed there was one hell of a story behind his knowledge. "Just get it over with. Six of them."

"No!" Jedda put herself between Razr and Shrike. What the hell was she doing? He was a stranger to her, and yet she was trying to protect him.

Unaccustomed to being the recipient of such kindness, he hung his head, at a loss for how to handle this. His wings, bound so tightly that they ached, quivered under his skin as if wanting to erupt from his back and shield her from what she was about to witness.

He lifted his head and looked at her from over his shoulder. "Jedda," he said roughly, "it's okay. Don't look. It'll be over quickly."

For the span of a dozen heartbeats she hesitated. And then, reluctantly, she nodded and moved aside for Shrike, but she still cried out as the first blow fell across his shoulders, which, although fully healed, were still sensitive from the last flogging he'd taken at Jim Bob's hand.

Pain exploded and blood splattered. He clenched his teeth and bore the second blow with a grunt. His ears rang, but through the buzz he could hear Jedda pleading with Shrike to stop.

Nothing she said would stop him. She *couldn't* stop him. This was something Razr had earned, and he'd learned the hard way that it was much less painful to take the blows than to suffer for days sometimes until an angel showed up to flay him with ten times the number of strikes.

Sixty fucking blows.

He normally healed within a few hours, but it took him days to recover from that kind of angel-inflicted torture.

Another blow landed, and his vision blurred.

He didn't even feel the next one.

* * * *

"Gods, you're heavy. You're damned lucky my species is freakishly strong." He was also lucky that there was a Harrowgate just a block away from Jedda's house or she'd have been forced to explain to a taxi driver why she was hauling around an unconscious, bloody man in the middle of the night.

She gasped with effort as she unceremoniously dumped Razr's unconscious body onto her bed, and so much for her new jade and amethyst comforter and sheets. All ruined by sticky smears of blood.

What was up with that, anyway? Why had Razr needed to be tortured? And why did she care? She hadn't cared about anyone since the day an angel killed one sister and sent the other into the wind. She'd been lonely at times, but mostly being alone meant not having to compete with anyone else for anything. Like the gems that kept her alive.

Oh, their parents had planned ahead of time to avoid competition between Jedda and her sisters, and for the most part it had worked. But her species was naturally competitive, and honestly, she was surprised that she and her siblings had stuck together for as long as they had. Most gem elf siblings lost touch within a couple of years of reaching adulthood at the age of sixteen human years.

She wondered where Reina was, if she was even still in the human realm. The last time Jedda had seen her sister had been a decade ago at an underworld gem and weapons show on the outskirts of the Ca'askull region of Sheoul. They'd run into each other at a display booth for cursed magnetite, and it had done nothing to heal the hurt between them.

Absolutely nothing. Reina knew how to contact Jedda, but she hadn't.

Not that Jedda was totally blameless. She'd followed up once, but after finding that Reina no longer lived at the location she'd given Jedda, she'd given up. Sure, she could attend the weekly gem trade in the elven realm where Reina would surely be on a regular basis, but Jedda was stubborn, and she wasn't going to be the one to make overtures at this point.

A sound outside her front door followed by a wave of intense evil jolted her out of her thoughts and raised the hackles on the back of her neck. Silently, she slipped to the living room window and peeked between the sapphire curtains. There, hanging in the shadows just off her porch, was a demon she recognized from the sacrificial dinner. He just stood there, his back against the side of the house as he looked out toward the street.

What the hell?

She whipped open the door. "What are you doing?"

He turned to her, flashing sharp, ugly teeth. "Shrike wants me to keep an eye on you. Make sure you deliver what you promised."

"Tell Shrike he can go fuck himself. I don't need a babysitter."

The bastard started toward her, but screw that. She wasn't

giving him a chance to so much as lay a finger on her. Throwing out her hand, she summoned the power of the very gem Shrike wanted her to find, the ice-blue diamond of myth and legend. All around her the air shimmered as heat built. With a mere thought, she released the energy, hitting him with a shockwave that sent him tumbling all the way to the street, where he landed in an awkward heap against a lamp pole.

"Stay off my property," she shouted. "Or next time that wave will take you apart." It wasn't true, but he didn't need to know that. Oh, she could have summoned twice as much power, but she lived in a human neighborhood, and there was no sense in drawing attention to herself. Especially since many humans were aware of the existence of the supernatural thanks to recent near-apocalyptic events, and nothing good ever came of humans and their fear.

Still, she'd always wondered how truly powerful her gem would be if paired with its mate and the angel who possessed it. Before he killed Manda, Ebel the Angry Angel had said that the paired gems were capable of widespread destruction on an atomic level, and she believed it. Even now she could feel her gem's power like a pulse inside her, as if it wanted to unleash everything it was capable of.

Shivering, she went back inside and fetched the med kit from the bathroom. Razr was still passed out cold, so she gently stripped off his slacks.

He didn't wear underwear. *Oh, my.*

Her mouth went as dry as the sand forest in her elven homeland as she took in his magnificent body. Everything began to burn, parts of her she'd all but forgotten she had in the five years since she'd last been with a man. The fallen angel was about as perfect as anything she'd ever seen. Made sense, she supposed—she'd never thought angels would be anything less than perfection. But seeing one naked and up close? No one could blame her for wanting to take pictures and post to all her friends on Instagram, right?

Cursing her ethics, she arranged him on his belly to allow access to his shredded back. Shame at the fact that she'd just ogled him shrank her skin. Gods, he must have been in so much pain. She'd nearly passed out herself during the beating, unable to stomach the sight of muscle and bone exposed by the deep lacerations.

Making matters worse, Shrike had reveled in the gore, growing angrier with each strike, as if he'd been taking some deep inner pain out on Razr. When it was over, he'd thrown down the cat and fled the office without a word, leaving her to gather Razr's unconscious body and find her way out of the castle.

At least the wounds had stopped bleeding and were already starting to heal. Still, this was one of the times she wished she'd chosen the garnet Gem of Enoch instead of the diamond. Jedda and her sisters hadn't known what power each of the gems had possessed at the time they'd chosen and assimilated them, but neither Jedda nor Reina had been completely happy with the outcomes. Manda had embraced the killing power of her stone, but Reina had no desire to heal anyone and had been furious. And while Jedda's gem had given her an ability to violently repel demons that she actually used sometimes, being able to help now and then would have been cool too.

Very carefully, she cleaned Razr's wounds and applied bandages, each one drawing an elven curse from her. Such a perfect body, torn to shreds on a regular basis. He had no scars—at least, none that were visible. She'd heard there were species of demons that could see scars no one else could, and she wondered what one of those demons would see if they looked at Razr.

Jedda saw a very fit, very toned male.

Bronzed skin stretched over thick veins that helped define the sharp-cut muscles of his shoulders and arms, and if there was an ounce of fat on his body, she'd turn her jewelry store into a yogurt shop.

Tenderly, she ran her fingers over his biceps and forearm, all the way to his fingers. His ring fascinated her, and when she touched the black diamond in the center, she felt the oddest buzz, as if it contained an enchantment that was restrained and trying to get out. Even stranger, enchanted gemstones were always aligned with good, evil, or neutral energy, and she couldn't get any kind of read on it. Was he aware of its potential power? Or its alignment?

Putting her questions aside, she followed a thick vein up the back of his hand and then laid her hand over his, marveling at how much bigger his was. As an elf, she was naturally on the delicate side, but he truly created a stark contrast in not only their size, but their coloring. Where she was light, he was dark.

Even the tattoos that looped around his shoulder blades and ran up the back of his neck in twin Celtic-style braids before disappearing under short-cropped black hair were dark. Not in color—although they were deep blue—but in nature. She recognized the symbols woven into the rope-like pattern. They were often burned or carved into objects, like cursed or enchanted gemstones, to dampen their power.

Were Razr's tattoos more punishment for whatever he'd done?

Gods, what *had* he done? It had to have been bad to get kicked out of Heaven, but then to be saddled with extra punishment?

She eyed the door. Maybe she'd made a mistake bringing him home. She'd heard there was a clinic right here in London that treated demons and fallen angels and the like... She could drop him off and then check on him tomorrow.

He shifted, wincing at the slightest motion, and she sighed in resignation. After all, a girl had to bring home the wrong guy at least once in her life, didn't she? And hey, he'd tried to warn her, tried to get her out of the dinner party before everything went to hell. If she'd listened instead of arguing, maybe she wouldn't be in this mess.

She owed him for trying.

Plus, he seemed to know a lot about the Gems of Enoch. It made her a little nervous, but at the same time, she'd love to learn more. She and her sisters had only discovered them because they'd felt them in use, and they'd stolen them before they'd learned what they were. Since that day a century ago, Jedda had done as much research as possible, but very little was known about them.

Seemed that very few angels published books about their greatest weapons. Go figure.

After she finished patching him up, she went to the kitchen to prepare something to eat and to plan her next move. Clearly Shrike was serious about getting what he wanted, and if he'd really enveloped her in some sort of sacrificial demonic magic, she was in trouble. Maybe she could get her hands on the horn he wanted, but there was no way she could give him her gem, even if she wanted to. It was part of her. It was why her heart was beating and her blood was pumping.

Without it, she would die. The thing that sucked, though, was that if she didn't give it to him, the result would probably be the same.

Chapter Seven

Coffee. Fuck, Razr needed coffee.

That was always his first thought when he woke up. Even as an angel waking up in Heaven, he'd wanted that uniquely human beverage that so many of his angelic brethren turned their noses up at. Hot, cold, black, with milk...it didn't matter to Razr. Just hand it over or get out of the way.

He yawned, opened his eyes and blinked, startled at the sight of Jedda sitting in a chair next to the bed he was currently sprawling in. He'd dreamed about her, except she hadn't been wearing a bright turquoise silk blouse and shimmering black leggings that showed off toned thighs and calves like she was now.

She'd been naked. Her luxurious silver-blue hair had blanketed her perky breasts, but everything else had been gloriously free of any kind of covering. She'd been walking on a beach of white sand and pink shells, and as she sauntered up to him, she'd held out his Enoch diamond.

Razr had extended his hand... But he still didn't know if he'd been wanting the gem—or her. The dream had flickered away as consciousness interrupted.

"Hey, you." Jedda reached for a pitcher of water on the bedside table. "You weren't out as long as I thought you'd be. You heal fast."

Confused, he rolled onto his side and pushed up on an elbow, feeling the pinch of something on his back. Bandages. She'd bandaged him? "Where am I?"

"I brought you to my place." She poured water into a glass and handed it to him. "I couldn't just leave you there bleeding on Shrike's floor. Who knows what he'd have done to you?"

His stomach rumbled—he'd missed the sacrificial dinner, after all—and he took a drink of water to quell it. It wasn't coffee, but he wasn't going to complain to someone who had helped him out.

"Where are my weapons and clothes?" When she pointed at a pile on the floor, he relaxed and set the glass down. "How did you get me here? And where *is* here?"

She offered a small smile. "I'm stronger than I look, and *here* is London."

Oh, right. He'd gotten that info when he'd gone to Scotland. "Near your shop?"

She shrugged. "It's walking distance in good weather. One stop on the Tube in bad weather. But this *is* England, so I ride the Tube a lot." She made a circular gesture with one bejeweled finger. Besides her gem-encrusted fingernails, she wore a lot of rings. As many as three on each finger. "Turn over and I'll remove the bandages."

He could do it himself, and he didn't generally like taking orders, but he suddenly wanted very much to have her tending to him. Touching him. The dream was still fresh in his mind, so what the hell.

Besides, while it was technically forbidden for angels to fraternize with demons, he was, for all intents and purposes, considered a fallen angel. Which meant all bets were off, and Heaven could suck it.

She could suck it.

Groaning at the inappropriately erotic thought, he flipped onto his stomach, and oh, look at that, he was naked. She'd stripped him bare and he hadn't awakened? That had happened only once before, when Zhubaal had carried him from Azagoth's office after a particularly brutal flogging and laid him out on his bed in Sheoulgra. He'd awakened confused and sore, but at least he'd been in his own bed.

"So." The mattress dipped as she sat next to him, her warm thigh pressing against his hip through the purple satin sheet. She liked her jewel tones, didn't she? Everything in the room, from the bright citrine lampshade to the jade rug and ruby wall accents screamed, *I hate subtle color and earth tones.* "What's the deal with this punishment thing?"

His cheeks heated with humiliation. "I did something stupid, and I got in trouble for it."

"Yeah, I guessed that much. Must have been pretty bad to get you kicked out of Heaven and to be cursed with eternal punishment."

"I also spent a few decades in prison," he muttered into the pillow.

His two team members, Ebel and Darlah, had rotted in jail with him while all their fates were decided. Ebel had been released first, with no restrictions on his power and without an *Azdai* glyph. It had taken him only two years to track down his gemstone and destroy one of the thieves who'd stolen it from him, but the amethyst had been tainted by the evil of the one who had possessed it, an evil that darkened his soul and turned him against his own kind.

He'd been hunted down and slaughtered. His gem and his pendant now sat uselessly in some archangel's office until the other two Gems of Enoch could be recovered and a new team could be formed.

Next, they'd released Darlah to find her gem, but this time, she'd been hobbled like Razr, her wings—and consequently, her power—bound, and she'd been branded with an *Azdai* glyph.

She'd disappeared three years later and was presumed dead.

Now it was Razr's turn. Returning to Heaven with his gem would redeem him. Returning with both his diamond and Darlah's garnet would make him a hero. Heaven would once again have the three Enoch stones, and he could put together another team to combat demons.

He *needed* those stones, and one was within his grasp. He just had to exercise a little patience and be smart.

Jedda's finger smoothed over the bandages, and he nearly purred. No one had touched him like that since Darlah. And even then, their relationship had been sexual, frantic, and intense, with zero intimate moments. At least, not by his definition of intimate.

"Can I ask what you did?"

He inhaled sharply, wondering how to play this. He could lie, tell the truth, employ avoidance... He had a few options. In the end, he settled on a generic version of the truth, figuring that offering a little information might help him draw info out of her, as well.

"I was part of an elite demon-slaying team. We got careless one day, and our carelessness cost lives and property."

Anger and regret burned through his veins at the memory. They'd been battling hordes of demons advancing on a shithole village in what was now Somalia, and Razr had ordered Ebel to station the stones and their human guardians on the edge of town near Razr and his team. But Ebel had misunderstood, placing the trio of humans and gems in the center of town, leaving them out of sight and vulnerable to demons who somehow slipped through the barrier generated by Razr's Enoch diamond. It had been a clusterfuck of epic proportions, and one Razr would never forget. Not even his dreams gave him respite from the sight of the death and destruction.

"I'm sorry," Jedda said softly. "I know exactly what that's like. I lost my entire family because I was careless too."

"They're dead?"

She peeled a bandage away with surprising tenderness. He'd have ripped the sucker off. "My parents and one sister are. My other sister and I might as well be strangers."

Okay, so now he *had* to know. "What kind of demon are you?"

She shifted, planting one warm palm on his waist, and his body stirred to sudden, hot life. Beneath his hips, his shaft swelled, and the satiny sheet rubbing it like a caress made it even worse.

"I'm not a demon."

He laughed. "Bullshit."

"I'm not." She pulled off another strip of bandage, and he welcomed the slight burn of the adhesive tugging on his skin. He needed the distraction. Badly. "I'm a gem elf."

"A what?" Talk about a distraction.

"A gem elf," she said slowly, as if he was hard of hearing. Or a toddler.

"I heard you. I just don't know what a gem elf is."

"Aren't angels supposed to know everything?"

How cute. Angels seemed to be kept in the dark about everything. "Obviously not," he said, adjusting his hips to accommodate his pinched erection. "But I do know you're a demon."

She removed another bandage, this time less gently. A lot less gently. "I think I'd know if I was a demon."

"How would you know?" he shot back. "Does a giraffe know it's a giraffe? Have you been classified by science or Baradoc, the demonologist?"

She huffed in indignation, and he hid his smile in the pillow. "My people aren't part of the demon or human worlds. We don't have any kind of corresponding religions or lore. We even have our own realm."

He snorted. "Angels don't know everything, but we *are* familiar with all the realms. If there was an elven realm, I'd know."

"That's pretty arrogant."

He shrugged. "What can I say? I'm an angel. A fallen angel," he corrected.

"Angel or not, you're an asshole," she muttered, and he laughed. She was adorable. And clearly, a demon. So was she lying to him or did she truly believe she was an elf?

A fucking *elf*. Ridiculous.

Her fingers fluttered over his bare shoulder blades, and he went taut at the first probe of the scar-like streaks from which his wings would emerge if they weren't bound.

"What are these?"

"Those are wing anchors."

"That's where they cut your wings off?" There was a startling note of sadness in her voice that left him off balance. She didn't know him. Not really. And yet, she felt bad for him? "I'd have thought they'd have healed by now. When did you fall?"

"A couple of years ago," he hedged, not wanting to get into this, especially because his wings hadn't been severed. Just bound so tightly with special golden twine that they ached every minute of every day.

"But the stitches—"

He sat up quickly to change the subject, but the sudden move knocked her off balance and sent her sprawling on the floor. Right on top of the insanely bright rug.

"Oh, shit." He leaped off the bed to help her up. "Sorry. I..." He trailed off as he lifted her to her feet, the look on her face as she stared at him leaving him even more off balance than before.

Those amazing eyes glittered as she took in his nudity. His cock, already rock hard, jerked under her gaze. Desire hammered through him, becoming a rapid pounding in his groin that grew more intense the longer they stood there, both frozen by what was happening.

He wanted her. He'd wanted her since the first moment he'd seen her, even though he'd believed that things could only end badly between them. Especially if she was responsible for the theft of his gem and the death of its human host, a young man named Nabebe whom Razr had all but raised.

But dammit, he liked Jedda, and he was beginning to doubt she'd had anything to do with the events that got him banished from Heaven. As a gem dealer, she could have acquired the Enoch diamond at any time during the last century or so, and it made sense that she'd deny knowing anything about it, given that the most powerful forces in Heaven and Sheoul were after it. Hell, Razr had even heard that Satan had put out feelers before he was locked away by Revenant, Sheoul's new king, and his brother, Reaver, the most famous battle angel in history.

But she's a demon. You hate demons. You were born to fight them. To destroy them.

Yes, that was true. But during Razr's service to Azagoth, he'd been around enough demons to know that they weren't one-size-fits-all. Baby battle angels cut their teeth on the knowledge that all demons were pure evil and must be destroyed, but he knew better now. Just like humans, each demon was unique down to the depth of malice or decency in their souls.

He'd bet that Jedda was one of the decent ones.

Her face tilted up, and his knees nearly buckled at the need that turned the clear ice blue of her eyes into opaque azure pools. She wanted this as badly as he did.

"I don't usually do this," she whispered in a shaky voice that punched him in the place deep inside that made him male.

"I don't either," he whispered back.

"I...I can't get pregnant," she said softly. "Not until I absorb an azurite."

He had no idea what the hell she was talking about, but it

didn't matter. Fertility had been one of the things taken from him when his wings were bound. No illegal half-demon babies for him.

Dying to taste her—and to get away from an incredibly uncomfortable subject—he lowered his mouth to hers.

He'd intended the kiss to be gentle. Exploratory. But she wasn't having any of that.

Throwing her arms around him, she deepened the kiss, her tongue meeting his in a violent clash. Her legs came up and wrapped around his hips, and he hissed at the feel of her warm center grinding against his hard length. She undulated wildly, her firm breasts pressing against the hard wall of his chest. Man, she felt good. So good he had to slide a hand between their bodies to reduce the friction that was threatening to ruin this whole thing.

She moaned at the contact of his fingers on her core, so he pressed against the fabric of her leggings, letting his touch both soothe and inflame. The scent of her arousal stoked his, making him crazy, making him want more.

Now.

He spun her against the wall and, using only his severely reduced angelic powers, he lifted her up next to a painting of loose rubies and a pearl necklace spilling out of a gold chalice. The surprise in her eyes turned hot as she hung there, exposed to his gaze and his mercy. With his hands free and her body pinned so she could barely squirm, he peeled off her leggings, leaving her only in her silk shirt and bright aquamarine lace underwear.

Stunning.

His mouth watered as he skimmed his palms up her creamy thighs and hooked his thumbs under the elastic of her panties.

"Yes," she breathed, her body quivering with anticipation. "Touch me."

She said it as if he was capable of resisting. No chance of that. He'd love to take the time to tease her, to make her beg, but he was like a man who had been wandering in a scorching desert for days and who had just come upon an oasis.

Greedily, he pushed one thumb between her folds and stroked her silky moisture through her slit, circling her swollen nub before dropping lower to penetrate her deeply. She threw her head back and arched into his hand as much as the angelic hold on her would allow.

Damn, she was beautiful, her hair whipping around her face as she tossed her head, her cheeks glowing with a rosy tinge that matched the color of her tongue as she held it between her clenched teeth.

Eager for more, he tugged off her panties, careful to not tear them when they caught around her ankles. As he straightened, he kissed and licked his way up her leg, savoring her smooth skin and every little catch of her breath. His own breathing was labored, his heartbeat hammering inside his rib cage as if urging him on. Not one to ignore the signals his body was sending him, he flicked his tongue over the swollen hills of Jedda's sex. At her cry of ecstasy, he dipped his tongue into her slick valley, making her cry out again and making his cock jerk with the first stirrings of orgasm. He didn't want this to end, wanted to lick her until she begged him to stop, but it had been a long time since he'd been with a female, and his body was humiliatingly ready to go off.

With a snarl of both regret and anticipation, he roughly parted her thighs and entered her in one smooth motion. His power still held her against the wall, so he planted his forearms next to her head and steadied himself as he surged against her.

"Razriel," she moaned, jolting him out of his lust with the use of his angel name, but only until she locked her legs around his waist and arched, taking him so deep he didn't think they'd ever come untangled.

His blood pumped like he was in battle, adrenaline searing his veins and skin until every part of him felt more alive than he'd been in years. Decades. His balls throbbed and tightened, and panting, he pounded into her, her delicate whimpers mingling with his groans of pleasure.

She came with no warning, stiffening against him, a muffled shout tearing from her throat. Her silken sheath squeezed him, catapulting him into his own electric explosion of ecstasy that made him see colors that put her hyper-bright room and clothes to shame.

As they came down, he realized he'd released the power that held her against the wall, and now she clung to him so tightly that not even a drop of perspiration could get between them.

Damn, that had been good.

"You know," she murmured into his neck, "you never told me why you tracked me down at the conference and what it is you wanted me to find for you."

This probably wasn't the time to show his hand, but he didn't have to bluff, either. "Must be something in the air," he said, pulling back just enough to gauge her response in her expression, "because I actually want what Shrike wants."

She stiffened against him, and panic flared in her eyes. "I don't understand."

"The gems," he said. "The remaining two Gems of Enoch. I want them, and I believe you're the key."

Chapter Eight

It was all Jedda could do to not erupt in a full-blown panic attack. And gem elf panic attacks were messy. Sort of an explosion of fine diamond dust poofing all around her in a massive, choking cloud. And that shit got everywhere and into everything. The last time she'd had a panic attack, the abrasive particles had clogged her vacuum cleaner's air filter and scratched her glass coffee table.

Slowly, so she wouldn't arouse suspicion, she lowered her stiff legs, allowing Razr to slip from her body.

He was still hard. Could he go again? Because she could. Over and over.

Damn, that was the best sex she'd had since...well, ever, the intensity and abruptness making it all the more intoxicating. His complete dominance of her, immobilizing her so she was helpless to do anything but surrender to his touch, had been unexpected, exciting, and something her human partners had never done.

She was still a little dizzy as she pushed away from him and grabbed a silk robe from the closet. Peridot green, of course.

"Look," she said, sounding like she'd just gotten up after a wild night of partying and not enough sleep, "I don't know why these gemstones are suddenly on the radar, but you heard me tell Shrike that I can't find them. And even if I could find them, I'd have to give them to him or that Lothar curse is going to make my life a living hell."

Gods, what was she going to do? Breaking the curse, if it was even possible, would buy her some time, but given that Shrike had sent a goon to watch her, she didn't think she'd get *that* much more time.

And really, why were the stones in demand after decades of

obscurity? Both her gem and Reina's were safely ensconced in the most secure vault in the universe, and it wasn't like the dhampires gave tours of the facility for people to see what was inside. *She* couldn't even get inside, and she was a client.

Something must have happened with her sister. But what? Was she in trouble? Had she told someone about the gems?

Was she dead?

An ache of despair centered in her gut at the thought, but no, she'd have felt her sister die, just as she'd felt it when Manda took her last breath. But still, something might be terribly wrong.

Razr watched her, his thickly-muscled body still bare, his skin coated in a fine sheen of sweat, his impressive length glistening with her arousal. Even though she'd just had the most amazing orgasm ever, she still felt a swell of desire expand between her legs, diminished only by the sobering subject at hand.

Two fallen angels wanted the one thing she couldn't give up.

Razr scrubbed a hand over his face as if trying to scour away the disappointment in his expression. "We'll figure something out. Shrike is an overconfident douchebag, and I have faith that you can produce at least one of the gems." He gestured to the bathroom. "Mind if I use your shower?"

Relieved to put this off, even for just half an hour, she nodded. "Towels are in the cupboard by the sink, and there are some travel-sized toiletries like toothbrushes and soaps in the drawer beneath the towels. There's a steam feature in the shower too—might help if your back still hurts. Take your time." Hopefully he'd take a lot of time, because she needed to figure a way out of this mess. "I'll make some lunch if you're hungry."

His naughty smile nearly made her already shaky knees threaten to collapse. "I'm starving," he said in a low, husky voice. "That little taste of you wasn't nearly enough."

When he turned to walk away from her, the flex of the muscles in his ass and legs pushed her over the edge, and she sank into the bedside chair to collect herself for a moment. How could she be so attracted to someone she barely knew, at a time when her life was in danger?

Groaning, she buried her face in her hands. What the hell had she done? How much trouble was she in? One fallen angel seemed bent on torturing her until she gave him what he wanted, and the other seemed determined to seduce her into giving him what he wanted.

Not that she could. But what a way to go.

She wallowed in self-pity until she heard the water turn on, and then she went to the guest bathroom to clean up and dress in an azure sweatshirt and jeans before checking to see if Shrike's minion was still outside. He was, but he was smart enough to be hanging out on the other side of the street. People walked past him as if he wasn't there, and she figured he was using whatever trick it was some demons used to make themselves invisible or unnoticeable to humans.

Shit, she was screwed.

Muttering obscenities in both English and Elvish, she threw together a quick version of her favorite shepherd's pie recipe and Yorkshire puddings. Although Jedda had grown up in France, her mother had been a fan of British food, and Jedda liked to recreate her mother's dishes now and then, even if she had to eat them all by herself.

Sometimes she invited her employees to dinner, six humans whom she considered friends but who didn't know the truth about her. But for the most part, when she cooked she did so for herself.

While she prepared the meal, she considered her options. She had to look for the crystal horn Shrike wanted, for sure. But clearly, she couldn't give up the gem that had become part of her body and soul. She wouldn't give up her sister or her stone, either.

She did, however, need to find Reina.

As the food cooked, filling her flat with the savory, warm scent of beef, she peeked out the window again. Ooh, new goon. Shift change, she supposed.

"Something interesting out there?" Razr's deep voice, coming from down the hall, made her shiver.

"Not interesting," she said as he stepped up next to her, dressed in his clothes from last night. The male could definitely fill out a suit. "Annoying. Shrike sent some creep to keep an eye on me."

Razr yanked the curtain aside with a growl. Menace billowed off him, and for a moment she thought he'd go right through the window. "Stay here."

"What?" She tried to stop him as he threw open the front door. "No, wait!"

He didn't stop until he was nose to nose with the demon across the street. She couldn't hear the conversation, but she could see it getting heated, with Razr backing the guy up against a light post. A few seconds later, the demon scurried away in the direction of the nearest Harrowgate.

"What did you say to him?" she asked when Razr came back inside.

"I introduced him to a few of my friends."

She frowned. "What friends? I didn't see anyone."

It was his turn to frown at her. "You didn't see the *griminions*?"

The oven timer went off, and she started toward the kitchen. "What are *griminions*?"

"Seriously?" His heavy footsteps followed behind her. "I mean, I know not every demon knows what a *griminion* is, but you didn't even *see* them? Creepy little short dudes in robes? Glowing eyes, claws for hands..."—he held his hand at just below groin level—"...about yea high?"

"I told you, I'm not a demon. And no, I did not see any *griminions*, and from the sound of them, I'm glad I didn't." She eyed him askance. "You say they're your friends?"

"Well, not friends, exactly. More like coworkers. They were in the area."

She was about to ask what their job was and who Razr worked for when the oven timer went off again and the phone rang simultaneously. "Do you mind getting the food out of the oven while I get the phone? I'll just be a minute."

It was Sylvia from her shop with a question regarding the pricing of a couple of rare stones from Australia. By the time Jedda worked out the kinks and got off the phone, Razr had set the table and dished up.

"This looks amazing," he said as they dug in. After a bite, he made a sound of ecstasy that had her remembering what they'd done in the bedroom. "It *is* amazing."

"It's nothing special." She shrugged, outwardly nonchalant, but inside, her heart did a little happy dance at the compliment. "Do you cook?"

"Nah." He reached for a Yorkshire pudding. "I mostly eat cafeteria food."

Cafeteria food? She studied him, realizing she knew absolutely nothing about him. She'd brought him home, cared for him, slept with him, fed him...and he was a complete mystery.

If this were a movie, it would either be a fun romantic comedy or the setup for a slasher film. She swallowed dryly and got up to fetch something to drink, taking note of the knives next to the stove. As if they'd be any help if he decided to chop her up. The weapons he wore on his body made a mockery of her little cooking knives.

Not to mention that he was a fallen angel, probably capable of melting her in her socks.

She fetched a couple of sparkling waters from the fridge and sat down. "So why is it that you eat a lot of cafeteria food?"

Razr took a break from shoveling down shepherd's pie to unscrew the top off his bottle of water. "I live on sort of a campus. It's a training facility for a special kind of angel called Memitim." She must have looked as confused as she felt, because he added, "Memitim are basically earthbound human guardians. They have to earn their way into Heaven."

"Oh. Well, that must suck. Are you—*were* you—one of these Memitim?"

He shook his head. "I was born in Heaven, a full-fledged angel. Right now I'm helping to train the Memitim."

Jedda gave herself a moment to process that. She'd really never given the Heavenly realm much thought, and it had certainly never occurred to her that there would be more than one kind of angel, let alone earthbound ones.

"You know, you're not what I would have expected from a fallen angel."

He paused with the mouth of the water bottle near his lips. "Yeah? What did you expect?"

"Shrike." She spread her napkin in her lap. "I mean, other than you, he's the only fallen angel I've ever met. He's what I would have expected. You don't seem as...damaged."

"I'm...not sure how to respond to that." He smiled, his charm proving her point. "I feel like I need to defend myself and insist that I'm all kinds of damaged." He tipped the bottle up, and she became mesmerized at the way his throat worked with each swallow, his supple skin rippling over straining tendons. "So," he said after he'd downed most of the bottle, "you say you're an elf."

"I *am* an elf." She tucked her hair behind one pointy ear so he couldn't miss it. *She* didn't miss the way he'd changed the subject. Now she was super curious about his damage.

His mouth quirked in amusement. "A lot of demons have pointy ears."

"I'm not a demon." How insulting. And how many times did she have to tell him that? Annoyed, she reached for her bottle of water, but in her haste, she knocked it over, striking the marble napkin holder. The bottle shattered, spilling foamy seltzer everywhere. "Dammit." She reached for a napkin, but once again her haste cost her, and she sliced her arm on a broken piece of glass.

Blood splashed on the table, and before she could mop it up, tiny emeralds, citrine, lapis, and a dozen other gemstones formed in the splatters of blood.

"That's...interesting," Razr murmured.

"It's nothing." She swiped her hand through the mess, and instantly the gems disappeared into her palm. "I'll get this cleaned up—"

"Wait." He seized her wrist and pulled her hand close. "What just happened?" Gently, he pressed a napkin against her wound, which was already healing, but was also spilling out a couple more gemstones. "What's going on, Jedda?"

At his no-nonsense tone, soft but steely, her breath burned in her throat and her blood burned in her veins. Gem elves did everything they could to hide this secret. If people knew the truth about them, they'd be hunted into extinction, slaughtered for the wealth they carried within their bodies.

Jedda didn't know Razr. Didn't trust him. And yet, there was something about him that made her *want* to trust him.

"Jedda?" he prompted. "You can tell me."

"No," she rasped. "I can't." All around her, diamond dust

poofed into the air, turning the kitchen into a priceless snow globe.

"Okay then." With a little cough, Razr released her, keeping the blood-soaked napkin. As he turned it over, a couple of sapphires pinged onto the tabletop. "I'll tell you what I think's going on. You sweat diamond dust and bleed precious gems, and you're worried I'll hang you by your feet and bleed you out for them. Am I right?"

He'd called it. Son of a bitch. She supposed there was no point in lying anymore, so she stared at the sparkling water as it *drip, drip, dripped* to the floor.

"My species...we don't locate priceless gems just to sell. We use them like fuel. They're what our bodies are made of. Our bones, our muscles, our organs. We can sense them. Not to toot my own horn, but that's why I'm such a successful gemologist."

He cocked an eyebrow. "Do you need different kinds of gems to survive?"

"You mean, could I live off, say, rubies, exclusively?" At his nod, she shook her head. "Every gem has a different chemical and mineral composition, and our bodies need certain types of stones for different functions. I need diamonds to cry and for the protective coating on my skin, for example."

Reaching out, he trailed a finger along her bicep, leaving behind a heated tingle. "Protective coating?"

"See how I sparkle in the right light? It's diamond dust. When I'm in a mine and my body detects deadly gasses or excessive heat, it absorbs the worst of it and lets me go deeper and stay longer than humans. Topaz gives me night vision. Stuff like that." She gestured to the large gemstones she kept all around the flat, many displayed as works of art, some just filling glass bowls, and others lying around waiting to be dusted. "They all give off their own unique, life-giving vibrations. We don't absorb them all—we surround ourselves with them too. Their energy is our fuel."

Sitting back in his chair, he appeared to contemplate what she'd told him. "Is their energy infinite? Or do you have to replace the gems when their energy is depleted?"

She reached out and spun the table's centerpiece, a crystal dish containing a mix of uncut gemstones, and watched the colors swirl in a multicolored blur. "Stones we keep around us provide infinite, but mild energy. For more intense energy and special abilities, we have to absorb the gems. The small ones are drained within a few months, and even the larger and most powerful ones can be depleted if we don't return to our realm every decade or so to recharge them. We can also hit capacity."

"Capacity?"

She nodded. "I'm so full of hematite that I can't absorb another one unless I break a bone and need more to heal."

"Are there ever any that you can't be around?"

"Oh, yes. Some are so powerful that they can have a corrupting effect on us, like a drug that never wears off." She'd seen that more times than she wanted to admit. "Of course, part of what makes us what we are is that we can't resist gemstones like that. We want them, even though we know we shouldn't actually use them. Those go into storage. At least, those of us who aren't crazy put them into storage."

There was a long pause as he stared at her with such intensity that she started to squirm. "Do you have any like that?"

"Several." She pushed a piece of carrot around on her plate, her appetite ruined by the topic. "Most of them are there because they're infused with evil, and I don't want them getting out into the world. I mean, can you imagine what would happen if someone like Shrike got hold of a lapis lazuli that could turn water into arsenic on a large scale?" She shuddered.

"You have a lapis lazuli that can do that?" Razr stood and headed into the kitchen.

"I have a lot of gems that are even worse," she sighed.

No way was she letting any of them go, and she'd paid the dhampires enough to keep the things stored for eternity. She especially didn't want them to fall into the hands of evil gem elves. Members of her species were just too self-destructive when they went evil, as Jedda knew all too well. Never again would she allow an evil gem to leave her possession.

Razr fetched the garbage and started to clean up the broken glass, refusing when she offered to help. "Okay, so you have this incredible affinity for gemstones. What makes you think you can't find the Gems of Enoch? Sounds like if anyone can, it's you."

"I can't just wish a gem into my possession," she said, because that was the truth. "In order to find an enchanted stone at a distance, it has to be in use. That's the only way it'll send out a strong enough signal. But even then, I have to be somewhere close."

He wiped up the last of the broken glass with a paper towel. "How close?"

She shrugged. "Once, a Svetnalu demon princess in northern Vietnam was using runes made from a lava beast, and I felt it from Malaysia. But that's rare. Really rare."

She and her sisters had felt the Gems of Enoch in use from twice as far away, but there was no way she was going to share that precious nugget of information.

"So you're saying you have no idea where any Enoch gems are, and you don't know how to find them."

She took intense, sudden interest in her plate so she wouldn't have to look at him. "That's what I'm saying," she mumbled.

There was a long silence, and she sensed disappointment rolling off him in a wave so strong that she swore she experienced it as well. Did she actually feel bad that she couldn't give him the diamond?

Finally, as he sat back down across from her, he broke the silence. "What if I can get you the crystal horn? We can get Shrike off your back with it. At least buy some extra time, and I'll help you find the Enoch gems."

Help her? It wouldn't make any difference. She couldn't give up her diamond. But the crystal devil's horn? Was he serious? "What about the horn? How can you help me get it? I thought you didn't know what it even was?"

"After you and Shrike described it, I realized I'd seen it before." He waggled his brows. "I just happen to know who owns one."

She rolled her eyes. "That's next to impossible. Probably a replica. I told you, according to legend there are only two—"

"And one of them happens to belong to my boss."

He really was delusional. But she played along. "Okay," she said. "I'll bite. Who is your boss?"

"I call him Azagoth, but you probably know him as the Grim Reaper."

She wasn't sure if she should laugh or laugh...harder. The Grim

Reaper? Demons were always calling themselves all kinds of crazy shit. She'd met a dozen idiots who swore they were Lucifer. And a dozen more who claimed to be Jack the Ripper. Hitler. Caligula. The list went on.

"Tell you what. You prove you work for the Grim Reaper, and I'll prove I'm an elf. Deal?"

"Deal." Razr grinned, that killer one that made her ovaries clench. "Come on, Dobby. Let's go."

Chapter Nine

Dobby? Jedda revised her opinion about Razr. He was clearly broken.

Also? Sheoul-gra was super creepy.

Jedda had spent most of her life in the human realm, with occasional jaunts to the elven and demon realms, but the Grim Reaper's home was, by far, the most unsettling place she'd been. Razr had explained it as being a holding tank for the souls of dead demons and evil humans, but apparently there were two distinct sections. One was for the living, and the other, known as the Inner Sanctum, was where the souls were kept, presided over by a fallen angel named Hades, but not until Azagoth checked out every one of them.

At first glance upon materializing on the arrival pad, everything seemed fairly normal. A green, grassy landscape stretched forever, broken by a forest in the distance. Ancient Greek-style buildings formed a small city dotted by fountains and sculptures, all lending a peaceful vibe.

But once inside the largest of the buildings, things got bizarre, weird, and a little scary. From the room filled with tortured, twisted statues to the zany little demon things Razr called *griminions*, Azagoth's home left her wanting only to go back to *her* home.

"Why is it that I can see the *griminions* down here but not in the human realm?" she asked as one of them skittered past, chattering in some language that reminded her of the squirrels that scolded her every morning on the walk to work.

"It's probably because you're an elf. Humans can't usually see them, either."

"Oh, now you believe me?"

He cast her a sideways glance as they started down a shadowy hallway. "It's actually starting to make sense."

"Hmph." She poked him in the ribs. "I told you so."

"Don't get cocky, Keebler," he warned her, but his tone was teasing and his made-for-sin mouth was quirked in mischief. "You still haven't proved it."

Stubborn male. "Don't worry, I will." A dark, intense buzz vibrated through her, coming from a room ahead. When Razr stopped in front of it, she eyed the iron doors with curiosity. "What's in here?"

"A bunch of shit Azagoth has collected from people who owe him." Razr waved to a big guy with a blue Mohawk at the far end of the hall. "Or people he blackmailed. I don't know. In any case, it's a museum of rare and valuable crap."

She couldn't tell if he was kidding about the blackmail, but she didn't really care. She'd shoved a precious gem up a dude's ass. Who was she to judge?

"Like enchanted stones?" She bounced on her toes in excitement.

"Yeah." He grinned. "Want to see?"

"Did you really have to ask?"

The hard clack of booted feet echoed through the hallway as Razr went to open the door.

"Hey, Razr, hold up." The Mohawked guy was walking toward them, shirtless, his color-shifting pants making Jedda dizzy. A statuesque female, her shiny mink-brown hair piled in a knot on top of her head, walked a step ahead of him with the authority of a queen. She was a bright light in the gloom that surrounded them, her flirty yellow sundress flapping around her knees, her matching flip-flops snapping against her heels.

"What's up?" Razr asked.

"Azagoth wants to see you in the library. Lilliana will take care of your female."

"I'm not his female," Jedda said, hoping she didn't sound as flustered as she felt. "We're...business partners." She held out her hand. "I'm Jedda Brighton."

Mohawk stared at her hand. The female *tsked* at him and took Jedda's palm in hers. "I'm Lilliana. Azagoth is my husband." She jacked her thumb at the Mowawked guy. "That's Hades. He sometimes forgets basic manners."

"Don't need 'em where I live."

Razr snorted. "Don't believe him. His mate keeps him in line."

"Pfft." Hades waved his hand in dismissal. "She knows who rules the roost."

Lilliana laughed. "Cat does."

Hades's shoulders slumped. "Yeah." Suddenly, he grinned and waggled his brows. "But she has sex with me, so it's all good."

If anyone had told Jedda she'd ever be standing in front of *the* Hades, she'd have given them the same colorectal procedure she'd performed on Tom the Walking Whisky Dick. The thought made her realize she could use a drink, and she really wasn't even a fan of alcohol.

"Come on, asshole." Hades clapped Razr on the shoulder and started him down the hall, leaving her alone with a complete stranger. In a strange place. Full of strange things.

She was going to start poofing diamond dust at any moment.

"Don't worry, Jedda," Razr called back from over his shoulder. His gaze bored into her, assuring her with a look that he meant what he was saying. "You're safe here. I promise."

Was it crazy that she believed him? Someone she'd just met? Probably, but she'd never encountered anyone whose energy synced so well with hers. It was as if he was somehow reaching inside her and holding her life-stone's essence, streaming directly from the Enoch diamond, in his palm. Was this what love felt like? Was she as crazy to think that as she was to believe in him?

"Would you like a tour?" Lilliana asked, thankfully interrupting Jedda's insane thoughts. "The boys could be a while. Razr will find us when he's done."

Jedda agreed, not having anything else to do. Besides, she was curious. This was a once-in-a-lifetime opportunity, and she might even discover some new gemstones in the material that made up this mysterious realm.

The tour proved to be fascinating. She and Lilliana walked through forests full of animals from the human realm, and they watched dozens of Memitim angels spar and play team sports. Apparently, the team sports were Razr's idea to develop their teamwork skills. Lilliana said there'd been a lot of complaining and even fights at first, but now the Memitim—who were, unbelievably, all Azagoth's children—were getting along better.

Jedda even got to meet a few Unfallen angels, which was a strange concept, and an ugly one. Apparently, Unfallen angels needed to enter Sheoul-proper in order to complete their fall and make them true fallen angels, and these people had chosen the sanctuary of Azagoth's realm to stay safe. They lived in fear of being forcibly dragged to Hell, which would destroy any chance of redemption. Jedda shuddered as she and Lilliana walked back to the main building.

"You okay?" Lilliana asked, stepping behind Jedda to usher her through the front doors.

"I'm fine. I guess I just didn't realize what Razr is going through. He must be terrified that he won't be able to get back into Heaven."

"Well," Lilliana said wryly, "Heaven isn't all it's cracked up to be."

Jedda thought about Becky, one of her dedicated church-going employees. "I know a few humans who would be very upset to hear that."

Lilliana laughed. "Humans have it pretty good in Heaven. For angels...it's all work and politics." She turned down a narrow hallway. "You hungry? I had Suzanne put out some tea and scones."

As if on cue, Jedda's stomach rumbled. "My favorite."

Lilliana led her to a small but elegant dining room, where a table with the promised refreshments had been set out. A tall brunette female wearing jeans and a skimpy black tank top entered from an arched doorway carrying a tray of finger sandwiches.

"It's all ready," the female said as she placed the tray on the table. "I know you didn't ask for the sandwiches, but I like making them."

"Suzanne likes cutting food into tinier food," Lilliana explained, a note of affection in her voice. "When it's her week of kitchen duty, everything we eat is miniature."

Suzanne jammed a fist on her hip. "If it's bite size—"

"It's the right size," Lilliana finished with a teasing roll of her eyes.

"Very funny," Suzanne muttered. "Now, if you don't mind, I'm going to go check on my human."

Jedda took a seat. "Her human?"

Lilliana poured tea into two delicate, gold-rimmed teacups shaped like human skulls. Sheoul-gra was the strangest, most disconcerting mix of normal and horrifying.

"Remember when I said Memitim are charged with guarding humans called *primori?*" Lilliana asked.

Jedda nodded, recalling Lilliana saying that *primori* were humans, and sometimes demons, who were in some way important to the fabric of existence.

"Well," Lillana continued, "Suzanne just got her first *primori*. We're very proud."

Grinning, Suzanne held out her wrist, revealing a small, round mark. "This is an *heraldi*. It represents his life. If it burns, he's in trouble. He's fine right now, but I should still check on him."

Lilliana leaned close to Jedda and said in a conspiratorial whisper, "Suzanne has a crush."

"I do not." Suzanne's cheeks flamed hot, betraying her. "But he *is* to die for. He just needs to dump the necrocrotch skank he's with."

Lilliana's smile faltered a little. "Don't get involved, Suz. You know better."

"I know, I know." Suzanne gave a cheery wave as she started toward the door, probably anxious to avoid a lecture. "Sex with humans is bad. But come on, give me some credit for necrocrotch."

"Necrocrotch?" A blond male munching on a bag of chips came out of the kitchen with another male whose long hair, a couple of shades darker, swung loosely around his shoulders. Both were dressed in leather, their chests, waists, and hips slung with weapons. "Sweet. I'm totally borrowing that."

Lilliana gestured to the two males. "The mouthy one is Suzanne's full brother and mentor, Hawkyn. The Fabio wannabe is Cipher. He's Unfallen."

"I call them the Unholy Alliance," Suzanne chirped affectionately.

Cipher frowned. "Who's Fabio?"

"He's a cover model from the—" Lilliana cut off as Cipher puffed up like a rooster.

"Cover model? Fuck, yeah, I could do that."

Hawkyn punched his buddy in the shoulder, and they squabbled good-naturedly as they left, leaving Jedda to marvel at the moment of normalcy in this incredibly bizarre place. She would never have guessed that people who lived in an underworld purgatory could be so...well, happy.

"I'm outta here, too," Suzanne said. "My *primori* is waiting."

"Just be careful," Lilliana called out, but all she got for her effort was a flip of the middle finger as Suzanne disappeared around the corner.

"Suzanne seems like an odd name for an angel," Jedda mused as she stared after the Memitim.

"Memitim are raised by humans, so they usually have common human names representative of the time period and region in which they were raised. Suzanne is relatively young."

"Wow." Jedda shook her head as she stirred honey into her tea. "Are any of the Memitim your children?"

Even before the question was fully out of her mouth, she kicked herself for asking it. Lilliana had explained that there were scores of Memitim baby-mamas, but it had only just occurred to Jedda that Lilliana might be one of them. Or not. Either way, it could be a touchy subject.

Fortunately, Lilliana didn't appear to be bothered by the question. "Azagoth and I don't have any children yet." She dropped a cube of sugar in her tea. "This is our time, and we're enjoying it."

Wow. Jedda hadn't spent a lot of time around demons or in the demon realm, but most of what she'd experienced when it came to demons was pure chaos. These people were focused, smart, and genuine. Reaching for a sandwich, she shook her head in amazement.

Lilliana's mouth quirked. "What is it? You look surprised about something."

"It's just that I expected the Grim Reaper's realm to be...well, not this."

"You expected torture and misery and a whole lot of scary."

Bingo. "I didn't want to say it out loud, but yes."

The other woman blew steam off the surface of her tea. "That's how it used to be. When I got here, in fact." She took a sip, and then she put the cup down with just the slightest *tink* against the plate. "Everyone's content here now, but make no mistake, this *is* a hell realm. This is where demon souls and the souls of evil humans are stored. And my mate can be as evil as anything you've seen."

Jedda swallowed a bite of cucumber sandwich in a painful gulp. "Can I ask you something? Something personal?"

Lilliana shrugged. "Go for it."

"On our walk, you said you lived in Heaven and got to time-travel for a living. You gave up so much to be with Azagoth. Don't you ever resent him? Even a little?"

"Never." The fierceness in Lilliana's voice made it very clear that she meant it. "I mean, I get mad at him because he can be a major asshat sometimes, but I knew what I was getting into. I make him happy, and he makes me just as happy. I'd sacrifice anything to keep it that way."

Scuffling noises from out in the hall drew Jedda's attention. Hades was striding toward them with a bloody body in his arms, and it took her a second to realize who it was. When she did, her heart skidded to a painful halt.

"Razr." Terror welled in her chest as she jumped up and darted out into the corridor. Her foot slipped in blood and she nearly went down, but she caught herself on the wall just before she crashed spectacularly. "What happened?"

Lilliana grabbed her arm from behind and pulled her around, preventing her from chasing after. "His punishment. He must have gotten the signal during his meeting with Azagoth."

"I hate that," Jedda yelled. Adrenaline coursed through her body like a billion tiny, uncut diamonds that abraded every nerve and made her tremble with rage and helplessness. She knew Razr's condition wasn't Lilliana's fault. It wasn't anyone's fault who lived down here. But it was sick and twisted, and what kind of whack job devised such cruelty anyway? "It's bullshit, and dammit, I want to help him. Right fucking now!"

Lilliana inclined her head as if she knew exactly what Jedda was going through. It didn't even make any sense. Jedda didn't know

Razr that well. But she couldn't fight the pull to him, the one that made her crave him and want to care for him. To watch over him when he couldn't do it himself. She'd always been a bit of a nurturer, but she'd also been a loner, not needing anyone but herself for survival or even company.

But Razr had challenged everything she'd ever known about herself. Everything she'd ever been.

"Please," Jedda said more calmly. "Take me to him."

Lilliana didn't argue. In a matter of minutes, Jedda was inside Razr's small flat in what Lilliana had called the "instructors' dorm," patching him up the way she had at her own place. Other than a few hisses and groans when she'd cleaned his wounds, he'd been silent...but awake. His eyes, dulled by pain, had locked with hers now and then, and each time, she'd had to blink back tears.

He finally passed out, and she climbed into bed beside him, wondering where they went from here.

* * * *

Jedda woke to the prod of a very impressive erection against her hip. Smiling, she stretched, letting her body slide against Razr's as he spooned her from behind.

"You awake?" he whispered into her hair. She shivered at the feel of his warm breath fanning the back of her neck like a slow caress.

In answer, she reached back and slid her hand between their bodies to grasp his cock. He gasped, arching into her palm. He was so hot, so hard, steel and satin and a drop of silken moisture. Gently, she slid her grip from the broad head to the thick base and back up, letting her fingers memorize every bump, every ridge, every smooth plane. Each stroke made him churn his hips as he nuzzled her neck and dropped his arm around her to cup her breast.

Oh, yes. This was what she'd missed when they'd had sex the other day. Not that she was complaining, but to be able to touch, to play... The decadence of it made her entire body go liquid with desire.

He pinched her nipple and rolled it between his thumb and

finger, tweaking it until it was so sensitive it felt like it was directly connected to her core. An orgasm hovered between her thighs and they'd barely gotten started.

"Jedda..." His voice was so tortured, so...male, and she went utterly wet.

Twisting, she looked over her shoulder at him, and in the glow of the nightlight from the bathroom, he was incredible. Passion and raw hunger lurked in his half-lidded eyes, his full lips parted on panting breaths, and she suddenly wanted that mouth on her body. Tasting her. Licking her. Kissing her. Didn't matter.

As if he could read her mind, he reached over and caught her chin in his hand to tilt her face toward his. As he captured her mouth, he flipped her onto her knees so they were upright, her back against his chest, his erection cradled in the seam of her ass, and his other hand playing between her legs. He was rough with her, like before in her bedroom, his tongue thrusting in her mouth, his finger thrusting in her core.

Her body jerked wildly, chasing what only he could give her.

"I don't know why I want you so badly," he murmured as he tore his mouth away from hers to kiss a blazing path down her neck. "You're just so...damned...beautiful. Every time I look at you, I want to be inside you."

Now she'd wonder what he was thinking whenever he looked her way, and she loved it. Half-crazed by his words, she angled her pelvis to give him better access and cried out as his other hand joined the first, one fucking her with fingers, the other tweaking her clit.

"You're so wet," he murmured. "You're going to drench me when you come..."

Pleasure ripped through her, and she came in an explosive blast that took her by surprise and threw her right out of her ever-loving mind. She barely noticed how he bent her forward roughly, urgently, and entered her in a powerful, dominating thrust that banged the headboard into the wall.

She came again before he was fully seated inside her, her walls pulsating around him, grabbing him.

He ground his hips into her, cursing, shouting, his fingers scoring her hips.

Bucking against him, she begged for more, *demanded* more, and he gave it to her. Lifting her hips so her knees came off the mattress and limited her control, he drove into her with powerful thrusts, shoving her toward the headboard with every slap of his thighs against hers. Pressure built as each wild stroke of molten friction reduced her to a mass of quivering need.

She screamed into the pillow as the stinging heat of release tore at her again. His primal shouts joined hers, and his hot jets filled her even as her breath left her.

As she collapsed onto the mattress, him on top of her, all she could think was that he was as perfect and rare and special as an expertly cut, flawless diamond. A girl's best friend, for sure.

How many girls had considered him a flawless diamond?

Not that it mattered, she supposed, but still, the thought might as well have been a cold shower.

"Hey." He shifted his weight, rolling onto his side but keeping one hand on her back, massaging gently. "You okay?"

How had he known? "Yeah." She smiled and turned over. "I'm just wondering what we're doing." Her face heated as she glanced at his fabulously naked body. "I mean, besides the obvious."

With a heavy sigh, he flopped onto his back and stared at the wood beams in the ceiling. "I don't know. I didn't expect to be so...enamored of you."

"Enamored?" She grinned, basking in the compliment. But something about the way he said he hadn't *expected* to be enamored with her left her unsettled. Maybe it was nothing. But what *had* he expected? And why had he had any expectations of a stranger at all?

"Enamored," he agreed, but he didn't sound too happy about it, leaving her with even more misgivings. "It's strange because I only needed one thing from you...and this wasn't it." He turned to her, his gaze locking with hers with such intensity that it stole her breath. "You've taken care of me when you didn't need to. You protected me from Shrike when you didn't have to. You even fed me and trusted me to bring you here. Why?"

"I don't know," she admitted. "I usually avoid your type, but I was just...drawn to you, I guess."

Plus, if she was going to get out from under Shrike's dinner party curse, she needed help, and Razr had offered. Granted, it might only be because he wanted her to "find" the two remaining Gems of Enoch, but still. She didn't have any other allies at this point, one of the downsides of only having human friends.

"My type?"

"Otherworldly," she explained. "Demons, shapeshifters, weres, angels, fallen angels."

He leveled an are-you-kidding look at her. "Ah, I hate to break it to you, but you're an otherworlder too."

"Elves don't consider themselves part of your world. We identify more with humans. More of us live in the human world than in the elven one, in fact."

"Why is that?"

Faintly, from somewhere outside, she heard a whistle and someone yell, "Foul!" The Memitim playing some sort of sport, she guessed.

"The elven realm is kind of...unreal. It's like living in a medieval dream." She reconsidered that. "Well, a clean, cheery medieval dream."

Razr gasped in mock horror. "Sounds awful. I can see why you guys would rather live in the human realm."

She laughed, enjoying this exploratory time with him. It was easy to talk to him, something she'd never been able to do with her human lovers. "What's your favorite food?"

"What does that have to do with life in...what? Middle Earth? Shannara? I don't know...Pandora?"

Torn between annoyance and amusement, she settled for shaking her head in exasperation. "Just tell me your favorite food. Maybe a dessert. Also, Pandora doesn't have any elves."

"The Na'vi have pointed ears," he shot back with a playful grin that tugged at her heart. "And salted caramel pie."

That did sound tasty. "Well, imagine your diet consisted of only salted caramel pie. That's it. Every day. And imagine having nothing to do but look for gemstones. Everything around you is perfect and bright and people rarely even argue." Mostly, elves just vacationed in their realm or lived like American snowbirds, people who summered in a northern state and wintered in a southern one. "It's nice to visit and recharge, but peace is tedious, and living in the chaos of the human world is, in its own way, more rewarding."

His expression turned contemplative. Maybe a little sad, and she wanted to hug him.

"I get that," he said softly. "Heaven is kind of like that. People argue—angels are hotheads—but for any kind of real challenge or entertainment, you have to get out of there." He smirked, and her heart tugged again, harder. She loved the playful side of him. "That's why I know about Pandora and Dobby and Shannara. Humans might be inferior creatures, but man, they know how to tell a story." Reaching out, he trailed a finger around the shell of her ear, and she shivered with delight. "What do you tell them about your Spock ears?"

"Nothing. Their selective cognizance renders them blind to our physiology unless we point it out or they're already familiar with the otherworld."

"So...do you date humans?" He made it sound like he was asking if she dated dung beetles.

"Since I live in the human realm, humans do tend to make up the majority of the dating pool." Although she had dated a werewolf once. Just once. They were grumpy as hell.

"So that's a yes." There was an underlying note of, what...jealousy, maybe?...in his voice that both flattered and annoyed her. "Are you dating someone now?"

The annoyance turned to anger, and she levered into a sit. "I wouldn't be here if I were, and if it bothers you, maybe you should have asked before we fucked the first time." She started to swing her legs out of bed, but he captured her wrist and held her back.

"Wait. You're right. It's just that I didn't expect this to happen. I figured I'd meet you, have the gemstones within a few hours, and I'd be back in Heaven by now."

She felt like she'd been kicked in the gut. "Back in Heaven? So soon? Don't Unfallen have to save the planet or perform some great heroic act or something?" Lilliana had been pretty clear about that. It wasn't easy to get back into Heaven, and according to her, only a handful of Unfallen ever had.

He flinched. The barest twitch of his facial muscles, but it was there. "I'm not Unfallen." His voice was gruff, as if he had to force the words out, and an uneasy feeling tightened in her chest. Where was this going? "I was tossed out of Heaven and put into Azagoth's service, but I can earn my way back into Heaven if I complete my mission. I can end the torture of the *Azdai* glyph and throw away that damned cat-o'-nines I carry around. I just need the Gems of Enoch to do it, and only you can help me."

It was her turn to flinch. She couldn't help him. It was impossible. "Surely there's another way you can earn your way back into Heaven," she said desperately. "I can help you with anything else. Anything. You name it."

"It has to be the Gems of Enoch." His voice was as rough as the floor of a mine shaft. "One of them, at least. The Ice Diamond. I need it."

"Why?" Immediately after she asked, the tightness in her chest became excruciating, and she realized she didn't want to know.

Dark shadows flitted in his eyes as he held up his hand. The ring on his finger, the one that had previously sported what she'd believed to be a black diamond, now shone with a familiar silver-blue light. His words from back at her house when she'd asked him what he'd done to get thrown out of Heaven screamed through her brain.

"I was part of an elite demon-slaying team. We got careless one day, and our carelessness cost lives and property."

Oh, gods. Oh, no. Oh, please, *no*.

But no amount of pleading or denial changed what, deep inside, she knew to be the truth.

"Because its loss is why my wings were bound and my powers were stripped. It's why I have to be flogged half to death and why I was kicked out of Heaven." He spoke through clenched teeth, his voice thick with emotion. "That gemstone is mine, and I want it back."

Chapter Ten

Razr had fucked up. Big time.

Oh, he didn't regret telling Jedda that the stone he'd wanted her to "find" belonged to him. She'd either cop to having it or she wouldn't. What he regretted was that he'd let this get personal. He'd gotten too close to her, and the crazy thing was that he didn't even know how it happened. Or when.

All he knew was that when she'd started talking about dating humans, he suddenly wanted to find every one of her past lovers and put them in the ground while he was still considered enough of a fallen angel to get away with it.

And now his feelings were going to make shit real fucking awkward if she didn't admit to sending his Enoch gem to Scotland for safekeeping.

After dropping the truth on her like a two-ton bomb, he let her process the news. As he showered—alone—he told himself that he hadn't given her even a second to respond because he'd needed to clean up. But the truth was that he didn't want her to lie to him. He'd give her time to do the right thing on her own.

Please do the right thing.

His chest tightened as he considered what would happen if she did hand over the stone. He'd go back to Heaven, and she'd... Well, she'd be stuck on Earth, dating inferior human men and scouring the planet for valuable stones for evil assholes like Shrike.

Shrike. Shit. Razr was going to have to do something about that douchebag. The original plan had been to placate the guy with the crystal horn, which Azagoth had agreed to give up under one condition: That even after Razr had been restored as Razriel, he would continue training the Memitim twice a month.

For the next century. And after the century of work was up, he wanted the crystal horn back.

No, Azagoth didn't give away anything for free or out of the goodness of his black heart. The Grim Reaper put a price on everything, and he always got the better end of the bargain.

After showering, Razr turned the bathroom over to Jedda, intentionally keeping the conversation limited so they didn't have to discuss his Enoch gem. Yet. While she showered, he dressed in the only clothes besides his burlap robes he had, the faded Levi's, plain black T-shirt, leather jacket, and black boots he'd worn to Scotland. He didn't need much since he rarely left Sheoul-gra, after all.

Jedda came out of the bathroom in the outfit she'd worn here yesterday: black skinny jeans, an oversized jade button-down shirt, and leather ankle boots. Her wet hair hung in a cascade of shimmering silver-blue down her back, a few strands curling around her chin and flushed pink cheeks. Her delicately pointed ears peeked out from the curtain of hair, and if he hadn't seen the elf in her before, he did now.

Was it really true? In the library last night before his *Azdai* glyph had demanded a sound whipping, he'd asked Azagoth and Hades if they were aware of the existence of elves. Hades scoffed at the notion, but Azagoth had been less skeptical.

"I've heard tales of their realm," Azagoth had said, "supposedly shared by fairies, as well. But if they exist, their deaths aren't governed by demon law."

"Meaning you've never had an elf soul come through Sheoul-gra," Razr mused, disappointed in Azagoth's answer. He'd hoped the ancient fallen angel who seemed to know everything would have some insight into Jedda's story.

Azagoth had confirmed the fact that he'd never seen an elf soul...and then he promptly flogged the hell out of him.

Razr couldn't fucking wait to be done with this shit.

"So what now?" Jedda shifted her weight with uncharacteristic nervousness as he finished tying his boots. She had to be wondering what to tell him about the diamond. She might even be wondering if he knew she had it.

"Now we grab the crystal horn and get a bite to eat. We can plot our next move over breakfast." Hopefully, *her* next move would be to tell him she had his gem, but one thing at a time.

She offered him a fragile smile. "Sounds good." She glanced over at the closet and then back at him. "Why is your closet full of robes? Is that your uniform down here?"

He went so taut that even his brain shut down for a second. He'd never told anyone about them. Not even Azagoth.

Back at Jedda's apartment, she'd mentioned that he didn't seem damaged, but those robes... Those were his damage. No, he wasn't broken and bitter like so many fallen angels, but he carried scars and remorse like everyone else, and sometimes self-flagellation was more effective than anything others could do to him.

"Razr?" She moved closer, until he could smell the pine-scented soap she'd used in his shower. "What is it? You can tell me."

"Can I?" He stood, towering over her in a move meant not to intimidate, but to make an impression. "If I tell you, will you promise to give me a straight answer when the time comes?"

She blinked, confused and caught in a trap. If she said no, she'd be admitting she had something to hide. If she said yes, she'd be obligated to tell the truth no matter what he asked.

"I...ah...of course."

He swung open his apartment door and ushered her out. His voice was mortifyingly hoarse when he spoke. "The robes aren't a uniform. I choose to wear them because they're abrasive and painful on my back when it's sensitive from the floggings, and they constantly remind me why I'm here."

Sometimes, when his guilt was extra intense, he'd actually give himself a lash or two, just so he felt more pain. But that little shameful secret was his and his alone.

He felt her eyes on him as they exited the dormitory building and walked across the lawn to Azagoth's manor.

"Doesn't being here remind you of that?"

"It isn't enough," he snapped, years of regret and anger spilling into his words. "People died because my team and I lost valuable weapons in the fight against demons." He mounted the massive staircase, his booted feet clanging loudly in the still air. "If we don't recover my diamond, the garnet, and the bracelet that goes with it, we'll be that much weaker in the Final Battle. Worse, if those stones fall into the wrong hands, they could be used for evil."

As they entered the building he glanced over at Jedda, who looked a little green. Now she *really* looked like an elf.

"I'm sorry." Her voice was ragged and her eyes haunted, and he wondered what she was thinking. What she was feeling. Guilt, maybe?

Inhaling deeply, he calmed himself, forcing the past behind him. For now.

He paused in front of the room they had been about to enter yesterday before Hades summoned him to Azagoth's library. "You're going to love it in here."

"I know." Shadows still flitted in her eyes, but her skin had brightened with excitement, glittering faintly in the light from the sconces on the walls. "I can already sense the power emanating from at least a dozen gemstones."

He threw open the door, and she didn't wait. She was practically a blur as she raced around the room, stopping in front of various display cases and stands. Some things she touched, some she avoided, and when she saw the crystal horn she both smiled and backed away, muttering something about quartz crystal and kryptonite. She reminded him of a delicate hummingbird, flitting from treasure to treasure, and when she finally came to rest at a brilliant ruby the size of her fist, he joined her.

"This one practically vibrates with power," she whispered. "It's so evil, but so...tempting."

He remembered what she'd said about some stones acting like drugs on her species, and he wondered if she was falling under the ruby's intoxicating spell.

"That," he said, as he peered at the gemstone from over her shoulder, "was given to Azagoth by Lucifer himself."

She jerked back with a hiss. "Satan?"

He was close enough to feel her heat and smell her natural, spicy scent beneath the artificial pine of his soap, and his cock stirred to life again. Not that he could do anything about it here, in Azagoth's plunder room. Disrespecting the Grim Reaper landed you in the statue room as a living work of grotesque art.

"Satan and Lucifer are two different people," he told her. "Lucifer is dead, but some say his spirit lives on in that stone." It wasn't true—Azagoth would know if that were the case. But it was hard to kill rumors like that.

And sometimes, you didn't want to kill them. You wanted to encourage them.

"So much malevolence in that one." Jedda shuddered and moved on to the slightly smaller blue topaz next to the ruby. "This one, too. My sister Manda would have loved it." She turned to him, her expression troubled, her crystal eyes glassier than usual. "Don't let Azagoth trade these, or sell them, or give them away. They're dangerous." She swallowed. "Really dangerous."

"I don't have much influence over him, but I'll tell him what you said."

She nodded absently and moved on to the next gem, a grape-sized tanzanite that sparkled atop its black velvet base. Closing her eyes, she trailed her finger over the shiny surface. "This one is incredibly powerful. Full of neutral energy. So much that an elf could absorb it, but the stone itself would have to be warehoused."

He stared at her, confused. "Wait. When you absorb gemstones, don't they disappear into your body?"

"Ideally, yes." As she spoke she looked down at the tanzanite, her long lashes casting shadows on her face. She was mesmerized by the gem, but he was mesmerized by what she was saying, unsure if he liked where this might be going. "But some stones are too large or too strong to be fully contained in our bodies. We can absorb their properties, but the stone itself must be stored somewhere safe."

He froze as the implications of what she'd just said sunk in. If she'd absorbed his Enoch gem, it could be lost to him. "Somewhere safe," he repeated, almost numbly. "Like a dhampire vault protected by Wardens?"

"Exactly," she said with a nod, and ice formed in his chest. "The stones need to be protected because if one were to fall into the wrong hands, it could destroy us." Her gaze flew up as if she sensed his mood, and she laid an apprehensive hand on his arm. Her touch was gentle, her voice concerned, and he wasn't ready for any of it. He stepped away. She followed. "Razr? What's wrong?"

"What's wrong?" he rasped. "What's *wrong*? I saw the Enoch diamond in Scotland. *My* diamond. And I'm thinking I might not be getting it back."

"What?" Her head snapped back as if he'd slapped her, shock written all over her face. But on its heels was anger, coming in fast and hot. "Wait." She advanced on him, finger pointed like a weapon. "You've known all along that I had it? You've been lying to me this whole time? Why the charade?"

"Because I didn't know you," he said. "I didn't know what you do with the gems. And it was too important to fuck up. I thought you were just storing it, but... You absorbed it, didn't you?" It was part of her. He knew it. That was why, at Shrike's castle, his ring connected to her like it was linking to Wi-Fi.

Silence stretched, the room growing so quiet that Razr heard his own heartbeat pounding in his ears. Jedda took a step back, and he smelled fear in the air. Dammit, he hadn't wanted it to go this way. And he still had questions. Lots of them.

"Jedda?"

"Yes," she whispered. "It's..." She swallowed hard and took another step back, her gaze locked on the floor. "It's my life-stone."

"Life-stone?" He didn't like the sound of that. Sounded...permanent. "What is that?"

She scooched to the side, edging toward the door. Reaching out with his mind, he locked it.

"It's my life. It's the building block on which all the other stones sit. Only my death will release it." A cloud of diamond dust formed around her, glittering in the overhead lights, coating the artifacts nearby.

Fuck. This just kept getting worse. "Can you replace it? Obviously you survived before you got it, right?"

It wasn't cold in here, but she shivered and wrapped her arms around herself. And she still inched toward the door. He hated that she was so afraid of him, but hell, if someone wanted the one thing that kept him alive, he'd be a little nervous, too.

"A replacement for the Enoch gem wouldn't be easy. It would have to be a stone at least as powerful as the Ice Diamond." She gestured to Azagoth's jewels. "Not even these would do. Well, maybe the Lucifer ruby, but it would turn me so evil I'd have to be destroyed." She swallowed so hard that the sound echoed around the room. "And even if I found a gem that would work, removing the energy the Enoch gem gives me would be dangerous. I'd have to be bled out and mutilated almost to the point of death. I'm sorry," she whispered.

He cursed, long and hard. "So what you're saying is that if I want my gem, you have to either be tortured or killed."

Her gaze snapped up to his, and more dust billowed out of her. "Yes," she croaked.

Mother. Fuck. He couldn't kill her. That just wasn't an option. But he was going to kill *the fuck* out of whoever stole the thing and gave it to her.

"Where did you get it?" When she didn't reply, he felt the first stirrings of unease. "Jedda," he prompted again, "where did you get the gem?"

"Don't," she begged him. "Please..."

Oh, shit. *No.* Son of a bitch, this couldn't be. The unease veered sharply to dread, the same gut-twisting, heart-pounding sensation he'd felt when he'd sensed something wrong with the custodians of the gems but hadn't found them yet.

"We had a deal," he ground out. "I tell you about my robes, you tell me whatever I want to know." That wasn't exactly the deal, but he doubted she'd quibble over it. Not now. But he wished she would. He wanted desperately for her to have a solid reason to not tell him what he feared the most—that she had taken the gems in the first place.

It made sense. The gems had been in use at the time, one turning all demons in a mile radius to ash, one healing all injured angels within a ten-mile radius, and one creating a barrier through which no demons could pass to reach the humans who stood at the center of a fifty-foot circle with the gems. He, Darlah, and Ebel had been miles away, using the harnessed gem power to devastating effect on hordes of advancing demons. He'd never been able to figure out how demons had broken through the barrier, but now he knew.

Demons *hadn't* broken through. An elf had.

Jedda started inching toward the door again, but this time he didn't feel bad for her fear. Some vengeful part of him welcomed it, and whatever shame he felt for that was drowned out by the memories of the screaming custodians.

"Tell me!"

Jedda jumped. "I...my sisters and I...we found the gems. In a cave—"

"Bullshit!" The obvious lie broke his last tenuous thread of control, and with a roar, he seized her by the throat and backed her against a display case full of weapons from the Great Demonic War of Talas. "You stole them. You killed the humans who held them and you *stole them.*"

"No!" Clawing at his arm as he held it at her throat, she shook her head wildly. "Just the one human. My sister killed her. My other sister and I, we stole the gems from the other two humans and ran. They were alive when we left them."

Fury and hurt blurred his vision, so he got right up in her face. "They died right after," he snarled. "Their lives were bound to the gems and to us. When the gems were stolen, they died. Slowly. Their organs dissolved and their bones broke, and they collapsed in on themselves. Took hours."

He trembled with the force of his rage and the horror of the memories. The human who had been bonded to Razr's gem, a young man named Nabebe, had been chosen by Razr, rescued from certain death as a baby abandoned in the streets of eighteenth-century Baghdad. Razr had raised him, trained him, and given him eternal life as long as he was in possession of the gem.

Razr's voice broke as he told Jedda exactly what had happened to the boy he'd considered a son.

"Nabebe screamed until his throat was raw and he drowned in his own blood, and *I couldn't stop it.*" All Razr had been able to do was hold the boy and vow to inflict the same punishment on the people responsible.

"Oh, gods," she croaked. "I'm sorry. I didn't know. I assumed only elves bond with gems. I mean, humans are...humans." She stopped fighting him, tears welling in her eyes, but it didn't move him at all. "It was a long time ago—"

"And that makes it okay?" he asked, incredulous.

"No, just listen. We...my sisters and I... Things were different back then." She reached up, attempting to peel his fingers away from her throat again. He loosened his grip, but right now he wanted to keep her where she was, where he could feel the beat of her heart in the palm of his hand. "Gem elves' moral alignment comes from the gems we absorb. Gemstones from the human realm are mostly neutral, and gems from the demon realm are usually tainted by evil. Then there are enchanted stones. The most powerful stone we absorb becomes our life-stone, the one we will die without. It also determines our alignment." She swallowed and licked her lips, as if needing time to collect her words. And her breath. "See, when gem elves are born, the parents have gems standing by, ready to infuse the infants within moments of birth."

He released his grip a little more, and she relaxed slightly, the heated flush in her cheeks turning mottled. "Neutral gems?"

"Not always. Obviously, the parents' alignments play a role, but so does the sibling factor." She cleared her throat. "Now, do you want to hear the rest? Because it's easier to talk when someone isn't threatening to kill me."

That was probably true.

"I'm not going anywhere," she swore. "Where would I go? I don't know how to get out of this place."

That was also probably true. Plus, the door was locked.

On top of all that, he didn't like manhandling females. And like it or not, he desperately wanted to believe she hadn't killed anyone on purpose. Which sucked, because he'd sworn to avenge Nabebe. He'd promised to slay the thieves and recover the stones and set the world right again.

Cursing, he released her and backed up, his anger receding enough that he was shamed to see the red marks his fingers had left on her pale neck.

"Thank you." She reached up and absently rubbed her throat. "So as I was telling you, gem elves are super competitive. Since we all need stones to survive, we can get really intense around them. Family members have been known to kill each other for a single, small ruby." She faltered over that, and he wondered if there was a story behind it. "When my sisters and I were born, my parents hoped to prevent us fighting over stones, so they gave us each an enchanted life-stone with unique alignments. Manda's was evil, Reina's was neutral, and mine was good."

He frowned. "Why would your parents align your newborn sister with evil?"

Her gaze drifted toward the Lucifer ruby, as if seeking its input. "Good and evil are subjective, are they not?" She smiled thinly. "In my realm, all gems and alignments are rendered neutral. Those who have absorbed evil gems can live in the elf realm and have normal lives. It's what's expected of those whose life-stones are evil. It just doesn't always work out that way." A tremor crept into her voice. "It didn't with Manda."

As strange as that sounded to Razr, he figured he didn't have much room to judge, given that some angelic traditions were just as callous and brutal. He scrubbed his hand over his jaw as he tried to put all this new information together.

"Okay, so I get the need for siblings to not fight, but how would these alignments prevent you from fighting over, say, some lady's non-enchanted diamond wedding ring?"

"Non-enchanted gemstones are common, so there's really no competition except for rare types like Taaffeite. But when it comes to enchanted gems, the alignment of our life-stone makes us crave gems of the same, or similar, alignment. Every stone outside of our alignment shifts how we feel, how we act, and it can even conflict with our life-stone and make us sick."

Interesting. And bizarre. "Can you ever change your alignment?"

"Yes. But only if we replace the life-stone, which we do a few times in our lives as we find more powerful gems. But since most of the minor gems we gather tend to match the alignment of our life-stone, if you change the alignment of your life-stone, all the gems of the old alignment will conflict with it." She glanced over at the Lucifer ruby. "Going from neutral to either good or evil isn't that risky, and even going from good or evil to neutral isn't always a disaster, but you *really* don't want to shift from evil to good or vice versa." She reached up and wound a long lock of hair around her finger. "Our life-stone also controls our hair and eye color."

"Well, shit," Razr breathed, unsure where to go from here. He hadn't exactly planned for this scenario. He especially hadn't planned to get physically involved with one of the very people he'd vowed to butcher horribly. This was extremely inconvenient. "So your sisters had the other two stones?" At her reluctant nod, he cursed. "One was found. Ebel's amethyst."

She closed her eyes and blew out a long breath. "Manda had that one. I don't know how he tracked us down, but he did. We were young and dumb, and it was before we learned to store the gems in a safe place."

She paused, and he knew that whatever she was about to say was going to mess with everything he'd always believed: that Ebel had done what was needed, and whatever he'd done was justified. But now that Razr had let Jedda into his life, his views were no longer black and white. They were now a million shades of jewel tones.

"What happened, Jedda?"

Her ice-blue eyes grew liquid, like water on the surface of a melting glacier. "He tortured us, killed Manda, and took the gem back. Reina and I barely escaped."

Irrational rage spun up at the knowledge that Ebel had tortured Jedda. Didn't matter that he'd pretty much planned to do the same thing. Which was what made the anger so irrational. Well, that and the fact that Ebel was dead, so Razr's anger was pointless.

Inhaling deeply, he cursed Ebel's name and refocused his line of questioning. "You said Manda's alignment was evil. The Gems of Enoch are good. So how was she able to absorb the stone's power without it changing her?"

"It did change her," she insisted. "But not as much as it should have. I don't know why. The gems changed all of us in different ways." She looked somewhere beyond him, somewhere in her mind he couldn't follow. "They aren't as good as you think."

That didn't make any sense. "They're infused with angel blood," he argued.

She shrugged. "I don't care if they're infused with the blood of all the archangels and Enoch himself. I'm telling you, their energy is like nothing any of us had ever felt, nothing like I've felt since. It's almost as if their frequency cycles at super-high speeds through all the alignments. We assumed they were neutral, but they're anything but."

He wasn't sure what to believe, but right now, he supposed it didn't matter. They still had a crazy fallen angel to deal with, and then he had to figure out what to do about his own situation. One thing was clear: he wasn't getting back to Heaven anytime soon.

And why didn't that bother him as much as it should?

"Razr?" Jedda's voice was small. Trembling. "Are...are you going to kill me?"

Fuck. The fact that she had to ask left him trembling as hard on the inside as she was on the outside. "No," he said, reaching for her.

With a small gasp, she shrank away from him, and he couldn't blame her. Mere moments ago, he'd yelled at her. He'd wrapped his fingers around her delicate throat. He'd terrified her.

Ashamed, he reached again, slowly, letting her come to him. It took a long time. Too long. But finally she eased into his embrace, and nothing had ever been so worth the wait.

He tucked her close, his heart breaking when she sobbed into his chest. "We'll figure something out," he swore. "We'll fix this."

How, he had no idea, and if she believed him, he deserved an Oscar.

She nodded, and then she suddenly jerked away from him. Alarmed, he instinctively looked around for an enemy, but she was actually smiling, even as a tiny diamond tear plunked to the obsidian floor.

"I have an idea. I mean, I don't know how much it'll help, but it can't hurt. Something happened recently to put the Gems of Enoch into play, right? I mean, that's why you were able to find mine in Scotland. And that's why Shrike invited me to that icky dinner party."

"Yes," he said slowly. "I've been wondering what's up with that, as well."

"Then let's grab the crystal horn and go."

"Where?"

She grinned. "Where else? Middle Earth."

Chapter Eleven

Razr could tell that Jedda was still shaken as they materialized in the elven realm, which she'd said was known to her people as *Filneshara*, The Timeless Lands. Maybe being here on her home turf would be good for her, would ease her rattled nerves and help them both find some answers.

That was, of course, assuming they could find her sister.

"That's a pretty cool trick," he said, as the tourmaline she'd summoned for travel between elven hotspots and the The Timeless Lands disappeared back into her palm.

"Tourmaline is the only stone that allows us to travel here. We can only possess one at a time, and it can't be heavier than two ounces. Any more than that can throw us into dead space that we can't come back from."

"That sounds kind of horrible." He checked out their surroundings, disappointed that they could be anywhere in the earthly realm. They were at the top of a grassy hill surrounded by forest and meadows, which was scenic and colorful, but nothing special.

"It probably *is* horrible," she said. "No one has come back to describe the experience."

He frowned at her. "Then how do you know it exists?"

She pointed to a pond nestled in the valley of more rolling green hills in the distance. Its mirrored surface reflected sunlight from overhead and bright, candy-colored flowers in the meadows, not a single ripple marring the image.

"We can see them in the reflection sometimes. No one goes there except kids looking to scare themselves." She shook her head. "It's like when human kids play Bloody Mary with a bathroom mirror. Except this is real."

"Have you seen them?"

She shivered and started down the dirt path toward the trees. "My sisters and I went to the pond when we were girls. We saw three...I guess you could call them apparitions." She swallowed hard. "I can't imagine being trapped like that, clawing at the surface and hoping someone will save you."

Er, yeah. Razr's punishment wasn't looking so bad now.

A lavender-scented breeze rustled through the trees as they entered a jungle forest unlike anything Razr had ever seen, and the deeper into the woods they went, the more he realized he had been wrong about this realm. The trees swayed with the fragrant wind, their limbs heavy with silver-laced leaves that sprinkled glitter with every gust of air. It was clean here, with no hint of industrialization. No smog, no chemicals, no man-made filth.

As they walked, the trees got taller and more ornate, and Jedda giggled when he stumbled to a stunned halt. Mushrooms littered the forest floor, lit up like little neon bulbs in every color imaginable. Tiny winged creatures zipped between them, bouncing off their caps before darting upward in sprays of sparks. And here, in this forest, the trees grew around gemstones of every shape and size, their trunks surrounding them like string art.

"This...is extraordinary."

"Yeah," she sighed. "It is."

"Do these gemstones provide energy?"

She nodded and continued down the path. "They power everything here. Every tree grows around a gem, and each gem grows bigger with the tree. In the center of my town there's an oak growing around an emerald the size of an elephant." She pointed ahead, where the forest parted to reveal a village of buildings fashioned from live trees and thick vines, and there, at the very center, was the elephant emerald.

He couldn't stop staring in awe as she led him through the village, which bustled with activity, from people hawking baked goods or tending to gardens to a blacksmith who set a gemstone into each weapon he crafted.

"They're enchanted stones," Jedda told him as they walked past. "His weapons sell for a mint in other elf realms and Sheoul."

"There are other elf realms?"

She inclined her head in greeting at an azure-haired female who passed them with a basket of apples. "There are two, both connected to this one. The elves of those realms aren't allowed in *Filneshara* except to trade."

"Why not?"

She shrugged. "They're kind of assholes."

Man, he really needed to learn more about elves.

From somewhere above, a bird screeched, but the canopy was so thick it could have been a pterodactyl and he wouldn't have been able to identify it. No one else looked up, so he assumed it wasn't a predator, but the way the village's denizens were looking at him said he could be.

"I'm guessing you don't have a lot of visitors here. That orange-haired dude looks like he wants to put his sword between my ribs."

"The only otherworlders who come here are guests of elves." She picked up her pace, making a beeline for what appeared to be a gem show at the edge of the village. "The people here aren't afraid, just cautious. They know you have no power here."

"I don't?" Instinctively, he reached for the weak abilities he'd been left with, but it was like feeling around inside an empty box. Damn, he didn't like this. As pathetic as his remaining powers were, they'd at least been accessible. Now he felt naked. Exposed. Not even the demon realm was this disconcerting.

"Only elves wield magic here."

Angelic powers weren't "magic," but he knew what she meant. And he really, really needed to learn more about these people and this realm. He couldn't believe he hadn't known it existed. Were *any* angels aware of it?

"Jedda!" A slender male with pale pink hair and eyes waved from a booth displaying gemstones in every shade of green. "I have freshly mined jade and a cursed malachite I know you'd love." He waggled his brows, but she just laughed and waved him off.

"Not today, Tindol, but thank you."

Another elf tried to sell her a sapphire shaped like a banana, and another was convinced she'd love an ugly puke-green stone linked to a Viking legend.

"I'm just curious," Razr said as they passed yet another silver-tongued salesman. "Why do you have a gem market when you could just harvest the gemstones that grow with the trees?"

"Gods, no," Jedda gasped, her gaze darting around as if making sure no one had heard him. "That's one of the worst crimes you can commit here. No one gets away with it. No one."

One of the winged creatures he'd seen in the forest buzzed his ear, and he gently waved it away. "What happens to those who try?"

"Death by hanging."

He blinked. "I thought you said it was peaceful here."

"It is. It's not us who do the hanging." She lowered her voice and leaned close. "It's the trees."

He eyed the forest with new appreciation. "That's pretty badass."

"If you think the trees are badass, wait until you see—" She broke off and stumbled to a stop, and he instantly went on alert.

It only took a second to follow her gaze to see what had brought her up short. Just ahead, a red-haired, red-eyed female dressed in brown leather pants and a gold tunic blocked their path. A sword with a glittering ruby pommel hung at her hip, but it was the daggers she stared at Jedda that made Razr put himself between the two females.

"Tell me that's not your sister."

"I can't do that," Jedda said, her voice tight. "Razr, meet Reina."

* * * *

"Hello, Jedda."

Razr's arm snapped out to catch Jedda around the waist before she even knew her legs had wobbled. A surge of emotion flooded her, because no one had been there to catch her in a long time. His support meant even more to her given how everything had crashed down on her so hard back in Sheoul-gra. She couldn't believe she was still alive. Hell, she couldn't believe she was still alive *and* that Razr had forgiven her.

And now she was sharing her realm with him, something she'd never shared with anyone. She just had to hope the experience wouldn't take a nasty turn.

"Reina." Jedda wasn't sure what to think or how to feel, but it was a relief to see her. She looked the same as the last time she'd seen her, with sleek garnet hair and garnet eyes that required colored contact lenses for visits to the human realm.

"I sensed your arrival," Reina said, her lips pursed in annoyance. "You haven't been here in years."

"I haven't needed to come." Jedda wanted to hug her sister, but Reina had never been comfortable with physical affection, and Jedda wasn't sure where their relationship stood anyway. "Have you been here all this time?"

Reina waved her hand dismissively, but not before Jedda caught a flash of fear in her expression, gone so fast she might have imagined it. "I've always liked it here."

Jedda gave her sister a skeptical look. "You *hate* the elven realm."

With a shrug, Reina turned to Razr, her assessing gaze a little too appreciative for Jedda's taste. "Who's this?"

There wasn't going to be an easy way to introduce Razr and explain who he was, so Jedda just blurted it out and let Reina sort it out in her own head. "His name is Razriel, and he's one of the angels we stole the Gems of Enoch from."

It took about five seconds for that to sink in, and then Reina gasped and stepped back, her face draining of color. "Surely not..."

"It's true." Razr held up his hand and wiggled his ring finger.

Reina lost more color, and a massive cloud of diamond dust exploded around her. Through the glittering cloud, a faint crimson glow outlined Reina's body, a giveaway that she was drawing on the powers of her gems to use as a weapon. And here in The Timeless Lands, elves were twice as strong as in any other realm.

"Reina, you need to calm down—"

"Why did you bring him here?" Reina rounded on Jedda. "Otaehryn herwenys es miradithas?" *What the hell were you thinking*? "Cluhurach!" *Idiot*!

"He has no power here, Reina." Jedda kept her voice calm, trying to talk her sister down. "You know that." As she'd told Razr, only elves had power in *Filneshara*, but that didn't bring back any color to Reina's face. She still eyed him like he was going to smite her where she stood.

"Why is he here?" she demanded again, her voice at a near shout that made everyone in the nearby booths stare.

"Because we have questions." She slowly moved toward her sister, casually putting herself between Reina and Razr. "The Gems of Enoch are suddenly in play, and we need to know why. Did something happen to you recently? Something that would explain the fact that two fallen angels want them when no one has bothered us since...since Manda?"

"Not recently," Reina hedged, her voice low, as if Razr couldn't hear. "Well, mostly."

"Dammit, Reina, just tell me. What's happened since the last time I saw you?"

Reina nervously smoothed her hands down the belted gold smock she wore in the elven tradition over leather pants. "I don't want to talk in front of—" She glared at Razr. "—*him*."

Razr snarled, and before Jedda could blink, he had Reina backed up against a tree. He didn't touch her. Didn't need to. His anger and size got his point across with ease.

"When you stole from me and my team, you caused irreparable damage and death. I've forgiven Jedda, but you?" He bared his teeth at her. "I don't know you, and I don't give a shit what you want. You *will* answer her questions, and you'll do it in front of me."

"We owe him that," Jedda said softly but urgently. "We owe him at least that."

"Fine." Reina slipped around Razr and moved a few feet away, twitching like an angry cat. "But you aren't going to like it."

Razr folded his arms over his chest and leaned casually against the tree he'd just backed her into. His hip hit the bright yellow topaz in the trunk's center, and he just as casually stepped away, probably remembering what the trees did to those who tried to steal the jewels.

"I already assumed as much," he said. "Start talking."

"Start talking, *please*," Reina scolded him with as much sarcasm as she could fit into three words and her voice. She made a sound of disgust and turned to Jedda. "Right after I saw you last, an angel named Darlah found me."

"Darlah." Razr went as stiff as the tree behind him. "The Enoch garnet is hers."

"Yeah, no shit," Reina snapped. "I was dating a couple of Charnel Apostles, and—"

"A couple?" Jedda shook her head. One Charnel Apostle was unbelievable. But two? Those sorcerers weren't just evil, they were nuclear-level evil. "Why?" Before the floral-scented breeze even carried away her question, she knew. Charnel Apostles could create gemstones full of powerful magic, gemstones with limited life. Basically, they were like drugs, delivering an intense boost of energy or strength or spell power for any gem elf who ingested them. Plus, they were apparently gods in bed. "Never mind. So what happened?"

"This Darlah chick found me somehow. But I was with my guys at the time, and there was a battle... Long story short, Darlah got her hand chopped off and I got her bracelet."

Razr sucked in a harsh breath. "You have it? What happened to Darlah?"

"Who the hell cares?" Reina narrowed her eyes. "Oh, wait, was she your lover?"

The heartbeat of hesitation before Razr spoke was confirmation enough for Jedda, and while she had no right to be jealous, just thinking about Razr with someone else left a bitter taste in her mouth.

"It was a long time ago," he said, catching Jedda's gaze as if to make sure she understood that. "Now, what happened to her?"

"No idea where that bitch went." Reina clacked her long nails together in irritation. "As for the bracelet, well, I *did* have it. Then I started dating this fallen angel who was climbing the political ladder in Sheoul."

Jedda's gut clenched. "Don't tell me you did what I think you did..."

Reina winced. "I did. I gave Slayte the bracelet so he could harness the garnet's power. He told me he was going to rule Sheoul. I was going to be his queen." She swiped her hair out of her face with an angry shove. "Obviously, that didn't happen." She sniffed haughtily. "Oh, and whatever you do, do *not* fuck the person wearing your gem's jewelry."

Uh-oh. Jedda shot a furtive glance at Razr. "Why not?"

"Because it'll bond you to them." Reina studied her nails, which were studded with peridots on top of black polish. "Found that out the hard way."

"What the fuck are you talking about?" Razr's eyes flashed, reflecting the same mix of anxiety and confusion Jedda felt. The situation with Razr had already been complicated enough.

"I mean that they can control you. You know how I can heal people with my gem? Well, apparently, my gem can also be used to tear people apart." She smoothed her top again, clearing it of imaginary wrinkles. "That bastard used me to slaughter hundreds of demons at a time. Thousands." Her voice wavered with emotion, something Jedda hadn't heard from Reina since Manda died. "It was awful, but I had these feelings for him because of the stupid bond. I *wanted* to help."

"Where is he now?" Razr asked.

"Dead. A couple of months ago."

"How?"

"You wouldn't believe me if I told you."

Razr's leather jacket creaked as he folded his arms over his chest. "Try me."

Reina sighed. "The bastard was using the power to tear through an army of demons that belonged to some guy named...Revenant, I think it was. We were in some shitty region in Sheoul, and then out of nowhere, these four psychos with hellhounds rode in on horseback like the damned Horsemen of the Apocalypse and went all kinds of crazy on him. I escaped, but not before I saw Slayte get hacked to pieces and then eaten by the hellhounds."

Ew. Jedda wished she had a soda to wash the taste of bile out of her mouth. "Where is the bracelet?"

"I don't know. Probably in a pile of hellhound shit somewhere."

"Disturbing details aside," Razr began, "that explains why the gems suddenly came onto the scene. I didn't hear about that particular battle, but the Horsemen must have told angels about it, and those angels recognized the use of the Enoch gem."

Jedda looked over at Razr. "Who are these Horsemen?"

"Reina just told you. The Four Horsemen of the Apocalypse."

Reina snorted in disbelief and Jedda laughed, but quickly sobered. He wasn't kidding. "The actual Four Horsemen? They're real? You know them?"

"They're real." He crouched to pick up what elves called "clover agates," because of their color and shape. They were pretty, but their weak energy was suitable only to nourish the tiniest of infants. "I don't know them well. I've only seen Limos and Thanatos—Famine and Death—in passing. They visit Azagoth sometimes, and they often travel with hellhounds. I don't know why. Hell, I didn't even think the beasts could be tamed."

"If those things I saw were *tamed*," Reina said, "I'd hate to see what feral hellhounds are like."

Jedda nodded in agreement. Hellhounds were some of the worst fiends she'd ever encountered. Right behind Shrike. "So is that why you're here? You're hiding from whoever has the bracelet now?"

"I'm hiding from Darlah. She swore to destroy me. I felt safe while Slayte wore the bracelet—I mean, he was a cruel psychopath, but he wouldn't let anyone hurt me. Now that he's gone..." She drew in a ragged breath. "I'm cool with hanging out here for a while." She glanced at Jedda and Razr. "So what's up with you two? How'd you end up here?"

"Long story," Jedda sighed.

Reina arched a reddish eyebrow that almost matched her hair. "You guys fucked, didn't you? Oh, man, Jedda..."

"It's okay." Jedda hoped. Shit, this was a complication she didn't need. But it also explained why she felt the way she did about Razr.

Razr must have sensed her unease because he came up next to her and took her hand. "We need to talk. Can we catch up with your sister again later?"

Reina nodded. "If you're for real and truly forgave Jedda, where does that leave me?"

"I don't know," Razr said in a quietly ominous voice, "but I give you my word that I'll protect you as much as I can. *If* you give me your word that Jedda can always locate you."

For way too long, Reina considered Razr's deal, and finally, just as Jedda began to sweat beads of sillimanite, Reina agreed. "Just know this, angel. If anything happens to Jedda, you'll never find me again. I can hide here literally forever."

Razr inclined his head in acknowledgement and then, to Jedda's surprise, Reina came over and embraced her. "Let's not lose each other again," she murmured. "Losing our parents and Manda was enough."

Jedda didn't point out that Manda was responsible for their parents' deaths—over a stupid ruby—or that Reina had defended Manda until the end. Which was why Jedda and Reina had gone their separate ways after Manda died. But maybe now was the time to put all of that to bed. Or to at least open the door for it to happen.

"Agreed," Jedda said as she pulled away. "Someday...let's talk."

Reina smiled. And then, in a gesture of goodwill, she opened her fist and offered Jedda a shiny round moonstone. Jedda's hand shook as she took it and held it in her palm. It vibrated with Reina's energy, a tracking device of sorts that would allow Jedda to locate her sister at any time, in any place.

Summoning her own moonstone took a little effort; Jedda had never been as skilled as her sisters at producing gems at will. Still, a few seconds and a few silent curse words later, she offered Reina a rough oval moonstone containing her own energy signature.

Reina took the stone, gave Jedda another hug, and disappeared inside a tree-formed archway to the elf grand hall where everyone would be gathering for supper soon.

Razr squeezed her hand, a comfort she was learning she didn't want to live without. "What was that about?"

"Healing," she said with a faint smile. "It was about healing. I think my sister is finally embracing her life-stone."

Chapter Twelve

It was dark when Razr and Jedda arrived at her apartment. At first, the time of day didn't seem important. It wasn't until she turned on the TV that he realized they'd been gone three days.

Her eyes, which had been bright with hope when they left the elven realm, were bloodshot now, and her face seemed a little drawn, hints of shadow in the hollows under her high cheekbones. He wondered if travel between the realms took more effort than angelic travel, sort of like jet lag for humans.

With a heavy sigh, she tossed her keys into a basket filled with gemstones near the door. "I hate how time runs differently in the elven realm."

He was familiar with the concept since parts of Heaven and Sheoul operated with similar time anomalies, but he generally avoided those places. They always made him feel like he'd missed out on something, as if he'd wasted his life, and if there was one thing he'd learned in his centuries of existence, it was that every minute was precious, even for immortals. After all, immunity to natural aging didn't mean one couldn't be killed, and no matter what, everything changed. He didn't want to miss the changes.

"Okay, so." Rallying with squared shoulders and head held high, she headed to the kitchen, her long hair brushing against the swell of her fine ass with every step. He could watch that all day. "What's this bond thing Reina was talking about?"

"Ah. That." Yeah, this could get a little sticky. Repressing a groan, he scrubbed his hand over his face, partly because damn, he was tired too, and partly to buy a little time to figure out how to explain this without freaking Jedda out too much. Finally, he dropped his hands and got on with it. "The human custodians of the Gems of Enoch went through a ritual that bonded them to the gems. Then Darlah, Ebel, and I bonded ourselves to the humans."

Halting mid-step, she looked back over her shoulder at him. "You had sex with them? Isn't sex between angels and humans forbidden?"

"Ah...yeah. I mean, no. We didn't have sex with them." Well, Ebel had fallen in love with his human, but to this day Razr didn't know how intimate they'd been. "We exchanged blood. But obviously, there are a lot of ways to bond to someone."

"Can we break it?"

Razr flinched, stung. Which didn't make sense. Hers was a reasonable question. Who in their right mind would want to be tethered to someone else for life? For centuries. For all eternity, even. The idea should bother him, too.

But for some reason, he couldn't dredge up an ounce of give-a-shit. He'd been intensely attracted to Jedda before the sex, and afterward, nothing had felt different. He'd known almost from the beginning that he couldn't harm her to get his gem back, and that had nothing to do with any mystical bond. She'd been unique. Special. Decent. She'd proved as much when she'd gotten him away from Shrike and helped him recover.

She hadn't needed to do that. Truly, it hadn't been the smartest of decisions. Had he been, say, Ebel, he'd have slaughtered her without a second thought the moment he knew that doing so would release the gem.

"Razr?" Jedda turned fully around. "Can we break the bond?"

"Not while both of us are alive."

Grief swirled in her remarkable eyes, sending another spear of hurt right through him. "Well, that sucks," she muttered, and his hurt abruptly veered to anger.

"Don't worry," he snapped. "Once I tell my superiors that the two remaining Gems of Enoch are unrecoverable without destroying you and your sister and that I refuse to kill you or give up your locations, I'll probably be executed. Problem solved. The bond will be broken."

Her eyes flared in horror, making him regret his show of temper. Nabebe had taught him how easy it was to needlessly cause pain with words, a lesson he seemed to have forgotten in the years since the human's death.

"Oh, gods." Jedda closed the distance between them and laid a comforting hand on his forearm. "Are you serious? They'll kill you?"

"I don't know," he said grimly. "I don't even know if I'll tell them."

"What do you mean?" There was a desperation in her voice that called to every one of his possessive instincts, demanding that he assuage her fears, but he couldn't. All he could do was reach out and cup her cheek, telling her with a touch that, while this situation was a shit sandwich, at least they were eating it together.

And wasn't *that* all kinds of romantic? Cupid, he was not.

"I mean that I can lie indefinitely about searching for the gems," he replied. "No one has to know about you and your sister." Azagoth and Hades knew the truth about Jedda, but they wouldn't squeal. And Jim Bob knew that the Ice Diamond was in storage with the dhampires, but seeing how he wasn't exactly being upfront about who he was or what he was doing visiting Azagoth in secret, Razr doubted he was much of a threat.

"So you'd just live the way you've been living? With your wings bound and subjected to torture for the rest of your life? That's bullshit. Isn't there another way?"

He shrugged, unable to come up with any other way that made sense. "I could come clean, but that would put you at risk. Even if they don't execute me, they could take my ring and give it to another who will hunt you and your sister down." Damn, he was screwed. "No, I think it's best to never tell them. As I'm concerned, the gems are lost and will never be found."

She opened her mouth, probably to argue, but just then, the phone rang. "Hold on," she said in a stern voice that reminded him of one of his old battle coaches. "We're not done talking about this."

While she answered the phone, he considered their next move. They had to get Shrike out of the picture, both for Jedda's safety and to make sure the fallen angel's interest in the Gems of Enoch came to a permanent and, with any luck, a painful end.

Maybe if they—

He doubled over in sudden agony so intense he looked for

blood and a spear wound to the gut. Clenching his teeth, he checked the back of his hand and sure enough, his *Azdai* glyph was lit up like a neon fucking sign as days' worth of pain-free time caught up with him.

"Razr?"

He heard Jedda drop the phone, and then she was there beside him, her arm around his waist as she helped steady him against the back of the couch.

"Need...to get...to Azagoth," he gritted out. "Hurry." The nearest Harrowgate was close, barely a block away, but it was going to feel like miles.

Jedda guided him to the door, effortlessly bearing his considerable weight on her diminutive frame as he leaned on her through spasms of pain. Even through the searing agony, he had to admire her strength and determination. He'd always been attracted to athletic, fighter-type females like Darlah, but he was rapidly learning that one didn't have to be big and brawny to be a warrior.

Keeping him braced against her side, one arm wrapped around him, she reached for the door with her other hand and tugged on the knob. "Oh, shit." She tugged again, this time more forcefully, but it wouldn't open.

"Is it...locked?" He felt like a jackass for asking, but sometimes the obvious got missed.

Fortunately, she didn't take offense, simply shook her head. "It doesn't feel stuck, either. More like—" She broke off with a curse. "Stay here."

As if he could do anything else. His bones felt like they were melting and taking his muscles with them. As she gently pulled away, he sagged against the wall.

She hurried to the window and let out a string of angry words in what he assumed was Elvish. He also assumed they were creative obscenities. "We're trapped."

A groan rattled his chest. "Trapped?"

"Shrike's minions. At least a dozen. They must have been watching for my return. I think they've trapped us with wards."

Every breath was labored now, as if he was breathing whips of fire. "Can you...get us to...ah, Rivendell?"

"It's Filneshara." Diamond dust filled the air, shredding his already compromised lungs, and he knew they were in real trouble. "The travel stones to my realm only work from *faeways*." Her voice was pitched with alarm, and he couldn't blame her.

But now wasn't the time to panic. As he told his Memitim students, stay active. No matter how much shit you're in, do something, anything, to stay focused.

"My pocket," he rasped. "In my pocket."

Quickly, she fumbled around in his jacket and pulled out the cat-o'-nines. Which she promptly dropped on the floor with a hiss. "You can't be serious. I can't, Razr. I can't. Please don't make me do it."

He inhaled, riding a relatively mild wave of pain as he straightened. "You have to. If we can't leave, you have to."

Her face contorted in misery. "I don't want to hurt you."

He hooked a finger under her chin, lifting her gaze to his, hating that this was hurting her. His pain didn't matter. It was hers that was tearing him apart right now. "I'm used to it. And I heal fast. You've seen it."

"I've also seen you pass out. And I saw how you looked just before you did." She turned away, her breaths coming in panicked wheezes. "I can't."

His skin was starting to blister, and inside his body, a firestorm of agony ripped through him as his bones began to fracture with audible cracks. "You can do it lightly," he said, desperately trying to keep his voice level so she wouldn't know how much this was making him want to scream.

Except that he was silent in his pain. He always had been. *Keep it inside*, his father used to say after a harsh training session. Which was all of them. One of the hazards of being born to two high-ranking, militant battle angels who expected their offspring to go down as legends, he supposed.

They'd been pretty disappointed in him, given the whole *fuck up an elite team and lose all their magic gemstones* thing. They hadn't even visited him in prison. Not once.

Jedda shook her head. Her entire body trembled and dammit, he couldn't make her do this.

"Okay," he croaked. "Get one of Shrike's guys in here." Something inside him popped, and he stumbled, catching himself on the fireplace mantel. "Hurry."

"I'm not letting some psycho stranger hurt you!"

He coughed, spewing blood. She cursed, came around him, and stripped off his shirt. She tossed it to the floor and started on his pants, which he would have enjoyed if he wasn't in agony and she wasn't about to torture him.

Something else inside him snapped—a rib, he thought, as he dropped to his knees. Shit, he was in so much pain right now that the cat in Jedda's hand would feel more like a loving stroke than a vicious rake.

She hesitated, and he had to clench his teeth to keep from screaming at her to get on with it. "Go...ahead. Do it, Jed. You can do it."

The straps came down on his back so lightly he would have laughed if he'd had the breath to do it. It hurt, but what hurt more was the cry that tore from her at the sound of the leather striking his flesh. He was so preoccupied by the misery he'd caused her that he almost didn't notice that all his other pain unrelated to the cat-o'-nine was gone now that the punishment was being executed.

He sagged in relief. "Again, Jedda. Five more." His voice was as shredded as his back was going to be.

"No," she whispered, her agony thickening the air, but a moment later she slapped the cat across his back. The blow was gentle, which somehow made it even worse. She was trying so hard not to hurt him.

"Again."

"I hate you for this," she cried out as she brought the straps down.

He hated himself, too. But it would never happen again. Once they took down Shrike, he'd take his sorry ass back to Sheoul-gra and let her have a normal life. One where she didn't have to hurt him or see him hurt.

One where he didn't have to watch her *be* hurt.

"Again, Jedda. Harder. The more painful it is, the more time I get between sessions." Usually. Sometimes the intervals were utterly random, as far as he could tell.

"No. I—"

"Do it!" he shouted. He needed her to be harsh. Make it hurt.

Give him more time. And if he had to piss her off to get it, he would. "Dammit, Jedda, fucking hit me!"

She did, a little harder. But barely. Then again. Her cry of pain tore through him, reaching all the way to his soul, and when she struck again, for the first time in his life, he screamed. Screamed not for himself and his shredded back. He screamed for her, for hurting her so deeply.

"Oh, gods, I'm so sorry," she sobbed, hitting the floor in front of him to gather him in her arms. He clutched her close as the *tink* of tiny diamond tears hitting the floor played like background music.

"No, I'm sorry," he whispered. "I am so, so sorry. Please forgive me, Jedda. *Please.*"

When she didn't say anything, he knew, and the dull ache that compressed in his chest became the most horrific torture he'd ever endured.

She didn't forgive him. But maybe that was for the best. It would make leaving her so much easier.

Chapter Thirteen

Razr wouldn't let Jedda tend to his wounds. She'd watched him suffer, bleed, and withdraw into himself as she held him in her arms, unable to give him the one comfort he'd asked for.

Her forgiveness.

It wasn't that she didn't forgive him for making her hurt him. There was nothing *to* forgive. She'd done what she had to do, even as she hated him for it. Hated *herself* for it.

Because ultimately, it was her fault he was going through this torment in the first place.

Jedda couldn't let this go on. She couldn't let Razr live the rest of his life like this.

She had to give up his gem.

The moment they were done with Shrike—assuming they survived the meeting—she'd scour the human and demon realms for a gemstone more powerful than the Enoch gem, and if she couldn't find one, maybe Azagoth would be willing to do what needed to be done to her.

She'd die, but Razr would no longer live a life of suffering. Suffering that she was directly responsible for. If she hadn't stolen his gem, he wouldn't be in this mess.

Rain pelted the window she'd been staring out of for hours, her gaze fixed on Shrike's minions. The soaking-wet demons lurked on the sidewalk, their beady eyes as dead as she felt on the inside. On the outside, she looked the way she felt: exhausted and bruised, a result, she thought, of Shrike's Lothar curse. The last time she'd checked herself in the mirror, she'd been shocked at how gaunt she looked, and even now when she glanced down at her arms, her breath caught at the purple bruises spreading under skin that had grown dull and grayish.

She and Razr were quite the pair, weren't they?

Footsteps pounded in the hallway, and her stomach turned over even as her heart fluttered. She was an emotional disaster, something she'd never been. Probably because she'd never had strong feelings about any male, let alone one who needed things she couldn't give him. Because one thing was certain: she could never, *ever*, hurt Razr again. Nor could she watch it. Or even know it was happening.

She'd always thought she was strong, but the events of the day had proven that she was nothing of the sort.

"Jedda?"

She couldn't even look at him. Her shame had tied her in knots she wasn't sure would ever be untangled. "What?"

"I think we can kill Shrike."

Shame took a backseat to surprise, and she finally glanced up. Razr looked like hell, his expression bleak, his eyes haunted. Gods, she'd hurt him so badly, hadn't she? "What do you mean? How?"

"My powers are bound, but the Enoch gem's aren't. Through the bond we share, I can access it."

Her heart gave an excited thump. Her world might be shit right now, but this was good news. Shrike had cursed her to growing misery, and although she hadn't told Razr, she could feel the crushing pressure of it even now. The moment they'd come back to the earthly realm from the elven one, she'd experienced a painful squeezing sensation, one that made her skin feel like shrink-wrap. She could only imagine how much worse it would get over the course of the next couple weeks.

"What kind of power are we talking about?"

"A concussive blast that will blow apart any demon it touches, including fallen angels." He gestured toward the door. "We'll tell his buddies out there that we have what he wants and we're ready to go."

"They'll want proof."

"We have the crystal horn. That'll get us inside the castle."

As far as suicidal propositions went, this was a good one. "And afterward? Assuming we survive?"

"Then you come back here and resume your life. I'll return to

Sheoul-gra and pretend to keep looking for the Gems of Enoch. No one has to know I found them. You and your sister will be safe."

It was how it had to be and she knew it. At least, it was how it had to be until she found a replacement gem or died trying.

But she couldn't let it end like this. She moved to him, and when he tried to step back, she persisted. "I know this is going to sound crazy, but I... I think I love you." His eyes flared wide, but she didn't regret her words. "Thank you for finding me. I'm so glad it was you."

Razr's gaze was tortured, but etched in his expression was something else. Something she wished she hadn't seen.

Love. He loved her too.

Very slowly, he reached out and cupped her cheek, his thumb smoothing away the teardrop rolling down her face and the tiny gem that formed behind it. She moaned as he lowered his mouth to hers and kissed her with so much tenderness and passion her knees nearly buckled. Heat spread through her veins, followed by a chill that sat on her skin like frost.

This was it. Good-bye.

When he pulled away, it was clear he knew it too.

Chapter Fourteen

The journey to Shrike's place, mostly via Harrowgate with a little walking, was silent. Shrike's goons weren't the talkative type, for which Razr was enormously grateful. And Jedda...she just seemed broken.

Because of him. Because he'd made her hurt him and because there was no point in trying to earn her forgiveness or make her feel better. The angrier she was at him, the better.

But it sucked. More than having his wings bound by gold rope. More than being flogged on a regular basis. More than being kicked out of Heaven in disgrace.

On top of it all, he was going to lose her. She would eventually move on to a new male, maybe some hot fucking Legolas from Pandora. Or whatever.

Fuck.

He kept an eye on her as they approached the ballroom where Shrike was playing a game of darts. The dart board was unique, though: a demon's crucified body, with no discernible point system. Well, Razr would spot Shrike points for creativity, as well as a handicap for his mental disorder.

Ramreels with their unholy halberds stood like statues at evenly spaced intervals around the room, their piggy eyes watching Razr and Jedda's every move. They were big bastards, over seven feet tall with thick muscles under their fur. Or did they have wool? Razr had never asked, even though he'd encountered hundreds over the years. Ramreels were sort of all-purpose demons, common and plentiful enough to form armies but capable enough to act singly as bodyguards or even butlers. Apparently, they were even good cooks.

One thing they weren't, though, was subtle. Not when they resembled giant rams, carried halberds, and stomped their hooves on the floor in anticipation as they were doing now. They wanted to fight, and the tension in the room only fueled their bloodlust.

"We have what you want," Razr announced, getting right to it.

Shrike's lips peeled back from his straight, white teeth. Dude had a good dentist. "I knew you'd come through for me. Let me see."

Jedda had carried the horn in a black velvet bag to the castle, but now she gave it to Razr. She'd said she couldn't touch quartz crystal, but she hadn't said why. Doing so would have required more talking than she was apparently willing to do.

He reached into the bag and pulled out the heavy crystal sculpture.

"That wasn't easy to acquire," she said, following the script they'd worked out before leaving the apartment. Shrike needed to believe she'd found it and not that Razr had borrowed it from Azagoth.

Shrike's eyes, locked on the horn, glittered with greed. "That's why I hired you."

"Hired?" Fists clenched, she took a step toward him as if she wanted to throttle him. *That's my girl.* "Seriously? *Hired?* You gave me no choice. You forced me."

"Forced?" Shrike asked innocently. "Such an ugly word. I gave you *incentive.* But I don't go back on my word. I'll pay, of course."

"Yes," Razr said softly, "you will."

He moved toward the fallen angel as if to hand him the horn, but with every step he drew on the power of the Enoch gem, power that streamed from Jedda in a shaft of light that was blinding to him, but invisible and undetectable to everyone else. The energy building inside him churned and swelled, filling him with a unique ecstasy he'd not experienced for a century.

Battle lust scorched his veins, and anticipation made his fingers flex. He'd needed this for a long time. This was what he was born to do, and he had a lot of fury to unleash.

"Wait!" A familiar voice screeched from somewhere in the building. The sound of running footsteps pounded toward them. Could it be...

A female in black leather pants and a silver crop-top burst into the great hall at the top of the grand staircase, her short chestnut hair curling around pierced ears Razr used to nibble.

He stumbled backward in shock, severing his link to Jedda. "*Darlah?*"

"Razriel?"

They stared at each other, and he wondered if she was as numb as he was.

"Darlah?" Jedda eased up beside him. "As in, *Darlah?* Your gem angel buddy? Your *lover?*"

"Ex-lover," he muttered. By the look on Shrike's face, the lover thing was news to him, and he wasn't happy about it.

"Someone had better explain what's happening," Shrike growled. "How do you know each other? Besides intimately."

Darlah, her face pale, didn't take her golden brown eyes off Razr as she descended the stairs. "Razriel was one of the Triad."

Suddenly, everything clicked into place. Razr's ex-lover was why Shrike had known about the *Azdai* glyph. He'd been meting out the punishment Darlah required. And she was also his source of information about the Gems of Enoch. But he hadn't known everything, which meant Darlah had been sparing with the details. She'd been smart to keep some things to herself, but Razr wouldn't expect anything else from her. He might have been the team leader and Ebel had been the brute force, but she'd been the strategist.

"Darlah, what are you doing here?" He gestured to Shrike. "With this crazy motherfucker."

Laughing bitterly, she stepped onto the landing. "Did you really think I'd go back to Heaven without my gem? Ebel found his and they still killed him. Imagine what they'd do to you or me."

"Bullshit," he snapped, angry at this betrayal. She'd been hiding all this time, and worse, she'd been hiding in a psychotic fallen angel's tacky lair. "Ebel is dead because his stone was tainted by evil, not because he returned to Heaven with it."

She cocked an eyebrow. "And how was he tainted by the evil?"

Razr threw up his hands in frustration. "Obviously, he must have bonded with the host. And because she was evil, he went insane and..." He trailed off, sickened by the implications of what he'd just voiced.

A glance at Jedda, at the trauma in her expression, confirmed his suspicion, and now it all made sense. Ebel's proximity to Manda and the evil taint of the stone had released evil in him, too. He must have raped her, sealing the malevolence in his soul. When he killed her and took the stone, the evil went with him, and he'd had to be destroyed.

How much of that had Jedda witnessed? No wonder she'd been terrified back in Azagoth's treasure room when she'd learned the Ice Diamond was his. She'd seen an angel behave in the most heinous of ways. And Razr's own behavior hadn't exactly been exemplary.

"It doesn't matter," Darlah said. "I'm not going back. But I do want my fucking stone." She snarled at Jedda. "I was close. So close. But your bitch of a sister had powerful friends."

Jedda sucked air. "You know who I am?"

"Fool," Darlah spat, her lips twisted in an ugly knot of rage. He used to kiss that mouth. Now he just wanted to gargle with kerosene to get the bad taste out of his own mouth. "That's why we chose you to find the gemstones. We figured you'd know where to find Reina."

"And if Jedda couldn't? Or wouldn't?" Razr shot back. "What then?"

Shrike tossed a dart, and it made a sickening squishy noise on impact with the dead demon's third eye. It really was an impressive shot, Razr supposed.

"We were hoping Jedda could find the bracelet as well as the matching gemstone." Shrike swung back around to Razr and Jedda. "But if not, we figured we could still get Jedda's."

"Jedda's is useless without my ring," Razr pointed out. "And you couldn't have known I'd randomly show up at the dinner party."

Darlah laughed. "I admit, that was a stroke of luck, but I would have found you eventually." She held up her arm to reveal her severed hand, making clear that she'd have done the same to him to get the ring.

Ah, shit. This situation could go bad, and fast, because clearly, they'd been prepared to kill Jedda to get the stone, and now they were prepared to kill or dismember him, as well. Wasn't going to happen, though. No way.

"Well," Shrike said with a dramatic sigh—because fallen angels were fucking drama queens, "I admit I'm kind of at a loss. I'm not sure where we go from here. I'm guessing you didn't bring Darlah's gem and bracelet."

"Even if we had," Jedda snapped, "do you think we'd give them to you now? You were planning to kill me, you bastard." She pegged Darlah with an accusing glare. "Bastard*s*."

"Darlah," Razr warned, "you know Heaven is going to find out about this. They'll never let you back in."

"Good!" She threw out her arms and her bound wings popped from her back. They'd been beautiful once, white with shiny mink tips. Now they were trussed like a roast turkey, with thick gold rope strangling the feathers and bones. Razr's looked like that too, and seeing hers made them throb. "Let them find out. Let them sever my wings so I can have the power of the Fallen when they grow back. This is where I belong." She made an encompassing gesture. "This is where I will make my name. Here I can rule demons instead of serve angels."

"I've heard that story before," he said, as every tale of Satan's rebellion filtered through his mind. "It won't end well for you."

"No, my love," she whispered. "It won't end well for *you*."

Suddenly, a flash of light and a massive swell of scorching heat slammed into him, knocking him into a pillar twenty feet away. Jedda screamed as she careened off another pillar and into a wall with a sickening crunch. Another blast hit Razr before he could recover. Fire seared his skin, and the stench of singed hair filled his nostrils. Every muscle screamed in agony at the cellular level from the impact of the energy wave.

Only Shrike would have been capable of using that particular fallen angel weapon, and with Razr's power bound by angels, he couldn't fight it. He needed Jedda.

He reached out with his mind for the power of the Enoch gem... But there wasn't so much as a spark. What the hell?

Groaning, he rolled to his feet as Darlah heaved the blade of a sword down so close to his head that he felt the gentle kiss of it passing next to his ear. Sweeping his legs out, he caught her at the knees, bringing her down in a clumsy sprawl. But she was quick, and she was on her feet before he made it halfway to Jedda, who hadn't moved since the initial blast. Blood and gemstones formed in a puddle around her, expanding with alarming speed.

Be okay. Please be okay—

Something hit him from behind, knocking him to his knees with the force of the blow and the intensity of the pain. Warm blood splashed down his back and hips, and holy fucking shit, he might have lost an organ or two as well. As he hit the floor, realization clobbered him as hard as the blow had.

He'd taken a strike from a halberd, its sharp, foot-long head buried deep between his shoulder blades.

His ears rang, and he wasn't sure which was louder: his pounding pulse or Shrike's maniacal laughter. He was going to die like this. And so was Jedda, if he couldn't rouse her to consciousness.

Desperately, he dragged himself toward her, the halberd's heavy pole-handle scraping the floor and sending fresh rounds of agony clawing through him with every inch of progress he made.

Almost there...almost there... "Jedda," he rasped. Her eyes opened, dazed and lacking the brilliance he loved to see. "I need your power, baby. You can do it."

All around her, the ice-blue glow of the gem's power flickered to life. But "flickered" was the key word. Her power was fluctuating, weak, and they were in some serious trouble.

* * * *

Jedda wasn't afraid of dying. Especially not if dying meant Razr could return to Heaven and be reinstated as an angel and would no longer suffer the horrific torture he'd been subjected to for years.

But dying for any other reason was bullshit, and the sight of him trying to drag himself to her, a weapon impaled in his back, misery etched on his handsome face... It made her angry and heartbroken and dammit, her will to live was stronger than this.

Even as her mind rallied, her body failed. Gemstones formed all around her, large ones, powerful ones. She wasn't just bleeding; her organs were failing.

A smile twisted Shrike's lips as he threw out his hand, and a sizzling strike of lightning hit Razr in the neck. He tried to scream, but the only thing that came from his ruined throat was smoke.

"No," she croaked. "*No!*"

Gritting her teeth, she found one last surge of energy. One last chance to end this. With a shout of agony, she lunged at Razr, sliding through her own slippery blood. Somehow, her hand found his, her fingers closing around the glowing gemstone in his ring.

It was enough. As if she'd plugged them into an electrical socket, they both lit up with an ice-blue aura of energy.

"Stop them!" Darlah shouted. Frantic, Razr's bitch of an ex reached for the nearest weapon, a dart, and hurled it at Jedda. But, just like in the mines, her body sensed danger, her skin hardened into a diamond shield, and the dart bounced harmlessly to the floor.

Oh, that *necrocrotch skank* had to die. And if Jedda survived this, she was going to give Suzanne a huge high-five.

Shrike produced a ball of fire at his fingertips, but he wasn't fast enough. Razr, energized by the gem connection he shared with Jedda, triggered an atomic shockwave of death in an expanding circular wave. The entire building shook, and a chorus of screams filled the air. Blood and body parts rained down in a gruesome tempest of death, and when it was over, nothing was left standing.

Not even the necrocrotch skank.

Pain throbbed through every cell, but it was the exquisite pain of regeneration, and Jedda welcomed it. Groaning, she swept her arm through the gemstones on the floor, absorbing them back into her body to accelerate the process.

"Razr?" Weakly, she lifted her head, expecting to see him picking up his own pieces.

Instead, she saw him lying in a pool of blood, his eyes open and glazed with pain. Sure, the halberd impaled in his back probably had something to do with that, but worse, so did the fact that his damned *Azdai* glyph was lit up.

"Fucking angels." Emotion choked her, leaving her voice completely wrecked. "How can they do this to you? How?"

Tears streamed down her face, and the gems that formed from them clinked on the floor, creating a heart-wrenching score for what had turned out to be both a victory and a defeat. She'd survived, they'd *both* survived, but Razr's life hadn't changed.

Sobbing, she crawled over to him and wrenched the halberd from his body. He didn't make a sound, and for a moment afterward, she thought he was dead. Diamond dust poofed in a massive cloud as she gathered him in her arms, but when he took a deep, ragged breath, she cried out in relief.

"What can I do?" she asked. Begged, really. "I won't hurt you again. Anything but that."

Blood dripped from the corner of his mouth. "Stop," he wheezed. "Let it happen."

Let *what* happen? "I don't understand. Razr? Please..."

"Shh." His hand shook as he reached up and traced a finger over her lips. "You need...to go."

"No—"

"You..." He swallowed. "You said...you'd do anything. I want you to go."

"Why?"

"Angels." He shivered violently. "They're coming."

Terror turned her blood to ice. They'd kill her. They'd kill her to release the Enoch gem from storage. Panic threatened to swamp her, but before the diamond dust made another glittery show, she pulled it back. No. She would not give in to fear. And she would not give in to Razr.

If angels were coming, she'd stay.

One way or another, Razr's nightmare was coming to an end.

Chapter Fifteen

Razr writhed as Jedda held him, her soft hands stroking his hair, the only place her touch didn't make him want to scream in pain. Why wouldn't she leave? They'd won the battle, which meant she was free. If she didn't get the fuck out of here she was going to get caught by whoever showed up to either kill him or torture the hell out of him, and, while he could accept his fate, there was no way he could allow harm to come to her.

They would *have* to kill him if they hurt her.

He wished he could see her, but Shrike's lightning strike had burned his eyes, and now everything was in fuzzy grayscale. Jedda's beautiful face was nothing more than a blob of haze.

"I hate this." She sniffled, and his heart ached. "I hate this so much. I hate angels for doing this to you!"

"We're not overly fond of you, either," came a deep voice.

Jedda jumped, sending a fresh wave of hellish pain and dread through Razr's body. "Who the hell are you?"

"My name is Gadreel."

Gadreel...Razr panted through another wave of misery as he ran the name through his weary brain. "Gadreel," he murmured. "Archangel?"

Jedda gasped. "You're an archangel?"

"Last time I looked."

"Can you do something about Razr? Can you stop his pain?"

Instantly, the agony melted from his body, and he sagged against Jedda in blessed relief. Relief he had a feeling would be short-lived. At least his vision had cleared. He'd be able to see death coming.

Today, death was a big dude in black slacks, a black shirt, and a long black trench coat. Fitting, Razr supposed. All he was missing was an executioner's hood.

"You two made a mess." Gadreel looked around the castle ruins, his long blond hair blowing in the breeze from the gaping hole in the south wall. "And if I'm not mistaken, that decapitated head over there belongs to Darlah."

Razr struggled to sit up, his body feeling as weak as a newborn's. He blinked up at the newcomer. The angel looked familiar, but he couldn't figure out why. He'd have remembered meeting an archangel. Maybe he'd seen the guy in passing at some point. It wasn't as if every angel knew every other angel in Heaven, after all, and archangels were especially reclusive.

"I didn't expect you to be here so soon." Razr rolled his head to work out a kink in his neck. "My *Azdai* glyph just triggered."

"That isn't what drew me here." Gadreel pinned Jedda with his steely gaze. "The power of the Enoch gem did."

Razr inhaled a ragged breath as he shoved awkwardly to his feet. "Don't touch her," he growled. "Do *not* touch her."

"Why would I?"

Razr blinked in confusion. Did Gadreel not know that Jedda possessed the stone? "I don't understand."

Gadreel flared his gold-flecked white wings. "That's because you're a lesser angel." He sighed as if he felt sorry for those who weren't sitting at the top of the food chain like he was. The prick. "Your gem elf friend here is qualified to wield Gems of Enoch."

Jedda and Razr exchanged glances. Now Razr was really confused. "I thought only humans could do that."

"No, the rule is that demons and angels *can't*. Which means humans and elves *can*."

Relief nearly sapped Razr's energy right out of him. "Until I met Jedda I didn't even know elves existed."

"Few do," Gadreel said with a shrug. "They don't belong in our...reality, I guess you'd say. Their lives and deaths happen on another plane of existence. But because they are neutral forces, they can wield the Enoch gems as well as, or better than, any human."

Jedda stepped forward. "Mr., ah, Gadreel, can I ask why the gems don't have exclusively 'good' vibes surrounding them? They're not even neutral. They're hard to pin down, really."

He inclined his head. "That's because each contains a small amount of demon blood."

Well, Razr hadn't seen that coming. "Why? Angel blood is far more powerful."

"Because the gems are used to fight demons. How would their energy know the difference between humans and demons without a baseline?" Gadreel's massive wings folded behind his back, the tips just barely kissing the floor. "Probably something we should have told you."

"Yeah. Probably." Razr couldn't keep the sarcasm out of his voice, and Gadreel shot him a glare. But hey, it could have been worse. A lot worse.

"Come on." Gadreel waved his hand, erasing the demon and fallen angel remains and sending their souls to Azagoth. The *griminions* would be disappointed to have their job stolen from them. "I'll zap the elf back to her realm and take you home."

Oh, fuck that. Razr took Jedda's hand and tugged her close, ignoring her little squeak of surprise. "I'm staying."

Gadreel wheeled around, his coat flapping at his calves. "What do you mean, you're staying?"

Razr took a deep breath and blurted, "I mean that I'm refusing reinstatement as an angel."

"What?" Jedda tugged on his hand. "Are you serious?"

"Yeah," he said, grinning. "I am."

The archangel stared. "No one refuses angelic reinstatement."

"Uh, dude." Razr couldn't believe Gadreel had said that. He knew of two angels who had refused in the last few years. "It's happened a lot recently. You guys are breaking rules left and right."

Gadreel flared his wings again, either out of boredom or irritation. Probably irritation. "Armageddon is nigh."

Okay, sure, as an angel battling demons, Razr had known that Armageddon would eventually come, and every fight had been considered preparation. Thanks to the Four Horsemen, it had almost happened. But, also thanks to the Horsemen—as well as a few angels and demons—it had been pre-empted. World saved. Humanity rescued. Whether that was a good thing or a bad one had yet to be seen.

"I hate to tell you this," Razr said as he bent to retrieve

Azagoth's crystal horn, "but we just stopped Armageddon. We're cool now."

Gadreel's eyes glowed so bright that Razr and Jedda stepped back. "I'm talking about Satan. He's contained, but he'll be loose soon. We must prepare."

Jedda's breath caught, and she let out a strangled squeak. "How soon?"

"Nine hundred and ninety-ish years," Razr replied as he kicked aside the halberd that had nearly split him in half. "Give or take a couple of years."

She gave him a you've-got-to-be-kidding me look. "You're alarmed now by something that won't happen for almost a thousand years?"

"A thousand years is the blink of an eye for angels." Gadreel turned to Razr. "Now stop being a fool and come with me. The Archangel Council will want to see you."

Razr tucked the crystal horn in his pocket and stood his ground. "I'm staying here."

"Razr, no." Jedda drew him aside, keeping her voice low. "I can't watch you be tortured over and over. Not for me."

"Oh, for crying out loud," Gadreel snapped. "We can reinstate you as an angel and you won't have to live in Heaven." He cocked his head and drilled Razr with a look he could only describe as cruel. "But there's a catch. Naturally."

"Naturally," Razr muttered.

"Azagoth likes your work with the Memitim. You will live in Sheoul-gra and continue in his service except when you and Jedda are needed for battles with the Enoch gem. And you'll continue your search for the remaining gem and jewelry."

Razr's heart pounded against his ribs as both excitement and worry squeezed his chest. He didn't want to lie about Jedda's sister, but he'd promised to protect her, as well. "What happens when I find them?"

"Since we have the amethyst set, we'll assign it, and you'll form another Triad."

Jedda grinned. "We'll be like the Avengers."

Gadreel scowled. "The what?"

"Nothing," Razr said. "I agree. To everything."

"Wait." Jedda pulled Razr aside once again. "What if *I* don't agree?"

His heart stopped pounding. Just seized up like an engine. "What are you saying? That you don't want to be with me?"

"Of course I want to be with you." She licked her lips and cast a worried look at Gadreel. "But I need to know you want that too. I know you just said you did, but earlier, before the battle... It was good-bye, and you know it."

He pulled her into a tight embrace, sorry he'd put her through that. "I had to, Jedda. I was afraid for your life. I didn't want to lead anyone to you."

"So you really want me?"

"I've never wanted anything more."

Gadreel huffed. "I give up. Come to the Archangel Council on your own. You have forty-eight hours." He waved his hand, and ecstasy tore through Razr as his body filled with light.

His wings, once strangled by rope, burst from his back in a twenty-foot span of iridescent pearl, and power surged through his veins in a cascade of glorious heat. A zipper-like sensation skittered over his skin as the tattoos meant to add an extra layer of restraint on his angelic powers dematerialized.

He was free.

"Razr," Jedda whispered in awe as she fingered one silky feather and sent shivers of pleasure through his every nerve ending. "Your wings... They're beautiful."

"Razriel," Gadreel corrected her. Then he disappeared in a flash of light, leaving them alone in the wrecked castle.

"Call me whatever you want," Razr said as he pulled her against him. "I'll always answer."

He felt her smile against his chest, and it warmed him like nothing else ever had. "You have no choice now that we're bonded."

Gently, he pressed a kiss into her hair. "I had a choice," he reminded her. "I chose you."

Chapter Sixteen

"Well, what do you think of our new home?"

So excited she could hardly contain the happy gemstone tears, Jedda looked around the manor Azagoth had chosen for them on the outskirts of his little city. The decor was exquisite in jewel tones and a mix of ancient Greece and modern London, complete with a MIND THE GAP sign hanging in the kitchen.

But it was the bedroom that had Jedda finally shedding a couple of tiny diamonds.

All of Razr's hideous burlap robes were gone, replaced by a closet full of new clothes. Even now, he looked absolutely edible in a pair of jeans, an untucked sapphire shirt...and flip-flops. Well, she couldn't fix everything.

Even better, a bed made to sleep four people comfortably took up half of the room, there was a hot tub in the corner—a gift from Zhubaal and his mate, Vex, both of whom seemed to have an affinity for them—and in another corner was a reading nook full of fiction and nonfiction books about elves and gemstones.

The most fascinating thing, though, was the item lying in the middle of the bed. The note attached to it said simply, *Enjoy ~ Azagoth.*

Razr scowled and picked it up. "Why would he give us a crystal dildo? You're like, allergic to quartz or something, right?"

Her cheeks burned so hot she thought she might catch on fire. "Not...exactly."

"You said you can't touch it."

"I said I can't touch it in public." She gave him a sheepish grin. "Or if I plan to get anything done."

He narrowed his eyes at her. "What are you not telling me?"

Emboldened by his curiosity, she slowly peeled out of her clothes, making him watch as he held the sex toy in a white-knuckled death grip. When she was completely naked, she gestured to him. "Your turn."

Cursing, he tossed the dildo on the bed and stripped out of his clothes so fast he might have set a record. He stood before her, his massive erection curving upward into his flat belly. Lust rolled off him in a wave of heat, and a rush of liquid desire dampened her core.

Not yet. First, she had to taste him.

She sauntered over, loving how his breath hitched as she went to her knees in front of him. When she looked up at him, her own breath caught at the worship in his expression. He wanted her as badly as she wanted him, and nothing had ever been such a turn-on.

Licking her lips, she gripped his shaft with one hand and cradled his sac with the other. He moaned when she closed her mouth over him and took him deep.

"Jedda..."

Desire curled in her gut at the sound of her name, spoken in a breathy, needy rasp. Sucking at the tip of his cock, she pumped her fist, drawing a pleasured hiss from him and a sigh of anticipation from her. His balls swelled as she rolled them between her fingers, and with each flick of her tongue on the underside of his shaft, he jerked and let out whispered curses.

She loved the power she had over him in this moment. She could do anything she wanted to him, and he'd beg her for it.

She eyed the dildo on the bed and...nah. Not now. But soon. They'd play with it, and he'd let her put it anywhere she wanted to.

"Don't...stop..." His guttural voice told her he was on the edge, was right there, and sure enough, he came with a roar, his hips bucking so hard she had to grip them to steady herself. He tasted like honey and sunshine, which was a seriously pleasant surprise after dating only human men.

Angels were pretty awesome, she decided.

She gave him a final lick, from the base of his shaft to the top, and then she climbed onto the bed, the dildo within reach. "So," she said saucily, "wanna see what happens when I touch quartz crystal?"

"Oh, yeah." Razr's half-lidded eyes took her in as she palmed the penis-sized dildo.

Instant ecstasy washed over her, and she moaned as the vibrations inherent to quartz filled her body. This was why gem elves avoided it...except in private. Contact in public could end in humiliation and sometimes, she'd heard, arrest.

Razr joined her on the mattress, and when he touched her, he too was swept up in the seismic eroticism.

"Ah...damn," he choked out. "This is like... It's like..."

"Like being held at the verge of orgasm," she finished hoarsely. "Just wait...until I show you...all the things...we can...do with...it." She tossed the dildo aside, needing to catch her breath, but more importantly, needing to be with *him*. There was time for toys and exploration later.

Panting, she pulled him to her and kissed him as he settled his heavy body on top of her.

"Be with me," she whispered.

"Always." He spread her legs and kissed his way down her neck, her breasts, her belly, nipping and licking, teasing her so brutally that she was trembling by the time he dipped his head and kissed her center.

"Yes," she moaned, but he denied her.

He nipped her inner thigh and then nuzzled her sex, his fingers feathering light strokes in the crease of her thigh. Desperate for more, she jammed her fingers through his hair and guided him where she needed him to be.

He chuckled softly, but he didn't spend any more time torturing her. Easing his fingers inward, he penetrated her with one as he flicked the tip of his tongue across her clit. She whimpered with need, bucking when he did it again.

Fiery lashes of pleasure whipped through her as he tongued her and pumped his fingers in her slick core, and with every second that passed, the fever inside her built.

"You taste like cinnamon." His voice was rough. So male. She loved it. "I'm going to have you for dessert every night."

On that promise, he replaced his fingers with his tongue, lapping at her hungrily, his masculine purr of need vibrating her from her core to her breasts, setting her off like an erotic bomb.

She panted through the detonation, the orgasm shattering her, emotionally and physically. She didn't even have a chance to recover before he mounted her, impaling her with his hard shaft and setting her off again.

He rocked against her, every stroke of his cock hitting a spot deep inside that kept her riding the wave of ecstasy that went on and on. How was this even possible? Her thoughts were a blur as he kissed her deeply and surged into her like they were riding waves in a stormy sea.

His wings erupted from his back and came down around them both, sealing them in a cocoon of safety and sensation. And as he shouted in his own climax, she joined him. Loudly. Breathlessly.

This was power. Not the kind that came from gemstones or spells or Heaven.

This power came from love, and it was the strongest of them all.

* * * *

Also from 1001 Dark Nights and Larissa Ione, discover Azagoth, Hades, Z, and Hawkyn.

About Larissa Ione

Air Force veteran Larissa Ione traded in a career as a meteorologist to pursue her passion of writing. She has since published dozens of books, hit several bestseller lists, including the New York Times and USA Today, and has been nominated for a RITA award. She now spends her days in pajamas with her computer, strong coffee, and fictional worlds. She believes in celebrating everything, and would never be caught without a bottle of Champagne chilling in the fridge…just in case. After a dozen moves all over the country with her now-retired U.S. Coast Guard spouse, she is now settled in Wisconsin with her husband, her teenage son, a rescue cat named Vegas, and her very own hellhound, a King Shepherd named Hexe.

For more information about Larissa, visit www.larissaione.com.

Also from Larissa Ione

~ DEMONICA/LORDS OF DELIVERANCE SERIES ~

Pleasure Unbound (Book 1)
Desire Unchained (Book 2)
Passion Unleashed (Book 3)
Ecstasy Unveiled (Book 4)
Eternity Embraced ebook (Book 4.5) (NOVELLA)
Sin Undone August (Book 5)
Eternal Rider (Book 6)
Supernatural Anthology (Book 6.5) (NOVELLA)
Immortal Rider (Book 7)
Lethal Rider (Book 8)
Rogue Rider (Book 9)
REAVER (Book 10)
AZAGOTH (Book 10.5)
REVENANT (Book 11)
HADES (Book 11.5)
Base Instincts (Book 11.6)
Z (Book 11.7)

~ MOONBOUND CLAN VAMPIRES SERIES ~

Bound By Night (book 1)
Chained By Night (book 2)
Blood Red Kiss Anthology (book 2.5)

Discover More Larissa Ione

Hawkyn: A Demonica Novella by Larissa Ione, Now Available

As a special class of earthbound guardian angel called Memitim, Hawkyn is charged with protecting those whose lives are woven into the fabric of the future. His success is legendary, so when he's given a serial killer to watch over, he sees no reason for that to change. But Hawkyn's own future is jeopardized after he breaks the rules and rescues a beautiful woman from the killer's clutches, setting off an explosive, demonic game of cat and mouse that pits brother against brother and that won't end until someone dies.

Aurora Mercer is the half-wytch lone survivor of a psychopath who gets off on the sadistic torture of his victims. A psychopath whose obsessive psyche won't let him move on until he kills her. Now she's marked for death, her fate tied to that of a murderer...and to a sexy angel who makes her blood burn with desire...

* * * *

Azagoth: A Demonica Underword Novella by Larissa Ione, Now Available

Even in the fathomless depths of the underworld and the bleak chambers of a damaged heart, the bonds of love can heal...or destroy.

He holds the ability to annihilate souls in the palm of his hand. He commands the respect of the most dangerous of demons and the most powerful of angels. He can seduce and dominate any female he wants with a mere look. But for all Azagoth's power, he's bound by shackles of his own making, and only an angel with a secret holds the key to his release.

She's an angel with the extraordinary ability to travel through time and space. An angel with a tormented past she can't escape. And when Lilliana is sent to Azagoth's underworld realm, she finds that her past isn't all she can't escape. For the irresistibly sexy fallen angel known as Azagoth is also known as the Grim Reaper, and when he claims a soul, it's forever...

* * * *

Hades: A Demonica Underworld Novella by Larissa Ione, Now Available

A fallen angel with a mean streak and a Mohawk, Hades has spent thousands of years serving as Jailor of the Underworld. The souls he guards are as evil as they come, but few dare to cross him. All of that changes when a sexy fallen angel infiltrates his prison and unintentionally starts a riot. It's easy enough to quell an uprising, but for the first time, Hades is torn between delivering justice — or bestowing mercy — on the beautiful female who could be his salvation...or his undoing.

Thanks to her unwitting participation in another angel's plot to start Armageddon, Cataclysm was kicked out of Heaven and is now a fallen angel in service of Hades's boss, Azagoth. All she wants is to redeem herself and get back where she belongs. But when she gets trapped in Hades's prison domain with only the cocky but irresistible Hades to help her, Cat finds that where she belongs might be in the place she least expected...

* * * *

Z: A Demonica Underworld Novella by Larissa Ione, Now Available

Zhubaal, fallen angel assistant to the Grim Reaper, has spent decades searching for the angel he loved and lost nearly a century ago. Not even her death can keep him from trying to find her, not when he knows she's been given a second chance at life in a new body. But as time passes, he's losing hope, and he wonders how much longer he can hold to the oath he swore to her so long ago…

As an *emim*, the wingless offspring of two fallen angels, Vex has always felt like a second-class citizen. But if she manages to secure a deal with the Grim Reaper — by any means necessary — she will have earned her place in the world. The only obstacle in the way of her plan is a sexy hardass called Z, who seems determined to thwart her at every turn. Soon it becomes clear that they have a powerful connection rooted in the past…but can any vow stand the test of time?

Arranged
A Masters and Mercenaries Novella
By Lexi Blake

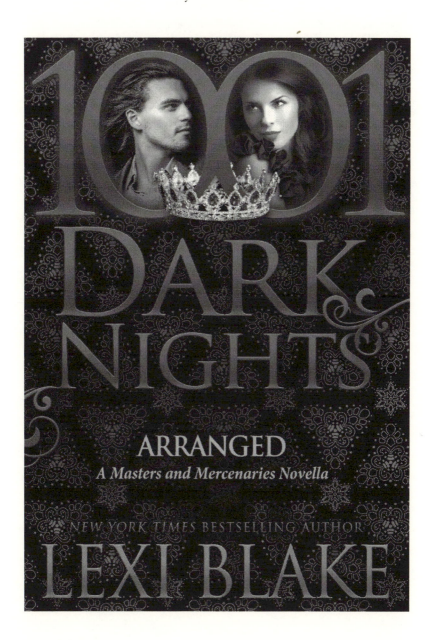

1001 DARK NIGHTS

ARRANGED
A Masters and Mercenaries Novella

NEW YORK TIMES BESTSELLING AUTHOR
LEXI BLAKE

Acknowledgments from the Author

As always thanks to Liz and MJ and their crew—Kim and Pam, Fedora and Kasi on the editing side, to that weirdo they have formatting (I can say that. I gave birth to him) and the amazing Jillian Stein working on social media and making pretty things to show off! Thanks to my publicist Danielle Sanchez and the entire crew at Inkslinger.

We all come across hard times in life and in our work. When those two worlds collide into a raging heap of toxic waste, you really need your friends at your side. This book is dedicated to two amazing women—Mari Carr and Lila DuBois. You helped me through a very hard time and I'll never forget it. I love working with the two of you around because you speak my language and make me comfortable. And this book would likely be very different without Lila helping me to see how Kash and Day could work, how even dominance can be light and feminine and lovely.

Prologue

Fifteen Years Before
Oxford, England

Kashmir Kamdar lay back on the blanket, his face to the sun. He loved England, genuinely adored the years he'd spent here, but sometimes he missed the sun of Loa Mali. It could be so dark here, but on a day like this, he found his way to one of the parks and let the sun soak into his skin and he felt the connection to his island home.

"You don't care at all about quantum mechanics today, do you?"

He didn't open his eyes. He didn't have to see Dayita's frown. Her perfect lips would be turned down, but there would also be a light in those hauntingly gray eyes. "You could read the chapter to me."

"While you snore? I think not."

He felt her settle down beside him, their arms barely touching. Yes, that was better. Dayita Samar was the only other Loa Mali resident here at Oxford, and in the last six months he'd pretty much decided that she was the only Loa Mali resident he needed.

He even adored her name. Day. She scared off all the other guys by putting that insanely thick mound of hair up in a mousy bun, hiding her glorious eyes behind bulky glasses, and wearing somewhat shapeless sweaters. He suspected she simply hadn't figured out how to dress for the cold weather. He wanted to see her on their island home, her body wrapped in a sari that would allow him hints of her copper and gold skin. She scared the men off with her incredible intellect as well. They were all intimidated by how freaking smart she was.

It hadn't intimidated him. After all, he'd lived in his big brother's shadow for all his life. He was absolutely used to being the second smartest person in a room.

"I suppose it won't hurt to take a little nap." She sighed beside him. "Or to watch the clouds. They're different here. I'm thinking about taking a meteorology class in my spare time. I'm fascinated by how different the weather is here in England."

He turned on his side and smiled down at her, his head propped in his hand. "You should feel the way the winds can whip around the Himalayas. There's nothing like a storm at base camp one."

Her eyes came open. "You're telling me they let you climb Everest? I would think the guards would have a problem with that. Did you force poor Rai to be your Sherpa?"

Naturally she knew what he was talking about and that he would need someone to guide him. And she was right about the guards. "I went to Nepal in Shray's place. He got a horrible cold at the last minute, but Father didn't want to cancel the trip. They let me go up to the first base camp. It was more than enough. A storm hit and I froze my poor backside off. I got back to the beach as quickly as possible."

She laughed, the sound musical to his ears. "Did you cuddle with the guard?"

"I have a 'no cuddling' policy with my royal guard. And you know they only really stay close when I'm working for my father. There aren't many people here in Oxford who want to hurt the spare heir of a tiny island country. Shray, on the other hand, oh, let's just say I've learned to be happy that I'm a second son."

"It's one of the things I like about you, Your Highness." She rolled over too, and they were side by side. "I think it would be hard to have your whole life laid out for you. I like that you're not jealous of your brother."

Yes, this was the Day he'd come to... Had he come to love Day? He certainly felt more for her than he'd ever felt for a girl before. He hadn't slept with a single model, or anyone else, since he'd met her, and he hadn't even tried to kiss her yet.

"Most people think I should be saddened by the idea of being the spare. By being so close to the crown and yet so far away. They think I should be jealous of Shray, but I feel sorry for him. Don't get me wrong. I adore my brother, but I don't want to be him. You're right. His life is laid out for him. He'll marry some woman my father approves of, have children as soon as possible, and settle down to be the perfect king one day. Did you know they forced him to major in economics and political science?"

He shuddered at the thought. And Shray hadn't been allowed to go so far from home. He'd studied in India so he could be close to the palace. His leash had been so very short.

Day's nose wrinkled. "How boring. Except the math part. That's probably fun. Maybe I'll study it in my free time."

He had to smile. "You don't have any free time. I'm forcing you to study something else. It's called human dynamics. We're going to a pub tonight and we'll drink and eat and watch the crowds."

Now her eyes went wide. "I need to study. I have a test in differential equations next week."

"Which you can pass in your sleep." Day had forgotten more mathematics than most people ever learned. Still, he knew she would prepare. "You can study later, Day. Tonight you're going to play. You never play."

She sat up and started to gather her books. "I don't and I should remember that, Your Highness."

Okay. That was bad. Even he knew that particular tone in a woman's voice, though he rarely heard it in Day's. It meant he'd screwed up. Normally that tone of voice represented an off ramp, and after a few weeks with a woman, he tended to look for those.

He didn't want one with her. He liked her. They were friends and he was starting to think they should be something more. He wasn't a child. He was twenty years old and maybe Shray wasn't the only one who was thinking about settling down. Not right away. Not marriage anyway, but it would be nice to settle in with her and see where they could go. The truth was he was tired of models and actresses who had no idea who Stephen Hawking was. The playboy was tired and wanted his brainy girl.

"What did I do wrong?"

She stopped, hugging her books to her chest. "Nothing. I'm

being exactly what I promised myself I wouldn't be. I'm being a foolish girl. I have a unique chance to make something of myself and here I am mooning over a boy I can't have. I'm sorry, Your Highness. I need to go."

He reached out, gripping her wrist gently. "Stop calling me that. Please call me Kash. I'm not my brother. I'm not destined for the throne. I'm nothing more than a young man trying to ask a lovely woman out for a date and screwing it up terribly."

Those gray eyes went wide. "A date?"

There was something about the breathy way she said the word that let him know all would be well. He got to his knees in front of her, facing her so she could see how serious he was. "A date. It's when a boy and a girl go out into the world and have fun."

Her eyes never left his, never shifted coyly away. It was one of the things he loved about her. Day took charge. "I'm not one of your fun-time girls, Kashmir. You should understand that about me. If you think I'm going to giggle and hook up and walk away happy I screwed around with a prince, you don't know me at all."

He liked the strength in her voice. "That's what I've been trying to do all these months. Get to know you. We've become friends. I would like to see if we could be more. Dayita, I know you think you're nothing but a brain on two legs, but I see you as something more."

"More?" She stared at him as though trying to find the definition in her head.

Yes, this was one of the things he needed her to understand. "You're brilliant, but you're also a woman. You treat all the men around you as if you couldn't care less."

"I don't think the men around me like me."

"I like you," he said quickly, not willing to let a moment of misunderstanding pass. "I like who you are."

Her cheeks had flushed, a deep color coming to them. "They don't think I'm especially feminine."

Because she knew what she wanted? He liked that most about her. "How do they know what femininity is? You're a woman because your body is different, but I...I like your soul, too. You don't have to be different with me. You can be exactly who you are and I'll still like you."

"If this is some kind of game to you…" she began and he could see the shimmer of tears in her eyes.

The last thing he wanted to do was ever make her cry. She was so strong. He wanted to add to that strength, never take from it. "It's not a game. I like you, Day. Even better, I like me when I'm around you. Does that make sense? I like how I feel when you're with me."

"How do I make you feel?"

How to explain it? It was something he thought about a lot lately. He'd started to study it like a scientist would, considering all the angles, measuring his feelings versus others and coming up with the theory that Day was the right woman for him. "I feel peaceful around you. I feel secure."

He knew it was a risk. Some women would see that as unmanly. He should have talked about protecting her. He wanted to protect her from everything, but he'd never in his life felt like a woman wanted to protect him, too.

She bit her bottom lip and seemed to think things over before she reached up and pulled the tie out of her hair, shaking it out. "Let me kiss you."

He stopped, his whole body going on high alert. His dick twitched in his slacks. When he'd proposed this little picnic, he'd known he was going to start to ease her into a more traditional male/female relationship, but he hadn't expected this. He'd thought he would get her to go to a pub with him and they would have fun, and after three or four outings she might not even recognize as dates, he would kiss her.

He should do it now. He should lean over and fist his hand in her hair and show her how masculine he could be.

"Yes." He stayed still because she hadn't asked him to kiss her. She'd been clear and plain in her intent. She wanted to kiss him. She'd asked his permission as though he was something precious.

Women threw themselves at him. They plopped themselves down in his lap and offered him all manner of sexual favors. Not once had anyone asked if they could kiss him. Certainly not in that strong tone that let him know he really should say yes because he would miss out on something if he didn't.

Her lips curled in a smile he'd never once seen from her. That smile was wicked and it got his cock hard as a freaking rock. He hadn't touched her yet and he was erect and ready.

She reached her hand up, fingertips brushing his skin. "Don't move. Let me touch you. Let me learn you."

For Day, learning was serious. She studied him, her fingers moving along his jawline. She was studying him, assessing and categorizing him. It wasn't a bad thing. No. Day wouldn't find him wanting. Day viewed the world itself as something marvelous, something to explore.

How would she explore him? The question made his body tighten, his whole being focus on her. The rest of the world seemed to fall away as Day leaned in and finally, finally brushed her lips against his.

He felt a spark deep inside. Her hands moved up, sliding into his hair and twisting ever so slightly. His scalp tingled and his breath caught. She kissed him softly, the ease of her lips contrasting with the sharp tingle to his scalp. Her chest came up, rubbing against his, and he felt something he hadn't before. He felt...wanted. Not for his royal position. Not for his money.

For himself.

She went up, as tall as she could get on her knees. He was sitting back and he found the way she towered over him incredibly sexy. He didn't have to do a damn thing. Day was in control. She would take what she wanted and what she wanted was him.

"Open your mouth for me. Let me in."

He found himself giving in, the whole moment spiraling out of control. It wasn't what he'd meant to do, but that was all right. He didn't have to decide. All he had to do was follow her path and she would lead him somewhere incredible.

He was so hard he could barely breathe as her tongue slid along his. It didn't matter that they were in a park. It wasn't that crowded at this time of day. The River Cherwell was off to his right and there was a lovely copse of trees to his left they could go into when she wanted to fuck. Yeah, he would move the blanket, open his slacks, lay back and let her ride the hell out of him.

He'd known it would be good.

The *thud thud* of a helicopter broke through the intimacy of the moment. Damn it. They needed to go away. He leaned in, but she was already pulling back. Her face turned up to the sky.

"I think they're landing," she shouted over the hard scream of the blades rotating.

She leaned in as though to try to cover him.

He wasn't having that. Not for a second. He moved out from under her, placing his body over hers. He felt her stiffen but he wasn't giving in.

"Your Majesty!" A familiar figure moved toward him. His guard. Rai. He'd come with him all the way from Loa Mali. He'd left his family and spent the last four years of his life here, only short visits home connecting him with the ones he loved. Rai had been his steadfast companion, giving him space when he needed it, taking care of him when he got too wild.

Why was Rai calling him "your majesty"? He stood, reaching down to help Day up. "What's wrong?"

Rai had a grim look on his face. "I have to get you to Heathrow, Your Majesty. There's a plane waiting for you. Something's happened at home. We need to go as soon as possible."

Kash shook his head. He wasn't leaving in the middle of a semester. "I'll call Dad. And what's wrong with you? It's 'your highne…'"

He stopped, the world shifting and twisting and turning until he couldn't quite stand. Day was there, holding him up.

There was only one reason to ever call him "your majesty." No one should have called him that. Not ever in his life. It was what his people called the king and queen. Only ever the king and queen.

"What happened to my father?" His gut twisted and he choked back a cry. "My brother?"

Rai shook his head. "There was a car accident, Your Majesty. The king and your brother were caught in a storm. Your brother was driving and he lost control and went over a cliff. I'm so sorry." He went down on one knee. "The king is dead. Long live the king."

King Kashmir.

Day's arms went around him, but now they were surrounded by guards. Rai had brought an army with him.

Because he was no longer the spare. Because he was the last of the Kamdar line and he was king.

"We have to go." Rai was back on his feet, nodding toward the helicopter.

Kash felt himself being pulled away from Day, but there was nothing he could do. He had to go home. He glanced back, saw her standing there with tears in her eyes.

And he knew the whole world had changed.

Chapter One

Present Day
Miami, Florida

Kash woke when the pillow beneath his head shifted. Confusion set in even as his head started to pound. His mouth was dry as the desert. Why was the bed moving?

He wasn't going to wake up this morning. There was no reason to. He was going to lie here and pretend he had absolutely nothing to do.

In some ways it was true. He was fairly inconsequential recently.

He groaned as he realized the pillow he'd been lying on wasn't a pillow at all. It had been a woman's hip, soft and warm.

Where the hell was he?

"That's right, Your Majesty. Time to wakey, wakey," a male voice said. "I'd offer you eggs and bakey, but I saw what you drank last night. We might want to hold off on the food for a while. Wish I could let you sleep this off, but I got orders."

The voice was familiar, but he struggled to attach a face. Whoever had invaded his bedroom was speaking English with a Western accent. Kash didn't want to open his eyes. The world was far too bright. "Well, I'm the king so I can override any orders you've been given. Where is my guard? And who the hell are you?"

"Yeah, I take my orders from Big Tag. I think he's far scarier than you are. Especially right now." More light invaded his previously darkened room. "That's right, darling. You should get dressed. The king is thankful for your company last night. And your sister's. And whoever the other lady was."

"Oh, good lord. Does he owe you cash?" An upper-crust British accent split the air and Kash did recognize that one. Simon Weston. And his partner, Jesse Murdoch, was the laconic Western guy.

"They're not hookers." Why the hell was McKay-Taggart here?

"Yes, we are," a feminine voice said. "And we agreed on a thousand for each of us. Are you telling me we're about to get stiffed?"

"I'll make sure you get everything he promised you and a bit more if you'll please avoid the paparazzi outside," Weston was saying. "If not, you'll find I'm good at suing people. Your choice, ladies. Easy cash or a nice lawsuit. Jesse, would you please escort his majesty's friends to the taxi that's waiting for them?"

"Sure thing, partner. You going to deal with our charge?" Murdoch asked.

"Hopefully our charge isn't about to vomit all over the hotel suite. Let management know that we'll be leaving soon and will require a security escort off the grounds. Michael will be here with the limo and Boomer is watching to ensure none of those reporters get to this floor. I'll have the king down in thirty minutes."

"We'll be ready. Ladies, let's get you home. You should probably put on some clothes…oh, huh. I didn't know those counted as clothes. All right then."

The door closed and Kash forced himself to sit up. The room immediately started spinning, but he wasn't going to give in. "Where is my guard? I don't remember much about last night, but I do know I didn't call McKay-Taggart. I certainly didn't need you to rescue me from three lovely ladies."

Weston looked perfectly neat and clean in his three-piece suit with shiny loafers. He crossed the suite to where someone had brought in coffee service. He poured a cup and started back across the room. "One of them isn't a hooker. One of them is a reporter and she's about to discover that the film she took last night of your antics is going to go missing. Jesse's quite excellent with sleight of hand."

He frowned. "A film?"

"Some would call it pornography." Weston placed the cup on the nightstand. "I'll choose to call it a reality show that will never be aired. As for your guard, apparently he quit last night. He was fed up because he'd figured out who the lovely lady was, but you refused to listen. He called home and explained the situation and your mother hired us. You're lucky you were here in Miami. If you'd been in Europe, you would be dealing with a cranky Aussie. I assure you I'm going to handle you with more care than he would. Well, unless you give me trouble."

Kash reached for the cup. Some of it was coming back to him. He'd fought with Rai. The man had been his personal guard for years, but lately they'd been squabbling like an old married couple. Rai knew him, knew how to deal with him even when he was a complete ass. Lately Rai kept getting on him, pointing out all the ways Kash was failing.

Shit. Rai had found out about Lia. Shit. Shit. Shit. Someone had told Rai about the fact that Lia had once been in his bed. Years before she'd married Rai. It had meant nothing to either one of them. It had been one night of pleasure and he hadn't seen her again. Fuck, he'd meant to go to the grave with that secret.

"Damn it. I certainly didn't mean to fire anyone. Is he still here in Miami?"

He needed to talk to Rai. He had to put things right. There was also the added problem that if he didn't have an approved guard, he would be forced to go home. Kash had come to Miami to attend a meeting with a company that claimed it could help protect the pipeline that brought Loa Mali's oil to the refineries. His country spent millions to ensure the drilling they did left their natural resources and the beauty of their island untouched.

Until such time as Kash found a way to get rid of fossil fuels altogether. That was the ultimate goal, to find a way to free the world from its dependence on oil. Well, and then to license the technology and make an enormous amount of money, but first and foremost it was about the science.

He'd been close. So close when an asshole rabid former CIA agent had blown up his fucking lab and killed several of his best engineers. Good men and women who were trying to help the world and now they were gone.

Their research had only survived because of Simon Weston's boss. Ian Taggart and his wife, Charlotte, had saved Kash, too. So he owed them.

And damn, but he owed Rai.

"He's already gone home." Weston sank into a chair beside the big bed. "Your mother has hired him to work a position that allows him to stay in Loa Mali most of the time. Apparently he's recently married and wants more time with his wife."

Guilt swamped him. Since that CIA bastard had ruined years of Kash's work, he'd dragged Rai around the globe, partying and pretending to enjoy life. The last few years had been one long sinkhole he couldn't seem to come out of.

He was even tired of sex. Not that he was going to let anyone know that. He had a reputation to uphold. A bad, horrible, playboy reputation.

"That's good for Rai. I need a younger guard anyway. I need one who can keep up with me. Rai has become an old man. All he cares about is his job and his wife."

"Yes, how boring of him."

Kash nodded. "I'm glad you see that. I offered him a world of travel and to be surrounded by the most beautiful of all women. He gives me lectures on how I should settle down. He tells me my liver will die soon. My liver is as strong as I am. My liver is a bull."

"Well, I do suspect you're full of bullshit, as my cousins would say. You should think about getting dressed. Our plane leaves in two hours. I need to get you out of here. The paparazzi will be swarming the place by now."

The coffee was starting to work. He was vaguely beginning to remember that Rai had called him an idiot. That hadn't been polite of him. He could remember Rai's dark eyes rolling and him saying something about how he'd given up, how he'd become everything his father would have detested.

Rai had been so sanctimonious. Then his own guilt had caused him to hit the bottle hard. It was why he'd brought those women to his room even though he'd figured out one of them wasn't a well-paid call girl.

Still, he was fairly certain he'd performed admirably, and what was one more sex tape? Why did everyone overreact?

"Don't worry about the paparazzi. They're perfectly harmless. How many do you expect? Five? Prince Harry's in New York. Most of the royal watchers will be after him. He's only shown his willy off a few times. Mine is everywhere. The Internet is awash in my beauty. The upside of that is the paps merely want a picture of me smiling and then they'll leave me alone." He stood up, feeling infinitely better.

Rai had poked his personal buttons, but Kash had behaved abominably. He needed to get Rai on the phone and apologize. The truth was he *had* neglected his research for the last few years. It was a setback and nothing more.

And the last several months had been particularly bad, and he blamed the Taggarts. He'd hosted the wedding of the youngest Taggart and it had left him feeling restless. Being around all those happy families had done something terrible to him. It had made him wonder if he wasn't missing something. Those smiling men with their women and children had caused him to wonder if his life wasn't a bit on the shallow side.

And for the first time in forever, he'd thought of her. He'd stood as Theo Taggart had promised to love Erin Argent for the rest of his life and he'd had a vision of Day with her gray eyes and silky hair. Day, with those ridiculous glasses.

Innocent Day.

They were worlds apart now. She was probably married and teaching somewhere in the States or England. She would have a professor husband who would argue fine points of theory with her and she would be raising a couple of genius-level children. He wondered if she saw him in the papers and laughed about the time the playboy prince had kissed her.

He hoped she was happy.

And for a moment, he'd mourned. Not for his father and brother. He did that every day. He'd mourned the Kash he'd been. He'd ached at the thought of what that Kashmir would think about who he was today.

"Good lord, man, put on some clothes." Weston stood and walked back to the coffee service. "Everyone else might have seen that, but I've been careful not to."

He wasn't sure why Weston was such a prude. The man was known to be a member of Sanctum. It was a club in Dallas that catered to people in the BDSM lifestyle.

"My mother has overreacted. I'm sure she was terrified when she learned I was over here in America without a proper guard, but she certainly shouldn't have called McKay-Taggart to escort me home. I assure you I can find my way. You don't have to make the twenty-hour flight." Who had he brought with him? Yes, that lovely girl from the east side of the island with the pretty breasts was the flight attendant. He could spend some time with her.

"There are currently around two hundred members of the press outside waiting to get a statement from you."

Kash stopped. "Two hundred?"

"Give or take a few. That's why we're going to require a police escort." Weston continued on as though nothing was wrong. "I've got my man with a limo in the parking garage. We'll meet Jesse down there and Boomer will join us in the lift. The hotel has agreed to shut down one of the lifts so it only stops on this floor and the parking garage. Boomer will ensure no one gets through. Miami PD has offered an escort to the airport. You should hurry and shower. We don't have much time."

His head was reeling in a way that had absolutely nothing to do with the unholy amount of vodka he'd downed the night before. "Why is the fact that I had sex with three women news? Believe me, it happens all the time. Second, why would I need a bloody police escort? And what is a Boomer?"

"A Boomer is one of two new former Special Forces bodyguards your mother has hired until Jesse and I train a new group to protect the royal family since it's expanding. I hope you have a large refrigerator. Boomer eats constantly, and you should watch out for any erratic behavior. He's a nice lad, but he's been hit on the head more than anyone could imagine. However, he's a bit of a savant when it comes to marksmanship. No one cares that you had sex with three women last night because no one knows. I took care of that and your mother is not going to be happy about all the bribes I had to expense to accomplish that. You need a bloody police escort to get through the throngs of reporters, as I mentioned earlier. Now could you please put that thing away? My wife is meeting us at the airport. I would like to be able to tell her the amount of nudity I witnessed was minimal."

He was getting irritated. He tossed on last evening's slacks. If the Brit wanted to power play him, he could get with the game. It wasn't like he would allow them to come in and drag his ass home like he was some kind of wayward child. He was a king. "Don't bother to bring your wife. I'm sure she's lovely, but my mother has overstepped herself. I will choose my guard and I will select who will train them."

Weston checked his watch. "How soon can you be ready?"

"Have you heard a word I've said? I thank you for helping me out last night and keeping that tape from hitting the web, but I can manage from here."

Weston picked up the newspaper that had been delivered along with the coffee service. He tossed it Kash's way. "If you feel that way, I can certainly let Michael and Jesse know they should stick to her majesty's side and allow you to be brutally murdered if it comes to that."

"Mother already has guards." He clutched the newspaper. She'd had the same set of guards for years. She liked to call them her girls. Four women who'd served in the military and had been trained by...well, by McKay-Taggart. Had something happened? "Why is Mother so afraid she needs more guards?"

"Not for your mother," Weston replied casually. "It's for your future bride. As for firing me and Jesse, you can't. We've been hired by your parliament to provide security and assistance for the royal wedding and to train the new queen's guard."

Yes, he'd had far too much to drink. He was still sleeping and having the oddest dream.

Weston shook his head. "It's all right there in the paper, if you don't believe me. Now hurry and take that shower. You've got to get home because the formal engagement ceremony is in two days."

Kash opened the paper and stared down at the headline.

Playboy King to Claim His Bride

"I'm not getting married."

Weston stepped up and patted his arm. "You are or you'll give up your throne. I'll explain it all on the plane. The other reason your mother hired me is I have a degree in law. I've read the clause in your constitution that your mother intends to use to force you to marry. I assure you, it will hold up. You can attempt to change the constitution but that requires a two-year review process, another year of public forums, and a vote. You'll be replaced by then. Like I said, I can explain it all on the incredibly long plane trip. Are you all right, Your Majesty? You went a bit green."

Kash ran for the bathroom.

He'd been right. He shouldn't have bothered to wake up.

* * * *

Dayita Samar stepped into the queen's private reception room with a smile. Not for the stunning décor or the view of the ocean in the distance, though both were worthy of great praise. No, Day's smile was for the woman herself. Queen Yasmine was one of the kindest women she'd ever had the pleasure of meeting. The queen mother was a stabilizing influence on the country, someone to look up to and admire for her willingness to serve her people.

How she'd managed to produce a son who was a walking venereal disease was beyond Day's comprehension.

Day curtsied even as the queen waved off such formalities.

"Darling Day, come here. It's been so long," the queen said, enveloping her in a hug.

She was far too thin. It had been a while and the queen seemed frailer than before.

"Your Majesty, it's always a pleasure to see you." Day had learned how to maneuver her way around a bureaucracy, but she genuinely enjoyed dealing with the queen. After the morning she'd had, it was a nice way to spend her afternoon. "You said it was urgent. How can I help you?"

"Oh, my dear, you won't simply be helping me. You'll be helping your country. You might be helping the world." The queen took a step back and there was no way to miss the sheen of tears in her eyes, though she took a deep breath and seemed to banish them. She turned and walked to the sitting area, a cluster of lush chairs on a carpet that was likely worth more than Day's yearly salary at the ministry.

The queen took a seat, gesturing for Day to take one of her own.

"I'm certainly intrigued, Your Majesty." Day studied the queen. There was a weariness to her that couldn't be missed, even though she smiled like nothing was wrong. "How can I help?"

"You can marry my son."

Day smiled and couldn't help the laughter that bubbled out. The queen was also quite funny. The idea of Kashmir marrying anyone was ludicrous. He was far too busy screwing supermodels and actresses and other men's wives. After a long moment, she sat back with a sigh. "Thank you, Your Majesty. I needed a laugh today. I've spent the morning fighting with parliament over funding for my elementary science education program."

The blustery old men who ran parliament didn't see the need. She'd argued that early science and math intervention worked to get more girls involved in those areas of study. By the time they hit junior high it was too late, and certain societal norms took over, making the classes less interesting to female students. Apparently that was perfectly fine with parliament. One of the men had even told her she would be far happier if she quit her job, got married, and had a husband to occupy her time.

Oh, how she would love to take a whip to that bastard, and not in a pleasurable way.

The queen frowned in Day's direction, getting her attention quickly.

Day sat up. "You're serious? About me marrying the king? I haven't spoken to the king in years. I hardly think he wants to marry me."

The queen's hands tightened around the arms of her chair. "I'm dead serious. The time has come and passed and I can't wait another second more. Have you ever heard of the Law of Rational Succession? It's a tiny clause set into our constitution over two hundred years ago."

She'd read the constitution, of course. History, and in particular Loa Malian history, was a subject she enjoyed. Since becoming the head of the country's education department, she spent her time reviewing public school books. She didn't remember the law, however. "I've never heard of it."

Her majesty seemed to relax a bit, as though she'd half expected Day to run for the hills. "I'm not surprised. Few people outside of constitutional lawyers have, but I've been assured that it will hold and that it's perfectly legal. The Law of Rational

Succession states that the king can be forced to marry or give up his throne if he has not selected a bride by his twentieth birthday."

"Twenty?" Kash was thirty-five.

"Yes, well, it was written long ago when men and women were expected to marry and reproduce at a young age," the queen explained. "I've given him fifteen years but there's no end our sight. According to the law, the king or queen's parents have the right to select a proper spouse, and the wedding must take place within two weeks of the invocation or the king's crown is forfeit. It was placed into law in an attempt to avoid the kind of trouble that comes from the line of succession being broken. There is also a clause about being able to remove a monarch who will not abide by the constitution or one who is too sick to care for the people."

"Has it ever been used?"

The queen shook her head. "It has never been invoked before. Now, I am going to assume that my son will work to block me, but I've got a legal team on that as well. Changing the constitution will require roughly three years. I can end the monarchy in two weeks. The only place for the crown to go is to my nephew, Chapal, and he will refuse it. He has already signed the documents of abdication in case Kashmir proves stubborn."

End the monarchy? Day tried to process the idea. The Kamdars had held the crown for centuries. The family had been the one to put into place the constitution that protected the citizens—even from a bad king. Kash's grandfather had been the one who shared the revenue from the country's oil with every Loa Malian, making them the wealthiest citizenship in the world.

Loa Mali had a parliament, but the crown worked hand in hand with them and the king could have the final say if he chose to use his power.

Not that King Kash paid much attention anymore. He was far too busy running around the world having his picture taken at parties.

"You would have us move to a purely representative government? I don't know if that is a smart move, Your Majesty. Some people in this country are still extremely set in their ways. I spent all morning arguing with a group of elected officials who believe a woman's place is in the home and that educating our girls in anything beyond how to keep a house is a waste of time."

The queen's lips curled up in an encouraging smile. "Excellent. As queen, you will be able to direct education from a much more powerful position. They won't be able to refuse you. Smile when you force them to eat crow, darling. That is the one thing we shall have to work on. You frown far too much. I know it's not proper to ask a woman to smile these days, but a queen is different. You must never allow them to see anything but strength. A good smile while you're gutting some idiot's argument is a perfect show of strength. Come along. Give me one. I know you can do it."

What surreal dream was she having? She was going to wake up any minute. She had to. "Your Majesty, I don't understand."

"It's easy. Look." The queen's mouth curled up in a restrained smile. "You see, the key is to not look too joyous. Save that for moments when you need the public to see you as a woman and not a queen. Those times come too. The key is knowing when and how to use the power to its best effect."

"What?"

The queen waved away the question. "I know you young people love your resting bitchy faces, but you have to save that for particular people. Like those men today. You may use this bitchy face on them to show your queenly power, though I assure you smiling will set them off their games more. And don't let the cameras catch you frowning or they do those miming things on the Internet now. There was a terrible one of me and some Harry Potter character. If you smile, they can't do this to you."

Day had seen it. Some Potter fan had likened the queen to Professor McGonagall. It had been Day's screensaver for over a month.

"I think you're talking about memes. No one makes memes of the head of education." Of course, no one really listened to her either.

"But they will make the memings when you are queen," Queen Yasmine announced solemnly. "Now, we must talk about your dress. I think traditional is best for the actual ceremony, but you should wear couture to the reception. The whole world will be watching. We need to present a true vision of our country as a cosmopolitan nation. I've already called the heads of three fashion houses to submit designs. And, darling girl, I love you, but we must pluck those eyebrows. They're growing together. They're not supposed to do that."

She wasn't... She felt her forehead and grimaced. Technically hair was supposed to grow. Plucking it was the unnatural force here. It was also not the point. "Kash hasn't spoken to me in fifteen years. Why would he want to marry me now?"

The queen sighed. "Have you listened to a word I've said? Kash doesn't want to get married at all. I'm rather certain he doesn't want to come home. That's why I hired guards to drag him here. I was even smart enough to hire the particularly handsome one with the British accent and the law degree. Even now he's explaining to Kash that there's no way out of the trap I've set and that he should accept this beautiful gift of love and stability I'm offering him."

"Is it a gift or a trap?" The queen had used both words, but it was definitely starting to feel like a trap to Day.

The queen's smile turned beatific. "It's both, of course. That's the beauty of it all. You're going to be perfect for him. You're the girl to keep him in line. My boy is lovely and so smart, though he often forgets to use his brain. I wish his penis wasn't so large. I think that was where we went wrong. It has to have come from my side of the family, because my husband certainly wasn't that large. And I was happy with that. It meant he didn't feel the need to use it on every woman who walked by. And you must get Kashmir to stop having it photographed. It's unseemly."

Day felt herself blush. Damn it. She didn't blush. Ever. She'd seen almost everything there was to be seen and she was cool with it all. Sex was part of a good and natural life. Accepting her own sexuality had been important. But something about the elderly queen talking about Kash's penis had Day's skin flushing. "Your Majesty, I'm not marrying Kashmir. He's been a halfway decent king, especially in the early years, but he would make a terrible husband."

"But he won't once you show him the way."

"The way?"

"Dayita, there's a reason I chose you." The queen was quiet for a moment and then she looked back up, not even attempting to quell the tears in her eyes now. "You can save him. You can give him the stability he needs. You can show him he doesn't have to destroy himself."

"I don't know why you think I can do that."

The queen seemed to come to some inner decision because she sniffled and then sat back, her head coming up regally. "You are smart enough to lead this country. You are perfect to be the face of the monarchy. If I allow Kash to continue, we will be obsolete and our country will go the way of so many other small nations. You are right. At this point we still have a faction that would love to see us go back into the Dark Ages. I worry that there is a group of men waiting to take over. They would privatize something that has always been public. That oil was found on public land and therefore belongs to all of us. They would change this and that would send many of our people into poverty. Women and girls, most of all. Are you willing to risk that?"

Something was wrong with the queen. Day had never seen her like this before. Her majesty was so gentle and gracious. "Your Majesty, I understand that you're upset with Kashmir, but I'm not going to marry him. You need to talk to him about this. You need to make him see reason. He should marry, but he needs to find the right woman."

"You are the right woman, but he is far too foolish to see it. He's spent fifteen years avoiding you."

"He doesn't remember my name." He'd refused to see her the one time she'd shown up to the palace in person. He'd never written her back. She'd sent him letters for more than a year until she finally realized he was ignoring her.

"Then introduce yourself, darling, because I won't be swayed," the queen announced. "I will see the two of you married and settled and working for a brighter future or I will destroy it all and let the cards fall as they may."

"Why are you doing this?"

"Because it's my last chance to make things right for him. He wasn't raised to be the king. The pressure has been too much. He chafes at the bit because he was allowed too much freedom in his younger years. I must leave him with a woman who can handle him, who can direct him in how he should go. Someone who can be a partner to him, even lead him when he needs to be led. Someone strong, and if I allow him to he will choose poorly. If I had more time... I do not so I will place this bet on the table. I will put everything I have into it and see if you will call me. I'm not bluffing, Dayita. I will do this."

Day felt her breath flee as she realized the truth behind the queen's words. "Does Kash know you're dying?"

"No."

"You have to tell him."

"I will, when the time is right." She waved a hand and the door to the hallway opened. A servant rushed in, carrying a tray. It was as though she'd been hovering outside, waiting for the moment when the queen would call upon her, anxious to do her part.

Was Day's country calling her now? It was insane to think that in this day and age she would be asked to marry in order to help her country, but some of what the queen was saying made sense.

"I'm a commoner." She tried to come up with any way out of this trap.

The queen took the pills her servant had brought her. She reached for them and clasped the older woman's hand when they touched. This wasn't a mere servant. Day had seen Mrs. Pashmi Indrus every time she'd met with the queen. She hovered in the background, but it was obvious she was close to her majesty. She handed the queen a glass of water.

"So is the English girl and she's done quite well," the queen replied. "She is the new royalty and you are very much like her."

"I'm not a virgin."

That made the queen laugh. "Darling, no one is anymore. And to marry a virgin off to my son would be like handing one over to a dragon and expecting her to know how to slay it."

"I'm afraid I would be more likely to kill your son than to find happiness with him."

"You cared for him once." She swallowed the pills and that proved to Day more than anything how serious the queen was. Her majesty would never allow herself to do something so personal around anyone but her small family. By showing Day her weakness, she was bringing her in. "I know the two of you were close in England. You can find this again."

Day shook her head, even though she knew damn well she was already sliding down the queen's slippery slope. "We're two entirely different people now."

"No, you're not. You're merely older and time has worn off some of your joy," the queen said quietly. "It will do this to you, time will. Only if you let it. It's easy to let time and pain change you into someone less than you were. Less able to love. Less able to forgive. Less able to look at this world of ours and see that it is so beautiful. Time teaches us to see the ugly parts so we can protect ourselves. But, darling, when we spend all of our energy protecting ourselves we miss out on all the reasons we're alive in the first place."

Day felt a tear slip down her cheek and missed her mother so much in that moment. Her father had moved on, starting another family and leaving her behind, but she could hear her own mother in the queen's words. Perhaps they were the words of every mother to her child, the prayer that her child would find love, joy, happiness. And a place in the world. A reason to be.

"I cared for him a long time ago," Day admitted. "But even then I didn't think it could work."

"Then what fun it will be when it does," the queen replied. "Am I taking you away from someone you truly care about? My intelligence says you haven't had a serious man in your life for years."

Not since she'd made the decision to move home. She'd dated a few men in England and then had a more serious relationship when she'd taken the head of education job back here. It hadn't worked out and now she threw herself into work. She was nearly thirty-six. There was plenty of time to find a mate.

But would she find a calling as well? Already there was a part of her that wondered what she could do with that crown on her head. She could ensure that a whole generation of children got what they needed. She could be an ambassador for science around the world. The Professor Queen.

She didn't have to love Kash. She merely had to be a good partner to him. Perhaps some people found their true love in the form of another human being, but Day could find it in helping her people.

"No, Your Majesty. I'm not in love. I don't think I've ever been in love." Except she'd thought she'd loved Kash. Those months with him had haunted her for years. She could still remember how it felt to brush her lips against his.

If the queen knew how she spent some of her nights, would she want her as a daughter-in-law?

"There are personal things we should talk about." Day couldn't not be honest.

"Is this about that club you go to? And the one in Paris? What was it called?"

Mrs. Indrus piped up. "The Velvet Collar."

"Yes, that is the one." The queen's eyes lit with mirth. "Pashmi and I looked at their website. Very interesting place."

The queen's servant giggled a bit behind her hand and suddenly looked years younger.

And Day found herself blushing again. "It's for relaxation. I rarely indulge myself physically."

"Well, that's good because I'm sure that my son does. He needs a good spanking, if I do say so myself. You both like those clubs. That's one thing you have in common. Excellent. It's a start." The queen clapped her hands together. "Now let's talk about your wedding. Pashmi, could you get us some tea and then perhaps you will join us? You have such a good eye when it comes to colors. We shall fill the palace with flowers."

Pashmi strode away to do the queen's will and Day realized she was trapped.

Utterly and completely trapped in a cage she couldn't force her way out of because there was a piece of her that still wanted to know if it could work.

That was the most dangerous trap of all.

Chapter Two

Kash strode into the palace, well aware every single person he met had taken one look at him and fled the other way. The guards at the gates hadn't questioned him, simply waved him by as they attempted to not look him in the eyes. The maids and servants he'd passed hadn't offered a single greeting.

The only person standing between him and his mother now would be the lord chamberlain. He had heard one of the maids calling for him. It wouldn't do any good. Hanin Kota had taken over the running of the palace a few years before the king and Shray had been killed. He was a somewhat cold man who lived for formality. His family had worked for the Kamdars for decades. Kash had always thought it would be fun to fire him, but he'd deferred to his mother's wishes.

If Hanin gave him trouble, Kash would boot him out. There was a freedom in what his mother had done.

He was angry. As angry as he could ever remember being.

"You might chill out before you scare the shit out of the entire palace, Kash." Jesse Murdoch easily kept up with him.

He ignored his so-called guard. Murdoch wasn't alone. The Boomer was with him. Yes, Kash would fire him, too. All of them.

The one thing in his life that should have been his choice was being taken from him. Everywhere he turned he had responsibility weighing on him. Lately he'd tried to handle it by giving more and more to parliament. They seemed happy. Now he was supposed to give up his much-needed time away and take some unknown wife and stay at home and deliver a brood of mewling children to his mother?

Chapal could have the crown. He'd decided that after the Brit had explained the situation he was in. His mother had used some antiquated rule of law to force his hand? Oh, she would find out he couldn't be forced into this.

"This is a real palace. It's cool." The mass of muscular flesh the others called Boomer was smiling at everything like this was all one long vacation. "Hello, ma'am. Real nice place you got here."

"She's a servant," Kash shot back. "The palace doesn't belong to her."

The young woman, who had to be all of twenty, turned back to her dusting, but not before he'd seen the way her skin had flushed with shame.

When had he taken to hurting young women with careless words? He wasn't this man. He was a charmer. He never shamed anyone for their position in society. Bloody hell. He was going mad.

"Please accept my apologies," he said quickly before turning back toward his destination. The queen mother's wing was off to the left.

"Don't you mind him," Boomer was saying to the maid. "He's a massive asshole."

"He's the king," the woman whispered.

"King Asswipe," Boomer replied. "I was told he was cool and everything, but he's real mean. He even sent away the lady with the mints on the airplane. Do you happen to know where the kitchen is? I'm a little hungry."

Good god, the man had eaten everything on the plane and he was complaining again? "Boomer" apparently meant never-ending gut in American English. "Ana, would you please escort Mr. Boomer to the kitchen and inform the chef that he's in need of sustenance? He's only eaten two full meals in the past few hours."

"Thank god. I'm starving." Boomer let himself be led off.

Which left him with only one intrusive guard. He'd managed to ditch Weston and the Texan, Michael Malone. They'd declared they needed to do a quick tour of the grounds so they could get something called a "lay of the land." Now all he had to do was get rid of Murdoch and his life would be perfect. "Why don't you go with him?"

Murdoch simply smiled. "Because I would rather be with you."

"I'm going to yell at my mother," Kash explained. "I would

prefer to do it alone."

Murdoch shrugged. "I can stand out here. Please don't try to run off."

"I'm not being run out of my own palace." Kash turned for the door. His mother would be in her parlor at this time of day. He'd snuck in the back way in the hopes of catching his mother off guard. Surely she knew his plane had landed, but he'd moved quickly. She would be expecting him in another thirty minutes or so. He wanted her off guard so he could tell her exactly what she could do with her bloody wedding plans.

His anger had been building over the course of the long flight. How dare she throw this at him? With everything else he had to deal with, the last thing he needed was his mother losing her mind.

Yes, perhaps that was the way to go. His brain was working overtime and on almost no sleep. He'd tossed and turned all the way over. Not even drinking had helped ease him into peace. The whole time he'd fumed and raged, and he was ready to play as dirty as she was.

Dementia. It wasn't so surprising at her age. So what if she was only seventy and had all her faculties? The fact that she'd decided to take him on was proof enough that she'd lost her mind.

He'd have her in a nice home shortly, and then when she cried and begged him to allow her to come home, he would. But only after she'd taken back that stupid invocation. She would go to parliament and explain that she would never question her son again.

And anyone who ever did would find out that he was the damn king.

He was about to open the doors when the lord chamberlain showed up, stepping right into the way. "I think you should wait, Your Majesty. The queen mother is busy at this time. I'll set an appointment for you if you like."

Hanin stood there, a smug smile on his face and his suit in perfect condition.

"I would like to fire you and punch you in the face on the way out. If you don't move out of the way and allow me access to my mother, I will."

"You always were a bit of an animal, weren't you, Kashmir?" But he stepped aside.

"Don't ever forget it. And that's 'Your Majesty.'" At least it was until he shoved the crown somewhere the sun didn't shine.

He opened the outer doors, ready to have it out with his mother.

"Be quick, Pashmi. They say he's on his way. I can't have my son seeing this."

Seeing what? Oh, he would see everything. He would control everything since it seemed he was never allowed to be out of control. They came at him from all sides. When he wasn't dealing with parliament, he was fighting with OPEC or some other oil cartel. When he finally found something he felt good about, some asshole ex-CIA guy blew it all up, and now he was expected to take this from his own mother? No way.

He shoved through the inner doors and stopped.

Hanin moved past him. "Your Majesty, I'm so sorry. I tried to stop him but he threatened me with physical violence."

"It's all right," his mother was saying. "He would have found out anyway."

His mother's long-time maid was helping her to sit up and a woman in medical scrubs was wrapping up an IV that had obviously been used on his mother.

His mother, who had taken to not eating supper. Or breakfast.

His mother, whose clothes hung off her lately and she'd waved off his worry by telling him she was trying a new diet.

His mother, whom he'd neglected so much he hadn't seen that she was ill.

Hanin turned on him. "Can I expect that his majesty will be civil to the queen mother? I told her you wouldn't take this well. She insisted. As you can see, she's not strong enough for a fight, much less a wedding. You should convince her not to do this."

All thoughts of yelling fled as his whole soul seemed to sink. How had he not seen this? How had months gone by and he hadn't recognized that his mother might be dying? "Please allow me to talk to my mother. I'll take care of her."

Hanin strode out the door, closing it behind him.

"What is it? Is it cancer?" The thought made his heart seize. He moved to her side, dropping to one knee. Grandmother had died of cancer. He'd watched her waste away even as she'd smiled and tried to pretend everything was all right.

The lines around her eyes tightened. "I didn't mean for you to know."

She would probably tell him there was nothing to worry about. Pashmi wouldn't care that he was the king. Pashmi had changed his damn diapers at one point. She was practically a second mother, so he turned to the one person in the room he could intimidate.

He stood and faced the nurse. "What does my mother have? What is this treatment you're giving her?"

"A blood transfusion, Your Majesty. She was down two pints, a side effect of the chemotherapy for her cancer. She'll feel better now. She'll have much more energy." The nurse looked back at his mother. "She's very sick, Your Majesty. It's stage four ovarian cancer. She had a full hysterectomy but the cancer had spread to her colon and the doctors no longer think the chemo is working."

He felt as though the wind had been knocked out of him. Those words kicked him in the gut and left him gasping for breath.

This was why she'd done what she'd done.

"You're going to die and you don't want to leave me alone."

"Could we have the room, please?" His mother straightened up, her shoulders going back in a regal fashion.

Pashmi led the nurse outside.

He felt sick. How had he missed this?

"It's not your fault, Kashmir."

"I would disagree. How long has this been going on?" How long had he been out there partying while his mother was dying? How many women had he gone through while she'd fought for her life, gone through round after round of hell?

"Please, Kash," his mother implored. "Please sit with me. It's not as bad as the doctors say."

He found the edge of the couch, balancing on it. He wouldn't sit back in case he needed to carry her out. "I'll have the doctors tell me themselves."

"Of course. Don't be angry with them. I asked them to keep things quiet. I didn't want to make a fuss."

No fuss over the fact that she was dying. "Tell me how long you've known."

"I was diagnosed six months ago. I told you I was having

surgery."

"You told me it was routine. You then told me they found nothing serious. I didn't go to the doctors because you told me it was all fine." And because he hadn't wanted to believe. He'd been in a bad place, dealing with the fact that he'd come so close and couldn't replicate the experiments that had gone well before. He'd come up against failure after failure so he'd done what he did now. He'd found a party and become the life of it. For a month.

He'd offered to come home for the surgery but he'd been somewhat relieved when she'd told him not to, when she'd waved off his worry and laughed that she would rather be alone. She'd told him if he came home, the press would come with him.

He should have come home. He should have been sitting at her bedside when she woke up. She'd had no one. Her husband and eldest son were dead. Shray would never have allowed their mother to go through this alone. Shray would have seen.

Why had God taken Shray and left behind the lesser brother?

"Kashmir, listen to me. I know you're angry."

He was angry, but it was muted now. The rage he'd felt was buried under an avalanche of pure guilt. And pain. "You have no idea."

She sat back, looking older than he remembered. "Yes, I do, and I don't blame you. I hoped I could get better, but it looks as though I will not."

"I'll call in all the doctors." He would take her anywhere he needed to take her. He would find the best specialist and bring him or her in. "There are new therapies coming out every day."

"I don't want them. I'm tired, son. I've fought my battle and it's time to be with your father and your brother."

All he heard was it was time to leave him alone.

"Please forgive me. I didn't want to disrupt your life," she said quietly.

Nope. He couldn't sit at all. "Not disrupt my life? You don't allow me to take care of you because you don't wish to disrupt my life, but you come up with this insane plan to force me to marry?"

Despite her obvious weariness, there was a light in her eyes. "It's not insane. It's quite good, my plan. And you will marry, won't you, Kashmir?"

So neatly was her trap sprung. Still, he couldn't say the word. He couldn't give this up. She would be gone and he would be trapped in some loveless, sexless, hopeless marriage.

"I want to see you happy." The words sounded more like a plea coming out of his mother's mouth.

"Then don't ask me to marry." He stood in front of the floor-to-ceiling windows that looked out over the city. In the distance, he could see the Arabian Sea. When he'd been a child, he and Shray had played on those beaches, building sand castles to rival their home.

He was going to be alone. No one would remember who he'd been. He would be who he was now for the rest of his life. He would be the player king, the party boy.

"What do you think of this one, Your Majesty?" a feminine voice said. "I like it but I worry it's a bit revealing."

He turned as a woman in a brilliant yellow dress walked in from the side room.

For the second time in minutes, he felt the world flip and realign.

"Day?"

She turned and her spine straightened. Her body, so relaxed before, seemed to grow a few inches, and her gaze took him in.

She looked like a queen with her steely eyes.

"Hello, Kashmir," she said, her voice deeper than he'd remembered. That voice of hers washed over him. "I wasn't expecting to see you today."

Dayita Samar. How many years had flown by? She didn't look older, merely more mature. As though the beautiful girl he'd cared for had turned into a gorgeous woman who knew exactly who she was.

Day. The first woman he'd ever thought about settling down with.

God, was she really the only woman he'd ever thought about settling down with? He'd had a few girlfriends over the years, women he'd spent time with, escorted to the world's glittering events, but none of them had ever been like Day. None of those women had talked science and politics and put him on his ass when he needed it.

"Hello, Day." He couldn't help but stare at her. It was like a ghost had walked back into his life at the precise moment he needed to be reminded of his past.

"Well, are you going through with it or should I take off this dress and get back to work?" There was no mistaking the challenge in her eyes.

Oh, she should take off the dress. He remembered vividly how he'd wished he could get her out of those ridiculously prim clothes she'd worn at Oxford. Gone were the heavy sweaters and thick, too-long skirts. The gossamer yellow fabric skimmed her every curve and she was luscious.

More than that. She looked like home, a home he'd long thought lost to him.

His mother looked up at him expectantly. "Well, I thought if I was going to force you into a quickie marriage, I should at least give you a bride, too. Should I tell you why I selected Dayita? She's lovely and of the right age and you have much in common. She has a master's degree in physics from Oxford, so she's intelligent. We don't want an uneducated queen."

"I thought you planned to go for your doctorate." He couldn't seem to take his eyes off her. While he was looking at Day, he didn't have to acknowledge that his mother was dying.

"Circumstances changed," she replied, gathering the flowing skirt around her. "My father required help at home so I returned to Loa Mali and I eventually took over the education department, with her majesty's blessing."

His mother smiled Day's way. "She's been brilliant, but the parliament is giving her trouble about funding for elementary education. It seems they would prefer to spend it on other things."

Day had been here on Loa Mali all this time? She headed his education department? And what the hell was his parliament doing? "There is nothing more important than our children receiving the best possible education we can afford."

"Our girls and our boys," Day said with a quiet will.

Those old men were giving her hell about educating girls? Another thing he'd allowed to slip by. "You'll have your funding."

"Will I have my wedding?" His mother started to stand, her hands shaking. "Or should I prepare the lawyers?"

She was really going to do it. His mother was lovely, but when she decided, her mind was made up. She would force them into a constitutional crisis and he had no idea what the fallout would be. Day had reminded him what was at stake. Education and equality for an entire generation of Loa Mali's daughters.

"You'll have your wedding." He rushed to steady his mother, her hand so small and frail in his.

Small of body, great of will. That was his mother.

"Excellent." She straightened up. "Let's talk to the seamstress, darling girl. I think the dress is perfect, but they must bring the hem up slightly. We can't have you tripping at your wedding. And Kashmir, I have a tailor coming for you as well. The appointment is at four. Please don't be late. We shall dine tonight as a family. Seven p.m. sharp."

He watched as Day led his mother back toward the room they appeared to have set up as a dress shop. Of course. Day would need new clothes.

Kash walked out, ignoring Murdoch, who followed behind him. He strode through the palace until he got to his room. He ordered everyone out, locked the doors, and when he was absolutely certain he was alone, he sat at his desk. He stared at the picture of his family, his father and mother, smiling and proud. Shray at twenty-two, the almost king. Himself, grinning though the photographer had asked them all for restraint.

Kash stared at the photo and wished he could cry.

* * * *

The papers didn't do the man justice. He was far more beautiful in person. Even more handsome than she'd remembered him.

Day sighed as she walked out onto the balcony. Their small family supper had turned into a twenty-four-person state dinner after the parliament heads learned that Kash was back home and a bride had been selected.

Her first lesson in politics—family couldn't come first when one was the king.

She'd sat at the opposite end of the table from Kash, but she'd managed to watch him. He'd been charming and witty and he'd deflected many of the rather rude questions about how his marriage would change the way things were run.

On her end of the table she'd been asked numerous questions about what she would wear and who would arrange her hair for the ceremony, and did she worry about how the public would take a commoner queen?

She rather thought they would prefer a Loa Malian on the throne. Unfortunately, all the females who could claim some royalty were related to Kash, the downside to one family holding a crown for so long. If Kash wanted royalty he would have to marry a foreigner.

That was the moment the minister of infrastructure went back to asking about her hair. Apparently he had a niece who was a hairdresser.

She took a deep breath and stared out over the city. At this time of night, it was quiet in this sector, though she could see the lights twinkling downtown and closer to the beach. All the tourists and young people would be dancing the night away or sipping a cocktail after a long day of surfing and fishing.

God, she loved this place.

Was she doing the right thing? Perhaps she was for her country. For herself and Kash, she wasn't so sure.

She'd watched him from across the long, formal table and she hadn't seen any hint of the boy he used to be. Somehow, in the back of her mind she'd thought they would meet again and he would be the same.

So foolish of her.

"Did you enjoy the dessert? They had been planning on serving crème brûlée, but I remembered you like gelato. Strawberry."

She turned and Kash was standing in the doorway, the tie to his tuxedo undone and the first few buttons of his shirt open, showing off golden skin.

Oh, how the girls must swoon over that man.

Unfortunately for him, she was a woman and not a girl. She curtseyed, recalling her etiquette classes and going down deep, to show her respect for the crown. "I thank you, Your Majesty."

"Come now, Day. I asked you not to call me that long ago, and now it appears there's even less reason. We were friends then. We're going to be husband and wife in a week. Shocking how quickly that woman can move when she wants to."

He looked so composed, but she couldn't forget that he'd only found out his mother was dying this afternoon. That was when she'd seen the real man. She'd interrupted them with her silly dress and she'd seen the shock and pain on Kash's face before he'd smoothed it out and gone back to being the polite royal he'd become.

"Are you all right?" She asked the question for two reasons. First, she wanted to know the answer and second, to see if they really were still friends.

His lips curved up slightly. "I'm faring quite well. We Kamdars are made of sterner stuff than this. Did you enjoy the dinner?"

So, not so friendly he would talk about private things with her. It was good to know where they stood. They needed to have a long conversation about how this was going to work. They might be marrying to protect the Kamdar line and to give his mother some peace, but they needed a plan of action about how best to achieve their goals.

Partners. That was how she'd decided to look at this. They were partners. And if she ended up governing the kingdom while he was out fucking around with supermodels, she wouldn't get her heart broken.

Just humiliated.

Yes, they needed a talk and perhaps a contract.

"I enjoyed the meal very much. The company left something to be desired, but I suspect I'll get used to dining with windbag politicians." She turned back to the balcony, leaning against it. The view from here was spectacular. Beyond that, it was soothing in a way.

"Yes, Mother told me they're giving you trouble." He joined her, leaning beside her, their bodies so close but not touching. "I'll talk to them, ensure you have your funding."

"Don't. It can wait a few weeks. I need to go back to them and introduce myself as their new queen." She wasn't about to let them think she sent her husband in. If he behaved as he so often did, he wouldn't be around much and it would be up to her to keep everyone in line.

"Is that why you agreed to this arrangement? Because you wanted power?"

"I agreed because I care about this country. I've spent the last ten years of my life working here and trying to ensure that our children get what they need to make it out in the world. I agreed because your mother is excellent at putting one in a corner. I agreed because someone has to and I wasn't sure who you would bring home if given the chance." She shuddered at the idea of some brainless model attempting to be a role model for Loa Malian girls.

"Ah, you don't think I have good taste in women."

"I think you have an unquenchable appetite for them, Your Majesty, and that is something we should talk about."

"Ah, the wifely lectures begin," he said with a sigh. "Please proceed. I'm anxious to get this over with so I can be properly chastened."

"I only ask that you attempt some discretion, Kashmir. I don't expect you to be faithful in any way, but I do expect you to not humiliate me."

He turned, frowning a bit as though she'd surprised him. "You don't expect me to be faithful?"

It was time for some honesty. "I don't think you can be. How long have you kept a single woman? A month? Three?"

"Six," he replied. "I was with Tasha Reynolds for six months before we went our separate ways."

"And were you faithful to her?" She already knew the answer to that question.

"We had an agreement." He frowned as though the conversation wasn't going at all as he'd expected. "She was on set much of the time. She knew I had a highly stressful job, so she was understanding. I gave her the same options."

"Excellent, then let's be fair with each other. As long as we're both discreet, this marriage of ours doesn't have to mean the end of our lives."

"You have a man?"

"No, but I do have a life and I can't imagine never sleeping with someone again."

He stopped, his body going still for a moment. "What is that supposed to mean? I'll be your husband. You'll sleep with me. I know biology wasn't your field of study, but do I have to explain how babies are made? That's what my mother is doing. She's buying your womb."

So he wasn't as sanguine about the marriage as he'd seemed earlier. That was another thing she needed to know. "There are many ways to make a baby, several of which don't involve sex."

He frowned. "You can't be serious. We're going to be married. We're going to have sex."

"When I decide I'm ready, we'll talk about it." This brought her to the place she needed to be. "I think we need to negotiate our own private marriage contract. I would feel much better if we understood the parameters. It would help us both to know how to act and what our roles are."

"Your role is as my wife, and part of that is sleeping with me," Kash insisted.

"Not until you've had an STD test and I'm certain I want to sleep with you. I've already confirmed that it's traditional for the king and queen to keep separate rooms."

"There's nothing traditional about this."

She had to laugh. "I think it's quite traditional."

"Not for my family. My father was deeply in love with my mother. He met her at a ball in Bombay. Her father was the king of a small South Pacific island. I was told they danced all night and he went to her father the next day and demanded her hand in marriage or there would be war. As neither country had much of a standing army, they chose wedding."

She'd never heard the story. "That's sweet, but it's not how most royals wed."

"My grandfather selected his own bride as well. I'm the first in a hundred years to be arranged by someone else. I suppose my mother thinks I'm incapable of selecting a proper bride."

She had to offer him an out if he wanted one. They would both be miserable if he truly thought he could do better. "You should talk to her if you have someone you care for. I don't think she wants you to be unhappy. If there's a woman you love, you should present her to your mother."

Kash huffed, a disdainful sound. "After she's presented you to the parliament? I think not. Anyone I could bring in would be less than perfect. You really are, you know. I spent the last several hours studying up on you. Top of your class at Oxford. Accepted into MIT's doctoral program, but you turned it all down because your mother was sick. You had the whole world laid out for you, but you came home and took a job so far beneath you it's ridiculous. This one is beneath you, too, you know. You should be in a lab somewhere mapping the universe, not trying on designer dresses."

"I assure you I can make a difference." There were times when she wished she'd been able to follow through on the plan she'd made so long ago, but things changed. Dreams changed. "I have a purpose here. There are many brilliant minds working on the universe. The former head of education barely passed her O levels, much less university. I've thought this through. I can have a voice in this position, a unique one."

"Yes, you'll be my better half. My smarter half. Everyone will know the only way a woman like you marries a man like me is because it was arranged."

He was being frustrating, threatening to bring out the piece of herself she'd decided to suppress. No matter what the queen said, she wasn't sure Kash would be able to handle her when she got into that state of mind. She forced her voice to be gentle. The last thing she needed was to hear from another man how unwomanly she was. "What are you worried about, Kash? I told you if you have another woman, I'll step down."

He pushed away from the wall. "And I told you there is no single woman. Do you know where they found me? The bodyguards my mother hired to drag me home, that is."

"Miami, I heard." She was curious where he was going with this. Something seemed to be raging in the king this evening. Something that needed soothing, but she wasn't sure that was her place.

"They found me in bed with not one woman, but three." He said it like she was supposed to gasp and quiver with shock and distaste.

Did he think she didn't read the papers? Didn't see the way the press covered his antics? "Hence my offer to negotiate a path that will please us both."

His eyes narrowed, anger flaring as though he wasn't getting the reaction he wanted. "You think I was pleased?"

"If you weren't then you were doing it wrong. And with three women. You would think one of them would know how to do it right." She wasn't about to feed into his beast tonight.

He chuckled but there was no humor in the sound. "I wasn't talking about the sex. Or maybe I was. Maybe I was talking about how hollow it is now, how nothing fills me. There is no other woman, but there won't be any love for you either. Don't think you can win me back by following through on this ridiculous plan of my mother's."

It was her turn to laugh. "I haven't thought of you that way in years."

He was quiet for a moment. "You never think of that kiss?"

She wasn't going to lie. Despite what he'd said, she'd had time to think. This wasn't a ridiculous plan. This was the queen's way of knowing someone would be watching out for her country after she died. Day did want this to work. Not the relationship. Not in any romantic way. Rather, she wanted the job. She was ready to do her duty, and only Kash could keep her from it. That meant if they couldn't be friends, at the very least they had to respect each other. "I think about it from time to time, but we were two different people then. Those children are gone. I get wistful when the memory washes over me, but I don't mourn for some lost love between us."

She sometimes wished things had turned out differently. She certainly wished Kash hadn't lost such a huge chunk of his family. But she knew the Kash whom she'd kissed that day by the river wasn't the Kash standing with her tonight. He'd changed in that moment. He'd become a king, and it was obvious the weight didn't sit well.

"Well, it's for the best that you didn't. Did you even think of me after I left or did you move on to the next bloke? I heard later on that you dated Neville Hightower after I left. Quite a step down, I should say." He turned to go. "I'll bid you goodnight. I'm sure there's something Mother has planned for us tomorrow."

"Stop right there." She wasn't putting up with that. She needed to make that clear. "You will not talk to me like that again."

He turned, his lips quirking in an arrogant smirk. "I'll talk to you any way I like. Haven't you heard that I'm the king?"

Now she was finding a little rage of her own. "I don't care who you are. You will not speak to me like that. If you have a question, I'll answer it. If you need comfort, I'll talk to you. Do you think I don't see through this? This behavior is one of two things. Either you are truly the arrogant ass you're presenting to me or the day has been too much and I'm a convenient punching bag."

His face lost that smooth smile. "I didn't mean to hurt you. It has been a long day."

There was the moment she'd been waiting for. When he realized what he was doing, he backed off. For that, she could reward him. She moved closer, putting her hand on his shoulder and leaning in. "Kashmir, you found out your mother is dying. Of course it's been a long day."

His head shook. "I can't. I can't even process it right now. Answer my question. It's easier to focus on this, on us. Please."

The *please* did it. Something about a polite man always softened her up. His question. Had she thought about him after that day by the river? "I wrote you letters for a year or so. I came home for the coronation and tried to see you, but they wouldn't let me through. Too many people and I wasn't important enough, I suppose. I don't blame you, Kash. I was some girl you knew at university. You had other things to deal with back then."

She didn't blame him. Not anymore. In those first years, she'd been angry with him, mad at herself for letting him in. Now she saw them for what they'd been. Two children trying to navigate a world that constantly attempted to drown them. They were all swimming as hard as they could and there was no blame to be placed.

He stiffened, coming to his full height. "You did what?"

She stepped back. "I wrote you."

"You wrote me a letter?"

"No, I wrote you probably fifty or sixty. I was lonely after you left. I knew after you didn't reply to the first five or so that you weren't going to, but I still liked talking to you. It was probably a silly thing to do. I should have gotten a journal or something, but I didn't."

He put his hands on her shoulders, looking her straight in the eyes. "Dayita, I never got a single letter from you."

He hadn't sent one either. It was so long ago. "I sent them to the palace post office. I suspect they deal with hundreds of letters."

"I should have gotten them. I asked my secretary to send me anything from my friends at Oxford. I got nothing. I was desperate back then. I wanted something, anything to make me feel normal, but all my friends deserted me. I wanted to see you. How can you say you came to the coronation? I offered to send a plane for you. You refused. You said you had too much to do. Why are you lying to me?"

Oh, someone had lied and she could guess whom. Her heart twisted at the thought of Kash being all alone and longing for his friends only to have none reply. "Kash, I never got any correspondence from you. No offer at all. Why would I have turned you down? I came to try to see you. I have pictures of me and my father at the coronation celebrations outside the palace. I assure you I wouldn't have made a twelve-hour flight in economy if you would have sent a plane. I know Matthew and Roger tried to contact you, too. Your friends didn't abandon you. They couldn't get to you."

"Why?" Kash let go and seemed to stumble a bit before regaining his balance. "Why would she do that to me? My mother is the only one who could have done this. No one else in this palace would have kept something like this from me."

The last thing he needed was to get angry with his mother. "I'm sure she had her reasons. You needed to be focused on your new duties. You couldn't spend all your time mooning over a beautiful girl."

His hands, fisted before, relaxed, and he gave her the first genuine smile she'd seen from him all evening. "Mooning? You think I would moon over you?"

Yes, she was remembering how to handle him. Perhaps there was a bit left of the happy boy she'd fallen in love with all those years ago. "I'm sure you did, Your Majesty. I can picture you right here, staring out and wishing for your lost love. Maybe you even bought a guitar and learned how to play. You wrote sad songs about how much you missed me."

He laughed, a magical sound. When Kash laughed, his body shook with it. It reminded her of how passionate he'd been about everything. Kash had an enthusiasm for life that brightened a room when he walked in, that made her look at the world around her differently. He'd been the one to bring her out of her shell.

Had she gone back into it for years because he'd gone away?

He smiled down at her, his hands coming up to frame her face. "I did miss you, Dayita. Those first years, I missed you like crazy." He sobered a bit. "But I've changed. You're right. I'm not the man I was back then."

Her heart twisted in disappointment. She'd almost been sure he would kiss her, but he moved back. She tried not to show how much that hurt. A few hours back in his life and she was the one with longing in her heart. It was dangerous, but luckily she was a disciplined woman. She wasn't a girl anymore. She knew better. And deep down, she'd always known that they'd had their chance and it wouldn't come again. "I'm not the same either. I'm older, more restrained. I'm comfortable with myself now so I can go into this arrangement with my eyes wide open."

"Can we not make any more major decisions tonight?" Kash asked.

He looked so tired and she wondered if he had slept at all. She was worried that if she left him alone, he might confront his mother, and they all needed cooler heads to prevail. The past was the past and they had to deal with the future. If she was going to be his wife, she needed to be his friend again, and friends took care of each other. "Come to my room and I'll get you a drink."

He cocked a single brow.

Yes, she still remembered how to speak Kashmir. "No, I'm not inviting you into my bed. Have a drink with me and I'll tell you all about our friends, if you want to know. I'm still close with Roger and Matty."

He frowned. "And Neville?"

Such a jealous man. "Neville got a bit handsy, and once I broke his fingers he seemed to lose interest in me."

"Ah, that's what I like to hear." Kash reached a hand out. "Are we really going to do this, Day?"

"Only if you want to, Your Majesty." It had to be his choice in the end, even if most of his options had been taken from him.

He seemed to come to some decision and he pulled her hand

to his lips. "All right then, my bride-to-be. I hope Mother stocked your room with whiskey. I could use some. Don't mind the bodyguards. They follow me. I think they think I'm going to run."

She'd seen his new American guards. She'd been assigned a couple herself. Michael Malone was a lovely man, and the oddly named Boomer was like a beautiful, massive golden retriever.

She nodded to Mr. Murdoch as they walked back into the palace. He'd been hovering close all night and seemed like a perfectly kind man.

Kash began talking about the old days.

It was time to figure out what kind of man her future husband was. And if he could handle what she needed.

Chapter Three

Kash came awake and sat up in bed. Something was wrong. Different. Definitely different. He was also dressed. He was wearing a pair of pajama pants because he'd sat up for the longest time with Day, talking about old times. They'd started out drinking Scotch, but when she'd switched to tea, he'd gone along with her. They'd called down to the kitchens and had tea and sandwiches and tiny cakes sent up.

He'd been sad to leave her.

"I feel odd."

"That's what it feels like when you don't wake up with a hangover, Your Majesty," Simon Weston said as he strode into the bedchamber. "I know it's terribly odd to realize you remember the evening before, but that's how it goes. I need to talk to you about security for tonight's official engagement announcement and celebration. I'm afraid things are going to move quickly over the course of the next two weeks."

Yes, he did remember. He was getting married to Day. His mother had set it all up, but then it had been his mother who had kept Day from him in the first place. "I need to talk to my mother."

"She'll be here in a few moments." Weston nodded toward the door and the flood of servants began. "She's coming in with the lord chamberlain. I've had breakfast brought in."

Yes, Kash could see that. His normal breakfast was usually coffee and a protein bar, but this was a full breakfast. Full English. He hadn't had a full English since his college days. Mostly because it was absolutely terrible for him. He smiled, the memories wafting over him as he smelled the sausages and fried eggs, baked beans and bacon. There was toast and hash browns and tomatoes. "Did you order this? I don't think my mother's ever had a fry-up."

Weston shook his head. "This is for you. I've gotten to be too American to possibly handle that breakfast. I've got an omelet and some fruit. Your fiancée ordered for you. She's attempting to take over some of the queen's duties."

His stomach grumbled and he couldn't help but smile. Day remembered. They'd often had breakfast together and he would always order a full English breakfast. She would wrinkle her nose as she ate some tiny thing and drank an enormous cup of coffee. He'd never had a woman other than his mother order breakfast for him.

There were only four plates. He hoped Hanin was sitting off to the side somewhere and he could ignore him, but somehow he doubted the world would be so kind to him. That meant there wasn't a place for Day.

"Should we invite my…?" He'd almost called her his wife. It was weird. He would have a wife in two weeks' time. "Should we invite the future queen? She might have something to say about her schedule."

Weston took a cup of coffee from the young woman serving breakfast. "Ms. Samar is also indisposed. She's having a spa day. I hope you don't mind, but my Chelsea and Jesse's wife, Phoebe, offered to join her. Apparently Ms. Samar doesn't have many close girlfriends, and spa days are much more fun when shared. I also think we should talk about a few specific threats that could be rather stressful for your bride-to-be. I thought I would talk about those before your mother gets here."

"Threats?" He smiled at the maid, who handed him a perfectly brewed cup of coffee. Usually he gulped it down, desperately needing the caffeine. It was nice to savor it, to truly taste the unique flavor. He'd missed this coffee. Loa Mali coffee was unlike anything else he'd ever tried. "Are you talking about the antimonarchists? They love to threaten me. They never do anything at all about it."

All talk. Blah. Blah. Kill the king. Blah. Blah something boring and political. Death to the Kamdars. Blah. So typical and yet they never even tried to murder him.

"I think there's something different now," Weston said.

"Why now?"

"Because up until now you've shown no signs of any chance

that you would marry soon. Without marriage there was always the possibility that the monarchy would end with you."

"I'm not the last Kamdar. My cousin could take the throne if something happened to me."

"Chapal?"

"Yes, he is obnoxious but quite intelligent." After all, he was a Kamdar.

"He's also gay."

Kash waved that thought off. "Yes, though he is a terrible dresser. No style at all. What his husband sees in him I will never know."

"By constitutional law, he can take the throne, but unless he is willing to procreate, the line would end with him."

Ah, he hadn't thought of that. He'd always thought that Chapal would carry on and be the absolute worst-dressed homosexual king in the world. His husband, Ben, would have to do all the hard work of making things livable in the palace. Chapal was too attached to his bloody computer.

But after Kash, Chapal was the last Kamdar. "I'll start the wheels to change that. The world is not where it was two hundred years ago. If Chapal adopts, his child should not be punished. We're not in the Dark Ages, though the antimonarchists would have you believe it. So you think they're serious this time because I'm getting married?"

"You've gotten threats?" His mother walked into the room, her voice strong but her body seemingly so frail.

Kash stood and walked to her, offering her his hand to steady her. He ignored Hanin, who walked in behind her. Hanin would be gone soon enough. He would allow the man to stay around because his mother favored him, but the minute she was gone so was Hanin.

His stomach turned. Had he really just thought about his mother being dead?

"Are you all right?" His mother stared up at him.

"I'm fine. I'm adjusting." And not well. He was floundering. "Come along. We have much to talk about and your breakfast is ready."

She waved him off but found her chair. "I'll have some tea,

please."

"Your son's fiancée ordered you tea and toast," Weston said.

"I told the cook the queen wasn't interested in food." Hanin sat down to his own breakfast, setting aside his ever-present planner.

"And my daughter-in-law-to-be wished to give me the choice." His mother picked up a knife and began to butter her toast. "I think this should be quite nice. My stomach can't handle much right now, but this looks good."

Day was getting his mother to eat even when she wasn't here. Still, he was angry with her. Oddly, not as angry as he'd been the night before. He'd wanted to rage at her, but hours in Day's company had defused the anger and what that hadn't calmed, seeing his mother's frail figure had. He settled himself into his chair, his appetite coming back. "Mr. Weston was talking about the antimonarchists."

Hanin's mouth curled in obvious distaste. "Animals, all of them."

"I'm sure they would say they're fighting for democracy," Weston replied.

"They're threatening my son?" His mother carefully scooped out the jam Dayita had sent with the toast. "They do this all the time. I'm sure they're particularly nasty now that the wedding has been called and they know the monarchy shall persevere."

"They're threatening to stop the wedding." Weston sat back. "I've sent each of you my plans for security. It will be very tight, and everyone will be vetted by my firm. I suggest allowing in one sanctioned photographer and one reporter. The queen-to-be would like to auction off the photos, with all proceeds going to a charitable fund for education."

The future queen was practically a saint. "Whatever she would like. I don't think I want to do a ton of press though. How are we framing this? Does the world know this is an arranged marriage?"

"Of course not," his mother replied. "As far as anyone knows, you and Dayita met in England and drifted apart but now you've gotten close again. Everyone knows you're a bit on the reckless side. They will assume Day is pregnant and that is the reason for the hasty wedding. If you could make that happen on the honeymoon, it would be wonderful."

Ah, there was his irritation. Not even the lovely eggs could get rid of it. "My procreation will be my choice, Mother. You've interfered enough."

Hanin sat straight up. "You can't talk to the queen mother that way."

"Bah," his mother replied. "I'm happy he's talking to me at all. If I have one thing to be grateful to the cancer for, it's the guilt that's kept my son from running away to be with loose women. He always runs for the loose ones."

"Or the spies," Weston added helpfully. "When I first met him he was entertaining several hookers and a couple of undercover spies."

Ah, the beautiful Kayla. Yes, he'd called her his Asian lily, and she'd been an American double agent. She'd quite scared him at times. Brutal girl, but lovely. "Could we forego hashing through ancient history? Well, not entirely. I would like to know why you chose Day as my bride when you did everything you could to keep us apart fifteen years ago."

His mother flushed but remained steady as a rock. "Because I figured out I was wrong all those years ago. You have to understand that everything was crazy after your father and Shray died. You came home and all you would talk about was some young lady I'd never met before. I needed you focused on taking the crown. We were desperate at the time. I was desperate at the time."

She'd been alone, her whole world washed out from under her. Perhaps a few years before he wouldn't have been able to see things in such a fashion, but he could now. Still. "I only wanted to see her. I wanted something that was mine."

"And I needed you to see the crown as yours. I needed you focused on the country." His mother reached out, sliding her hand over his. "I was wrong, but at the time I thought I was right. I thought the feelings you had for Dayita were nothing more than a childish crush on a girl who likely reminded you of home. You didn't fight hard. You sent her a single invitation and then we heard nothing more. She sent years of letters. I thought it was one sided."

Had that really been it? At the time he'd felt so crushed. She hadn't answered a single request and he'd given up, moved on. Day had written him letter after letter. She'd flown a thousand miles to see him.

He'd been the faithless one.

"You read the letters? Are they still around?"

Hanin put his fork down. "I kept them for history's sake. Your mother asked me to keep them from you, but I always worried she would change her mind. So I kept them instead of trashing them. Three years ago she asked about the young woman, asked me if I knew her. I said no, but I did know a way her majesty could get to know her. And I gave her the letters."

"And I fell in love with Day," his mother said quietly. "I found out she was here in Loa Mali and I did everything I could to bring her into my sphere so I could watch over her. When the time came, I made my move to bring her back to you. I don't know if I was wrong to do what I did in the beginning. I don't know if she would have been a steadying hand or a distraction, but I do know you need her now."

"You had no right to keep those letters from me." But he kept his tone calm. He hated the fact that he couldn't let his rage fly. And he truly loathed the reason why he couldn't. How could he be angry with his dying mother? There was someone he could deal with. "Hanin, you became my employee the day my father and brother died. I consider following my mother's orders in this case tantamount to treason. Would you like me to have your head cut off?"

The man had gone a nice shade of gray.

His mother gasped. "Kashmir!"

Weston merely chuckled. "You have the right, Your Majesty. Still, I think a public execution might overshadow the wedding."

Hanin stood. "I did my job. I serve this country and the palace. Do you have any idea how hard you make my job? She was right to do what she did. Getting you to focus is like being forced to work with an untrained monkey."

"Hanin!" At least his mother was shocked by all of them. "Please don't refer to his majesty in such a fashion or he'll be right to fire you."

"He's planning on firing me anyway." Hanin stepped back. "The minute you're gone, I'll be gone, too, and he'll probably get rid of his bride as well. A man like him doesn't change. I feel sorry for your poor bride. She'll either find herself divorced in a year or the object of everyone's pity because there's no chance that you don't go back to your partying ways within weeks of your mother's death. Perhaps before. After all, it's not like you ever cared what she and the world thought of you anyway. Her majesty is trying to save the country, but you won't care. You'll ruin us all in the end. I always saw that."

"Hanin, please," his mother began.

"Oh, no, Hanin, you continue on." It was good to see his lord chamberlain for who he really was. "Let me know exactly how you feel."

Tears had started in his mother's eyes. "I can't plan this without him."

Damn it. She shouldn't be planning anything at all. She should be resting, trying to maintain her strength.

Fucking fuck and fuck fuck.

Kash stood and attempted to moderate his tone and his expression. All the sweet words in the world wouldn't mean a thing if he looked like he felt—like he wanted to murder someone. He had to be the king, and the king remained calm and made reasonable decisions. "Hanin, please accept my apologies. It is true that I believe my bride and I will be happier with a new lord chamberlain after we're wed and I am in the palace most of the time. I would like to do things in a modern way, and you have always emphasized the traditional. Perhaps that is why we seem like we're at cross purposes. I do, however, promise to make your retirement a lucrative one. And I certainly won't ever speak of beheading you again. That wasn't well done of me."

Hanin turned and walked back to the table. "I will stay for your mother's sake."

His mother reached over and patted his hand as though he was a child and had done something well for the first time.

"Shall we talk about the guest list? I've got it down to seven hundred." Hanin opened his notebook.

"I'll need all those names. Every single person will have to be vetted," Weston replied. "We've got almost no time so I need a finalized list by this afternoon."

"Seven hundred." It horrified Kash. The one good thing he could think of about his two-week engagement was going to be the smallness of the wedding. No one could put together a true royal wedding in two weeks. "No. We have so little time and there are no plans. We should keep it small. No more than twenty."

His mother's face lit up, and for a brief moment he saw the woman who had raised him, youthful and full of joy and strength. "No plans? I've been planning for years. Everything is already in place. It will be the grandest wedding, Kashmir. I've already found someone who will release a hundred doves as you and Day are pronounced husband and wife. And, of course, we must be seen observing all the rituals."

He shook his head. "Absolutely not."

Weston was watching his mother. "Rituals?"

"Yes, Loa Mali has many beautiful rituals for the bride and groom." His mother put her hand over her heart. "The Palm Ritual is lovely. I have many pictures from your father's and mine."

"Mother, it's the twenty-first century. I'm not hiding in a group of palm trees getting my arse cut up so I can steal a woman who has already agreed to marry me. Nor will I allow my best friends to tie me up and beat my feet with fish."

What Loa Mali had was a group of crazy antiquated and downright ridiculous rituals meant to ward off evil spirits and generally make everyone getting married think twice about doing it in the first place.

He saw the glint in his mother's eyes and knew he was in trouble.

* * * *

Day sat back with a smile, the steam from the spa deliciously warm. "It's supposed to ward off bad spirits and build the groom's strength for the wedding night."

Phoebe Murdoch's lips curled up as she laughed. "Fish? They're going to beat Kash's feet with fish and that will give him virility?"

It was silly, but she suspected the queen mother was going all out with this wedding. "I suspect the practice was created by fish merchants. One of our main industries is fishing, but we have a problem with bycatch. These are the unwanted fish that are caught by our commercial fishermen. Several of our local fish are quite horrible to eat, but legend has it those fish are imbued with the potency of our ancient sea god, so they're prized for wedding and fertility rituals. Not only will Kashmir have his friends beat him with the fish, he'll have to eat a good portion of one raw in order to ensure our wedding night is productive. And since we haven't yet agreed to have relations on our wedding night, I fear it will be for nothing."

"You're not sleeping with Kash?" Chelsea Weston sat on the bench to Day's left. "I would love to have seen the look on his face when you told him. That man thinks he's God's gift to women. Not that I don't like Kash. He's fun to be around, but he does think a whole lot of that face of his."

Did he? Day wondered about that. "I think a lot of it is armor. I knew Kash before he became the king. In some ways he did everything he did to differentiate himself from his older brother. He became the playboy because Shray was so serious. But you have to understand that playboy prince was studying theoretical physics at Oxford when I met him, and he didn't get in because of his name. Kash is incredibly smart."

"Oh, I know that," Phoebe replied. "When Jesse first met him, he was close to a working prototype of a car that ran on water."

Day had been grateful for the company when she'd been told Chelsea and Phoebe would accompany her. Normally this day would be spent with Day's sisters and her female in-laws-to-be. She had some cousins, but they had mostly moved to Europe or the States. She'd been unable to see herself spending this time with the little mice who worked with her at the department. They were sweet women, but her two assistants were mostly biding their time until they could find husbands. She liked these two women. They were smart and strong of opinion.

It was interesting that she also thought they would be quite submissive when it came to sex. But then she had started to wonder the same thing about Kashmir.

"I'd heard a rumor that the explosion in the Arabian Sea wasn't an accident." She hadn't talked to him about it the night before.

They'd sat together and drank and talked about their old friends. She hadn't wanted to bring up anything that might make him sad or angry. He'd been in a good place, and she'd been the one to take him there. She wasn't one to undo her own work.

How would he feel if he knew she was looking at him as if he was a potential sub to top?

Chelsea shook her head. "Not an accident at all. It was all the work of a group of major douchebags known as The Collective."

Phoebe stared at her friend. "You are the worst CIA employee in the world. You know that's probably classified."

Chelsea shrugged. "It's also good gossip, and I don't work for them anymore. Right now, I'm a happy housewife. Well, a housewife who works ten hours a day writing code for the new business. And let me tell you, dealing with Adam is not a picnic. He thinks he's way smarter than he is. Satan's right about him."

Chelsea talked a lot about Satan. Day was fairly certain it was an oddly affectionate nickname for someone, and not that Chelsea had a weird religious bent. Still, she wanted to shift the flow of conversation back to the important stuff. "Why would this Collective come after Kashmir?"

Phoebe and Chelsea seemed to have an entire conversation through frowns and the narrowing of eyes.

Finally, Phoebe gave in. "Fine. It is good gossip and I don't work for the Agency anymore either. Also, you're about to become like the head of the country and stuff, so I think you could probably find this out on your own. The Collective was a group of the world's biggest companies and they basically Star Chambered the rest of the world. They helped each other out, you know. Some business needed to sell their firearms, so The Collective helped out by starting a civil war somewhere. They manipulated stock prices, practiced all the worst things humanity can do. Kash's experiments would have cost the oil industry everything, so they sent an agent to blow the lab up."

"They were also supposed to kill Kash," Chelsea explained. "But my Simon jumped off a cliff and saved him."

"I think Big Tag would say that's a gross oversimplification of that story," Phoebe continued. "But Jesse does say it was pretty cool. It was actually Kayla who got the king out."

Chelsea shook her head. "Don't."

Phoebe had flushed. "Yeah, uhm, but mostly Si. It was a team effort."

Day could guess what they were covering up. She hadn't been blind for fifteen years. His womanizer reputation had been the reason she'd held back during college. Until that moment when he'd allowed her to take control, when she'd realized she might truly have something to give him that no one else could. Of course, at the time she hadn't understood that there was a word for what she needed.

Dominance.

"I know what he used that boat for. He kept his harem out there. So did he seduce her after she saved him? Did he offer to pay her off with his body?" That sounded like Kashmir, the manwhore.

Chelsea winced. "She might have been a spy at the time, and he thought she was a supermodel."

Day let her head fall back as she laughed. It was a good play by the Agency or whoever had hired this Kayla person. Going at Kash through his cock was the only way to go. "I pray his cousin found out about that. Chapal runs the country's technology and security. I believe most of his migraines come from Kashmir's many women. I'm afraid your husbands taking over security even for a brief period of time will be difficult for them. Kash acts out when he's angry. I expect him to misbehave a lot before this wedding actually occurs."

"And after?" Phoebe was studying her.

It was easy to forget these two lovely women were both former CIA. Of course, that was likely exactly why they'd been so good at their jobs. "After, we will find our way. I suspect we will be friends and try to get along as much as possible. He'll have his life and I'll have mine."

"That sounds terrible," Chelsea shot back.

But Day had come to some terms with it. She hadn't expected to marry at all. Now she had the prospect of children. Oh, they might be implanted with the medical equivalent of a turkey baster, but they would have two loving parents. "I never thought I would marry when I made the decision to stay here on Loa Mali and work."

"You're beautiful," Phoebe remarked. "You're intelligent and kind. Why would you think you wouldn't marry?"

"There aren't a lot of prospects on this small island, and despite all of our wealth and our freedoms, we're still quite old fashioned in some ways. The king has done a good job by steering parliament away from laws that would curb a woman's freedom, but there are still many who believe a wife's place is at home. I'm not that woman. It would have been difficult to find a man here who wouldn't want me at home. Home is a place I go to after work. It's not that I look down on women who do stay home. My mother did and I loved her very much. I simply am not built that way. I wouldn't find the same satisfaction that she did. As I believe she would have hated working the way I do. We need choices. We need to be free to be who we are."

"A queen isn't free," Chelsea said.

She'd thought about this, too. "But a queen makes a contract with her people. She knows what she will do and what is not acceptable. I quite like a contract. My marriage to Kash will be contracted. We will have our roles, agreed upon between both of us."

"There is nothing wrong with a good contract, but don't write out spontaneity." Phoebe adjusted her towel. "You cared about Kash once. Why not see if you can again? Some men like Kash settle down after marriage and make lovely husbands."

"She should know. Her brother was the only person I've met who was worse than Kash. Well, I mean he didn't have a harem boat or anything, but Ten tore through some women, if you know what I mean," Chelsea confided. "And now he's faithful to his wife. Whose name is Faith. Yeah, that's terrible. Sorry about that."

"Faith is wonderful," Phoebe replied. "And Chelsea's right about my brother. He was a horrible manwhore. Kashmir is actually a nice man. I've always thought the right woman could settle him down. All the women I've ever seen around him are too superficial. They're flighty things. I think he picks them because he never has to get serious with any of them. At least that's what my husband thinks."

"Si thinks he's…" Chelsea bit her bottom lip and sighed. "Sorry. New friends."

"Thinks he's what?" Day was intrigued. She'd heard a bit of gossip concerning these friends of Kash's. She wasn't sure how to ask without embarrassing anyone, but perhaps direct was the best bet. "Does your husband, who I would guess is the top, think Kashmir would be happier as a bottom?"

Phoebe's jaw dropped.

Chelsea merely laughed. "Yes. Yes, that's exactly what he thinks. A lot of us do, but we wouldn't say it. He's a little sensitive. He's been to Sanctum, but he just played around. I've heard he's gone to several clubs around Europe and plays, but at least outside the actual bedroom he tops."

That was what she'd been a bit afraid of. Yet last night when she'd taken control of the situation, when she'd seen to his comfort and given him direction, he'd responded beautifully. He'd been happier at the end of that night, though she would have bet he hadn't realized what she was doing.

Phoebe curled her legs underneath her. "So, how long have you been in the lifestyle, Mistress?"

Well, that hadn't taken her long. "Ten years. I met a man in graduate school. He was lovely and he had certain needs that I found I enjoyed indulging. We broke up because I came home to Loa Mali. Not much of the lifestyle here. I go on retreats two or three times a year. I have Mistress rights at some clubs in Europe. I find it relaxing, but I worry my husband-to-be will prove very traditional in this sense."

"How will you know until you try?" Chelsea asked. "I doubt anyone has ever offered to top him before. Not in a serious way. You don't have to pull out a whip."

"You want me to be the sneaky top." What she'd been so far.

"I think some subs need to be eased into what they need," Phoebe explained. "I know I did. I thought it was distasteful until someone convinced me to try. And I probably still wouldn't have found myself if I hadn't been with a man I truly connected with. I can certainly see how Kash might need it. Submission for some of us is relaxing. It's a way to find a place where we don't have to think. For all his playboyness, he still has an enormous amount of pressure on him."

"He did back then, too. I can see now it was why we worked. I was different than the other girls. I thought he liked to talk to me because we came from the same place, that he merely missed home. Now I look back and realize he liked it when I would take charge. I didn't force him to make all the decisions. It's hard to make all the choices. And I wouldn't want a sub who needed me to direct him in his daily life. But sexually, I prefer to be in control. Again, it's the way I'm built, but it can be hard to be different."

It could be impossible. Lately, the trips to her clubs had been unsatisfying. She needed a permanent partner, someone she could connect with for more than a weekend or a few weeks. Someone who needed her.

She was coming up on a time in her life when she would have to decide if she would suppress that need for the rest of it. Perhaps that was why she'd given in to the queen mother so easily. Being the queen meant having a nation that needed her, a whole island of people she could fight for.

Or perhaps she'd done it because for years she'd dreamed of Kash kneeling for her, asking her for discipline, his face peaceful when she gave it to him.

That one kiss had changed her life in ways he couldn't have dreamed of.

Should she give her marriage an actual shot?

"He might surprise you," Phoebe said. "Ease him into it. Like I said, it really worked for me. He's already comfortable in the lifestyle. It doesn't scare him or make him squeamish. I know the few times he's visited Sanctum, he tends to like to watch some of the heavier scenes. But when it comes time to play at anything beyond spanking or light scenes, he won't participate even when there are other Doms to supervise and teach him."

"Because he's not truly interested in being the one holding the crop," Chelsea said with a smile. "He likes to watch and fantasize about those heavy scenes, but I would bet real money he's not the Dom in his head."

Day breathed in the steam of the room, letting it relax her. "I could run a test, I suppose. If I know my future mother-in-law, she's going to want all the bells and whistles a Loa Malian wedding can have. One of those is the Palm Ceremony."

"Do you get hit in the face with palm fronds?" Phoebe asked.

"That's still better than fish."

She had to chuckle at the thought. It was obvious Phoebe had never been hit with one. They could be sharp. "No, it's a ritual to honor the first king of Loa Mali. Supposedly, he found his bride wandering on a beach. He would hide and watch her from a copse of palm trees. He asked her father for her hand in marriage, but he refused because she was from another island. The king decided to steal his bride. He rode onto the beach and scooped her up on his stallion and whisked her to the palace, where he made love to her for the first time. Her father, seeing how happy he'd made the daughter, acquiesced and the couple was married one week later. So you see, the whole fish ceremony is silly because most married couples get it on after the Palm Ceremony. We might be one of the only cultures in the world that actively tell engaged couples to take a test drive."

"I like it." Chelsea stood. "I've got a massage in five. I think we should help the Mistress plan."

Phoebe winked her way. "You know I'm always up for a good plan."

It was probably a horrible idea, but sometimes a woman had to take a chance. Perhaps when her king stole her away, he would find he was the one who was claimed.

Yes, she liked the sound of that.

Chapter Four

"You're sure you want to do this?" Chapal moved a palm frond, sneaking a peek at the beach where Dayita would soon be walking.

Kash sighed and tried not to step on anything the horse decided to leave behind. "It's considered good luck."

His cousin looked somewhat ridiculous wearing traditional clothes. His chest was on display and he wore a pair of lightweight pants that reached just below his knee. On his head rested a headdress made of shells and palm leaves.

On Chapal's skinny, never-hit-a-gym-in-his-life, how-was-a-brown-man-so-damn-pale body, it looked a bit silly.

Kash rather thought it made *him* look dashing and romantic. Otherwise, he looked like an idiot douchebag about to reenact a bit of history almost no one gave a damn about.

Except for all those crazy people on the beach waiting to watch the ceremony. They lined the beach and the road that would take them back to the palace. Weston had the route guarded by a number of the new guard he had hired in the last week. He'd doubled the amount of palace guards and was working with the small police force and military to get them trained.

Even his old bodyguard Rai had agreed to come back for the royal wedding. He stood outside the staging area, his back to Kash and his eyes moving across the crowd.

"Do you really want good luck?" Chapal asked. "You want this marriage to work? I ask because I like Day. I've known her for the last few years and she's a lovely woman. I would hate to see her get hurt."

Days had passed and this was all he'd heard. It had been a solid week since he'd agreed to the arrangement and every moment he spent with Day made him think it wouldn't be so bad. Every moment he spent away from her made him wonder if he was a monster.

"Why would she be hurt? Have you ever once known me to hurt a woman?"

Chapal turned, crossing his arms over his chest and then uncrossing them because he was wearing a horrible necklace made of the aforementioned itchy palm fronds. "You would never physically hurt a woman. I know that. I'm talking about her tender heart."

He had to smile at that one. "Tender heart? Have you seen what she does to members of parliament who don't get on board with her education plans? She can eviscerate a man with that sharp tongue of hers."

Day had been keeping her appointments as the head of education despite the fact that the last week had been a whirlwind. He'd gone with her to an advisory meeting with the parliament's committee on schools. He'd stayed in the background as she'd requested, watching from the back of the balcony seats. They'd given her a rough interrogation about her budget and why they should increase it. At two points in time he'd nearly stood up and gone after a few of the bastards for the way they'd spoken to her. Day had been cool and calm, explaining everything patiently and then threatening to go straight to the press with a story about how the Loa Mali parliament had spent three hundred thousand dollars on a party to celebrate their own anniversary, a party the public wasn't invited to, but they refused to spend a paltry seventy-five thousand to update computer software for their children. They'd sputtered and cursed and Day had gotten her way.

And Kash had gotten a hard-on. A really massive, wouldn't-go-away-for-a-long-time hard-on.

That had felt good. It had been a long time since he'd wanted more than sex, since he'd wanted one particular woman, and for more than to prove he could have her.

Maybe he was a bit of a monster, but he never lied to the women he took to his bed.

And he wasn't going to lie to Day.

"She doesn't date often," Chapal continued. Why his cousin

believed he had to also be his conscience, Kash had no idea. "The whole time I've known her she's dated two men. One was a setup and she never saw him again. She spends all of her time on work. When she goes on vacation, she goes alone."

That didn't seem right. "Where does she go? And what happened with the other man?"

"She dated the minister of transportation for about six months. They seemed well suited, but then she broke things off with him and he was married to another woman within six weeks. She won't talk about what happened. I think he asked her to marry him, but only if she gave up her job and came home. I think she comes up against this quite a bit. As for her vacations, she goes to Europe. Ben and I asked if she would like company once, but she said she was fine alone."

He didn't like the thought of her roaming around Europe by herself. Not because she couldn't take care of herself, but rather because he didn't like the thought of her being lonely. He could see her wandering about museums and soaking up all the history, perhaps meeting with friends she'd made, but she would be essentially alone. There would be no one holding her hand or ensuring she had everything she needed. No one would bring her coffee in the morning or cuddle with her at night.

"I want to make this marriage work." He was saying the words aloud for the first time and they felt right. "I do not intend to do anything that would break my bride's heart. If I do this, I'm going to do my best to be a good and faithful husband."

Chapal's jaw dropped and he stared for the longest moment.

"You don't have to look at me like I've grown two extra heads," Kash complained. "I can say the word faithful. Listen to this one. Monogamy. See. It rolls off the tongue. Don't you back up, you ridiculous ass. Lightning is not going to strike."

"You have to admit you've never used those words unless they were accompanied by a vomiting sound." Chapal stepped closer. "I think you could hurt her if you aren't careful."

No one cared if she hurt him, of course. "Leave that to Day and me. We've been talking things through. We're going about this in an intellectual way, determining the best way to handle things. We've decided to make a contract between us and if and when we choose to have sex, we will be faithful to each other. If things seem to be difficult, we'll be honest and revisit the contract to allow more freedom."

He hadn't liked that thought. She was surprisingly open to…well, to being open if things didn't work. She said she would rather they had a healthy, happy friendship and partnership than put the country and whatever children they might have through a divorce. No married king and queen of Loa Mali had divorced before. He didn't intend to be the first, but he didn't like the thought of some passionless friendship between them.

"She's a sensible woman and it appears she's being realistic about this marriage, so I'm going to completely back off." Chapal held his hands up as if they were proof he would interfere no more.

He should leave it there. He wasn't some lovestruck idiot who needed to talk about his feelings. He didn't have feelings. He had responsibilities that he tried his hardest to forget about. Of course, they were the same responsibilities that Day had been bearing some of the burden of. He didn't need to talk this out before the evening came around.

It was simple. The tradition was that the groom and bride-to-be spent the evening together, getting to know one another. The groom attempted to seduce the bride.

That was one tradition he intended to keep up.

"Prince Chapal, it's time to do your part. Ms. Samar is about to start her stroll along the beach." Weston stepped out of the copse of trees, his three-piece suit completely pristine somehow, despite their walk in the forest.

Chapal shook his head. "I truly never thought I would have to do this. I'm so glad Ben and I eloped."

His cousin sighed and proceeded to step out into the clearing. He would be the king's "eyes," the servant who first saw the long-ago queen and told his sovereign about the beauty on the beach.

Kash heard a loud shout go up, the royal watchers all cheering as the ceremony began.

"I want you to move quickly when you get to the road approaching the palace," Weston said matter of factly. "The police are having some issues. I advised them that I believed the crowd would be quite a bit bigger than their estimates. They chose to disagree with me and now we're understaffed there. Smile and wave and move through quickly. It's the only place I worry about. I've got Michael and Boomer here, and Jesse and I will monitor the road."

"All right." He wanted to see her. He wanted to be done with all this pageantry. Which was odd, because usually the pageantry was what he craved.

"We've also had an issue with a woman claiming she needs to see you."

He sighed. Yes, he'd gotten several phone calls from Tasha Reynolds. "She's the only woman I dated for more than a few days in the last several years. She's an actress and she's very aggressive." He'd found her aggression, her take-charge personality, attractive in the beginning. He'd enjoyed having a strong woman who was capable of making decisions. Until she'd proven that all her decisions were based on what was best for Tasha and only Tasha. She'd been mean to her staff and rather cruel to him as well. He'd walked away after a terrible fight and refused to take her calls even after she'd threatened to go to the press. "Ignore her. It's best not to feed into her neuroses."

It was after Tasha that he'd taken to finding his gentle "flowers." Even the thought of how he'd called them that made him think of what Day would say. Likely she would roll her eyes and walk away, shaking her head and calling him a douchebag. She called him on his douchebaggery at every turn and yes, he liked that, too.

Day was take-charge, but without the hard aggression. Day made decisions based on what was best for the people who depended on her.

Day was the kind of woman he could depend on.

He wanted to see her. Why did Chapal get to see her first? Chapal couldn't even appreciate her curves. Chapal didn't want to let his hands skim her hips while he kissed her gently. He would have to be gentle with her. Like his cousin had said, she probably didn't have a lot of experience. He would have to treat her with the respect she deserved, but in a way that let her know he could take care of her. Herd her gently toward their bed. Once she was there, he would keep convincing her to stay there.

He found himself looking forward to the chase. He never chased any woman. They came after him. He winked their way and they fell into his arms.

And he wasn't so unaware that this behavior was far more about the type of woman he spent time with and how interested each of them was in his money and his fame. It was rarely about him.

Somehow he thought Day was different. Perhaps he was being foolish, but he couldn't help himself. Dayita was going to be his bride. His. No one else's. Dayita was going to be at his side when he needed her. She was the type of woman who would take an interest in his job, beyond smiling for the press and spending money on shoes.

He tried to peek through the palms but all he could see was Chapal's backside.

"I like your bride," Weston said. "So does my wife. She thinks Dayita is perfect for you."

He wasn't sure about perfect. He didn't believe in perfection. Even in his happiest moments there was always a sense that something was missing, but that wouldn't be her fault. It was because he was a fraud. Because he wasn't Shray. "I think we've got a good beginning. Now I have to convince her to actually give this thing a try."

"I thought she was doing that."

He sent the Brit a grin. "I'm talking about sex. I don't want a sexless marriage."

"Somehow I think you'll find a way, Your Majesty. But you should talk about it with her," Weston said.

He pulled back a frond and there she was. Dayita was dressed in all white, no shoes on her feet, and her glorious hair wild and free. He felt the tug of arousal in his groin. Yes, there was the unruly beast he'd known when he was younger. His cock didn't need any foreplay when it came to this one. All he needed to do was look at her. "I would rather show her how I feel."

A shadow fell over him and Rai was suddenly standing in the small clearing Kash would soon ride out of. "I hope you've taken all the tests, Your Majesty. Otherwise our fair queen-to-be might not last long."

"Excuse me?" Weston's whole body had tensed.

Kash put a hand up. He knew damn well what Rai was talking about and why they'd had the fight that had ended their friendship. "Don't, Mr. Weston. Rai has a long lead when it comes to me. He's more friend than bodyguard." He turned to the man who'd been at his side most of his life. Right up until the moment he'd realized Kash had slept with his wife. Oh, they hadn't been married at the time, hadn't even been dating, but Rai had taken deep offense. "And yes, I've had blood work done, but you know I'm careful."

"Careful? You're the single most reckless ass I've ever met." Rai turned his back. "It's almost time to move, you piece-of-shit player."

"You can't allow him to talk to you like that," Weston said.

Kash waved him off. "He's only doing it because we're alone and he knows you and I are friends." There was something he needed to know, something that had his gut in knots when he thought about it. "I need to know that you're not taking this out on Lia."

Rai turned, his face red. "Don't you mention her name, and no. She's innocent. You're the vile animal who seduced her. I would never harm my wife. She's been through enough."

She'd been excellent at fellatio. Not that being good at fellatio was a bad thing. It was a serious plus in Kash's mind, but apparently Rai needed a bloody virgin as his bride. Years before, Lia had come to Kash. He'd been having one of his blow-out parties. She'd wanted to spend time on the boat, and Kash had suspected she wanted a way out of her parents' house. He'd spent a single evening with the girl years before.

Six months before, she'd shown up on Rai's arm and they were engaged.

He'd barely recognized the girl when they'd been introduced. She'd been terribly embarrassed and had made him promise to never tell. God, if he'd ruined Rai's marriage, he would never forgive himself. "I'm glad you're happy with Lia. She loves you very much. She was young and a little wild, a bit like we used to be."

"Used to be? Perhaps I've matured, but I've seen none of that from you."

No, his actions of late weren't those of a mature man, but he was trying. "I'm so sorry for that night, Rai. I know I can't make it up to you, but I miss you, my friend. And I thank you for helping out today. Are you enjoying the new job?"

Rai simply turned away and moved back to his post.

"We can't use him again. I'll make sure he's never on your service." Weston had his phone out. "I have no confidence that man will take a bullet for you."

Once he would have. Once Rai had been his closest friend. It was probably fitting that a woman came between them. What he hadn't expected was how much he would miss his friend, how much he wanted to talk to Rai about Day. Still, Weston had a point. "You can move him around, but don't fire him and you can't move him to a lower position. No cut in salary. He has a wife and mother to take care of."

Weston nodded, but it was easy to see he was still suspicious. "You should get ready. It's almost time."

A great cheer went up and Chapal made his way back to the staging area. He was shaking his head. "I can't believe how many people are out there. I hope you don't fall off that horse. Good god, man, don't step back."

Because the horse seemed to have an active bowel. This could all go horribly south.

And then it did. He heard the crack of gunfire and the screams of people and Kash took off, running with one thought. He had to get to her. He had to get to Day.

A hard arm went around him and he was being pulled back. Kash fought like hell, right up to the moment another arm went around his neck and the world went black.

* * * *

Kash paced the floor in front of her, still garbed in his traditional clothes. He would have made a stunning Horse King if the ceremony hadn't gone so poorly.

"I'll have him killed. I'll use the horse that shits constantly. I'll find three more exactly like him. Terribly gassy horses. I'll tie that motherfucker to each of them and quarter him and then I'll allow the horses to shit on his corpse. His suit won't look so perfect then, will it?"

Day couldn't help but smile because Kashmir looked adorable when he was angry. Also very masculine and threatening, but adorable. She particularly liked the reason for his anger.

"They thought someone was trying to set off a bomb," she pointed out. "They didn't know it was merely fireworks. You know your guard was only doing his job."

"Rai would never have choked me until I passed out." Kash was off, his words spitting out in a rapid-fire volley of rage.

Day simply poured him a glass of Scotch. The poor man had had a long day. Kash had heard the chaos and tried to reach her. When Simon Weston had rightly attempted to get the king out of the line of fire, Kash apparently fought like hell to get to her. He was angry he hadn't been the one to protect her.

The instincts to love and protect and cherish were still there. He wasn't even fighting them. He cared about her, and that was a good thing, since the afternoon had brought on a revelation of her own.

She'd realized when she'd heard that sharp, shocking sound that she'd never gotten over him. Not really. She'd heard that explosion and her first thought had been to get to Kash. The idea that he could be hurt or even dead had chilled her to the bone. She'd known in that moment that she would hate herself forever if she didn't try with him. She'd started running toward where she'd known Kash was waiting.

The intensely large Mr. Boomer had simply scooped her up and run. She'd known she didn't have a chance against him and she hadn't thought to offer him a pizza to let her go. She'd found herself shoved in what was basically a tank masquerading as an SUV, and she'd been at the palace before she could breathe. Kash had come in a second SUV along with Chapal, who'd been forced to explain why her bridegroom was unconscious.

It was now hours later and they'd made an appearance on the balcony of the palace so everyone could see they were alive and unharmed. Her first balcony. She'd stood at Kash's side and waved, her free arm around him. She'd been the one to convince him to calm down and show his people that all was well. She'd also been the one to convince him not to kill the Brit who'd merely been doing his duty.

Now she had to calm him down again, and she thought she knew how she would like to try.

There was nothing holding her back. She wanted him. She needed to see if she could make this work between them. If what Chelsea and Phoebe had said could actually be true.

"Have a drink and let's talk about this."

His eyes narrowed, but he took the drink. "I don't want to talk. I want to punch Weston in the face. Rai would never have overreacted in such a manner."

"Rai was running toward me full tilt when Mr. Boomer tossed me over his shoulder. He reacted to that terrible sound in exactly the same manner as the other bodyguards," she explained. "I think we should have a talk with him about why he didn't stay with you."

Kash took a long sip. "To tell you the truth, I'm glad he went after you. He's unhappy with me right now. At least he thinks enough of his job to try to save you. I wish the ceremony hadn't been ruined. You know now a lot of people will say we're cursed as a couple."

"Only the superstitious ones." She knew there were already rumors spreading, but they didn't matter and he needed to see that they didn't. "We show them how uncursed we are by presenting ourselves as a happy couple."

He was suddenly still, his eyes on her. "Are we a happy couple?"

"I don't think we've had time enough to be sure of that yet, but I know we were once." She'd thought it through in a way she never had before. She had a much different view of those months with Kash in England. "You were courting me back then, weren't you? You wanted me to be your girlfriend."

He sat down in the plush chair that dominated the sitting area portion of his bedroom. Normally they stayed in the living room, but he'd wanted more privacy. This was the only place in his suite that wasn't covered by CCTV, the only place where they could truly be alone. Everything about the space was masculine and decadent, including the man himself. With his hair disheveled and his chest on display, it wasn't hard at all to see him as a primal male.

One she'd dearly enjoy taming.

"I don't think you realized it at the time."

She was willing to admit her faults. "I didn't. I had my nose in a book most of the time back then and I had little experience with men. No, I had no idea you were interested in me beyond copying my notes from class when you slept in."

"It would surprise you to know that I often thought about sleeping in with you." His voice had gone low and gentle. "I was crazy about you back then, Day. I find myself in the same position today, but I don't want to scare you. I know you think we should take this slow and I will honor your wishes, but I want this marriage to work. You see me as a playboy, but I don't want to be some forty-plus player who trades on his money to keep young girls around him. I think it might be time for me to find out if I can be the king my father would have wanted me to be."

It was all she needed to hear. If he wanted to try, she was ready. Despite his reputation, she'd fallen right back into a peaceful friendship with him. He'd been the old Kash, supporting her when she needed it. He'd asked her questions about her work with the education department and then gave her ideas on how to handle the parliament. He hadn't told her what she should do. He'd suggested, debated.

"I think you'll find me less averse to giving this marriage a real try than you think. I was planning on talking to you about using the Palm Ceremony to begin to explore what we could be as a couple."

He frowned. "I'm not sure what that means. You want to talk? Or have counseling? Because that sounds terrible."

"I was talking about sex, Kashmir. I thought we could use this time to see if we're sexually compatible."

He popped up out of his chair like an eager puppy. "Yes. I think that is a brilliant idea. We should start now. Don't worry. I intend to be gentle with you."

She didn't move at all. "Like you are with your lovely flowers?"

"Women deserve a man's care," he said quietly. "Day, I can't erase my past."

"I don't want you to." He misunderstood her problems with his statement. "But I do need you to understand that I'm not one of those flowers. I'm not here to sit at your side and bat my eyelashes in the hopes that you'll buy something for me. I don't work like that. I don't care about your money."

"That is easy for you to say. You're about to have access to all of it, aren't you?"

He had a point. "Even if I wasn't, that wouldn't be why I would want you, Kash. Sit down. We have some things to talk about before we get started." This was the point where she would normally introduce the idea of a sexual contract, but she had to ease him into this. Show him how good it could be to hand the reins over to her in this one part of their relationship. "Come here close to me."

He moved to the chaise she was sitting on, lowering himself down with a sullen frown. "I knew there would be talking."

She was fairly certain his lovely flowers did very little talking, but he would get used to it. "Why did you want me back then?"

"I liked you. I liked talking to you. I liked being around you. I rather liked who I was when I was around you." His expression softened. "I don't think you knew how alluring you were to someone like me. You didn't understand how beautiful you were, so you didn't use it against me. Most women do."

"Well, that happens when you surround yourself with women who are mostly valued for their looks. I don't blame them. They've been told their beauty is the only thing worthy about them. If you want to meet women who don't feel that way, you should probably expand out of models and actresses."

"Well, you would be surprised how many gorgeous, sexy physicists turn me down because I'm not smart enough for them."

Oh, she loved this part. She loved the flirtation, the push and pull of verbal foreplay, and Kash was a master. "Somehow, I doubt that. You're one of the smartest men I've ever met. You could talk about anything. It makes me wonder why you don't still study."

"Well, I have a busy schedule of smiling at the public and waving. Then there's all the ministry meetings I take. I note that you never once asked for a meeting with me."

There had been a reason for that. "You didn't seem interested. Honestly, you haven't been interested in much of anything for the last five years or so. Is it because your secret project was taken down?"

He seemed to freeze for a moment. "It was more than a secret project. It was a passion project. I suppose you know about it from Chelsea. She was there at the time, though I only met her briefly. I lost an entire generation of our most brilliant minds that day. Ten of the smartest engineers and scientists in Loa Mali. I did that. Is it any wonder I haven't gone back? You know if I'd reconnected with you, you could have been on that rig that day. I would have asked you to help me with the project."

So guilt had sent him on a half-a-decade bender. "Kash, it wasn't your fault. You weren't trying to hurt anyone."

"I would have hurt the oil companies."

"Including your own," she pointed out. "You weren't doing anything but attempting to push our country forward. Would you have kept the technology for yourself?"

"Of course not. It would have belonged to Loa Mali. I was doing it because someone will. I want to be the first. Our oil reserves won't last forever. Our country is in the unique position to move in a direction others can't. That's why I did it. To put my country on the cutting edge and honestly, so that I could patent the process and make money for us, money to keep our standard of living high."

She reached over and put a hand on his. "A noble cause and one only a man of your intelligence would even understand to pursue. Do you know why I was attracted to you?"

His lips curled up. "I do not have the same false impressions of my own beauty that you do."

Such arrogance and yet she found herself laughing. "Your masculine beauty was the least of your attractions. I liked how smart you were, how passionate you were about making a place for yourself in the world. I wanted to be a part of that. I wanted to support you and yes, I wanted to advise you. I loved how you never seemed intimidated by me."

"I wasn't intimidated. I wanted you. I wanted to get my hands on you and show you how hot you could get."

She was already heating up, but this wasn't going to go the way she feared his other encounters went. "You do know I'm not a virgin, Kash."

His gorgeous eyes rolled to the back of his head in a pure expression of disgust. "Of course you're not. You're thirty-five years old. I would worry if you were." He reached out, putting a hand on her knee. "But you don't have my experience, either. I have to remember that."

"And what kind of experience is that?"

"You know what I mean. I've slept with many women."

"But you haven't slept with me. You don't know what I want or what I need to get hot." She wasn't about to tell him that simply being near him was getting her hot. "I want you to forget about all those other women. I'm unlike any from before. Learn how to please me. Let me teach you how to make love to me."

She saw him still, his eyes heating. "All right. How do I start?"

"Show me what you have to offer me."

His lips curled up in a decadent grin. "Are we going to play games?"

Only the most important one of her life. "It's for pleasure, Kash. I enjoy some games. I find them relaxing, and they help us get to know each other better. If you would rather we simply went to bed, I can do that, too. You should know that I was going to run from you today."

"At the ceremony? Of course. It's part of the ritual. The beautiful bride is unsure of the king. She tries to flee, but he catches her."

She shook her head. "I was going to run. I was going to make you chase me. I was going to make you work for me, and in front of all those people. I would have struggled in your arms until you let me go, fearing you'd hurt me. And then and only then would I have placed my hands on either side of your face and brought my lips to yours. I would have touched you and found you worthy and allowed you to take us both away."

"You would have run from me?" He asked the question in an icy tone, but she couldn't miss the fact that his cock was already hard and straining against his pants.

She didn't move from her chaise. Already, her heart and soul were moving into top space, a place where she was in control, where she could relax and have her way. He would accept her or not. "I cannot be that queen from long ago who allowed herself to be kidnapped and taken away. The choice will be mine. The choice to be queen. The choice to have you. I will make these choices not because I'm about to be royal, but because I am a woman and that is what I do. I will not play that game with you, love. I won't give over and then protest that I had the choice taken from me. I will choose and accept the consequences. I wanted to show them who they are getting as their queen, not some gentle flower who will stand by her man and wave, but a woman who will fight for them as I fight for myself. As I would fight for you."

"You want to see what I have to offer you?" The chill was gone from his voice. His hands were on the medallion around his neck. He took it off and placed it on the table to the side of her chair. "I wonder what will please you. I don't think you're impressed by the palace I'm offering you."

She gestured to the room around her. "That's not yours. It belongs to the people. In essence, they're offering me this magnificent space."

"A hard woman to please," Kash mused. "How about wealth? By marrying me, you'll never worry about money again."

"All your money comes from oil," she replied, enjoying the fact that he was playing along. "Again, that belongs to the people. I should thank them with my service to them."

"Service you can only offer because of me."

"Is it you or your mother? Because you had no idea I still existed. So I have to ask you, Kashmir, what exactly are you offering me?"

He stopped and for a moment she thought he would laugh and give up the game. Instead, his hands went to the drawstring of his pants. His chest was already on display, each and every muscle beautifully defined. The man was sheer perfection physically. He shoved his pants down and he wore no boxers. No, when he shoved those pants aside, he was standing in front of her, proudly naked. "I can offer you my body."

She sat up because he was getting closer. "I have a body of my own."

His jaw tightened, but she saw the light of competition in his eyes. He might be frustrated, but he was also intrigued. He put his hands on his hips, perfectly comfortable with his nudity. "All right, my future queen. Let me tell you what I can offer you. I can offer you the touch of my hands on your flesh, skimming every inch of your body. I can offer the heat of my mouth, my lips and tongue exploring you, tasting your essence. I won't stop quickly because you're complex. I'll have to taste you everywhere, nipping and licking and sucking until I know you by heart." His hand went to his magnificent cock. "And I can offer the pleasure of my cock. I can offer you everything I have, every trick I've learned to bring you joy in bed."

She stood and closed the space between them, her eyes on him. She took in every gorgeous inch of his body. Like those delicate flowers he'd spent so much time with, so much of Kash's self-worth was wrapped up in his handsome face and perfect body. He was celebrated the world over for being beautiful. How many magazine covers had he graced? Likely more than she could count. She needed him to believe in more than his own looks. "Hold still and let me look at you. Don't move. And let go of that cock if you're offering it to me. How can I touch it if you've got it in those big hands of yours?"

He immediately let go, his cock bouncing slightly. He stared forward as she took him in, as though he knew instinctively that this was a moment for him to submit.

"You offer me a lot, Kashmir. Certainly you come in the most beautiful package I've ever been offered. You're the single most stunning man I've ever seen, but I need more." She ran a hand over his chest, letting her skin enjoy the warmth of his, the smooth touch of flesh against flesh. "I need that brilliant mind. I need your intellect. But I also need you to need me."

"I need you, Day," he said with a laugh.

She continued her slow exploration. She couldn't punish him, though later on such sarcasm would be dealt with if they signed a contract. He would probably enjoy the discipline. "Not yet. Right now you think I'm nothing more than another pretty female body, but you'll learn I'm going to be more."

He finally looked down at her. "Fine. What do you offer me, my almost queen? I've laid it all out for you. Tell me what I get."

She sighed as she moved around to his back, enjoying the play of his muscles as she continued to stroke him. He was a massive panther and she wanted to see if he could purr for her. She also liked that he'd asked the question. It made her more certain than ever that he was right for her. She didn't want a man who followed her blindly, even inside the bedroom. Certainly not outside of it.

Now she had to discover if she was right for him, if she could give him what he needed. What he might not even know he needed.

She ran her hands over his broad shoulders, enjoying the shiver that went through him. "I offer you the warmth of my hands on your body, the feel of my skin against yours, promising companionship and comfort. My hand in yours when you need to know you are not alone. I offer you the joys of my mouth. My lips and tongue tasting you, but more than this, my words will lift you up, will always be kind. I offer you my body for your pleasure, so that we can be one with nothing between us, no space, no lies, no heartache, only joy. I offer you my body to grow whatever children we're blessed with. It will be yours while I'm young and vital, and yours when I'm too old do to anything but hold you in my arms. This is what I offer."

"I need you, Dayita." His voice was hoarse.

This time, she believed him.

"Then we can begin."

Chapter Five

Kash gritted his teeth and felt his cock stiffen. He'd only thought he'd had the erection of a lifetime, but when she'd said those words—*then we can begin*—he reached monumental proportions. Any thought of this being some sort of test run was over. He wasn't thinking about anything but pleasing the woman in front of him.

His queen.

The last fifteen years of his life had been about the world revolving around him, being the ultimate authority figure. But here and now, he realized she could be his sun.

She could be his secret. She would never have to know how weak he was, how dark his wants were. He could pretend to indulge her and steal something for himself.

She would never know that all those "lovely flowers" were nothing more than a way to pretend he didn't want what he wanted. A way to pretend he was more of a man than he actually was.

She put her hand on his chest and he could feel his own heart beating. "I think I'd like to join you. You may take my dress off. Carefully and slowly. When you're done, I want you to fold it and put it on the counter. You may touch me, but only as I've touched you up until this point. Do you understand, love?"

He understood that her thick-as-honey voice was doing things to his cock. He couldn't breathe he was so hard and he hadn't touched her yet. He should take control. He should put them on a proper footing, but he couldn't. The words wouldn't form in his mouth. There was only one word that he seemed capable of speaking. "Yes."

She turned and offered him her back. The dress she wore had no zippers or buttons, merely two elaborate ties. She'd told him what she wanted. A long, slow adoration of her body. He didn't have to move quickly and plot out how to bring this woman to pleasure. She was giving him a map, offering him the secrets of her desires, allowing him to indulge his own.

He drew her hair up and swept it to the side, his fingers luxuriating in the silken cloud. How long had it been since he took his time, since sex was something to sink into and not some drunken nightcap to end his day? Maybe never. Maybe because this was more than sex.

He carefully undid the first tie, revealing the golden skin of her shoulder. She leaned her head to the left slightly, allowing him access to that first, precious patch of skin. He touched her, letting his fingertips play over the warmth of her flesh. He skimmed from the curve of her neck down to her shoulder and along her arm.

The worries of the day were floating away and all that mattered was learning her, discovering her every curve and hollow.

"May I kiss you?" The question came naturally.

"Yes. Gently. We're just starting out. This could take us all night."

He leaned over, letting his lips find the spot where her neck and shoulder met. He brushed them there, aware of the way she shivered. "Given that I've waited fifteen years for this, I think a full night is what I need."

"Did you only wait fifteen years?" He could hear the smile in her voice. "I think I waited a lifetime."

He ran his mouth along her shoulder, breathing her in. "You're right. It has been a lifetime."

He moved to the other knot, easing it apart and pulling the fabric free. The instinct was there to toss the clothing aside, but that wasn't what she'd asked him to do. She'd asked him for patience, and he intended to give it to her. His cock wouldn't rule with this woman. He carefully folded the dress, his focus on the task at hand, and yet somehow it made him even more aware of what was to come. His hands ached to cup her breasts, to spread her thighs and get his mouth on her.

Not until she was ready. Not until he was insane for her.

She turned and he saw her naked for the first time. His queen. His. He was vitally aware of the possession that sparked through him. He didn't want to share her with his people, but perhaps he could view it differently. She would be theirs when she was buttoned up and properly dressed. And when her hair was flowing around her like a silky cape, when her breasts were upthrust and begging for attention, when her pussy was on display, that was when she would be his queen. Only his.

And he, her only servant.

"You're beautiful, Day."

She smiled at him. "I'm glad you think so. I want everything you offered. Kiss me, Kashmir."

He moved in, eager to get his mouth on her and yet a bit disappointed the play seemed to be over. Not that she would call it play. Not that he would tell her why he wanted it.

He was the king in all things. No weaknesses.

He reached for her, but she put a hand between them.

"I wasn't talking about my mouth, love."

He frowned. "Then we should go to the bed. I'll lay you out and eat that soft pussy of yours like it's the finest treat. I'll lick you and suck you and fuck you with my tongue, but first we should find a comfortable place."

Her eyes turned steely. "Or you can get on your knees for me and do all of it right here. Can you do that for me? Get on your knees and show me the pleasure of your mouth."

On his knees? He hesitated, longing warring with what he'd been taught all his life.

"Don't think, Kashmir." Every word out of her mouth was velvet seduction. "Do as I ask. You don't have to be the king in this room. You can be whoever you want to be. When we're alone, we can throw off all the ideas of who and what we're supposed to be and let ourselves flow. Get on your knees and worship me. Show me what you can offer me and I'll reward you."

It was a game. Play, as his kink friends would call it. They didn't have to acknowledge anything. His bride was a bit kinky and that was something to welcome.

She didn't have to know how much the idea of worshipping her fed his soul, how throwing off the heavy mantle of responsibility, tossing away his crown for a brief moment, tantalized him and energized him.

He made all the decisions, bore all the cost. What if he could find one place where he didn't have to? No one would know. No one but him and Day. Their secret.

He dropped to his knees, embracing the possibility. "Tell me I can lick you. Tell me I can suck you and run my tongue all over you. Tell me I can make you come for me, my queen."

Her eyes were hot as she stared down at him. Those gorgeous breasts of hers were close, so close to his mouth, and yet he held back, waiting for the words he wanted to hear. He didn't have to decide. He only had to follow her lead in this.

She cupped his face. "Do you have any idea how happy you make me? How much I want you? Only you. Touch my breasts. Lavish my nipples with affection."

He let his palms find her breasts, cupping them and holding them. Her nipples were hard points against his hands and he could feel the way she breathed out, a low moan coming from her mouth. He teased her nipples, rolling them between his thumbs and fingers. Finally, he leaned over and licked one, the tip of his tongue running around the edge. Her skin smelled like the ocean, breezy and pure. He tasted the salt of her flesh and sucked the nipple into his mouth. He let his arms go around her and surrounded himself with Day. He sucked and played with her, letting himself take his time.

He moved to the other nipple, feeling her hands in his hair. Her fingers tangled there and she guided him where she wanted him to go. He loved the rough feel of her tugging at his hair, lighting up his scalp. He needed to please her, needed her soft moans of acceptance. Every sound that came from her mouth seemed to have a hard line to his dick.

He was going to die, but it would be a good way to go.

"Look at me." The words sent a sizzle through his system. Her hand in his hair tightened, gentle pressure showing him where she wanted him to go. "I want you to trust me. I want to be a safe place for you. Do you understand?"

He didn't. Not entirely, but he would have said yes to anything she'd asked in that moment. "Yes. I trust you."

He did. Certainly more than any woman he'd cared for before. Even all those years ago, he'd known Day was different. He'd known instinctively that she would be worth working for. Now he was caught in a trap, and suddenly that didn't seem such a bad thing.

She leaned over and her lips captured his. He gave in, letting her take control. It felt natural to give her sway. Her tongue came out, running along his lower lip and sending fire through him. His tongue played against hers. Finally she rose up over him, looking primal and gorgeous. A sea goddess looking to mate with a lowly sailor. She would bless him with her body and he would worship her forever.

"Carry me to the bed. I love how strong you are," she said.

He was on his feet in a second, leaning over and lifting her up. In this she was delicate. She weighed next to nothing and felt perfectly right in his arms. "You're so lovely, my queen. I like calling you that. My queen."

"Show me how good it is to be your queen." She stared up at him as he lowered her to the bed. She pulled him down, bringing their lips together once more. "Kiss me properly."

He rather liked her idea of a proper kiss. He moved down her body, touching and caressing as he went. She was a prize and he'd won. He settled himself on his belly as she spread her legs for him.

He could show her how he worshipped his queen. Her pussy was a perfect, ripe peach. Golden and succulent. Already he could see she was aroused, sweet cream softening her. He breathed in her scent, letting it wash over him before he leaned over and ran his tongue between the part in her labia.

"That's right, love. It feels so good. Your mouth feels so good. More. I need more." She stiffened around him.

So responsive. She responded so beautifully and held nothing back from him. He found her praise intoxicating, her willful lust addictive.

He fucked her with his tongue, spearing up inside and coating his lips with the taste of her. He let his finger find her clitoris, rubbing in a soft circle as he explored her.

"Stop," she commanded.

He didn't want to stop. He wanted to make her come and then thrust himself inside her until he was completely spent.

"I said stop." She tugged on his hair and her voice had gone deep.

Damn it. What had he done wrong now? He rolled off her, frustration threatening to overwhelm the lust of before. He stared up at the ceiling. What did she want from him? He'd done everything she'd asked and now she wanted him to stop?

He groaned as he felt heat on his dick. He looked down and Day was inspecting his cock, her mouth hovering over him. So close. So fucking close.

"I want to taste you, too." She leaned over and teased at his cockhead with her delicate tongue. "Hold on to the headboard. If you let go, I'll stop what I'm doing."

His hands floated up as though they were smarter than his brain and knew when to obey the lovely queen currently giving him head. Her hair spread out around her, tickling his skin and surrounding him with her. He gripped the slats of the headboard as he watched her work. Her tongue came out, licking at the slit on his dick and lapping up the pre-come she found there. She scraped her teeth lightly around his erection, the sensation making him stiffen and grasp the slats with desperation.

She was going to kill him. She was an evil queen, trying to take his crown through sexual frustration. Every time he was sure she would take him deep, her head would come up and she would be right back to teasing licks.

He groaned as she cupped his balls and rolled them gently in her soft hand.

His toes were curling, his body prepping to go off.

And that was when she got on her knees.

He groaned in frustration.

"I'm letting you off easy this time, love. Mostly because I can't wait either." She reached for the box of condoms he'd placed on his bedside table in a spark of optimism.

She wasn't leaving him hanging. She wasn't playing some cruel game. He relaxed as he realized Day wouldn't do that. She'd enjoyed playing with him, exploring him, and now she would bring them both to pleasure.

He gripped the headboard tight and she rolled the condom over his cock. He watched as she straddled him like a stallion she was about to ride.

Heat rushed through him as she began to lower herself onto

his stiff dick. It took everything he had not to hold on to her hips and force her down. She moved over him, taking him inch by inch. He would feel her sink farther and then draw back up, every second a brilliant mix of pleasure and maddening frustration. No woman had ever made him want her the way this one did. No woman made him want to bow before her, to offer up everything he had.

Day settled herself on him, taking every inch of him, and he could hear her sigh with pleasure. She rolled her hips and he groaned, his eyes nearly crossing as she gripped him tight. So small and sleek and soft. He watched as her breasts bounced while she rode him.

Over and over again she rolled her hips and worked him. He watched as her mouth came open and he heard her keening cry. She dropped down and looked up at him.

"Now, love. Take me hard and fast. Make me come again."

He had her on her back before he could take another breath. He was off the leash and he didn't think about anything but doing her will. There was no gentle flower here. He didn't have to treat her with delicacy. She was his match and she could take him. He spread her legs, loving how wild she looked with her hair flowing around her, her arms coming up to grip him. He thrust inside her, one long hard motion of his body.

Instinct took over and he growled as he felt her nails scoring his back. Yes, he liked that. He wanted her mark, to carry it on him and feel the ache so that long after, he could remember how good it was to fuck his wild cat.

He fucked her hard, grinding down on her. He felt her tighten around him and her climax forced his own.

His spine bowed with the force of his orgasm. He gave over and let it take him.

Finally, he dropped down, rolling to the side and taking her in his arms.

She cuddled against him, her head finding his chest. "You are perfect, love. No king ever worshipped his queen more. Thank you for the gift."

He held her until he sensed her breathing slow and steady as sleep took her. Kash stared down at the woman in his arms and wondered if he hadn't gone over the edge of a cliff he could never climb back up.

He'd loved how she'd taken control, but would she see him differently? Would he be less of a man for allowing her to use him like this?

He held her through the night, his body pleasantly tired but his mind troubled.

Chapter Six

Day looked out over the ballroom and wondered where her bridegroom had gotten off to.

"You look lovely, Your Majesty." Rai gave her a proper bow.

He and the other guards had done a wonderful job on the wedding. It had gone off without a single hitch. Between McKay-Taggart working security and the lord chamberlain running the wedding, she'd had to do little except wave and say the words that bound her to Kashmir and the Loa Mali throne forever.

Which was good because it seemed her Kash had a never-ending need for sex. Since that first night, he'd been voracious. He was sweet and so willing to please her when the doors closed and they were alone. There wasn't a doubt in her mind that this was the right thing to do.

They fit together, and tonight she was going to talk to him about more exotic play. Tonight, she was going to discuss punishments and rewards.

She wouldn't ever top another man again. Only her dashing husband.

"You practically glow with happiness," Rai said, his eyes looking out over the dance floor.

"Thank you." She felt happy. Maybe truly for the first time in her life, she felt at peace. Always there had been this nagging question in the back of her mind about whether she could find someone she loved who could accept her as she was.

Now that question had been answered. Kash had answered it when he'd said "I do."

It was funny how the more he gave her in the bedroom, the less she felt the need to be aggressive outside of it. She'd found herself compromising more and more, especially with him. When he wanted to sit in on her meetings with parliament, she didn't question it. After all, he never forced his opinion on her, but he did give wise counsel.

She was rapidly falling head over heels in love with him once again.

She turned to Rai, wondering if she could help her brand new husband out a bit. She knew he missed this man. They'd been friends for years. She didn't understand the nature of what had caused them to break. "I think Kash would dearly love to have you on his detail again. He misses you."

A bitter smile crossed his lips. "Somehow I doubt that. Or perhaps not. Perhaps he's simply so arrogant and self-centered that he doesn't understand how he hurts the people around him."

Or maybe that would be a terrible mistake. "All I've seen is his kindness."

"Then you haven't been watching, Your Majesty," Rai shot back. "You wait. Give him a month or two and he'll be right back to his old tricks. He'll crawl into the bed of any woman who will have him. And some who don't want him at all."

She stepped in front of him when he started to go. "What exactly are you accusing my husband of?"

Rai's jaw formed a stubborn line. "Nothing at all, Your Majesty. After all, what woman wouldn't want to bed the great Kashmir Kamdar? What woman would say no to him? Certainly not my own wife. If you'll excuse me."

She let him pass with a sigh. So that was what had happened.

"If it makes you feel any better, I believe Kash slept with the young Lia before her marriage to Rai." Hanin stepped up next to her, looking out over the ballroom with a keen eye.

The lord chamberlain hadn't been particularly friendly, but then he'd been under a bit of pressure. A royal wedding in a few weeks wasn't an easy thing to accomplish. Day was happy he seemed to be calming down. "Rai didn't find out until after the wedding, I suspect."

"Yes. He married the girl hastily. From what I understand, Rai discovered Kash had been his wife's lover. You know how palace gossip is. No one can keep a secret here. Kash should have immediately told Rai, if you ask me. No one ever asks my opinion, much less follows my excellent advice. If they did, their lives would all be the better for it." He turned to her. "Rai was right about one thing. You do make a lovely queen. Hopefully now that we will have a sovereign in residence full time, the country will be more stable. The king can wander as he may and we shall have your wise hand to guide us."

"Well, I think you might find that the king is much happier staying home now that he's married. I think he'll take his duties more seriously than he did before." She felt comfortable that Kash's wanderlust had more to do with guilt than anything else. She would gently start pushing him to restart his project. He'd come so close, and he had a true passion for innovation.

The lord chamberlain's lips pursed as though he was thinking about what he would say next. Or thinking about not saying anything at all. "I should hope so. Nevertheless, I hope you find me helpful. Anything at all that you need, I shall be more than happy to provide it for you. This is your household now. It's up to me to make sure it runs according to your desires."

"And the king's."

He bowed his head. "Of course. When he is here, I shall surely take him into account. When you return from your honeymoon, I hope we can sit down and plan the next few months."

"What do you know that I don't?" She wasn't going to beat about the bush any longer.

The lord chamberlain shrugged, an elegant motion. "I know he's planning a trip to Hong Kong a few days after you return from your time on the yacht. He's going to be gone for a week or more and he told security that you would be remaining behind. He's planning a series of trips and I do believe he intends to take them solo."

That couldn't be right. Hanin had simply misunderstood. Kash wouldn't leave her behind right after their honeymoon. If he had something he needed to do, surely he would have spoken with her about it.

She looked back over the ballroom floor where couples were dancing. The ballroom was glittering and elegant, but Kash was nowhere to be seen. She did, however, note that Jesse Murdoch was standing at the edge of the ballroom, his back to the hallway. He guarded the door that led to the more intimate gathering areas. There were several rooms in this wing that the royals used to entertain heads of states. They were cozy rooms, perfect for a talk with her husband.

She would ask him calmly and he would explain that it was all a mistake. Then they could start their honeymoon early. She was ready to leave the pomp and circumstance behind and focus on Kash. He'd had a long day. He would need some play to alleviate the stresses. She'd seen his forced smile, the stiff way he'd waved to the crowd on the balcony.

"Thank you, Hanin," she said politely. "I would love to sit down with you and plan everything out. I think we shall have a busy schedule."

Hanin nodded. "Excellent, Your Majesty. And let me know if you need anything to make this evening even brighter."

Because they should be heading off to bed in a bit. They would stand together and greet their guests and then retire while the party went on. It was custom.

So many customs. She stepped out onto the floor and was forced to smile and greet people whose names she barely remembered. Her brand new social secretary was across the palace, meeting with the photographers and helping the queen mother select the right photos to be published in the morning.

Where was Kash? He'd kissed her on the cheek and then frowned as he'd gone to dance with yet another guest. He'd been dancing all night long and only once with her. Kash had spent the evening charming all the ladies, and she missed having all that masculine attention to herself.

She worked her way through the crowd, trying to ignore the chatter around her.

"I don't know. I hope she's doing this for the right reasons."

"Such a beautiful wedding. He's so dreamy. She's pretty and all but I'm surprised he would marry a commoner."

"I don't know. I expected more from her. She's a bit on the plain side for a man who could have any woman he wanted."

"The right reason being money and power, since she's not going to be getting any fidelity from that man. Imagine actually marrying Kash. Not that he isn't exquisite in bed. I enjoyed my time with him, but the humiliation would be terrible."

"Who wants to bet how long it is before he's right back to his playboy ways? As soon as she's pregnant, he'll find a way. I've heard he's already seeing that actress again. She showed up at his wedding. What gall."

Day stopped.

"I can't believe he walked out with her. Everyone could see the way he was touching her. The poor queen. Not married more than a few hours and her husband is already cheating."

"Ah, well, we all know he married her because his mother forced his hand. He'll get her pregnant a few times and then he'll be done with her."

She could feel her cheeks heat, humiliation swamping her.

"Don't listen to them," a low voice whispered.

She turned and Phoebe Murdoch was standing beside her. Someone had figured out the new queen was walking among them and the gossip was now being whispered instead of openly talked about. She felt a hundred eyes on her and she steeled her spine. She'd stood up to professors who didn't think she had a place in their world, to parliament members who laughed openly at her suggestions. She wasn't about to crumble because a few people said some nasty things about her marriage.

Day gave them her brightest smile. "I hope you're all having a lovely time. His majesty and I are so glad to be surrounded by such supportive friends. I will let him know how much you care about him."

She caught sight of a few men and women who paled at her words, but she was done with them. If Kash had walked out with a woman, there was a good explanation. She knew something the others didn't. Kash didn't have a reason to hide things from her. He'd been given a clear choice. She would have accepted a marriage without the relationship. She would have been friends and partners with him. He'd chosen and she had to believe he meant to honor the choice.

Phoebe walked beside her. "You are really good at that. I'm fairly certain some of those people peed a little. You know they're always going to talk about you. You have to be able to separate

Dayita from the queen."

It was an excellent point and one she would take to heart. She stopped at the edge of the crowd and reached for her new friend's hand. "Thank you. I will try to remember that. Do you know where my husband went and who he was with?"

Phoebe didn't pale exactly but she did frown. "I think he's trying to avoid a scene."

"With a woman?" She was starting to understand what was happening.

Phoebe looked over at the place where her husband was guarding the door. He had a steely-eyed glare that turned away even the most avid curiosity seeker. He caught sight of his wife and they seemed to have a whole conversation with gestures and raised eyebrows. Finally Phoebe turned back to Day. "Apparently one of Kash's ex-girlfriends managed to get through our security. She snuck in as the date of one of the ambassadors. Before we could figure it out and toss her on her rear, she managed to get to Kash. I think he's trying to convince her to leave quietly."

So at least Day knew where she needed to go. "He'll struggle with that. He'll view her as something delicate and weak, and if she's got half a brain in her head, she'll manipulate him."

"I don't think he's trying to do anything but get rid of her," Phoebe said.

Day turned. She wanted to make something plain. "I never thought for a moment that he was. I believe in Kash. I trust him, but he won't understand how to deal with a woman like this. He needs me."

She strode to the double doors that led to the hallway. Murdoch touched his earpiece and muttered something she couldn't understand.

"Your Majesty." Murdoch nodded her way. "Is there something I can do for you?"

"Yes, Mr. Murdoch. You can stand aside and let me get to my husband, who is likely trying to ward off some bimbo."

Murdoch frowned his wife's way. "Seriously, baby? I told you to distract her, not tell her everything."

Phoebe shrugged. "Sorry. I thought that was your 'hey, you should help out your new friend' raised eyebrow. You should really be more specific. And she's not worried that Kash is cheating on her. She's worried he won't be able to throw that chick out on her rear."

Murdoch winced slightly. "Yeah, I'm worried about that, too. I tried to send Rai back there but he said something about Kash being able to handle anything and walked away. I think it's time to fire that dude, but Kash keeps overruling me. I'll escort you back if my wife will watch this door for me."

"I think I can handle it." Phoebe took her husband's place. Somehow, despite the fact that she was wearing a beautiful, filmy gown and heels, Phoebe Murdoch oozed competence.

Murdoch opened the door for Day and they slipped out into the hallway. The minute the doors closed, the sounds of the ballroom seemed to fade and she could breathe again. How did Kash deal with such scrutiny every day of his life?

"Take a deep breath," Murdoch said. "Not a one of their opinions matter. Get used to being judged and get used to smiling and giving them your happy middle finger. I know a bit about this."

"How so?" She hadn't realized how tense she'd been until she'd managed to get out of that ballroom.

Murdoch started walking down the mostly empty hallway. There were a few of the catering workers moving mounds of used glasses back toward the kitchens, and she could hear someone discussing the fact that they would need to open another case of champagne. "I've been the center of attention before, and not of good attention. I've had people think the absolute worst of me and I decided they were right. It got me into a lot of trouble, but I found a group of people who built me back up."

She smiled his way. "Your wife and friends. That's good. I'm usually all right being the focus of criticism. I've never followed what my father would have called the 'proper' path. I can handle it. However, I'm not allowed to use my happy middle finger. The queen has to be more subtle."

Murdoch whistled. "Damn, I wouldn't have gotten through most things without being able to shoot people the bird. I suspect you'll find other coping mechanisms. He's in that room to your left. I'll be out here and ready to escort you back to the ballroom when you're ready. Be careful, though. There are reporters and they've been using this hallway to move around."

"You don't need to get back to Phoebe? I'm sure I'm safe here in the palace."

He shook his head. "Nah, Phoebe's a pro. She can handle anything those people throw at her."

She strode to the door and heard the sound of a whiny female.

"Kash, we can make this right. All you have to do is divorce her. You don't even need a divorce. You can get this marriage annulled and we can start over."

Ah, she recognized the voice from one of the more popular British soaps. Tasha Reynolds was considered one of the world's most beautiful women and she'd dated Kash for the better part of a year before moving on to one of her costars. She'd been giving interviews in the last two weeks about how she felt Kash was making a terrible mistake with his marriage. The woman had gone on every talk and news show she could, spilling secrets about their sex life and how he'd told her he would never marry anyone but her.

So she was a crazy bitch. Luckily, Day had figured out how to deal with crazy bitches a long time ago.

She opened the door and got ready to save her man.

* * * *

Kash looked out over the ballroom, hoping to catch a glimpse of his wife.

His wife. Dayita was his. He should feel settled and satisfied, but something gnawed at his gut. He was falling in deeper and deeper with her, and he wasn't sure he knew how to swim in these waters. Day smiled as she shook the hand of one of the Swedish royals. So poised and perfect.

"She's truly going to make a wonderful queen." His mother came to stand beside him, her hand coming to his arm as though she needed him to balance her. The last week had taken a toll on her, but she'd shooed away any thought of resting. "I hope you'll forgive me someday."

He looked down at her. "It's all forgiven, Mother. I understand that you did what you felt you needed to do. You found a proper monarch for the country. She will be wonderful."

And he would be somewhat superfluous. Already all the serious people shook his hand, laughed and joked around him, and then asked the real questions of his bride. He'd heard the US ambassador asking her for a meeting about potentially inviting the president to Loa Mali for a state visit, and Prince Harry had spoken with her about sponsoring a new charity. Harry only ever talked to him about polo and beer.

His mother had lost Shray, the true king, and she'd finally figured out that Kash was never going to take his place. She'd found a daughter this time, someone lovely and kind and intelligent. Someone who *could* take Shray's place. He would be nothing but a sperm donor.

Yes, he'd heard someone say that, and now it played around in his head.

"What do you mean, Kash? You're the king. Having a queen doesn't take the crown from you." His mother blinked up at him as though she couldn't quite process his words.

He put a hand over hers. It wasn't a good time to have a fight. Hell, he didn't want to fight with her at all. He couldn't truly be angry with her. She'd given him an out. He could leave everything to Day and spend his time as he wished.

Why did that seem so hollow?

"Of course it doesn't, Mother. You're right, though. She is a perfect queen. The ambassadors are all happy about her." He gave his mother a grin. "They don't have to deal with me now. Of course, they will if I find any of them hitting on my wife again. I swear that Spaniard kissed her hand five times. There's no need to kiss her hand at all. Does he think we're back in the Victorian era?"

"You'll have to deal with the fact that your wife is beautiful and everyone looks up to her." His mother glanced to her right. "Ah, they're calling for me. I need to select the official portraits to go out to the press. I'll be back in a bit."

"Don't overdo it, Mother." He would hate for her to not be able to enjoy the festivities, but he couldn't stand the thought of her crumpling.

She waved the worry off as she started to walk away.

And he was left with the good Scotch and worry in his head

that he was slipping into something he couldn't come back from.

The night before, he'd gotten on his knees in front of Day and by the time she was finished with him, he was begging for her. He'd been on the ground, kissing her feet. At the time, it had felt like the perfect thing to do. He'd wanted to please her more than anything. He'd been happy and relaxed in the moment and he'd come like he'd never come before. He'd settled down with her and wondered what it would be like to have her use a paddle on his ass. Would it send sparks through his system? He'd loved it when Day gripped his cock and brought him to just the right side of pain. Could they explore more?

What would the world say about the pervert king who let his wife rule him? His father would be ashamed and he would be a laughingstock.

He had to stop this slow descent. He had to find a way to not want what he wanted. It was perverted. He was the man and she was the woman, and if they played those games, he should be the one on top.

Tonight, he would put their relationship on a proper footing.

Why did the thought make him infinitely sad? It was his wedding night. He cared about his bride. He wasn't sure it was love. Certainly it was lust and possessiveness and a deep and abiding friendship.

Was he falling in love with Day? Was that making him weak?

"I've been hoping to catch you alone."

He stopped, a chill rushing through his system as the familiar voice snaked along his skin. He felt a hand at his back and then he was staring down into big, blue eyes and pouty red lips. "Tasha, I'm surprised to see you here since you weren't invited."

A faint sheen of tears made those eyes a crystal blue. "I had to talk to you. I came as the guest of one of the ambassadors."

"You shouldn't have been able to get through security."

She shrugged. "I used my legal name. That should tell you how important this is to me, Kashmir. I made a terrible mistake, but you made a bigger one. How could you have married her? She isn't even pretty."

Day was gorgeous, but he wasn't about to argue with her. "You don't have to worry about me anymore. I've got a wife to do that."

Tasha frowned. "Yes, I've been looking into your wife. I've managed to dig up some facts about her that might shock you. Kash, please let me talk to you. That woman is using you. She doesn't love you."

Oh, but when he was on his knees in front of her and Day was smiling down at him, it felt like he'd imagined love would. In those stolen hours when they locked the rest of the world out, he was a different person entirely. Settled, happy.

And then she would sleep and he would deal with the storm of regret and guilt.

He glanced around but Weston wasn't in the ballroom. He was probably in the control room, looking out over the palace, trying to catch any threats that would come their way. He hadn't caught the real threat. Apparently, all a woman had to do was find some ambassador and she could waltz right in.

Still, the last thing he needed was a huge scene with Tasha. Despite her aggressiveness, she was quite fragile and needed to be handled with kid gloves. On more than one occasion she'd threatened to harm herself if Kash wouldn't do what she wanted him to.

He would let her say what she felt like she needed to say, and then calmly explain that he wasn't going to leave his wife and she should go back to London and her boyfriend. He could do all of this quietly and solve the problem before anyone realized there was one. He glanced around, looking for the photographers. When he realized they were busy shooting Day, he decided to make his move.

"Come on. I'm not going to do this in public. We'll talk in private." He began to walk toward the west doors. There was a sitting room that would serve as a good place to deal with the situation. He should have taken her calls and gently explained that he wasn't unhappy about the marriage. He'd been a coward not to talk to her, and now he had to find a way to make her understand.

She hurried to keep up with him and suddenly he felt her hand reach for his. She tangled their fingers together and held on tight.

Yes, he had to deal with this and quickly.

Murdoch's brows rose above his eyes as Kash approached the door he was guarding. "Problems, boss? You know I can handle any unwanted guests."

He felt Tasha's hand start to shake. She'd always needed someone to protect her. He had to get her to understand that it couldn't be him anymore. "I can handle her. Please make sure no reporters follow us out."

He slipped beyond the door and led her to the sitting room, closing that door behind them.

Tasha was immediately on him. She invaded his space, her head tilting up and lower lip quivering. "I've missed you so much. I know I was foolish to leave you, but you have to understand that woman isn't good for you. I know everything. I still have friends in the palace. I know you didn't want this marriage. Your mother forced you into it."

He tried to ease away from her, but she simply followed him until his back hit the wall. "Please, Tasha. You don't know her. We were friends for years. Yes, this was an arranged marriage, but I agreed to it."

"Because that woman convinced your mother to do it. I know everything. I know how they've been meeting in secret for years."

He worked hard not to roll his eyes. She did enjoy a bit of drama. "They were meeting because my mother was interested in Day's education programs. They became friends. I assure you my mother needed no prompting. She was sick of me acting like a horny teenaged boy, so she found a wife to help me settle down."

"She's not the right one for you. I understand why you did this, but you've taken it too far." Tears rolled down her cheeks. "I never thought you would actually do it. She's wearing the ring that should have been for me."

He would never have married Tasha. Not in a million years. She would have made a terrible queen.

Had he been thinking about it even back then? Had he chosen women specifically for their unsuitability?

He tried to get a hand between their chests, needing some space. "It was never that serious between us. Don't you remember? We agreed we were only having a bit of fun."

"We said that but then we fell in love. Kash, we can make this right. All you have to do is divorce her. You don't even need a divorce. You can get this marriage annulled and we can start over."

"That is not going to happen. Why are you doing this?" What the hell was he supposed to do? He wasn't the type of man to shove a woman, but she wouldn't let him go.

"Because I finally realize how much I love you."

"She's doing it because her show on telly got canceled last week," a familiar voice said.

His heart nearly stopped. Day was standing in the doorway, a fierce frown on her face.

Kash tried to hold his hands up. "It's not what you think."

Tasha turned around, but stuck close to him, her well-manicured hand clutching at his chest. "It's exactly what you think. He's mine. He's always been mine. I'm sorry, but this was all about making me jealous. He took it too far, but he's got my attention now. I know this will hurt you, but he doesn't love you."

Kash was damn near panicking. What the hell would he do if Day thought he was truly in here conspiring with an ex-girlfriend? "I swear, I brought her in here so we wouldn't make a scene. I didn't bring her in here to do anything but talk to her."

"Of course you didn't. You are not the problem here, Kashmir. It's all right." Day shook her head. "It's obvious to me that this woman is taking advantage of your good nature. Why don't you let me deal with this, love?"

She was using the same voice she used on him in the bedroom, the one that let him know she was taking over. For a second, he wanted to throw up his hands and leave it all to her. He could walk out and Day would deal with the crazy ex.

"He's not going anywhere." Tasha stepped away, moving closer to Day. "He's mine and if I don't get him back, I'll go to the press and tell a story that will ruin this family. Do you understand? I know things."

If Day was intimidated, he couldn't tell. "Really? Well, you should go and tell all. I'm sure it will make for excellent fiction."

"It's not fiction. I had an investigator look into you. I know all about your so-called vacations."

Day frowned. "What vacations?"

Tasha turned back to Kash. "Your sweet new wife is a complete pervert. She's into all kinds of nasty bondage things. But she can't even be normal there. Do you know what she does? She's a dominatrix. She abuses men."

Kash felt the whole room go still. What the hell? Day had done this before? She'd topped men and in a place where people could see her? Could know who she was?

Tasha continued on, every word out of her mouth threatening to make Kash sick. "She would take these vacations and she would go to underground clubs. She was little better than a prostitute."

"A prostitute gets paid," Day corrected as Kash watched in horror. "I did everything I did for pure pleasure."

Tasha shook her head, blonde curls bouncing. "I've got pictures of you. This scandal is going to make Kate Middleton's nude shots look like an innocent day in the park. How are they going to feel when they find out their pretty new queen is a pervert? That she tricked the king into marrying her? They'll know he would never marry a whore."

"Don't think you can use that against us," Day was saying. "We're perfectly fine with the way we are and no one else comes into it. So go ahead and spout all the nasty stories you like."

Tasha's mouth dropped open and she stared at him. "You let her do that to you? You let her tie you up and spank you like you're some kind of...naughty little boy?"

"We haven't gotten that far yet, but honestly it's none of your business. Now you can leave my home or I'll have you dragged out." Day took a step toward Tasha.

"Dayita, don't say another word." He had to take control. She'd lied to him. His gut twisted at the thought of her with other men, with submissive men. Was that what she was trying to do to him? Was she trying to change him into some plaything to be used for her own pleasure? So she could have the upper hand in all things? "You should leave this room and go up to the bedroom. I will deal with you later."

Day's eyes widened. "Excuse me?"

He hardened himself against her. He wasn't going to let her humiliate him like this. "You heard me. I said go up to our room and I will deal with you. Don't you even think about walking back into the ballroom. The evening is done for you. I will handle our guests."

"What are you doing, Kash?" For the first time since he'd

found her again, she sounded unsure of herself. Day was always so self-possessed. Now he knew why. She made the men around her bow down, and he'd allowed himself to become one of many.

He knew it wasn't fair. Deep down he realized he was being a terrible hypocrite, but he convinced himself that this was different. He looked at her, a chill coming over his whole body. "I'm going to clean up the mess you made for me. Get upstairs or I swear I'll have the guards take you up there."

"I'd love to see them try." She stood up to him.

He couldn't have that. There would be no backing down. This was far too important. He couldn't allow himself to look weak in front of a woman who could apparently destroy them all. He moved into her space, using his height to his advantage. "Do you want me to humiliate you, Dayita? I'll do it. If you don't walk out of here right now and go to our room, I'll carry you. I'll throw you over my shoulder and I'll slap your ass all the way through the ballroom."

"You wouldn't dare."

"Try me." He leaned in. "After all, that's what you want to do to me, isn't it? You want to turn me into a pathetic creature who licks your boots. I assure you that won't happen, my darling wife. You might have tricked me into this marriage, might have fooled my mother into believing you're some kind of a saint, but the manipulation stops now. If you push me, I'll have every newspaper in the world tomorrow running a photo of you being carried off, and the story the next day will be that I abandoned you. I'll leave and you won't see me until I'm ready to deal with you. Do you want that humiliation?"

She'd paled, her eyes shimmering with tears, but her hands were fists at her sides. "Why are you doing this?" She started to reach for him. "We need to talk about this, love."

He backed away. This was how she got to him. She offered him everything he couldn't have, like Eve offering up that apple of hers. "Now!"

She turned, but not before he'd seen the look of abject horror in her eyes. She held her head high and walked out of the door.

"Well, well, it looks like you always make the right choice." Tasha's satisfied voice made him turn.

"Oh, I don't think anyone in the world would agree with you." Kash stalked toward her, his hands itching to do some violence. He wouldn't, but the need was there. To destroy something. To smash it all into bits until his life was completely unrecognizable and he could start over again after sweeping up the ashes. "After all, I chose to bed down with a snake like you, my dear. Listen to me and listen well. You're going to find out what a king can do. If you tell your trashy story to another soul, I swear to god I will make your life hell. I'll be patient and wait. I won't come after you right away, and you'll never realize it's me coming for you. I'll find a way to ruin your reputation. If you're up for a part, I'll pay the producers to hire someone else. If you find a man foolish enough to marry you, I'll send my people in to let him know what marrying you will cost him. There won't be anywhere you can hide. If you destroy my wife's reputation, I'll spend the rest of my life making yours into a literal hell on earth. Am I understood?"

Tears, real ones now, poured from her eyes. "Kash, please. Please, listen to me."

He was done listening. "I can start right this instant. If you aren't off my property in the next ten minutes, I'll consider our war on. I have far more weapons in my arsenal than you do, so think about giving that interview. If I hear even a hint or a whisper of you spreading this story, I'll destroy you."

She turned and ran out of the room.

Kash followed her. Murdoch was standing outside the door, looking from right to left, as though he wasn't sure what was happening.

"That's the second crying female to come out of that room," Murdoch said. "What's happening, Kash? Day looked like you'd ripped her heart out of her chest. Tell me she didn't find you having sex with that woman. She was coming to save you from that chick with the crazy eyes."

Did everyone think he needed saving? "Tell Mr. Weston we won't need the bodyguards anymore this evening. I don't want to be disturbed. Do I make myself clear?"

Murdoch frowned. "I'm not sure what's going on, but I don't like the look in your eyes, Kash."

"Your Majesty." Perhaps his first mistake was trying to be

friendly with people. He wasn't a person. He was a figurehead, and it was past time he used the only thing his position afforded him that was worth anything at all. Power. "You will give me my due respect or you can go home, Mr. Murdoch. I'm going to speak to my bride and I won't be disturbed."

Because he had a few things to work out with her. A few questions that needed to be answered. By the time he was done with her she would know there would be no more manipulations, no more pretending. He would be the head of the household in all things and she would fall in line.

He strode to the secret stairwell the servants used. He could get to his apartments without being seen that way. All anyone would say was that the bride and groom had slipped away to start the honeymoon early.

He took the stairs two at a time, eager suddenly to get this over with. He would smash this whole relationship to pieces and see what they were left with. It had never been real. Not for one moment. Day had lied to him. She'd hidden huge parts of her life from him and he wouldn't take it. Not another second.

He opened the door that led to the hallway of his wing and was nearly shoved back. Simon Weston was sprinting down the hall.

Kash started to yell out to the man that he should be more careful, but that was the moment he realized Weston had a gun in his hand.

"Sorry, Your Majesty. I can't let you go down there." Murdoch had moved in behind him. He put a hand on Kash's arm. "You'll need to come with me. There's a problem in your room."

Day? What had happened to her? He started to drag his arm out of the other man's hold when he saw her being escorted out of their rooms. She was pale, her face tear streaked. She'd been such a lovely bride, but now she looked like a woman who'd seen a ghost.

She was escorted by Rai, one big hand on her arm. He strode down the hallway with purpose.

Kash started to move toward her, the instinct to hold her almost overwhelming. She looked so fragile that all he wanted to do was scoop her up and try to protect her. That was the moment she looked up at him. When she caught sight of him, her gaze turned blank and she moved like a zombie, her feet shuffling down the hall, all of her natural rhythm gone.

She walked past him like he meant nothing at all.

He could have sworn he caught Rai's satisfied smirk.

"What has happened?" He knew better than to go look for himself. One of his blasted guards would choke him out and he would wake up hours later looking like a fool.

That was something he did all too often these days.

Murdoch started to lead him down the hall, back the way Day and Rai had gone. "Apparently, one of the servants likes to sneak a sip of your Scotch at night."

Seriously? All of this over Jamil's nightcap? He stopped, forcing Murdoch to drop his hold. "If you're talking about the old man who turns my bed down at night, I told him he could have a glass when he likes. He worked for my father. He's been here as long as I can remember. For god's sake, don't arrest one of my bloody butlers over a tumbler of Scotch."

"He's dead," Murdoch said, his voice flat. "He died after drinking the Scotch that was brought up this evening. Simon caught it on camera. He tried to get here first, but the queen found him. She's very upset. Someone tried to poison you, Your Majesty. It's time to get you out of the palace for a while."

Kash felt the room go cold. Apparently, his evening wasn't going to end pleasantly.

Chapter Seven

Day sat in the chair offered to her, her whole body weary. Had it really only been twenty-four hours since Michael Malone had shoved her on a private plane? He'd been waiting at the security entrance to the palace to take her from Rai's custody. She and Kash had been taken to the private airfield in separate vehicles, and the plane had taken off before she could quite realize what was happening.

Now she was here in Dallas, Texas, and she felt numb. She'd slept little and spoken not one word to her husband.

Her husband, who'd looked at her like she was some kind of a freak. Her husband, who had made it plain he wanted nothing to do with her.

How easily they'd broken. As if what they had together had been nothing but spun sugar to dissolve in the slightest hint of rain.

"I know you're both tired, but I wanted to give you an update on what's happening in Loa Mali." A man with short brown hair sat behind a rather plain but sturdy desk. He was a large man, his shoulders broad and his jaw square, an all-American type. The name on the office said Wade Rycroft, but the man had introduced himself as Alex McKay. "Ian sends his sincere apologies, Kash. We've got a problem he needs to handle. It's a family situation."

Apparently the bodyguards had decided to ship them to home base.

"I don't care about Taggart's family issues. I would like to know exactly what's going on. I've heard nothing. We were given no choices, McKay. I will not be treated like some prisoner." Kash stood up. It was obvious none of his anger had fled over the course of the day.

"You're being treated like a man who was damn near assassinated," McKay replied, his voice even, but the narrowing of his eyes made his irritation clear to Day. "This is what you pay me for. You pay me to ensure your safety and the safety of your wife. More than that, you pay me to keep your monarchy safe. My employees did exactly what they should have done. They got you out of a dangerous situation. They shipped you somewhere no one will think to look, with the absolute best security you will find in the world. Two of my most experienced men are working to figure out who wants to kill you and also to keep the assassination attempt out of the press. If you find anything wrong with my plan, there's the door. You're free to go."

Kash turned and walked toward the door. He hadn't read the same body language she had or he simply didn't care.

Day stayed in her seat. One of them had to be reasonable. "I thank you for your quick service, Mr. McKay. My husband is going to act like an ass now. Let him. I would appreciate any update you could give me. Did they find out what kind of poison was used? Has Jamil's daughter been informed? She needs to know she'll be given his full pension."

"Jamil had a daughter?" Kash stopped at the door.

Naturally, the man had been sharing a Scotch before bed with Jamil for years, but he didn't know about his servant's family. In the few weeks she'd been living at the palace, she'd made it a point to learn about the family's closest servants. They were men and women who had devoted themselves to the palace for years. They deserved some respect. She kept staring straight ahead. "Yes. He took care of his daughter and her two children. His son-in-law died two years ago and he's the sole source of income while she's taking classes at university. I would like to offer to pay her tuition and to keep up Jamil's paychecks while she's in school."

Kash worked his way back to his seat and slumped down. "Jamil is really dead."

McKay's voice was the tiniest touch more sympathetic this time. "Yes, Kash. We wouldn't have hauled you out of your country for anything but true worry for your life. And as far as your servant's daughter knows, her father passed away of natural causes and the palace will take care of her. It's best we keep this under wraps for now. The press would swarm the island if they knew."

Kash looked infinitely tired as he sat back in the chair that seemed almost too small for his enormous frame. "The press was all over my island already. How do you expect them not to notice that the king and queen have been taken away?"

"I've set that plan in motion. Your yacht was seen launching last night after midnight for the Arabian Sea. Right now it's being captained by a friend of mine, and every now and then two of my employees who look a bit similar to you will be seen cuddling on the deck or taking in the sunset. Believe me, they know how to sell this. As far as the press knows, you and your queen are on a private honeymoon cruise and you do not wish to be disturbed. Rumor has it you've packed enough food and drinks for a full two weeks at sea."

Kash's hand tightened on the armrest. "Two weeks? You expect me to hide out here for two weeks?"

"Hopefully by then Simon and Jesse will have figured out exactly what's happening," McKay continued. "They've already identified the man who delivered the Scotch. He's being questioned right now, but he claims to know nothing."

"It will likely have been a young man named Gilad. I can't imagine he's an antimonarchist," Kash muttered. "His father was once the head of security. He grew up around the palace."

"We're gathering data," McKay replied. "We're going to figure out when the Scotch was poisoned and every single person who touched that bottle. When we know anything at all, we'll let you know. Until then I want to offer you the safety of Sanctum. Kash, you've been here before. You know all the rules. I've closed the club down to everyone but actual McKay-Taggart employees and their partners. We've converted the privacy rooms into suites for your time here. You may use the club, or if you prefer, stay in your rooms. I want you to have some company, if you would like. There's a full bar and a kitchen that will also be staffed while you're here. I thought I would have someone go over how the club runs with your new bride."

"Oh, I'm sure she knows," Kash said bitterly. "My bride is very familiar with all things BDSM. Does she not have a membership here? I'm surprised since she belongs to clubs all over Europe. Was the US too far to travel for your trips, my dear?"

McKay looked between them as though just figuring out there was serious tension there. "No, she's not a member, though she is welcome through your membership. Are you a member at another club, Your Majesty?"

Well, the cat was out of the bag and had been beaten half to death, so she might as well not hold back. She sat up straight, unwilling to allow Kash's sarcasm to bring her low. "I hold a membership at The Velvet Collar in Paris and a club in Berlin called The Tower."

McKay grinned. "Holy shit. Mistress Day." He stood up and held out a hand with what seemed like genuine happiness. "I knew you looked familiar. We haven't met, but I did attend one of your classes a few years back. My wife and I joined Ian and Charlotte Taggart on vacation and we spent a few days at The Velvet Collar. It was fascinating. You taught a brilliant class on suspension play. We use your techniques all the time. I'm so honored to host you."

She shook the man's hand, grateful at least one person in the world didn't think she was some kind of criminal for her desires. "And I am honored to be here. Rene at The Collar speaks highly of your club."

"I'll be thrilled to introduce you around," McKay said, warmth in his voice. He let go of her hand and then turned to Kash. "And if I didn't say it before, congratulations on the wedding. I'm sorry I couldn't make it, but we've traveled so much lately. Ian and Charlotte were sorry to send their regrets as well, but the wedding happened so fast."

"You didn't miss anything at all," Kash replied.

"I'm sure it was lovely." McKay frowned but moved toward the door of the office anyway. "I'm going to make sure the rooms are ready. I can imagine you're tired. I'll be back in a moment."

The door closed and silence hung in the small office.

"Would you like to explain why you're so angry with me?" She had to ask. She didn't understand what had really happened.

He stared straight ahead. "You lied to me."

"I never lied to you. I never told you I was a virgin or that I didn't have a past."

"You also didn't mention that past included being a

dominatrix. You didn't think that would be a problem? You didn't think that would open us all up to ridicule? The queen of Loa Mali wears leather and likes to spank naughty men. Some press statement that will make. It's a nightmare and you've brought this down on our heads because you were selfish and manipulative."

"They were private clubs, Kashmir. You've been to them too. It's all right for you to frequent clubs, but not me, is that correct? I would like for you to state your hypocrisy so I can understand its depths." Weariness was starting to be brushed aside in favor of a righteous anger. "Would the playboy of the Western world like to condemn me as a whore?"

He waved her off. "No one cares what I do. They will care about you, and that's merely me being realistic. It's already bitten us in the ass. We've already had our first blackmail attempt. How many more? How many times will I have to threaten or bribe some man you used to punish so he won't out you? My mother is sick. This could push her over the edge."

At least she could answer that particular fear of his. "Your mother knows. I brought it up to her in the beginning. I should have brought it up to you, but honestly, I didn't want to hear about your past. I was letting it go and moving into the future. I thought you would give me the same courtesy."

He finally turned. "My mother knows?"

"Yes, I told her, but she explained that she already knew."

He ran a hand over his hair, messing it up further. "And yet you didn't think to explain to me that you preferred feminine men? You merely decided to change me into one?"

Change him? Was that what he was worried about? "I'm not trying to change you in any way. I like the way you are. There's nothing at all wrong with it. You can be strong and still need to submit. It doesn't make you less of a man."

His jaw tensed, anger making his whole body rigid. "I do not submit. Not to you. Not to anyone. I'm the king."

"I never said you weren't the king. What we do in the privacy of our bedroom, it doesn't change who you are outside of it. And there's no weakness in submitting sexually to a partner who understands your needs and supports you. This is about finding one place in the world where you can give up control, where you know you're safe because your Mistress would never harm you."

He threw back his head and laughed, a terribly bitter sound. "Safe? You don't make me safe, Mistress Day. You want to make me weak and you've already placed my whole kingdom at risk."

Perhaps it was how tired she was or the fact that she'd heard it before exactly how wrong she was for being comfortable with herself and her needs, but she was ready to give him what he wanted. She stood and faced him. Blissful numbness had overtaken her and she couldn't work up the will to cry. She wasn't strong enough at that moment. It would come later, but for now she stared at the man she'd loved since she was nineteen years old. She wasn't strong enough to lie to herself anymore. It had always been Kash, from the moment he'd grinned at her in class and winked her way. Back then, he'd been the one who'd made it all right to be who she was, glasses and impulses and all. The funny thing was she would never have walked into a club, never have studied up on dominance and submission, had it not been for Kash. He'd given her the strength to accept herself and now he hated her for it.

"I'll contact a lawyer after I've had some sleep." There wasn't anything else she could do. She wasn't going to stay when it was so clear she was unwelcome.

"A lawyer? I've already taken care of it," Kash insisted. "This time. But there will be a next. I'm sure of it. My god, even Ian Taggart knows who you are."

She sighed as she walked to the door. "I didn't mean to take care of your ex-girlfriend. I meant to file for a divorce. Or annulment perhaps. We haven't actually consummated the marriage, so it might be possible."

"Divorce?" He said the word like he'd never heard it before.

What exactly did he want from her if he didn't want to end the marriage? "Yes, Kash. Divorce. You're so horrified by the fact that I like to take control during sex. You're horrified that my whorish past might come up, and despite the fact that you've slept with every woman on the planet, somehow this will make you less of a man. You're horrified by me personally. So the simple way to fix the problem is for the two of us to get a divorce. Since I handle everything anyway, I might as well be the one who files. Oh, you can tell everyone it was you, but we both know you'll be far too lazy to call a lawyer yourself."

Before she could open the door, he put a hand on it, holding it closed. "Lazy, am I?"

She shouldn't have said that, but her defenses were down. She shook her head. "We shouldn't talk anymore until we've had some sleep. If Mr. McKay has set us up with only one bed, I'll take the couch."

"Shouldn't the Mistress have the bed? Shouldn't I sleep on the floor like the good lap dog I am?" He seemed determined to see the worst in everything.

"I never asked you to do that, Kash."

"But you would have at some point. You were preparing me to be your boy. I believe the term is grooming. You were grooming me to accept being your slave."

Naturally he would see it that way. "I was trying to bring you comfort."

"I cannot be what you want me to be."

"Hence the divorce. Then you can go back to your delicate flowers and leave your manly wife behind. Perhaps they'll make you feel more like a man with their simpering neediness."

"Or I can go back to them anyway, keep my marriage and my crown, and turn you into what I need you to be," he shot back. "Have you thought of that? I can bend you to my will and then you'll know who the Master is."

There was no way she was taking that. "Or I could save us both an enormous amount of trouble and cut your balls off while you're sleeping and stuff them down your throat so you never threaten me like that again. If you lay a single hand on me, you'll find out how strong I can be."

That seemed to throw him. He stepped back, his hands up. "I wasn't going to hit you, Day. I would never hit you. I…god, I didn't mean it that way."

At least he wasn't about to become an abusive prick. He was simply feeling the stresses of the past few days, the same way she was. "I'm going to find a place to sleep. I can't talk about this anymore today."

He reached out, this time his hold on her arm gentle. "Dayita, I would never hit you. I'm sorry I made you feel that way. But you should have told me before we married that you need something I can't give you."

"You don't know what I need at all. I need to play in the bedroom. I never would have asked you to defer to me outside of there. I thought you needed someplace where you didn't have to be the king, where you could relax and let someone you trust take over. That was all I ever wanted. I wanted for us to explore and find what works for us. I wasn't ashamed of my past. If it gets out, I don't care. I didn't think you would either. I thought you loved me more than you loved your own image. A silly thing to think since this was an arranged marriage."

"We're not divorcing, Day," he said, but his tone was low and weary. "Royals don't divorce."

"Tell that to Charles and Diana," she replied. "Somehow the British monarchy is still around."

She walked out, closing the door behind her, and stepped out into the hallway. Naturally she had no idea where to go.

"Sometimes it's hard to accept the things we need." Alex McKay stood at the bottom of the stairs leading up to what she suspected was the dungeon portion of the club. "Especially those things that run counter to what we've been taught we should need."

"Why do you think I was gently working him toward a light form of submission?" She asked the question with the weary tone of a woman who knew she was about to be judged and found lacking.

"So you were being sneaky about it? You know he's been in this club a few times. He always tries to play the Dom, but it was obvious to me his heart wasn't in it. I actually suggested he scene with one of our Dommes. I suggested that he should do it because every Dom should know what it feels like to be the one on bottom. Most of my tops eagerly embrace the experience because they know it will make them a better Master or Mistress. Not Kash. He utterly refused, and when I insisted I couldn't give him Master rights without it, he left and hasn't come back until today. Oh, he's friendly enough, but I knew then I'd hit a tender nerve. But you did get him to submit, didn't you?"

Had she been wrong to lead him the way she had? She'd never demanded that he do anything. She'd simply gone on instinct.

Should she have turned it all into a long lesson about what she wanted from him that would have ended in a contract signed by the two of them? "I don't know that I would say that. I don't need his pure submission. I was only trying to give him what I thought he needed. He's not capable of telling me. You're right about that. It's why I did what I did."

"He has to be able to look himself in the mirror." McKay leaned against the railing of the stairs.

"He did nothing that he should be ashamed of." How could Kash even think that?

"I know that. You know that. I don't think he understands that at all. Sometimes the best play a top can make is to be patient and show some kindness to his or her submissive. Even when they don't really deserve it." McKay gestured to the stairs above. "Your rooms are on the third floor. I opened the connecting doors between rooms two and three to make a suite. My wife, Eve, stocked the rooms with toiletries and clothes. You made her day because that woman loves to buy clothes. There are two beds if you need them, but I would advise you not to make decisions today. I know he's a douchebag, but sleep on it before you dump him. I think he needs time. Two weeks isn't a lot of time to adjust to getting married and to changing his view of himself."

"I don't know that patience will win this war, but I will definitely sleep before I do anything," she replied.

"You'd be surprised how patience can be rewarded. I should know. I wouldn't be married to the most beautiful woman in the world without it. And her kindness. Goodnight, Your Majesty." He nodded her way before he walked back toward the office.

Day started up the stairs, McKay's words playing through her head.

* * * *

Kash sank into the chair despite the fact that his every instinct told him to go after his wife and beg her forgiveness. He wasn't going to do that. He didn't need to apologize. She'd taken what he'd said in the wrong context. He would never hurt her physically.

So what exactly had he meant? Fuck. He had no bloody idea.

He didn't even recognize himself anymore.

Here he was married for less than forty-eight hours and his wife was already talking about divorce.

How had he gotten here? Not two weeks before he'd been perfectly happy. He'd been carefree. He'd had everything he could possibly want.

He'd hated his life.

The door opened and Kash forced himself to sit up straight. He wasn't about to lose it in front of Alex McKay. He'd known the man for a few years, but only in a friendly acquaintance fashion.

This man had known more about his wife than he had.

Anger burned through him at her betrayal.

"So everything is set up," McKay explained as he sank back into the chair. "The only people who will be in and out of the club for the next forty-eight hours will be the Dom-in-residence, myself, and your bodyguards. I'll have Michael and Boomer on the daytime shift, and then Remy Guidry will take over the nighttime shift. I've left you dossiers on Wade Rycroft and Remy, so hopefully you'll feel comfortable. While Wade serves as the caretaker for Sanctum, he's also a former Green Beret. He'll back up Remy at night. Then we'll have the club open for select members the day after that. Unless your majesty would prefer to be alone, and then we'll close Sanctum for the full two weeks."

Kash shook his head. He would go crazy if he were stuck here with only his wife. He'd woken up the morning of his wedding certain that two weeks alone and naked with his wife was exactly what he needed. Two weeks where he didn't have to worry about anything but pleasing his queen.

Two weeks where he would have fallen further and further under her spell.

"No, I don't want that. Please tell Mr. Taggart that he should go on as though everything is perfectly normal. I'll be crawling the walls in a few days." Or he would be signing divorce papers.

It was the rational thing to do. He could spend a few days pouring over constitutional law and laying out the best plan to remove his inconvenient wife so he could get back to his real life. He'd fulfilled his obligations by marrying her in the first place. There was likely nothing that said he couldn't divorce her.

Why did the thought of divorcing Dayita make him almost as angry as what she'd done to him?

"Kash, do you want me to bring in someone for you to talk to? You've had a rough couple of weeks. Lots of pressure on you."

He'd found out his mother was dying, been forced to marry, fallen in love, been betrayed.

Was he in love with her? Was that why he was so angry? Had any other woman caused him problems, he would have gently ended the relationship. He would have moved on and not thought about her twice. He had the feeling Day would haunt him for the rest of his life.

"We have a man named Kai Ferguson who works in the building next door. You've met him before."

Kash frowned. "Yes, I've met him. I'm not going to sit in some room and discuss my feelings with his man bun. If he wishes to speak with me and have me take him seriously, he can get a haircut."

McKay groaned. "You're as bad as Ian."

He certainly was not, but he also wasn't going to get caught in some ridiculous discussion of what should be private feelings. All feelings should private. All of them.

Smile and wave and never let them see you're anything but happy, son. You cannot allow the press or any of your people to see you as anything less than a king. Kings do not have feelings. Kings have responsibilities, and we do them without complaint. I know your brother acts the fool much of the time, but he's not going to be the king. He can be the clown.

He'd been twelve and Shray almost fifteen. Kash had hidden in his father's study because he wanted, just once, to know what these weekly meetings between his father and brother were like. He was never invited. It was not information for the spare. In the early days, his mother would distract him by playing games with him or suggesting they watch a movie. At the time, it had felt like precious moments he got with his mother. It was only later that he understood she was trying to spare his feelings.

His father had cared for him, but Kash had always known his place was to be the spare, and once Shray had married and had children, he would be worthless. He would have been nothing but the clown-like uncle, only relevant because of his childhood.

It was why he'd studied, why he'd gone out into the world. He'd wanted to make something of himself. Yes, he would have been the spare—a footnote in royal history—but he would have been a man of learning, someone his father could have been proud of.

How had he still ended up the clown?

"Don't close the club. I would rather have something to do at night."

McKay nodded. "All right. I'll let Ian know. He'll be happy about that. He needs a night at his club, but you should know he was willing to give it up to protect you. He considers you a friend."

"I consider him a friend as well." His stomach was in knots. He stood up. He needed sleep but he wasn't sure he would be able to sleep with her in the room. There must be a bench somewhere. "I know you said you'd put together a room for us, but I suspect you didn't understand the nature of my marriage to Day."

McKay's face was a polite blank. "I've been given a full report on the state of your marriage."

"It's an arranged marriage. It was never for love or feelings. It was strictly to secure the crown." If he started explaining things that way, perhaps he could keep some much-needed distance. He simply had to view his marriage the way it was intended—as a pure exchange of need. He needed a wife. She needed all of his money and power.

Except she hadn't really gone out and spent much. He'd overheard her arguing with his mother that she didn't need a new wardrobe. His mother had been the one to insist that Dayita have what she called a "trousseau." Day had put her dainty foot down when Mother had suggested that she redecorate the queen's traditional apartments. Day had claimed it was lovely and all she would need was her desk from home to make the rooms livable.

"That's funny," McKay said quietly. "That's not what my men observed. I was told you were quite fond of the queen. They said you changed when you met her. You weren't fighting actively against the marriage once you realized who you were marrying."

Somehow things had fallen into place when Day had walked into the room again. His world had seemed brutally cold after realizing his mother was sick. He'd felt alone. And then Day had walked out as though the universe couldn't possibly take away someone so precious without handing him someone else. Day was the one who encouraged him to talk about his mother. He wouldn't talk about it, but there had been comfort in knowing she was there if he needed her.

Why was she there? Why had she done the things she'd done? Taken him down the dark path like some temptress leading him to sin.

Not sin exactly, but certainly something that could lead to his ruin.

"I calmed down and accepted the marriage after I realized my mother was dying." It wasn't a lie. It also wasn't one hundred percent truth.

"Ah, well, Kai could talk to you about that, too. I know you have to be concerned."

Numb was a better word. He still wasn't sure he'd accepted that she was terminally ill. She'd seemed so invigorated by the wedding.

According to Day, his mother had known about Day's past. Did his mother think so little of him that she believed he needed some kind of keeper? That he needed a top to show him the way? How his father would have laughed. Poor Kash, always the clown.

"I'll handle this on my own. I thank you for doing your job." He needed to put a good spin on this. He'd made a mistake by showing his irritation with his new bride. They had to present a united front even when he was so angry he couldn't look at her. He had to think of the crown. Not himself. He had to be the kind of king his father would have wanted. Strong. Dominant in all things. Never wavering. "Now that I've had a few hours to think about it, coming here is actually the best thing that could happen to us. We don't have to pretend we're in love. Day and I can relax and play without fear that someone will go to the press. You need to understand that if anyone goes to the press…"

"What you would do is nothing compared to what Ian would do. Trust me. You're safe here." McKay closed the folder in front of him. "I'll let you know if we hear anything from Simon and Jesse. Chelsea and Phoebe have come onto the team as well. Chelsea is searching around the web to see if she can find a hint of anyone talking about harming the king while Phoebe is sitting in on the interviews. She was Agency for years and she's got excellent instincts. You're in good hands."

He was sure they would find whoever had poisoned his Scotch. He stood up. "Again, my thanks. I'm going to get some sleep."

"Of course. The guards are already here. You're safe." McKay let him get to the door before speaking again. "You know Day had poured herself a glass of that Scotch before she found the body. It's why Simon was running so hard down that hallway. He'd seen Jamil fall and your wife enter the room. Your servant was out of her line of sight when she walked in. I've seen the video. She was seconds away from taking a drink. Luckily she was pacing and found Jamil. If she'd taken even a sip, you would be a widower today."

His stomach dropped at the thought. Day had almost taken a drink? A vision of Day laid out on the floor, her warm eyes cold and unseeing, nearly made him stumble and fall. He'd been the one to send her to that room. He'd been the one to upset her. He'd been the reason she'd reached for the Scotch. She tended to prefer tea before bed. She hadn't been getting ready for bed. She'd been getting ready for a fight.

He managed to nod McKay's way. He'd always hated the fact that palace security required CCTV cameras in the living portions of his suite. His bedroom and the bathrooms were the only parts of the palace where he had some privacy. This was one time he had to be grateful. "Thank you for telling me. She didn't mention it. I'm certainly grateful to Mr. Weston for getting to her as quickly as he did."

He walked out the door. He knew the way to the privacy rooms that would serve as his suite while he was here. He took the stairs two at a time but stopped when he reached the third floor landing.

What the hell was he going to say to her? He wasn't about to meet with a lawyer.

He'd almost lost her.

He was so fucking angry with her.

If this was what love felt like, Kash didn't want it. This was a terrible ache in his gut, a pendulum swinging between anger and insane grief.

He stepped quietly into the room and there she was. Day hadn't bothered to get undressed, though a gown and robe had been left out for her. She'd simply lain down and fallen fast asleep, her shoes still on.

What the hell was he going to do with her?

He shrugged out of his jacket and toed off his shoes. There was another bed in the adjoining room, but he didn't want to use it. Suddenly, despite the fact that he was angry, he didn't want to leave her alone.

Had what she'd done truly been so bad? He was a hypocrite of the first order and he knew it.

Her eyes fluttered open. "I'll go to the other bed if you want this one."

He found himself sitting at the end of the bed, pulling her feet into his lap as he unbuckled the straps at her ankles and eased the shoes off her feet. "Just stay here. Day, I'm...I was surprised by your background. I wish you had told me."

She sighed, a sad sound. "I suppose I knew deep down you would reject me."

Something about the lonely sound of her voice softened him. "I can't live that way. I can't be that way."

For a moment she looked like she would say something, and then she rested her head down again. "And I can't be anything less than who I am."

"Where does that leave us?" He was so tired. He'd been running on anger and adrenaline, and now he was flat out of both. He was a bit hollow, lost as to what he should do.

"It leaves us where we were before. We can divorce and you can find a more suitable bride, or we can be friends. We can understand that we don't work as lovers but we might be good partners. If we're discreet, it could possibly work."

The thought rankled but he couldn't fight more tonight. Today. God, he wasn't even sure what day it was. He only knew he seemed so far from the man who'd held her hand and promised to honor her forever.

"Go to sleep. We'll figure it out." He wasn't sure they could figure anything at all out.

He just knew he didn't have the strength to yell at her

anymore. He lay down beside her.

"Kash?"

The bed was soft and he wished he had the right to pull her into his arms. He would be warm if she wrapped herself around him. "Yes?"

"I'm sorry. I never meant to hurt you. I thought I was giving you what you needed."

But he couldn't need those things. He couldn't let himself even want them anymore. Still, as he lay there, all he could see was the girl she'd been. He'd given her up once for his crown. Could he do it again? How much would being king cost him? He reached out and brushed her hair off her face. She was so lovely. Of all the women he'd been with, why was it only this one who'd ever truly moved him, who'd ever fed his soul? "I won't yell at you again. I'm sorry. When you wake up tomorrow, we'll be friends again. All right?"

A tear slipped from her eye but she nodded. "Friends, then."

He watched her until her breathing evened out and she was asleep. Despite the heavy weight of the day, Kash lay there wondering if friends could ever be enough for him again.

Chapter Eight

Day looked down at the magazine in front of her, a deep sadness running through her heart. It had been a solid week since her wedding but seeing herself in that gorgeous yellow sari, Kash standing beside her in all his wedding finery, made her ache inside. For the most part she'd been able to avoid news coverage, but she'd walked down to the women's locker room to use the sauna and someone had left a copy of *People* magazine, with its cover story on the royal wedding, laying on one of the benches.

Had it been so little time since she'd been that happy woman?

"Hey, I was…that's weird. I was looking for that magazine. It's not every day you find the celebrity holding the magazine she's on the cover of. Well, unless you're my brother-in-law. I swear he keeps his own press clippings around at all times so he can pull out some sexy picture of himself and sign it." The woman in front of her smiled. She was a bit taller than Day, with a friendly face and a mass of curly brown hair tied back with a black ribbon. She held out a hand. "I'm Kori Ferguson."

Day shook her hand. She'd been told Kori might be in and out of the club. She and her husband, Kai, ran a clinic next door. They specialized in helping soldiers with PTSD. It was the kind of thing Day would have usually been interested in. She would have asked a million questions and wanted to know about the science behind their therapies. Now she could barely work up the will to return the woman's smile. "Dayita Kamdar."

Kori stepped back, the smile on her face turning a bit mischievous. "Should I curtsy?"

The Domme in Day recognized what a righteous brat that one would be. The woman in front of her would likely be fun to play with. Of course, she was sure Kash would see her even thinking the thought as a form of cheating. He didn't seem to be capable of understanding that play didn't have to end in sex.

He also wasn't capable of seeing how much he needed.

Day handed over the magazine. "No curtsies, please. I'm trying to be undercover. I don't think Mr. Taggart would take it well if his staff started curtsying to the royals."

Kori snorted lightly. "I'm so not that man's staff."

Naturally, she was offending everyone these days. "I apologize. I meant no offense."

Kori shrugged. "None taken. I'm sure Big Tag would call me staff. Then I would do something mean to his locker. Then he would laugh and handle it super well, and Kai would get all pissy and I would find myself tied up and well, you know where it goes from there. Big Tag is surprisingly good natured about practical jokes. I filled his locker with Jell-O once. Don't even ask. It was a week-long project. I thought he would flip his shit. He laughed hysterically and asked me if I could do it to Adam's car."

It was an interesting place she found herself in. She might have even loved Sanctum had she not felt so deeply alone. "And did you?"

"Still working on it. So, are you coming to the masquerade night?" Kori opened one of the lockers and stuffed the magazine inside. "Kai and I are getting things ready. I was surprised you haven't come to any of the play nights. Kai said you were active in the lifestyle."

She had to go with the united front she and Kash had agreed on. He'd been true to his word. He'd softened his stance and hadn't accused her of being a whore or trying to ruin his kingdom again. They'd sat down the day after they'd arrived and agreed that they could make no decisions and do nothing until they figured out who had tried to kill Kash. While they were stuck here in Sanctum, they'd decided they would work on being friends. After the first day, they'd slept in separate beds, kept up different rooms. They'd been polite, but there was a distance between them she'd never felt before. Not when they were together. Somehow, when they were in the same room, there had always been a connection she could feel. It had been cut now, and she wasn't sure they would ever get it back.

Kash didn't seem interested in finding that connection again.

He'd spent his time watching movies in the men's locker room or playing video games with the bodyguards. Day had been left to read or work out, or—worst of all—think.

"My husband and I are going to keep a low profile while we're here," she said simply. "We're on our honeymoon. I think we want to keep things private. You know how newlyweds are."

Kori whistled. "Dude, you have to get your stories together. Kash is telling everyone that this is nothing more than an arranged marriage and the two of you have an agreement. He's planning on playing tonight. One of the things I brought in was a set of leathers for his royal deludeness. Sorry about the dude, Your Majesty. I dude everyone."

Kash was planning on playing? Was he kidding? "My husband requested that you bring him a set of leathers?"

Kori's eyes went wide. "Whoa. Okay, I believe it now. I didn't before. When they said you were in the lifestyle, I thought it was kind of like Kash was in the lifestyle. Like you played around a bit, but you would be more of a delusional tourist than anything. I apologize for the rudeness, Mistress Day."

She was well aware that she'd likely turned on a dime, but something about Kash going behind her back to play rankled. "I appreciate your acknowledgment, but it isn't necessary. What is necessary is your honest answer to my question. Did my husband request that you bring him a set of leathers because he intends to play in the club this evening?"

"Yes, ma'am. If he doesn't intend to play, then he's going to be walking around your private suite in a full-on mask tonight. He's the one who requested the masquerade theme. Everyone wearing some form of costume means there can be a full play night."

"There have been several play nights already." Not that she'd attended them.

"Yes, but the club hasn't technically been open to the full membership. It's only been open to a close-knit group."

"Why would that..." The answer hit her square in the gut. "Are they all couples? No single submissives?"

Kashmir would want a sub. He would want some delicate thing to blink her eyes at him and never complain so he could feel like a man. It wouldn't matter that the delicate flower couldn't give Kash what his soul craved. All her husband cared about was his image.

Kori sighed and sank down to the bench. "Yes, it was all couples the last few nights. I think Big Tag was trying to make you more comfortable. He admires you as a top. Apparently some dude in France likes you, and Tag likes that dude, so there's a mathematical equation in Tag's mind that adds up to you being one of the good ones."

"I'm well known at The Velvet Collar. I believe Mr. Taggart is good friends with Rene, the man who owns the club. He's also a friend of mine." And one she should have listened to. "I was trained by Rene. One of the things he taught me was that I can't change a submissive who doesn't want to change. I should have listened to him."

A leopard didn't change his spots, and Kashmir Kamdar would never be faithful. Certainly not to her. He was probably keeping her quiet and focused until the moment that he could break ties with her. He would know a compliant wife was better than one actively fighting him. Hence his decision to stop haranguing her. He'd made his decision and now he was surviving as best he could until he could spring whatever plan he'd come up with on her.

Until then, if he could quietly have his fun, he would do it.

"Please excuse me." She started to turn to go.

"Arguing with him won't solve the problem," Kori said suddenly.

Day turned, arching a brow and then realizing what she was doing. They weren't playing. They were in a club, but the roles weren't rigid here. She was tense and upset and slipping into the one role where she felt in control. It wouldn't help her. It would only serve to cause her more trouble. "I wasn't planning on arguing. I was going to talk to him. You're right. We do need to get our stories straight."

"But it will end up in an argument, you know. Look, I'm not trying to overstep… Okay, I am, but it's totally what I do. Overstepping is kind of a hobby of mine. If you go find Kash, you'll get into an argument, and that won't solve anything. He's too stubborn to give in and you gave him an out. Is it so surprising that he took it? Kash has been fooling himself for years."

"An out?" Now she was confused.

Kori shifted on the bench, gesturing for Day to join her. "Kash talks when he drinks. He wasn't playing so Tag gave him a free pass to the bar. He came down to the club last night and after a couple of shots, he started talking to my husband. Oh, in the beginning it was all about how Kai should cut his man bun. Don't you underestimate the power of the man bun. Anyway, after another few shots, he told Kai that you lied to him and tricked him into a D/s relationship."

She couldn't help but roll her eyes in perfect disdain. "That's ridiculous. I didn't trick him into anything."

"So you outlined what you wanted from him?"

There it was, that creeping, completely unfounded guilt that seemed ready to overwhelm her at any given moment. This was why she hated all the time she'd spent "thinking." "I gave clear instructions and they led us both to incredible encounters."

"So you didn't work up a contract with him?"

And the wave was cresting. "It wasn't like that. I knew we wouldn't have that kind of a relationship."

"But you wanted one." Kori leaned in. "Mistress Day, you don't have to talk about this, but I know you're not talking about it with Kash and I don't think you have made friends here. You've been through something stressful and I understand pulling back. But talking can help. It's helping Kash."

He did seem happier. He'd had breakfast with her this morning and spoken more than a few words. They'd had a lively discussion about an article he'd read in a scientific digest. It had almost made her feel normal.

What would it hurt to talk to Kori? From what she'd heard from Kash, this woman and her husband were in some ways the mom and pop of the club. Big Tag and his wife were the king and queen, but Kori and Kai were the ones many of the members talked to when they had a problem.

"If I had sat him down and explained that I was a Mistress and wanted him to submit to me sexually, he would have run as fast as he could. Kash thinks submitting means he's weak. He can say he understands the lifestyle all he likes. He doesn't."

"I don't know about that. I think he does understand much of it. The thing he doesn't understand is himself, and tricking him into something he's not ready for wasn't the best plan."

"I wasn't tricking him."

"I understand that, but that's how he'll see it. Why didn't you tell him you had experience?"

How much had Kash talked? Little hypocrite. He'd told her they should show a united front and then turned around and given up their every secret. "I didn't hide it. I simply didn't talk about it. I didn't want to hear about Kash's conquests."

"But you knew about them."

She couldn't avoid it. "Everyone knows about them. His escapades are legendary."

"While yours were private. You knew much more about him than he knew about you. Doesn't that put him at a disadvantage?"

She caught hold of her anger. There was nothing in Kori's demeanor that indicated she was being judgmental. She was the wife of a therapist, and Day would be surprised if she hadn't picked up a few of her husband's techniques. It was a bit like a science experiment. She'd put forth a theory—that Kashmir had been "tricked." Now it was up to Day to prove or disprove the theory. Kash believed it. By examining her own actions with Kori, she could find a way to change his mind.

Or she would decide she owed her husband an apology.

"I don't view relationships as a game. I don't seek to have an advantage over him. I wasn't trying to trick him. I was trying to form a connection with him and it worked. When we were alone together, he responded to everything I asked of him. He enjoyed it."

"Until?" Kori asked.

"Until the moment he figured out someone knew about my background as a Domme. We were perfectly fine until he realized it was possible someone could find out."

"Interesting and not unsurprising. I did hear that Ian and some of the others were working to ensure your privacy," Kori explained. "I'm fairly certain after they're done, you won't have to worry about the press finding out."

"That's the real problem. I never worried. I didn't care. I'm not ashamed of myself. I take pride in who I am and what I can do. I've helped many submissives learn about discipline and to find their inner strength. There's nothing wrong with it."

"No, but it is seen as abnormal by many in society."

"And it always will be if we all hide."

Kori shook her head. "It can't be you. You gave up that right when you chose to take the crown, Your Majesty. You get to stand up for people who don't have a voice. You get to do amazing things for the needy people of both your country and the world, but you don't get this. The minute you decided to become Loa Mali's queen, you ceased being able to take that part of yourself public. I'm not saying there's anything shameful, but you have other fights to fight. Bigger fights. You can be whoever you want behind closed doors, but you belong to the people otherwise. That's what Kash has to deal with."

It hit her forcibly. Somehow she'd known it in an intellectual way, but she hadn't fully grasped what it all meant. Kash's life had changed that day fifteen years before. He'd gone from coddled spare son with all the choices of his life open to him to a man whose path was laid out before him with no exit ramps.

She was now trapped with him and Kori was right. She had to be realistic. There were many ways she could help the people of her country, but she couldn't do anything at all if she was so controversial a figure that no one would listen. She wasn't a pop star who could say whatever was on her mind and still expect to collect a paycheck at the end of the day. She wasn't even a politician. She represented the people of Loa Mali.

Kash had been submissive for fifteen years. Submissive to his crown, to his people. His sexuality was one way he could have some form of control. Still, even he couldn't walk into a BDSM club without causing a scandal. They had to keep that part of their lives private.

It wasn't going to work. Sadness replaced her anger with him. Anger would solve nothing. She'd been naïve to think she could show him how good it would be to submit to her, that he needed to submit.

"He isn't capable of giving himself what he needs," she said softly. "He won't ever give in. Not fully. That's why he was going to travel after our honeymoon. He needed distance."

"If it helps at all, I think you're right. I believe he would find great joy in having a place to submit to a strong top. It would help him realize he doesn't always have to be the king, but I fear he's spent too long with a crown on his head to be able to change his mindset. It's one thing for him to be known as a manwhore, something different for him to be seen as sexually submissive."

He wouldn't be able to do it. She could see that now. He'd indulged himself, but even right before their wedding, she'd felt him pulling away. He'd always intended to pull away. He'd been trying to stave off that moment when he would have to tell her he could never be that way again.

Had he dreaded it? Had Tasha showing up that night actually been some form of a relief for him?

"I should let it be." Talking to him wouldn't change a thing.

Kori frowned. "Oh, I didn't say that."

"You were right. Arguing isn't going to get us anywhere. I understand his position. I was wrong to try to be sneaky. I should have been upfront with him. It would have saved us both a lot of time and heartache and potential lawyers' fees. No, I'm going to give him the space he needs. I'll try to talk to him about what we need to do, let him know I won't fight him. I think that's what he's afraid of. He's afraid I'll cause trouble, but that's not my intention at all. I want to make this easy on him, and definitely easy on the queen mother."

She wasn't sure what made her sadder, the idea of losing Kash or that for a moment it had felt like she'd had a family again. For a few weeks, she'd felt like she belonged.

"I agree you should go easy on his mom, but you should totally give him hell. It's the only way they ever learn. Look, you're the Mistress. I get that, and you all have rules and shit, but sometimes a bit of bratty behavior goes a long way." The smile that lit up Kori's face let her know she played the brat a lot. All the more fun for her Master. "Sometimes you've got to change the game on a man to get him to see things in a different light."

That sub was probably so much trouble, but then again, she also seemed smart as hell. Day wasn't sure what she was thinking, but maybe it was time to change the game. After all, the rules had been stacked against Kash since the day he'd been born.

"What are you thinking?"

"You know what they say, Mistress. What's good for the goose…"

Was good for the gander. Ah, she understood. Perhaps it was time to start over, but with no secrets between them. He would likely still reject her, but if there was any chance at all, she would take it.

"I'm going to need some help."

* * * *

Kash stepped into the lounge with an uneasy sense of guilt. He'd told Day that he was going down to the conference room to play some video games. He'd then changed as quickly as he could and left via the back door of their suite, praying she wouldn't see him. He was dressed in the leathers the group had been kind enough to supply. He wore leather pants and boots, a thin leather vest, and a mask. With his hair pulled back in a tight queue and the mask covering half his face, he was certain no one who didn't know he was here would recognize him.

Would Day recognize him like this? Would she respect him like this?

He'd lied to her. Damn, why had he done that?

The lights had been turned on and heavy industrial music thudded through the club. It looked like Taggart had gone all out since there was a heavy layer of smoke running across the dungeon floor. It gave the space a hypnotic, other-worldly feel.

This was what he needed. To be out of his own head for a while, outside the world and the places where all the responsibility weighed him down, where he could be someone other than the king.

But wasn't that exactly what Day had been trying to offer him?

He shook off the question and jogged down the stairs, moving quickly toward the lounge section of the club. Guilt followed him. It kept pace with his movements, giving him not a moment's rest.

She was trying to be his friend and he was plotting against her. She thought he was going to give her some happy-ass divorce, but he couldn't. He fucking couldn't, and that pissed him off, too.

He needed this evening. That was what he told himself. He

needed a night to prove to himself that the thing with Day had been an outlier—an experience that varied from the norm. He wasn't the man who sighed and kissed his woman's feet. He was the top.

There would be no sex tonight. He couldn't. He…he was married to Day, and he felt that deep in his soul. But perhaps if he found a sub to top, the world would shift back into place.

Then he would be able to sit down with her. He might be able to deal with the situation rationally. When he really thought about it, he was doing this for the two of them.

If he could figure his own shit out, perhaps she would understand. Perhaps she would fall in line and he could be strong enough for the two of them.

Kash made it to the lounge area, where most of the group would start their evening. Some people were already out in the playroom area and some had scenes going in the dungeon, but he needed to find a partner.

To top. Because he was the top. He was the Dom. That was how it had to be.

"Are you serious? Dude, what is wrong with you? Is that a wig?" Taggart asked a man with long hair that very likely was a wig.

Taggart sat on one of the lounge chairs, leaning back and looking like a king holding court. Well, if the king of Sanctum also happened to be a long-haired rocker with a red bandana around his forehead.

Apparently the group had taken the whole masquerade theme seriously. Kash had thought they would all just wear masks, but some of the group were in full-on costume. Charlotte Taggart wore red thigh-high boots and a Wonder Woman costume that would certainly fall off her the minute she started taking out the bad guys. Although it could be effective. She had lovely breasts. She could distract her enemies with those.

"I'm not going to apologize, Axl Rose. Khal Drogo is a badass," the other man said.

"He's also about five feet taller than you," Taggart returned.

The other man shrugged. "I have about a billion dollars more than he has so I think I win. Also, my sun and moon is even prettier than the one on TV. Hey, gorgeous."

A lovely woman stepped into the lounge wearing a flowing

white gown and a wig with platinum blonde locks. She looked at the man who would probably have made a better hobbit and sighed, her hand over her heart. "And you look amazing, my love. Don't let the big bad wolf tear you down. I'll set some dragons on him."

Taggart grinned. "I got Wonder Woman to shield me."

The man with the fake swords at his sides stepped up and put his hands on the woman's hips. "I've got a billion dollars on Big Tag, too. Don't you worry about my ego. I can handle it. You ready to handle me?"

"You know I am, baby," the woman replied and then her eyes took on a steely look. "How do you greet me?"

To Kash's surprise, the man fell to his knees, his hands on his thighs as he offered himself up to his Domme.

The woman put a hand on his head and accepted the offer with a smile. "Come, my love. Let's go play. It's been a rough week. I think you need some serious discipline."

His face turned up and he was grinning. "Yes, after that last board meeting, I'm going to need a little something something, if you know what I mean."

She reached out a hand, helping him up, and then led him away toward the play area.

"That is one happy tech guru," Charlotte said with a smile on her face.

"I remember when he was all uptight and grumpy." Serena Dean-Miles took a seat. She was dressed in a schoolgirl outfit complete with pigtails and Mary Janes. "Hey, Ka… I mean, hi, Sir. We're calling him Sir tonight, right?"

"He's undercover, though I wouldn't have agreed to any of this if I thought he was in real jeopardy," Taggart explained, his hand on his wife's knee. "Every single person in this club knows the rules. No one is going to talk to the press because they know they would have to deal with me. And Mitch. He's a bloodsucking lawyer. He's like a giant tick. Once he settles in, it's really hard to get him out. Ask Laurel. One unplanned pregnancy and she's saddled with the man for life."

Charlotte shook her head. "Don't believe him. They're incredibly happy. And now Serena and I are going to help the Mistress set up for her demo. I've heard Harrison nearly had a heart attack when he found out a Domme was going to be doing a ropes demo tonight. He had a rough case this week and he's sure he can avoid the heart attack he sees coming his way if he can get in a good, long session."

"Harrison Keen? The attorney?" He'd met the man briefly when he'd been at Sanctum the year before. Keen had been on the board of a charity Kash funded. Harrison Keen was an all-American man who commanded attention when he walked in a room. "He's going to help this Mistress with her demonstrations?"

Taggart laughed, the sound booming through the lounge. "No. He's going to beg the woman to tie him up and beat his ass red. Keen's a big old bottom. Oh, don't get me wrong. He's the alpha male in the courtroom, but when he's in the dungeon, that man is all about kissing some dainty Domme feet."

"We talking about Keen or Milo?" a new voice asked. Adam Miles strode up. He was dressed in a perfectly pressed suit, his hair slicked back and a briefcase in his hand.

"Keen," Tag replied as his wife stood up. "Milo's lost his damn mind. I swear, the nerds are taking over. Between Milo's dragons and Phoebe and Jesse's weird wand fetish, it's getting sketchy around here. Now Adam's come dressed as Simon. It's a crazy fucking world, man. You know it's not normal for your wife's fantasy guy to be another team member, right?"

Miles shot Tag his middle finger. "Fuck you. Si doesn't have a copyright on three-piece suits. I'm not dressed as him. I'm a professor and that's one naughty schoolgirl."

Serena stood and cuddled up against her husband. "You know I am, professor. Very naughty. I didn't do my homework. I suppose someone's going to have to punish me."

"I think we can work something out, you bad, bad girl. Look at that pout." Adam growled down at his wife and then his entire demeanor changed. "Hey, babe, don't let me forget. We're out of wipes. Jake used nearly a whole box yesterday."

Serena nodded. "We're calling it the Great Poop Incident. I've never seen a baby poop so much. Jake was overwhelmed. We can steal a box from the nursery when we pick up the kids."

"I heard that," Taggart said with a frown.

Serena shook her head. "Nope, Axl Rose is an outlaw. He

would totally agree with my decision to move to a life of baby wipe thievery." She looked back up at her husband. "I'll see you later, professor. I'll try to stay out of trouble, but you know how naughty I can be."

Miles smacked his wife's backside, eliciting a squeal from her. "I've got a paddle with your name on it. Now go and do what you need to do. Jake'll be up in a bit and then you'll have to deal with two angry professors."

Charlotte kissed her husband and the two subs were off to help set up the scene.

Miles sank into the chair opposite Taggart. "I sent you the report on the masked one's latest threat."

Kash sat down with the two men. "What do you mean latest threat?"

Taggart had his phone out, pulling up files. "You ran down where they would have gotten the poison?"

"Of course," Miles shot back. "I'm a genius."

"What was the poison?" Kash asked. "It had to be fast acting. There are only a few poisons that could be used that would act so quickly. Was it cyanide?"

"It was a conotoxin," Miles replied.

Taggart was shaking his head. "Dude, I am never going to Australia. Everything wants to kill you there. Even the flipping snails. I do not get it. Charlie wants to go for vacation, but I think it would be one long attempt at survival."

"Snails?" He didn't need Taggart's sarcasm.

"There's a marine snail, native to Australia," Miles explained. "It's called a cone snail and it's one of the most venomous creatures on the planet. Unfortunately, Tag's right about Australia. Everything wants to kill you there. Have you ever seen a real kangaroo? They can punch and shit, and they are not unfamiliar with fight club."

"Where would the assassin have gotten this venom?" Kash needed to keep them focused.

"Probably from a pharmaceutical lab." Tag nodded. "Yep, there it is. A small lab working on the coast reported a break-in, and someone stole a small supply of the venom. They're studying it to see if it can be used to treat epilepsy and a host of other disorders."

"I need to check travel records, but I'm getting some pushback," Miles said. "They don't know why some firm in Dallas wants to invade the privacy of a bunch of Loa Mali's citizens. Perhaps if the king could call?"

"I'll do it in the morning. My cousin can get you all the information you need." Someone had tried to kill him. It still wasn't something he'd entirely processed. "So you think someone traveled to Australia, stole some of this toxin, and came back to use it to kill me. Why not use something simpler?"

"Despite what *Murder She Wrote* will teach you, it's actually hard to get your hands on a poison that works so quickly," Miles explained. "Most agents require time and will sicken the victim before killing him. Cyanide works well, but you have to have enough of it and it's highly controlled. I'll figure out who went to Australia shortly before the robbery and we should have a suspect pool."

"Australia is quite close." He didn't want them to think this would be easy. "We have an excellent relationship with them. We don't require visas coming into or out of the country. It will be a large pool. It's winter break back home. Lots of people on holiday."

He glanced out over the playroom and caught sight of the *Game of Thrones* couple again. That was when it clicked. He'd seen that man before. He'd met that man before. "That was Milo Jaye."

Taggart barely looked up from his phone. "Yep, that's Milo. Thanks, Adam. Did I punch your face for that lately?"

Adam's eyes rolled. "Sure, bringing one of the wealthiest men in the country into your circle of influence is a punchable offense."

"I already filled the tech guru nerd spot. Case married into a family of them," Taggart argued.

"Yeah, well, the Lawless clan has yet to accept your offer to come to Sanctum," Adam shot back. "And you know how the old saying goes. You can never have too many ridiculously wealthy tech gurus on the team."

"But he's one of the most powerful businessmen in the world." Kash didn't understand.

Taggart's eyes finally came up. "Is that a declarative statement or a question? I can tell you he's a smart fucker. I wasn't going to let him in. He found the weakest link in my chain, sued Adam, and voila, now he's happily getting his ass slapped by his girlfriend. They were pretty dumb in the beginning though. Milo thought he was the top."

Adam snorted a little. "That was pretty funny to watch, and I'm so not the weakest link. If you see Jake, tell him I'm in the conference room trying to trace a couple of flight manifests down, and that if he starts our scene without me, I'll kill him."

Adam strode off toward the stairs.

"Why so interested in Milo Jaye?" Taggart asked.

It was odd to be having such a personal conversation with Axl Rose, but he did have some questions. "He's not the type of man I would see as a submissive. As a matter of fact, I wonder about the other one, too. The lawyer. He seems to be so masculine."

A brow arched over Taggart's left eye. "How does masculinity come into this?"

He should stop talking right here and now. This wasn't a conversation he needed to have. "You know how it is. The woman submits to the man. That's how it's supposed to be."

Both of Taggart's eyes widened, and he looked around like a man who'd just realized something was about to kill him. "Dude, you do not say that bullshit in this club. Like seriously, not even outside of it. The subs have ears. They have ears everywhere, and those ears are attached to faces that have mouths, and those mouths talk, and then my wife hears that I was in a conversation where she and all womanhood was subjected to the patriarchy or some shit. She'll have a really long political term but what it really means is I sleep on the couch."

He should have known all he would get out of Taggart was sarcasm. "I'll try not to speak of the patriarchy around your wife."

"Hey, don't be so touchy." Taggart relaxed back and studied him for a moment. "You really think being Dominant or submissive has something to do with gender? Because in my experience, it doesn't. It's more about the psychology of the person and the way he or she deals with the world around them. It can be something as simple as a woman or a man was once in a position where he or she was out of control. Especially if that situation involved something sexual. They might need to be in control during sex. I control who plays in this club. I'm not going to allow a submissive in who is actively seeking to hurt himself. I would connect that person to Kai or another therapist. There's no room for self-hate here. It can be too dangerous. I deal with those people more magnanimously than the other side of it."

"The other side?"

"The ones who truly want to cause pain without pleasure, who seek to control their submissives in a way that is not healthy for the sub. It's why almost none of my friends in the lifestyle are twenty-four seven. Even the ones who started that way tend to ease up over time. You can cross the line into abuse if you get the wrong Dom and sub together. Don't get me wrong. That kind of a relationship can work, but it's rare. The submissive must be as strong as the Dominant for a relationship like that to work."

"I thought the whole point was that the Dom was the strong one."

"That's because you don't take any of this seriously. When I try to talk about the fundamental ideas of the lifestyle, you tend to take another shot and talk about spanking girls. The only reason I let you in here is because I trust you not to hurt the subs. Also, you tend to have terrible taste in women. I thought I might be able to save you."

"I do not have terrible taste in women." He'd been with some of the most beautiful women in the world. And many of them were horrible human beings.

"Dude, you can't even tell a supermodel from a spy. Hint, the spies are the ones who try to kill you."

He would never live that down.

Taggart leaned forward, his voice softening. "I like your wife very much. I have to wonder if she's not the reason you're suddenly asking questions."

"I know you've met her before."

"Have I met Dayita Samar, or Mistress D? I've certainly met the latter. She's a friend of a friend and she's considered one of the finest Dommes around."

His stomach clenched at the thought. He was trying to forgive her for not telling him. He was trying to see things from her point of view. "That is good for her and for whomever she chooses to top."

"Kash, she's a serious sexual top. From what I understand, it's merely a part of her personality. The same as it is mine. No damage or trauma forced it. Some of us are simply born this way. Like Harrison and Milo are bottoms. They gain great pleasure from serving their lovers in certain ways and from being served in the way only a top can."

"Yes, I understand this much. They enjoy having their backsides smacked and kissing a woman's feet."

Taggart's icy blue eyes narrowed. "Okay, that was judgmental, but I think you're new to this so I'll keep talking. There's more to it than getting spanked. I've gotten spanked. It doesn't do anything for me. I think if one of the male subs were here, they would tell you that what they get is a place where they don't have to be in control. Hell, the female subs would tell you that. There are some strong-as-hell boss ladies who grace this club. They come from all walks of life and they seek to relax, to have those few hours a week where this other part of their personalities gets to come out. They can indulge that piece of themselves. Humans are complex. Well, Adam isn't. Adam's a douchebag, but for the most part there are these whole other people who live inside us and never get to come out unless we're brave enough to explore. I might be the top here, but don't you doubt for a second that I wouldn't get on my knees in front of my Charlie. There's nothing weak about that. I love that woman. She gets every piece of me, with nothing held back. And you know what, she's the reason why I found that softer side of myself. She and our kids. I'm a completely different person without them. Colder. Alone. Some might have called that strength, but it was really fear." Taggart shoved his phone back into his pocket. "Have you talked to your wife about this? About how to move forward?"

"How do two tops move forward?" The words felt stubborn, but he couldn't admit the truth. He couldn't simply say what he wanted.

"I have a married couple here who are both tops, and they enjoy themselves mightily. And before you start talking about cheating, they don't sleep with their submissives. They give their expertise to the subs they top and then go at it like a couple of angry rabbits. Seriously, those two know how to tear up a bed, but then you go to hand them a bill and they get all legal on a man's ass. Note to self, no more fucking lawyers. We've got enough damn lawyers."

Jacob Dean strode in, wearing a suit that was only slightly less perfect than his partner's had been. "Hey, Tag, you seen Adam? I got stuck in traffic. Stupid 75."

Taggart nodded. "Yeah, he's working on a case. Said he'd be a while and you should start without him."

Dean gave him a thumbs-up. "Excellent. I'll go get our girl warmed up."

"You're an asshole." Kash watched as Dean strode away.

"It's all a part of my charm." Tag stood up. "I think the demo is going to get started soon. I'm going to go watch. Also, it'll be fun to watch Adam and Jake fight when Adam realizes Jake got that first piece of pie."

He wasn't sure what pie had to do with anything, but he followed Tag into the play space. All around him the members of Sanctum seemed to be embracing the idea of a masquerade. He caught sight of the ridiculously wealthy Milo Jaye and his girlfriend. Milo was on his knees in front of her, his eyes soft and a smile playing on his face. His girl lightly ran the tip of a cane down his chest, and it sent a shiver through the man's body.

Why did the image have to tighten his groin? Why couldn't he be normal?

What the hell was normal?

"So your wife didn't want to come down and play?" Taggart asked as they moved toward the largest of the stages. "She's more than welcome, of course. I have no problem giving her full Mistress privileges here."

"But I am given merely probationary privileges?" Naturally Day would be able to oversee him if she'd come down. She could stop him and instruct him if she thought he was doing something incorrectly.

Taggart nodded. "Oh, yeah, she's way better than you. You could learn a thing or two. I don't know why you wouldn't. She's a badass."

"In my country, women are not supposed to be badasses. They are supposed to be partners, to be helpmates to their husbands."

Had he honestly just said that? What the fuck was wrong with him? He didn't believe that. He fought against that kind of backward thinking. When he'd been running his lab, he'd made sure to bring in all the brightest minds, male and female.

And now the only use he had for anyone was to bring him his next drink, be his next body in a bed.

How had his life gotten so damn shallow?

Taggart slapped him on the shoulder, one of those American male gestures that let a man know he was both stupid and tolerated. "Maybe that's why you couldn't tell the difference between the chick who wanted to kill you and the ones who were in it for your cash. As for me, give me a badass chick every day of the week. You say you're looking for a helpmate? Badass chick will not only cook your breakfast, she'll take care of the assassins trying to kill you, give you the best blow job of your life, and scare off all the people you don't want around. You can keep your delicate chicks. Give me a Russian mob princess. There's a class of women who know how to treat a man right. Conversely, they also know how to cut a man's balls off if you don't hold up your end of the bargain."

"That being?"

He smiled, a bright, open expression that Kash wasn't used to seeing on Taggart's face. "Complete and total dependence. I'm joking. Though that is what I feel when she leaves me alone with the kids. Sometimes I think that's her way of letting me know what hell on earth is like. I'm ready to drop to my knees and beg her to never leave me and all she did was go buy groceries. Yeah, that's a clever plan of hers. That's my girl. She's always plotting. So you didn't tell me why Day didn't want to come down and play. You've been here. Why hasn't she?"

Because he'd made her feel so terrible about their situation that she mostly sat around the room like a prisoner waiting for her execution. She read a lot, used the gym when she was sure no one was around. She'd taken to sitting in the small alcove that contained the basketball net. He'd caught her sitting in the sun, her face turned up as though she missed the warmth. She'd been so stunningly beautiful in that moment that he'd wanted nothing more than to take her hand and lead her upstairs.

"Do you think a woman like Day could be happy with a vanilla relationship?"

"Why should she have one?" Taggart asked.

How did he make him understand? "It's not seemly. If we ever got caught…"

"You get caught all the time, dude. There are pictures of your junk pretty much everywhere. You know you have your own YouTube channel, right?"

"That's different."

Taggart stared at him for a moment. "How? Because you're a guy and you're supposed to fuck around, and she's female and should remain pure until she gets to marry the guy who's fucked around?"

"I don't think like that. I don't have a problem with the fact that she's slept with other men."

Taggart stopped, settling himself on an unused bench. "Good, because that would make you a really heinous hypocrite and I might decide you need assassinating."

They were in a scene space that had three walls around it. It looked a bit like an exercise room, except the barbells were alongside a number of paddles and crops. He understood why Taggart had chosen this space for his impromptu conversation about hypocrisy. Kash could hear him easily over the music, but they could still see the large stage.

"Would Day get to stay queen if you died?" Taggart asked, his eyes narrowed.

He had the sudden suspicion that only the truth might save him. Taggart often believed he was smarter than anyone else and that the world should work according to his rules. "No. That would be against the rules of our primogeniture. My cousin Chapal would become the king."

And then they would have the problems of succession because Chapal would be stubborn about divorcing his husband and marrying a female simply for procreation. A female who would be required to provide a son. He and Day could have ten daughters but if one son was born, he would supersede all his sisters.

Why was that the rule? Because some asshole a thousand years ago decided men were more important than women? That a man—any man—could lead better than a woman?

He had a sudden vision of a young girl. She would have her mother's silky hair and serious eyes. She would love science and she would be told to study housekeeping. She would be taught to wave and smile and defer to her younger brother because he would be king.

He'd made progress. He'd been the one to push for women to get their degrees. It had been in his coronation speech. He remembered writing it even when his father's advisors had told him not to push. He'd done it for Day. He'd done it because he'd been in love with a girl who'd wanted to discover the secrets of the universe.

And then his lab had blown up and the guilt had eaten away at him for five long years. He'd turned away from truly leading, and a whole group of nasty old men had gained power in his absence. They'd tried to turn the country back, tried to tell all those little girls who they should be.

The only person fighting them had been Dayita.

While he'd been off drinking his guilt away, she'd been quietly fighting for the next generation. So that both boys and girls received everything their country could give them. So when they became men and women, all were strong.

"Besides, dude, you're like the king and shit," Taggart pointed out. "What the hell does it mean to be the king if you can't tell everyone to fuck off about a couple of things? I get it. You can't behead people anymore, but you have some power. You can protect your wife. Unless you think your wife is wrong because she's not a simpering flower who needs you to protect her from everything life throws at her. Unless you think she's wrong for needing what she needs and being strong enough to ask for it."

Kash clung to the one thing he could be righteous about. "Ah, but she didn't. She didn't ask for it."

Why had he said that? He'd bloody well outed himself.

If Taggart was surprised, he didn't show it, which led Kash to wonder if this hadn't been the point of his conversation all along. "She tricked you into submitting to her?"

"Yes."

Taggart thought about that for a moment. "How does that work? Did she get you drunk? Blackmail you?"

"No. She didn't tell me what she was doing."

"She didn't give you instructions?" There was a suspicious tone to the question, as though he didn't really believe he had asked one at all. As though it all should have been obvious. "Because those are usually the norm in a D/s relationship. In vanilla relationships you sometimes fall into bed together and one partner naturally takes the lead, but you can usually tell who that is. Did she fight you for it?"

Nope. He'd lain down the minute she'd turned that sexy-as-hell voice on him. "It wasn't like that."

"Did she tie you up when you were asleep or something? You know that's assault and we should really talk about that."

Taggart was twisting his words, the bastard. "No, she didn't do that. And yes, she gave me instructions."

"She asked you to get to your knees? She asked you to let her take control? How was this confusing to you?" Taggart asked in a rapid-fire interrogation.

"I understood the instructions."

"And it seems as though you followed them," Taggart surmised. "Did she tell you she would stop the sex if you didn't obey her? Is that how she blackmailed you?"

He hadn't even thought to ask the question. He'd been so enthralled by the way she took control, by the relief he felt at the idea of not being in charge for a few fucking minutes in his day. "I did what she required. It didn't seem wrong at the time. But she didn't tell me about her past. She didn't tell me what she wanted from me."

"Did she require your submission outside the bedroom? Did she manipulate you into giving in to her when the subject wasn't sex? Women can use any number of manipulative techniques to get us to submit to their evil wills."

He had the feeling Taggart was making fun of him. It made him think though. She hadn't tried to manipulate him. She'd asked if he was going to come to her meetings with parliament, that he sit back and allow her to handle things, but that was her job. She understood it far better than he did. He'd spent the whole time getting hot because of the way she masterfully handled those men, but he'd also realized that she was competent.

They hadn't fought until that last day. They'd found a familiar friendship that had filled some place inside him he hadn't realized was empty.

"No, she hasn't tried, but that doesn't mean it wasn't part of her plan. She was grooming me." It sounded stupid even to his ears.

Taggart's whole body buckled under the force of his laughter. He was red in the face when he came back up. "Kash, man. That is the best. For a hot minute there I thought you were serious. Oh, you got me good. That was hysterical."

He was deeply appreciative of the fact that his face was covered with a mask because he could feel his cheeks heating. It was ridiculous. "Yeah, I thought it was pretty good. You know me, I am an incredibly funny man."

Taggart gave him a wide smile. "I was worried there for a minute. She's an amazing woman. Your girl is kinky and she'll keep you on your toes for the rest of your life. You totally could have done worse. You should thank your momma for picking a wife who's badass enough to be your queen. And Kash, it's time to let go of all that other shit and get the hell back to work."

"What are you talking about?" He feared he knew. Taggart was one of the only men on earth who knew what he'd been working on and how wrong it had gone.

"You've been hiding from that project for years. It wasn't your fault some douchebag decided to kill your project, and it's not your fault that your people died. And this time around, you'll have me working security, and I've heard that queen of yours is pretty smart, too. You've fumbled around for years. It's time to do what you're supposed to do."

"What's that, Taggart?"

Taggart's eyes went to the stage and they lit up as the lights came on. "Well, well, there's some manipulation. I should have wondered why Charlie was so hot to help set up. See, not all plots are bad things. Some end up leading to happy endings. You wanted to know how it would work with two tops, you can find out tonight. Or you can play with your girl and be happy and tell anyone who thinks it's wrong to go straight to hell. It's your choice."

Taggart started walking away. Kash put a hand on his shoulder to stop him. "You didn't answer my question. You said there was something I was supposed to do."

"Yeah, man. Some asshat who's no longer alive thanks to a badass babe set you back. Now it's time to step up again. Time to change the world. The world needs visionaries. You can't be a visionary if all you do with your life is worry about what other people think. Be brave. Be the fucking king, my man."

He glanced up and saw what Taggart had seen. A gorgeous woman wearing a black catsuit that clung to her every curve was walking onto the stage. Walking? That woman didn't merely walk. She strode. She owned the ground she walked on. A black mask covered her face, but there was no question of who she was. Between the long, midnight black hair that nearly reached her waist and those gorgeous lips of hers, he knew his wife. Although he'd never seen her look so confident, so secure in who she was than that moment she walked onto the stage.

Day was done waiting for him. She was here in the dungeon and she would move on.

Charlotte Taggart took the stage as Day looked over the ropes that had been left for her. Charlotte stepped up and looked out over the small crowd. "Thank you all for joining us tonight. We've got a special treat. A friend of ours is here in town for a few days. She's considered an expert at both bondage and suspension play, and she's going to give us a demo tonight. She's going to show you that with proper technique, a tiny Domme can handle her big, burly sub."

Was that what all that rigging was for? There was an elaborate system of ropes and pulleys connected to an apparatus obviously meant to suspend something in midair. It looked like she would be suspending a man there.

"Please welcome Mistress D."

There was clapping and shouts of hellos from the couples around him. They were all shapes and sizes, all colors and ages. There were men with women clinging to them and women with men resting at their feet. Some of the couples were same sex, and then there were the threesomes. Not a one of them seemed uncomfortable.

No one cared here. They were all seeking the same thing—to be happy.

Day took center stage. She didn't need a microphone to be heard. "Thank you so much for having me here tonight. I love rope. I love how it feels in my hands and how creative I can get when using it on a partner. I love suspension play as well because when my lovely sub is trapped in my web and suspended off the ground, he is completely vulnerable to me. There isn't a part of him I can't torture and touch, no ground beneath him to keep him from me. Of course, I prefer submissives who enjoy the sensation, and not all do. As with any play, this should be consensual and kind...even when it's quite cruel."

Because the cruelty was nothing more than a game. Because Day wouldn't want to hurt anyone. She merely sought to give her partners a space to explore their fantasy selves, to be someone different than they were in their daily lives, to give up control and feel free for a few hours.

Why should that be forbidden to him?

He saw what could be their lives flash before him. If he chose to stick to this path, they might very well find some friendship, but she would need this. If he forced her away from this lifestyle altogether, a piece of her would be lost, hollowed out. Or if he allowed her to play quietly, she would eventually find a man who wasn't intimidated, who wouldn't allow some societal norm to take away his choice, to define his masculinity.

What right did anyone have to choose who he would be?

He was the fucking king.

"I want to show you some of my techniques," Day continued. "I know the big Doms of the room have no trouble at all suspending their dainty subs, but I prefer my men with muscle. I want to show you how a smaller top can safely suspend and play with her bigger, heavier sub. Can I get a volunteer?"

Three other men held their hands up, one trying to crowd the stage as though willing to physically block out the other men.

He could sit back and watch. He could think this through and make a rational decision.

"I volunteer. Me. And if any one of you touches my wife, I swear I'll kill you where you stand, is that clear?"

Taggart gave him a big thumbs-up as he moved toward the stage.

Chapter Nine

Day frowned as she watched the man shove his way through the crowd. She hadn't been able to hear exactly what he'd said, but she'd gotten the gist. He was selecting himself and taking the choice from her.

He was about to find out she didn't play that way.

She looked over at Charlotte and Kori, who were standing off to the side, waiting to see if she needed any help. Serena Dean-Miles had been assisting until her big gorgeous brute of a Dom had explained that she had a meeting in the principal's office.

"I want that man taken out of here," she said to Kori. "Do we have bouncers?"

Kori nodded. "Sure we do, but I think they're going to make you take care of this one."

It wasn't her club, but this was her scene and she meant to make things clear. She was in charge and she would select her volunteer. It certainly wouldn't be some mouthy brat of a beast with no manners.

Oh, god, it was Kash.

She turned and there he was, stepping up the stairs. Another man put a hand out. She'd been introduced to Harrison Keen only moments before. She'd thought she would probably use him as her test subject. He was a lovely man, six foot with plenty of muscle. He was perfect to show her techniques off on.

"Hey, the Mistress gets to decide, asshole. Have you ever been in a club in your life?" Harrison was asking.

"Have you ever been thrown into a damn hellhole of a prison because you touched a powerful king's wife? I have this prison. Well, they might have turned it into a tourist attraction, but I can build a new one."

"What the hell are you talking about?" Keen shook his head.

That was her Kash. He could make some of the oddest threats she'd ever heard, and he didn't mind going medieval on people. Was he here to haul her off the stage? When she'd agreed to do the demo, she'd chosen to do it for herself, to have some fun and relax. Not to give Kash the middle finger. She'd thought about it and decided she wouldn't do it for revenge. Only for herself. She'd suspected he wouldn't even realize she was here. She'd thought he would have found some delicate sub and settled in for the night, and seeing them together would finally make her understand that her marriage was over before it had truly begun.

Of course, she might find out her husband was here to treat her like some child who couldn't make a decision for herself.

Kash hoisted himself up onto the stage, his body moving with the elegant grace of a panther. How could he seriously think that a tiny mask could hide his beauty? Anyone who knew him would know the brilliance of his eyes, the straight, square line of his jaw, those sexy broad shoulders.

She put her hands on her hips, completely unwilling to give up her space. He could reject her, but he wasn't taking this from her. She leaned in, making sure she couldn't be heard. "Kash, I'm not hurting anyone. I've got my mask on. No one knows it's me."

"I know it's you. I'll know it if you play with another man, and then I think our cover will be blown because I will kill the man. I have diplomatic immunity, but it could still cause problems and Big Tag would be upset. No one is getting topped by you but me." He loomed over her.

She wanted it more than anything, but how could she believe it? "You'll hate me when it's over."

His jawline softened. "I could never hate you."

She wasn't so sure about that. "I think it's a mistake. We don't have a contract. You were right. I should have sat down with you and explained everything."

"That seems dull. If you had tried that, I would have gotten bored. I am easily distracted these days and it's all my own fault. I've let my mind go to waste. I know it's an easy thing to do when you're in a body this beautiful, but it's been pointed out to me lately that I let the world down when I don't also exercise my gorgeous brain. I will stop playing so many video games and join you in your morning reading."

She shook her head. "Kash, everyone will be watching you."

He frowned. "Of course they will. Have you seen my body? It's stunning. I am a man in his peak physical condition, and more than that, I am a king, blessed with the body of a god. I've been told I have a glow about me."

Who the hell was this? This was the Kash she remembered, the Kash who joked about his own arrogance. The Kash who'd been such a good friend, who'd caught her heart. Still, he couldn't have changed overnight. "I can't go through that again. I'll go up to our room and we can talk about this. It's what we should have done the first time."

He shook his head. "I don't want to talk. I won't understand that way. I have to see a thing, to feel it, to experience it. I might get angry later, but I won't be angry with you. I'll be irritated with myself. I wasn't raised to be comfortable with something like this, but I don't want to take this from you. Let me be your submissive tonight. We're among friends, and none of them will talk. I don't have to be the king. I can be someone else, someone who can give you what you need."

It was all she could ask for, but she still found it hard to trust. "Why are you really doing this? You know I'm not going to have sex with another man."

His lips curled up ever so slightly, and he stared at her with something akin to wonder on his face. "Because I never thought you would look so beautiful, so sexy as a Domme. Because I want to be what you need, even if it's only for an hour or so. I want to pretend we're not fighting and that I can let go for a while."

There was a tension to his shoulders that told her he was still worried about it, a stiffness to the way he held himself that let her know the fight wasn't over. But if they never tried, if she didn't let him bend because she was so afraid he would break, they couldn't possibly know if it could work.

She could go easy on him. After all, this was merely a demo. She wasn't about to lead him into some crazy sexual sadism. She was teaching other club members how to safely secure their subs.

She didn't need to make him kiss her feet or to slap his ass.

She turned to the crowd. "Thank you all for your patience and thank you to all who were willing to volunteer. This lovely man will serve as my submissive this evening. Let me start by showing you how I've set up the rigging. Darling, you can kneel in the middle of the stage and wait for your turn."

His eyes tightened as though the command rankled, but he turned and took his place. Kash dropped to his knees and she began.

Four hours later, she walked through the dungeon, her mask off finally. It was funny how when she'd taken it off in the locker room, she'd barely recognized the woman looking back at her from the mirror. That woman seemed to have aged a bit, her glow dulled by regret.

She should have stayed in her room, given him more time.

The club was closed and the space quiet now. She wondered if Kash had changed and gone back to his room. He'd been quiet, too. Contemplative. During the demonstration, he'd been completely compliant, offering her nothing but his obedience, but she hadn't felt any joy from him. There had been no relaxing into the moment. He'd been an automaton, easy to use, but there had been no connection between them.

She stopped at the stage where she'd briefly had some hope. It was gone now, and she had to ask herself some hard questions.

Could she live without this the rest of her life? Could she give it up and truly be happy? Could she be happy without Kash?

"You didn't change."

She stopped, taking a deep breath because he'd startled her. She'd thought she was the last one left downstairs. "I was down in the locker room talking to Kori and her friend Sarah. I didn't have clothes down there. I changed up in my bedroom. I didn't think it would be seemly to walk around the club in nothing but a towel."

"Some people walk around here perfectly naked. I don't think anyone would mind." He was sitting on one of the spanking benches. The whole place had been cleaned by a group of efficient submissives and one or two tops who helped supervise them. Even when they were cleaning, they'd still played with the tops, offering up saucy comments that led to playful swats.

This was a place of happiness, and yet she felt so damn hollow.

"It would feel odd after-hours. There's something magical about the club when it's all lit up, something that lends itself to fantasy. Now it's back to reality." Back to figuring out what to do about their marriage. "Do you want to walk up with me? I can change and make us some tea. We should talk."

He was silent for a moment, his head hanging low. "I didn't like it, Day."

Her heart constricted. There was no anger left inside her, only a deep sense of loss. She moved toward him, putting her hands on his shoulders. "I know. I'm so sorry I put you through it. I shouldn't have. I pushed you. That's why we need to talk."

He groaned and swung his legs, jumping down from the bench. "You people talk too much. I've decided to forgive you for not talking to me about this in the first place, Day. You were right. I hate the talking."

She held her hands up. "All right. I won't mention it again, but we have to make some decisions and soon."

He stood in front of her. "What kind of decisions? Whether or not you leave me? Why do you need this so much?"

How to explain it to him? "It's a part of me."

It was a part of him, too. She was so sure of it, but it couldn't work if he never let himself be.

"I was embarrassed. I didn't like all those people watching me like that."

"Yet you don't mind having five or six sex tapes on the Internet at any given time." The words slipped from her mouth. Maybe she was still angry.

He shrugged as though none of it bothered him at all. Not the sex tapes. Not the million and one articles about his rampaging hormones. The only thing that bothered him was the one thing she needed. "The sex tapes are normal."

Frustration welled inside her. "This is normal, Kash. You use that word like it has meaning. And unless you've got the last name Kardashian or make your living off porn, I assure you having a bunch of sex tapes out in the public domain isn't something most people do."

He stared at her for a moment. "You're jealous."

She shook her head, ready to end this blasted evening. "Believe what you want to believe, Kash. I'm going to bed."

"I was embarrassed," he said quietly.

Which was exactly why this could never work. She stopped. The last week suddenly seemed so much longer than a mere seven days. "Like I said, I won't ask this of you again. I didn't ask this of you tonight. You volunteered."

"Because I was jealous."

She sighed. She'd known it at the time, known better than to allow it to continue. But the idea that he was willing to try had been far too tantalizing. "I told you I wasn't going to have sex."

He leaned against the bench. "Then what's the point? Explain it to me. I've been sitting out here for hours trying to figure it out. I don't want this, Day. I don't want a wall between us, but I can't seem to find a way around it. I tried tonight."

He had. She'd watched him struggle with it, completely unable to come up with a way to connect to him. When she'd tried stroking him, he tensed up. When she'd softened her words, she got the same response. "I know and it didn't work. It's not your fault."

She was fighting against years of ingrained belief that he couldn't be a man and show weakness. Oh, he could show drunkenness or promiscuity and still be a man. He could act like an idiot at a party, but this was forbidden. To show this kind of vulnerability was not something he could do and might never be able to accept about himself.

Was she willing to live without a piece of herself? Could she take that part of her soul and wrap it up and put it in a closet somewhere, never to be taken out again? She wasn't at all sure she could.

"I don't want you unhappy," he said quietly.

She reached for his hand. "And I don't want you unhappy."

Kash brought her hand to his chest, placing it over his heart. "Do I let you go? I don't want that, either. If we divorce, I'll be back in the position of giving up my throne. Maybe that's for the best. Maybe we should think about abolishing the crown altogether."

And give the power over to a group of men who thought women should stay in the house and not make waves? Who argued with her over whether or not girls should be educated? "Why are you questioning this? You're a good king."

"I haven't been good for five years," he said, his tone weary. He let her hand go and started to pace, his body moving with a restless energy. "I shut down after my project blew up. I told myself it was all my fault and I gave up. That's what I was thinking about tonight. I tried to clear my damn head, but I couldn't because I knew everyone was watching me."

Was that really what the problem had been? He'd never shown any issues with their play before, but then they'd always been alone. It was only when Tasha had threatened to out them that he'd flipped out and lost his damn mind.

What would one of the world's most famous men need to relax, to center himself? Would he need one thing for himself? One piece of his life that was utterly private?

"Kash, stop pacing. Sit down, for a moment, please." She eased behind him as he lowered himself to the bench, the expression on his face still and sullen. "Can you give me a few minutes? I want to try something. This isn't sexual play. This isn't me being your top. Just for a few moments, let me be your wife."

"I don't know what that means, Day."

She needed to show him. She eased the leather vest off his shoulders and put her hands there, stroking out and away, as though she could brush the tension from him. "It means whatever we need it to mean. It means that sometimes I need you to stop being the king for a while and let yourself be a man."

"I don't get to be a man. I can be a celebrity. I can be a king, but I can't be just a man."

That was where he was wrong. She started in on his shoulders, finding the pressure points and easing them. And perhaps this was where she'd gone wrong. She hadn't given him true aftercare because the scene had been so stilted and rushed. Day leaned over and kissed the back of his neck. "Who told you that?"

He breathed deeply and she could feel him starting to relax. "My father. He didn't tell me. He told Shray. He told me I could be anything I wanted because I didn't matter, though he didn't use those words, exactly. I got the gist."

She worked her way down one muscled arm and toward his hand. "I doubt he meant it like that. I know he loved you."

"Did he? Perhaps then, but I know I wasn't the one he taught to be king, and I screwed everything up."

"Because of what happened at the lab?"

He nodded slowly, but already she could see how much easier he was breathing, how he'd started to let her lead his body. "I should have been more careful. I should have known."

She massaged down his other arm. Sometimes he was like a giant tiger and he needed to be petted or he roared and roared. He needed to be eased into real intimacy because he distrusted it so. "I should have known someone would steal my car last year. I should have known that walking in that parking garage late at night would be a mistake. It's my fault he stole my purse, too."

Kash moved quickly, turning and catching her hand. His eyes were cold as ice. "Who?"

Another mistake. She leaned over and kissed his forehead. "He knocked me down and took my car. The police found it on the beach two days later. They never caught the man. Was that my fault, Kash?"

He frowned but eased up on her wrist, turning and offering his back again. Such a touchy tiger. "Of course not."

She smoothed her palms down his back, sending a shudder through him. "Should I have not driven again?"

"No. You should not have. Had we been married at the time, I would have escorted you everywhere. Your lovers were quite lazy if they did not. Nor should you have been allowed to walk alone at night, and I will ensure that you have all the bodyguards. Women, of course, fierce women who would slaughter anyone who dares to look at you."

She groaned but wrapped her arms around him. She loved him. So much. This was the Kash she adored. Why couldn't he see that he could be anything he wanted to be when they were alone? "I didn't have a lover at the time. And don't change the subject. What happened wasn't your fault, but how you reacted to it was."

He leaned back into her. "You're not the first person to point that out to me." His head rested back, bringing their cheeks together. "I don't want to think right now. I want you touching me. I want you needing me."

Longing rushed in again. How easy it was to turn the tide. "I always need you."

"Tell me what you want me to do." He whispered the words. "Tell me how to please you. I won't think anymore. I won't think about eyes being on me or my past sins. If you tell me to stop, I can do it now. We're alone."

"Are you ashamed of how I make you feel?"

He sat up straight, letting go of her hands, and she could feel the distance between them. "We should go to bed. You were right. We have to talk about this. We have to find a way to work through our differences because I need you to understand that we can't go on like this."

She wanted so badly to reach out to him, to have not ended the moment, but the thought of something sacred to her being a dirty secret for him wasn't manageable.

"Your Majesties," a deep voice said, and the bodyguard on duty stepped into the space. Wade Rycroft was a huge man with a slow Texas accent. She'd spoken to him a few times, enjoying his stories of living on a ranch with five brothers and more cattle than one could count. Now, though, his usually jovial face was set in deep lines.

Kash stood, stepping in front of her as though the man was going to hurt her somehow. Or perhaps he was embarrassed by the way she was dressed. "Yes?"

"I've been informed there's a problem back in Loa Mali," he explained. "Your mother has been hospitalized. We've got a private jet waiting to take you back."

His hand was suddenly in hers again. Though his face showed no expression at all, he tangled their fingers together. "Of course. We'll be down in a moment."

She followed him silently upstairs, wondering what the next few days would cost her husband.

Chapter Ten

Kash stood outside his mother's room, shaking his head at Simon Weston. "What exactly does that mean?"

Weston looked like he hadn't slept in a couple of days. The strain of taking over the household security, dealing with the press, and trying to find a killer had likely worn on the man. He'd probably thought this would be a cakewalk, a fun job that would be almost like a vacation.

Kash had fooled him.

"It means that I found a vial of the poison in your former guard's room. I had an anonymous tip come in that Rai's new bride had been to Australia recently."

"Her mother lives there."

"When I searched the room he used here in the palace, I found the vial."

Kash shook his head. "No. Absolutely not. Rai hates me because of something I did before he got married. Namely, his wife. He might cut my balls off if he had the chance, but he would never try to kill me. Not like that. He might do some froufrou historical duel thing because he watches far too much Masterpiece Theater, but he would never poison me."

Simon's expression didn't change a bit. "I understand that it seems convenient, but I did have him arrested. At this point he's being detained for possession of an illegal substance, but to hold him further, the police have to be able to announce the real charges. That's why he's not being held at the police station. He's in a guarded room here in the palace. I wanted to get the okay from you to go public so I can have him moved to the city jail."

He wasn't about to have his best friend slammed into a jail cell.

"No. There will be no charges. He didn't do this. Have him released immediately and let him know I want to talk to him. If I know Rai, he's got his own theories. And tell him not to punch me. It's been a long day. He can punch me later."

Actually, that wasn't a half bad idea. He was sick and tired of missing his best friend. He should allow Rai to beat the shit out of him, admit to having a tiny penis that couldn't possibly have pleasured Rai's wife, and see if they could move on.

Or he could ask Day what she thought he should do. She might be able to get him out of a beating. He didn't really care what anyone except her thought of his penis. Only Dayita needed to know it was a glorious beast that brought pleasure to its queen.

"Kash, as your acting head of security, I have to tell you that this is a mistake," Weston began.

"No, tossing Rai in jail when it's obvious he's been set up is a mistake," Kash shot back.

"Or we're making the real culprit feel like he's gotten away with something and giving ourselves some time to figure this out."

And allow Rai to hate him even more? "No. I want him released within the hour."

Weston's jaw tightened. "This is a mistake."

"It's my mistake. I won't allow him to rot in jail for something I know he hasn't done. Look in other places. CCTV showed nothing?"

"We believe the Scotch was brought in with the poison already inside."

"Then whoever this is has his conspirators. It's someone familiar with how the household is run, but not familiar with my habits."

Weston seemed to stop, as though that statement brought on some new idea. "Yes, you're right. Your own men would have known that Jamil typically joins you for a drink. They would have known he could potentially ruin everything. I see what you're saying. I have an idea."

"As long as your idea gets Rai out of his hellhole prison." One day Rai would forgive him for deflowering his bride—before she was his bride. But there would be no forgiveness if Rai himself was deflowered by some rough and tumble prison love.

"I'm calling now. And I'll set up a meeting that might be interesting." He pulled out his phone. "And Kash, she's not as bad as your lord chamberlain made her sound. I'm sorry for that. He told me she was on death's door, but the doctors claim she could be back on her feet in a few days if she'll rest. She's responding to the medication well. She's quite the survivor, your mother."

Hanin had always been a drama queen.

Kash shook Weston's hand and nodded to Michael Malone, who was standing guard outside his mother's room. He was relieved that she was better than he'd expected, but he'd seen her asleep in her bed, looking so pale and fragile.

He closed the door behind him. His mother was still sleeping and he didn't want to disturb her. Like Day was sleeping. He'd carried her out of the car and up to his room. He wasn't sure why, but he'd passed her own room by completely, choosing to settle her into his bed.

The two women who meant the most to him were sleeping and he couldn't. He was restless and wanting, and he wasn't even sure what he wanted.

Kash stared out the window of his mother's room, the slow sound of the monitors forming an odd rhythm. Each beep was another second of life, another breath, one more heartbeat. How many beeps would his mother get?

He stared out over the beach where he'd played as a young child, where he and his brother had built sandcastles and then pretended they were monsters destroying grand cities. And their mother would laugh at their antics. His father would usually be at some meeting or other. After Shray was old enough, it had been only Kash and his mother playing on the beach.

He'd run from that life, a pendulum swinging as far from his father's regimented existence as he could. As though he had to choose. The king or the playboy. Nothing else. Nothing in between. No compromises. He had to be a king like his father or a rogue so full of himself he never, ever cared about criticism.

Did he have to be one or the other, or could he find his own path, one informed by his father's love but free of his prejudices? One where he could be both king and man. Both sovereign and husband.

"What do you see when you look out there, son?"

He turned and moved to her bed, sinking to one knee in front of her. "Should I call the doctor?"

She shook her head. "No, I'm fine. I'm feeling better. I caught a terrible cold. It settled into my chest, but I'm breathing better now."

And any secondary infection would be made worse by the cancer. She would be weak and unable to fight off something Kash could easily handle.

"What do you see? While you've been gone, I've been thinking so much about your childhood. I wonder how you see it when you look back. Everyone asks you questions. I try not to bother you with them because I know how often you're surrounded by reporters and advisors and politicians, but I need to know. I worry we don't see the same things."

He glanced back toward the window. What did he see? He saw sand and sun and rolling waves. He saw ghosts. "I see the beach where I played with Shray when I was young. I see the beach where you would take me to play long after Father took Shray under his wing to teach him."

His mother frowned. "To teach him?"

"To be king. When Shray was a teenager, Father told him he couldn't play with me at the beach anymore. He had to be better than me because he was going to be king. Father never came to the beach. He never played."

His mother's eyes softened, a sheen of tears forming. "Oh, my darling, how can you say that? Your father played with you many times when you were young. Look through the pictures I keep. Go and get them. They're in a box in the bottom of the dresser."

He started to argue with her, that she needed rest, but he could see how desperate she was so he strode to her dresser like a dutiful son. He needed to smile and tell her everything was all right because she was sick and his own misery would only bring more to her. He needed to agree that his childhood was beautiful and everything was perfect.

He'd seen the pictures of his childhood. They were mostly taken by state photographers and again, they'd been interested in Shray. Kash hadn't minded because the thought of sitting still had been mind-numbing at the time. He opened the bottom drawer and found a metal box. He pulled it out and turned back to his mother.

He rushed back because she was struggling to sit up. "Mother, stop."

She frowned up at him. "I will stop when I am dead, and as that might be soon, you will leave me to make the decisions. There's a proper queen now. I can become the old bat who says and does whatever she likes. You see, you thought I brought in Dayita for you, but it was really for me. Where is she?"

"She was exhausted. She didn't sleep at all on the plane. I put her in bed about an hour ago." Likely because she was worried about everything, because he was giving her hell and causing her to question their marriage because he couldn't bring himself to bend even a little.

Are you ashamed of how I make you feel?

He could still hear the question, hear the small tremor in her voice. Day was always so steady, so strong, and yet in that moment, she'd sounded small.

He'd made her small.

His mother shifted on the bed, leaving a space for him. "Good, she needs her rest. Now come and let me show you. It's easy to forget, you know."

He sat down next to her. "Forget what?"

"That the truth of our lives changes given our perceptions. That time and experience can make things hazy. You weren't in a good place with your father when he died. I think that colored everything about your relationship with him. I can't let that go on, Kashmir."

He huffed, forgetting for a moment that he'd promised to be good. "So you think some photos you kept will change my perception of my childhood?"

"This isn't my box, love. This was your father's. This was precious to him."

Kash looked down at the rather plain metal box. It was the kind of thing people kept important papers in, sturdy and weatherproof. It had a piece of tape on the top with a single word written in neat, masculine script.

Kashmir.

He touched the box. "Why would he have a box with my name on it?"

"Open it and find out," she urged. "After he died, I found both of your boxes, yours and Shray's. For a long time it was hard for me to think about Shray's, but recently, I've enjoyed going through it and remembering how close our family was. This is what you've forgotten, what you have to remember before you have children of your own. He loved you."

He hated the fine tremble to his hand as he opened the box.

Inside he found a mass of photos, but not the kind taken by the press. These were personal pictures taken by an amateur hand, pictures of himself and Shray smiling in the surf, their faces splashed with the waves, of himself as a giggling baby held in his mother's arms, of his toddler self hiding beneath his father's ornate desk. In that photo he was grinning ear to ear and reaching up to whoever was taking the photo. This wasn't the picture of a child afraid to interrupt his father's work. This child knew he was the center of the world.

He took a deep breath, the sweetness of his childhood washing over him. Had he forgotten? He'd run through the palace like a little monster, and eventually he would be scooped up in strong arms and tossed into the air, giggling and begging for more.

He could feel it, feel how he'd flown up, the thrill rushing through him. He'd put his arms out and tried to fly, and never once had he thought about falling because his father was there to catch him.

His father. He would scoop him up and take him to the kitchens for coconut ice cream.

"Why did he stop coming to the beach with us? Why did he take Shray and forget about me?" Though it was easy to see he hadn't really. While the pictures seemed to stop around the time he was thirteen or fourteen, they were replaced with newspaper articles and report cards. There was a birthday card Kash had made tucked inside.

His mother's hand came out, so frail and delicate on his own. "When you were almost fourteen, your father was diagnosed with Parkinson's disease. He was taking some medication that made it unwise for him to spend too much time in the sun."

Kash felt like the world had shifted. "What? Father had Parkinson's?"

His mother nodded. "Yes. In the beginning he worried he would die very soon or be incapacitated. He needed to get Shray ready. He didn't want you to worry. He wanted you to enjoy your childhood. He always told me that he was lucky you were his second son and not his first."

"Because he thought I would be a terrible king."

"No, because you were so smart, so brilliant when it came to science. He was so proud of you. He said a mind like yours shouldn't be wasted on politics. He said a mind like yours could change the world, and that was so much more important than being a king." Her hand gripped his, holding him. "He was worried during those years. He thought if the parliament found out about his diagnosis, they might seek to abolish the monarchy on the grounds that his heirs were too young. I remember he would remind himself that a king must be strong."

He couldn't help it a moment longer. The world was a blurry place and yet he finally understood. His father hadn't been talking about him. Or perhaps at times he had been. Perhaps it didn't matter that his father had been a king. All that had mattered was he'd been an obnoxious teen, and they would have clashed no matter what.

What mattered was that his father had loved him, that his father had believed in him, that his father had been more than a king. He'd been a man.

A man with flaws and fears.

A man with love and regrets.

A man who could love his wife and children and make mistakes. He could follow in his father's footsteps and have a life filled with loved ones, with a woman who knew him as more than a king. A woman who loved him because he was her husband.

And maybe, just maybe, if Kash was brave enough, he could be a man who changed the world.

He leaned into his mother, holding her gently. "I'm sorry for staying away for so long. I'm sorry I didn't remember."

"He wouldn't let you see. I argued that he should tell you," she whispered. "But he wanted you to have as normal a life as you could. He saw how it aged your brother. He couldn't do it to you. And I was so lost after he died that I kept his secrets. You should know that I left you a letter detailing all of this in case I died. You have to know that the illness might be hereditary, though the likelihood is still low. You'll have to watch your health carefully as you get older. Your father was significantly older than me. He was sixty when he was diagnosed."

"Hush, we don't have to talk about that now." He wasn't going to worry about something that might or might not happen. He needed to focus on the now. Every family had something in their medical histories to worry about.

His mother looked up at him. "I don't want us to end the same way, with you angry with me. I made these mistakes, but I love you. I love you and I ask you to forgive me."

He shook his head. "There is nothing to forgive. Nothing, Mother. I love you. And things will be different now because I love my wife. I think I've always loved her but I was afraid to show it. I'm not going to be afraid anymore."

He made the choices. And if anyone found out that he liked to submit to his gorgeous, dominant wife, well, they could go to hell because they didn't understand what a woman like Day could do to a man.

No one got a say in his marriage except him and his wife.

He held his mother, the truth of his life sinking in and finally filling a place that had seemed hollow. "I don't want you to die. I command that you not die."

His mother smiled up at him. "Give me something to live for. You know I'll hold on for a grandchild."

He sighed.

"What is it?"

"I've screwed up so much with Day, I fear she won't forgive me, Mother."

Her hand slid over his. "Tell me."

He grimaced. "Much of it is sexual, Mother."

"Well, of course it is. It's you. You know, Kashmir, the one thing I thought you would get right was the sex stuff."

"Well, didn't I prove you wrong?" Perhaps his mother could help. She'd already given him the perfect woman. Now it was up to him to figure out how to keep her. "I think I've messed up with Day."

"Of course you have. You're a man. You can't help yourself. Tell me what's going on."

According to Day, it wasn't like she didn't already know. He was about to tell her everything when there was a loud shout from the hallway.

Startled, he slid from the bed. "Wait here, Mother. I'll be right back."

"Kash, you fucking bastard!"

That was a familiar voice. Weston had gotten Rai out quickly. Kash stepped out into the hallway where Rai was straining against the much larger Boomer. It was good to see Rai couldn't do everything. His best friend often seemed far too competent to be believed, too fit and perfect. Now he looked silly because Mr. Boomer had put a hand on his head and easily held him at arm's length.

"Uh, he wanted to go in without an appointment," Boomer said. If holding back the other man was any strain on him at all, it didn't show. "Si told me no one sees the queen momma without an appointment. Now, he didn't leave me an appointment book or anything, so I think what he was trying to tell me was that the queen momma needs her sleep and no one should see her except her son. I don't think he's her son."

While he found Mr. Boomer quite charming, he didn't want to piss off Rai any further. "It's fine. Please let him go so we can handle this here and now. And, Mr. Boomer, if he does hit me, let him. Unless he goes for my face. My face really belongs to the whole country, so you need to protect that."

Boomer moved his hand and Rai nearly fell to his knees.

"Damn you, Kash," he began.

"I would have thought letting you out of jail because I know, despite all evidence, that you would never harm me might put you in a better mood."

Rai shook his head. "Not mad at you. Need to tell you. It was never you he was after. I figured it all out a few minutes ago. It's Hanin. He wants to kill Day. He was always after Day."

Fear flashed through Kash and he took off running for his

room.

Nothing mattered if Day wasn't alive. Nothing at all.

* * * *

Day came awake to the sound of a door creaking open. She sat up, her head still cloudy from sleep. She glanced at the clock, the digital light shining, and realized her head was actually cloudy from lack of sleep. She remembered falling asleep in the car after the plane had landed. That had been a little over an hour and a half before.

She glanced around and realized she wasn't in her room. Her suite was done up in light, airy colors, and this place was a darkened tomb.

Kash's room. Had he brought her here? She suspected so.

She yawned and forced her body to move. Something was going on in the outer room of the suite.

She sat straight up in bed as her brain started to function, remembering exactly why they'd made that ridiculously long flight.

Her mother-in-law. Her sweet, lovely mother-in-law had taken a bad turn and they'd needed to get home in time to potentially say good-bye to her.

Day's heart constricted. How would Kash handle losing his mother? He tended to shut down when things got too emotional. He'd been alone for so long and here she was sleeping while he was facing one of the hardest moments of his life.

Some partner she'd turned out to be.

She scrambled to get out of bed. How far was it to the hospital?

She moved to the doors that led to the outer rooms of the suite, opening them and finding the cause of the noise she'd heard previously. A group of neatly dressed servants were busy setting breakfast up on the table in the living area. It was the table where she and Kash typically shared their morning. Michael Malone stood inside the door, dressed in an all-black suit, an earpiece in his left ear. He nodded her way.

So she had her guard back. They'd been much more subtle at Sanctum. She'd barely seen them, though she'd known they were there. Now that she was home, there would always be a guard on her door.

How much longer would she be here at the palace? How much longer would she have this family?

"Coffee, Your Majesty?" one of the maids asked.

Day sought her name. She was trying to learn them all because they were important to the family and needed to know they weren't mere cogs in the wheel. "Elissa, yes, please, but could you put it in a cup to go? I need to get to the hospital as quickly as possible."

"Why would you need to go to the hospital?" The lord chamberlain walked into the room, looking resplendent in his three-piece suit. "Is your majesty ill?"

She shook her head because all the servants had stopped as though the thought of her being sick was beyond what they could handle. "No. I'm fine. I need to go and see the queen mother. I assume that's where my husband is. I need to go and be with him. Can someone update me on how she's doing?"

Hanin shook his head, his eyes on her. "Now, now, Your Majesty. I can update you. You know how I adore the queen mother. I've worked for her and her family all of my life. I apparently overreacted. I was in a panic when I contacted the Americans to bring his majesty home to see her. I'm so sorry. At the time I truly thought she could die on us."

"And now?"

He moved across the room, picking up the silver server and pouring her coffee with an expert hand. "She's recovering in her room. Queen Yasmine is one of the strongest women I know. It's from her breeding, you know. She comes from a good family. That's important."

Relief spilled through her. The thought of losing Yasmine had nearly crushed her, and what it would have done to Kash… She didn't want to think on it. "I'm glad she's all right. Is my husband with her?"

"Of course." Hanin brought the delicate china cup to her. "Have something to eat, Your Majesty. When I saw them last, they were having a lovely conversation. There's nothing at all for you to worry about. After you've had some fortification, I'll take you down to her room myself."

Her hands were shaking. How long had it been since she'd eaten? She walked over to the table and set the coffee cup and its saucer down. Her stomach was a little touchy. Perhaps pouring acidic coffee on it first thing wasn't the best play.

"Elissa, do we have any tea? I think coffee might upset my stomach today. And perhaps some toast. All this looks lovely, but I need something simple. It was a long flight and I think all the stress is wearing on me."

Elissa nodded. "Of course, Your Majesty. The lord chamberlain didn't order tea for you, but I can pop down to the kitchen and be back in no time at all."

"Thank you." She glanced up to see Hanin frowning. Naturally she'd upset him. The lord chamberlain seemed to take offense easily. Kash had talked about pensioning the older man off when his mother was no longer with them, and Day was starting to agree with him. It was obvious the man had deep ties to Yasmine, but he didn't seem to like the younger royals much. When the time came, she intended to ask Chapal's husband, Ben, to take the role. He would have the palace running in a proper and modern fashion. Until then, she needed to get along with Hanin. "Thank you so much for the update and for this lovely spread. It's all beautiful, but it's too much for me this morning. I'll have a spot of tea and go join my husband."

They'd barely talked on the plane. Kash had sat in his seat, a beer in one hand, while he'd stared out at the night sky even as it had turned into day. She'd tried to sleep, but couldn't stop thinking about what had happened.

Was he ashamed? She couldn't overcome shame. She could handle him being shy, needing to go slow. She couldn't handle being his dirty secret.

"Your Majesty?"

She glanced up and Hanin was still standing in the room. The other servants had all gone, but he had stayed behind. "Yes?"

He glanced back to where Malone stood. "Might I speak to you privately, Your Majesty? It's palace business and I'm afraid it can't wait."

She couldn't think of what he needed from her that her guard couldn't hear, but she wasn't going to argue with him. He ran the palace and there were certainly plenty of secrets to be kept. She nodded. With her mother-in-law out of commission, she was in charge. "Of course. Mr. Malone, would you mind?"

"I'll be right outside. I'll knock when Elissa gets back and after you've eaten, I'll escort you to Queen Yasmine. She asked about you earlier." He stepped out and closed the door behind him.

"Are you sure you won't have some coffee? I can get you some cream and sugar, if you like," Hanin said, his hand on the ornate silver pot.

She shook her head. Tea sounded so much better. "No, but thank you."

"You don't mind if I pour some for myself, do you?" He was already reaching out for another cup.

"Feel free. Now, what is the problem, Hanin?"

He was silent while he poured the steaming hot coffee. When he turned around there was a frown on his face. "The problem is one of perception. I'm worried that when certain stories come out, and they will eventually, your past will bring down the royal family."

She stilled because the whole room seemed to chill. "What are you talking about?"

"Do you think Kashmir's whore of a girlfriend is the only one who knows about your past?" Hanin asked, his tone dark and nasty. "I have been the queen's right hand for years. I helped her investigate you."

"And I assume you disapproved."

"Of course I did. You're common. Worse than that, you're not even a proper female. You argue with your betters."

"My betters being men, I suppose." Oh, her mother-in-law was going to be disappointed, but Hanin was leaving the palace today. He would not be allowed back, but she was interested in seeing how far he would go.

"I'm sick of this generation of women not knowing their place. The queen has always known. She didn't argue with her husband or her son, and her son is an idiot."

"I assure you the queen had control. She might have done it in a sneaky way, but Queen Yasmine did not sit back and allow the men around her to run things. She simply didn't take credit for her work. My generation doesn't have to dissemble." She stood up.

Maybe she wasn't so curious. She was ready to go and be with her family.

She was ready to start the fight for Kash's heart because he was worth it, and she needed to tell him that. In plain English. Hanin was right about one thing. Her husband could be an idiot at times. Especially when it came to his own emotions.

"Your generation will bring down this monarchy with your disgusting need to expose yourselves, your every emotion, your wants and needs," Hanin continued. "No one cares about them. Society can't work when everyone is an individual. Can't you see that? We need the crown and the crown needs true royalty."

She held up a hand. "You're dismissed, Hanin. I don't want to see you here again."

He gripped the coffee cup like it was a lifeline. "You can't do that. You can't fire me."

"I can and I did. My husband will back me up, and once my mother-in-law has heard how you've spoken to me, she'll be on my side as well."

"The queen won't believe you."

Day gestured up to the camera that covered the living room. "She'll see you. She might not hear things, but there's no doubt you're being less than gracious right now."

His mouth turned up in a nasty smirk. "Oh, but I cut that camera out of the feed. With all the new security, it was easy to explain that the king wanted more privacy. No one questioned it. So we really are alone right now, dear, and I truly wish you'd tried the coffee."

That chill she'd felt before went positively arctic as Day glanced down at her own cup. "You poisoned the Scotch."

"I was watching the ballroom and I saw when Tasha hauled Kashmir off. I saw when you strode in and made a spectacle of yourself. I'd been watching for days and knew you liked to play the man. I knew you had a glass of Scotch with the king. So when he sent you up, I sent up Jamil with the special Scotch I'd had prepared. I knew you would get there first, and like the weak slut you are, you would need that drink. You almost took it. I almost had you."

She'd come so close to falling into that trap. "You could have killed Kash."

"It was a risk I was willing to take, but I planned to rush in and save him. Then we could have found a proper bride." He stared down at the cup in his hand. "I didn't know Jamil was a thief."

"He wasn't a thief. He was the king's friend." She started to back up, trying to put some distance between her and the man who'd tried to murder her only a week before.

"The king must be taught that he is above us all. He can't be friends with the help. He must be the king, exalted and revered. That's what we're missing. I believe a bride, a pure royal bride, could teach him this. Or at least she could have his child and we could start over again."

How long had Hanin been planning this? The idea chilled Day to the bone. "You advised the queen to arrange the marriage."

"Yes, but then she wouldn't listen to me when it came to selecting a bride. She'd found those letters you sent and decided it had to be you. She couldn't see you for the whore you are. Even after she knew about your sexual perversions, she couldn't understand that you were wrong."

Because the queen mother understood that a person was complex and that sexual differences didn't mean anything as long as a man and woman were in love.

She loved Kash. They could work it out. They just had to believe they could. They could get through anything as long as they held on to each other and promised to never let go. That was how a couple in love got through life. They simply held on.

"I'm going to leave now, Hanin. You should probably run." Would Malone hear her if she shouted out? The door was thick and the walls well insulated. How many steps before she could put a hand on the door and throw it open? Her guard would be there.

She backed up, slowly, unwilling to take her eyes off the snake in the room.

That snake slowly reached into his pocket and pulled out a gun. It was a shiny revolver. "Run? Why would I run? This is my home. It has been for as long as I can remember. Don't move another inch, Your Majesty, or I'll be forced to put a bullet in you. I don't want to. It could make for a much more salacious story for the tabloids."

She froze because there was nowhere to duck, nothing to hide behind unless she could get to the entryway. There were two columns on either side of the door that might offer her some protection. "I'm not going to drink your poison, Hanin. You're crazy if you think I'm going to do your work for you."

"So you're willing to let me kill Elissa when she returns? When that door opens, I intend to shoot whoever is standing there. I'll know my game is up. I'll shoot her and then you. I'm willing to die for my cause. I've served this crown with everything I have. I'll give my life to protect it. I will not allow a whore queen to take it all away from me."

He also wasn't as strong as he thought he was. Already she could see his hand shaking. Elissa would be back any moment, but she couldn't let that fact push her into obedience. She didn't want Elissa to get shot, but she wasn't about to help her would-be murderer.

Of course, he couldn't know that. He was crazy. He could likely be led to believe any number of things.

"You'll have to bring it to me. Bring me the cup you made for yourself."

He stared at her, his eyes narrowed. "Drink the one I made for you. They'll both work. It's right there. Hurry. Elissa isn't slow. She's good at her job. She'll hurry because she wants to please her queen. She's young and can't see you for what you truly are."

Which apparently was a whore. Very original of him. "I'm too scared. What if you shoot me? I can't. I can't think."

Better to let him believe she was far more scared than she was. It was odd, but the fear seemed to be in the background, as though she'd moved into survival mode and nothing else mattered.

Unless Kash was the one who walked through that door. If Kash took the bullet, she would want her own. She would want to curl up and go wherever he was. He would need her.

Hanin stood there, his hands starting to shake, and she wondered how much of Hanin was really there. "You ruined everything. Everything."

The cup in his left hand started to rattle and she saw her chance. She sprinted for the door. He might shoot her, but it was better to have the chance. The minute that shot rang out, Malone would come in.

Day screamed as she dove for the pillar.

The door blasted open and she caught sight of the one thing she hadn't wanted to see. Kash rushed in, his big body a massive target. He caught her in his arms and shoved her behind him. Rai was there along with Malone, all three men running into the room.

"Stand down!" Malone ordered.

"Hanin, you're caught," Rai explained. "Put the gun down."

The gun clattered to the floor. "It wasn't loaded. I couldn't risk hurting the king."

Kash still stood in front of her. "But you would kill my queen?"

The cup and saucer rattled, the sound jarring. Day had to peek around her husband to get a look at Hanin.

Hanin's eyes were wild as he spoke. "She's unfit to be queen. She isn't royal."

"She's my wife. She's royal now," Kash returned.

"And when they all find out what she does?" Hanin spewed his bile. "How she dominates men? Does she do these things to you, Your Majesty? Is that how she caught you? You're in her web."

Day's stomach tightened. It was the one thing Kash couldn't handle. Someone knowing.

Rai and Malone had heard that accusation. It could kill Kash.

"Let her go," Hanin insisted. "No one will follow her, Your Majesty."

"That's where you're wrong," Kash replied. "She already has one devoted servant. She has me. I'll see you hanged for this."

"No need." A hollow look hit Hanin's face. "This isn't my home anymore. This isn't my world anymore."

He brought the cup to his lips.

Day started to yell out, but Kash turned and caught her, his arms going around her. Even as he started to haul her out the door, she could see Hanin falling.

Kash rushed her out, taking her from the sight. He strode to her room, opening the doors and charging in. He turned briefly and yelled down the hall at his guard. "If that wasn't poison he drank, Rai, let me know so I can kill him myself."

"He's quite dead, Kash," Rai replied as he followed. "Malone is calling it in and staying with the body. Who could have guessed snails would be so poisonous? It's how I figured out it was him. He has a cousin who works at a lab in Western Australia."

Kash set her down. "And how did you know it was Day he wanted to kill and not me?"

"Because I heard him talk about how she would ruin the crown," Rai replied. "I thought it was idle gossip until I put together he was the one who had poisoned the Scotch. He was in the booth with me that night. He watched you send her away. We all heard that conversation."

Then the guards knew? Her hands were shaking.

Rai reached for one of them, pulling it up. "Your Majesty, you should know that the guards all take an oath of silence when it comes to the family we protect. You should also know that I've long believed Kashmir needed a woman who could spank his ass silly, and I'm glad to hear he found one. Not a one of my men sees you as anything less than the queen and Kashmir as anything but one incredibly lucky man. Well, they do worry that our lovely and intelligent queen has been strapped with such an ignorant ass for her husband."

Kash was standing beside her, looking down at her hand. "Thank you, Rai. Thank you for wanting to save her."

Rai kissed her hand and then let it go, turning back to Kash. "Of course I wanted to save her. You, on the other hand, I would have let drink all the snail venom in the world. I hate you."

Kash was grinning. "But you'll come back to your job."

Rai was already moving for the door. "Yes. I'll return to work but only because I love my wife and this pays better than anywhere else."

"Rai, I'm glad to have you home."

He stopped at the door, not looking back. "And I'm glad to have a friend who believed in me even when all the evidence was against me. Even when I behaved like an ass. Stay here. I'll post a guard on the door, but I don't think we can keep this out of the press. I'll try, but two bodies in a week is a lot to cover up."

The door closed behind him and Kash wrapped his arms around her. He hugged her close. "I'm so sorry."

She held on to him and hoped this wasn't the end.

Chapter Eleven

Hours and hours later, Day closed the door to her room with the full knowledge that none of this was over. Hanin was dead, but there was still such distance between her and Kash. Who would have guessed that the attempt on her life would have been the highlight of her day? Now she had to sit down with Kash and figure out what to do with the rest of their lives, with their marriage.

She looked back into the room. He was sitting on the couch in her sitting area, staring into space. Her bed was not more than ten feet away. How lovely would it be to sink into her comfy mattress and drift off to sleep?

Perhaps they should put this whole conversation off. The day had been tiring. "I think I should go to bed."

He didn't look her way. "No. We should talk. We can talk here. There are no cameras. We can't go back to my room. They're still working in there. In the morning the press will be swarming and we'll have to admit to everything. We'll also have to announce that Mother is ill. Tomorrow will be a long day."

"All the more reason to get some sleep." And to put off the moment where they would have to decide whether to even try to make this marriage work.

"Day, I can't go on like this. I want this over and done with tonight. I want to walk into that press conference tomorrow knowing I don't have anything further to announce. I want my world peaceful again."

Wow. That felt like a kick in the gut. One little demo and an assassination attempt and he was ready to blow up the marriage. Still, he was the one who'd been forced into it. She couldn't hold him to a marriage he hadn't truly wanted in the first place. "I understand."

It was going to be a much longer night than she'd planned. They would have to draft a statement and figure out how to deal with the constitutional crisis dissolving their marriage would trigger, but perhaps it was for the best. She wasn't sure she could stay married to him if they weren't going to try to have an honest marriage.

She was in love with him.

"I don't think you do understand, and that's what we need to talk about," Kash replied. "I've figured out what went wrong with the demonstration the other night at Sanctum. We can't go to clubs. It doesn't feel right. I'm not an exhibitionist. At least I'm not now."

What was he talking about? "Kashmir, I'm sorry you didn't enjoy the demonstration. I wish you had, but at least we know."

He stood up, gracefully moving toward her. He'd been stiff for hours and still seemed anxious. He shrugged out of his jacket and kicked off the loafers he'd been wearing, getting more comfortable. "Yes, we know that I don't like the thought of other people seeing me like that, but I have some reasons why I feel that way, why I might never be comfortable sharing that. I know there's nothing shameful about it, but I'm not there yet. I might never get there. I have to know if you need the crowd."

She wasn't sure what he was talking about. "The crowd?"

He moved to her closet, disappearing briefly inside. Kash walked out carrying a small leather bag and she winced.

Her kit. Not that it was actually her kit. That was packed away in the deep recess of a storage closet, along with most of her belongings from before her marriage. The brown leather satchel was the one Kori had put together for her back in Dallas. It was nothing more than a few hanks of jute rope, a paddle, some binder clips, and impact toys.

He walked over to her four-poster bed, setting the bag down. "Yes, the crowd. Do you require the crowd to fill your needs or is this something you'll be happy doing alone with me?"

Hope lit inside her, a tiny flame praying to be stoked. "Kash, what are you saying? I need you to be plain."

He turned to her, the look on his face so serious. "I know I didn't please you that night. I thought about it all the way home, trying to find some excuse. There isn't one. There's merely a preference. Let me try again. Let me try while no one is watching. Everyone watches me. Every minute of the day. I play into it. I use it to my advantage. But while I was with you that night, I hated that other people were watching. For the first time in my life, I truly needed something that was private, something that belongs only to me."

"I don't need the crowd. I don't need it at all." She needed him. Only him. If he could need her, that would be all the fulfillment she would require. He was telling her he was willing to try. Another need rose, hard and fast and nearly volcanic. She'd tamped it down before and maybe for the same reasons. Maybe because she was evolving. "Take off your clothes, Kash. I want to see you naked. No one's here except the guards, and they won't leave their stations. It's you and me and I want to play."

"Ah, there she is. Do you know when you lower your voice like that, I can feel it in my cock, Day?" His fingers were on the buckle of his belt, working it free. He shoved his slacks and boxers off his hips, freeing his cock. His shirt hit the floor an instant later.

His cock obviously liked her Domme voice. It stood tall and proud, almost coming up to his naval. He didn't have any problems with exhibitionism now. A thrill sparked along her spine. There was no playing now. No candy coating. No gentle easing in. He knew what she wanted. He knew she was the top and he'd done as she'd asked. The question now was how far could she push him? How much control could she get him to give into her hands?

"Was it only the crowd you didn't like, Kashmir?"

He stilled as she moved around him. "Yes. It made it hard for me to relax. It's been a rough time. I need you to help me be out of my head for a while. I want to be alone with you. I don't want to share you."

Given how often he'd shared lovers, she was taking that as a win. "There's no sharing now. You're all mine and I want complete and total submission from you. Can you give me that?"

"I don't know. I have to figure out what I can and can't give," he said, his eyes down.

She could handle that. That was exactly the point. "All you have to do is tell me no. If you say no, I stop everything and we go back to the start and there are no recriminations. I want to try this with you but I need you to understand that if it doesn't work, I'll choose you."

His eyes were suddenly on hers. "You would give this up?"

She'd thought about it for a long time. What was the scale on this question? How did it balance out? She knew what Kash's issues were and they ran deep, childhood deep. They were ingrained in his personality. Was she willing to give him up over what was only one piece of their relationship? She'd lost him to his responsibilities before. Could she do it again?

"I would give this up if you need me to. If this is a choice between you and having this in my life, I'll choose you."

His shoulders relaxed, that tense look around his eyes softening in an instant. His hand came out, brushing against her cheek. "I will never ask you to, love. I'm sorry I acted the way I did. If I can't give you what you need, we'll make accommodations, but I think you'll find I can learn over time."

"You haven't learned much if you think this is how you greet your Mistress." She gave him her best stare, the one that was sure to have every sub in a mile radius dropping to his or her knees.

Kash's lips turned up and he gracefully fell to the floor. "Not Mistress. I don't like the term."

So he was already attempting to push her buttons. "You think this is about you then?"

"I know this is about me." Confidence rolled off him. "I control this. This might be the one thing in the world I truly control. Everything is responsibility and politics, and those offer only the illusions of control. It's what I thought about while I was hanging in suspension that night. I thought about the fact that my life is a series of choices that are forced on me. This isn't forced. This is offered. I can take it or leave it and the world won't come to an end. No one goes hungry because I made this choice."

It was precisely why so many powerful men and women chose this way to play. They did it because their actions affected so many in the real world. They could choose to be a bit selfish for a few hours, to let go and allow themselves to relax and hide away for a while. To let that part of them that needed to be soft and submissive have some sway.

She opened the kit and picked up the crop Kori had purchased at her behest. It was a nice one, flexible with a soft leather tip. She could control it, her strength and the angle of impact determining how much pain she inflicted. Of course, it could also be a tool. She slapped it against her hand, bringing Kash's eyes up to hers.

"Spread your knees wide." She let the soft tip of the crop find his belly, running it up and over his muscled abs and perfect chest, all the way up to his chiseled chin. "Spine straight. Now tell me what you think you should call me, if not Mistress. This is my fantasy, too. If you want to spend some time being worshipped and adored, then I want to feel powerful. Needed. I want to spend a few hours being someone more than merely Dayita."

"You are always powerful," he whispered. "Always. You don't need a crown on your head to be a queen. That's who you are. You are my Queen and I do want to worship you. Show me how powerful you are, Your Majesty. Show this lowly servant what a queen is."

Every word that dripped from his mouth seemed to race through her veins, lifting her up and taking her higher. She looked down at her "lowly" servant, taking in every inch of his gorgeous flesh. She took her time, inspecting him carefully. She let her hands run through his raven dark hair. He kept it long and it had a natural wave to it. She tugged on it, pulling it to the point that he would feel the sizzle along his scalp. A shudder went through him and she watched his cock twitch.

Yes, that was what she wanted to see.

"Did you like it when I tied you up?"

His head was back, giving over to her hold. His eyes were on hers, as though he couldn't look anywhere but exactly where she wanted him. "Yes, but I couldn't relax because everyone was watching me."

She should have thought of that, should have realized that Kash tended to overcompensate for his flaws, for his fears. He would smile and play the fool in the press because he didn't think there was a way out. Every lover he'd taken before had been with him for the purpose of being seen. This was a chance to have something secret, something that belonged only to the two of them.

"Then I should reward you for being such a good servant. You did so well. You let me show our friends exactly the techniques I wanted to show them. I thank you for that and I honor you."

"What would you have done if I didn't mind being seen like that?" Kash asked.

"Like I've told you, I didn't have sex with most of the people I topped."

"But if I had merely been a submissive coming to the glorious Mistress Day, if I had been some random man who needed a bit of play, who let you tie me up and suspend me off the ground, what would you have done?"

He wanted to be different. Of course, he was, but he needed the words. He wanted some dirty, filthy fantasy? She could give him that.

"If you had walked into my dungeon, all of my rules would have flown out the door. I would have looked at you and known that you were everything I had been waiting for. I would have tied you up. I would have used my ropes to bind your arms and legs. They would cling to your body and you would feel them as an extension of myself, of my will. You would feel me all around you." She sighed and moved on, letting the crop trace the line of his spine as she continued. "You would be wound up tight and then I would suspend you. You wouldn't be able to fight me or to do anything at all but take what I give you. I can give you pleasure or pain and it's all my choice. You would swing in my trap, your body both heavy and light at the same time. You would be secure. You would know I would never, ever let anything harm you, that I would work my hardest to ensure your safety so you could enjoy the ride. Did I say I would wrap my rope everywhere? Because there would be one place I left untouched, open and vulnerable." She completed her circle, moving in front of him again. "Can you guess which part of you I would have left out? Which delicious piece would be dangling like ripe fruit for me to enjoy? Can you show me?"

His body had tightened, but not in a bad way. He reached down and gripped his own dick, stroking himself with a rough hand. "This part."

She slapped the tip of the crop over his hand, a gentle sting which had him releasing himself. "No touching what belongs to me. You're my servant and that means your cock is mine, a treasure of the royals like my crown or my scepter. You wouldn't like what happens to thieves."

Or he would, because it would lead to an insanely pleasurable round of torture.

The hint of a smile crossed his face before he schooled himself again. "No, Your Majesty. I wouldn't want to find out what happens to thieves. I apologize. Please continue your story. It was just getting good."

"I would suspend you so you were looking down, so you could see me moving underneath you. Did you like my rig?"

"It was perfect. I did love how you used science and engineering to such kinky ends. Our professors at Oxford would approve."

Likely not, but she had used their methods. "With my machine, I can move you easily up or down, and I would move you into the perfect position where I could touch your cock. Like I said, it's ripe fruit and I would pick it. You would be utterly helpless while I played with your cock."

She reached down, gripping him as he'd touched himself. Kash liked it rough. A growl went through him, but he managed to stay in his position. She eased down on her knees in front of him, holding that magnificent cock in her hand.

"You're going to kill me," he whispered, his jaw tight.

No. Just torture him a bit. "It's my right to play with you however I see fit. Rigging you up without someone around to help me if something went wrong would be unwise and would put my precious servant in potential danger, so I can't do that tonight. But I can give you a little taste of what it would have been like. Would you like that, my servant?"

"I am here to do her majesty's bidding," he replied, his voice thick.

She stroked his cock, loving the feel of him hardening in her hand. She could barely get her fingers to meet around the stalk. With a little twist that made him hiss, she got back to her feet. "Go to the bed and lie down, facing up. I'm going to tie your wrists down."

He grimaced, but managed to get to his feet and place himself where he needed to be. Kash laid himself out in the middle of her bed, on display for her pleasure. It would be easy for her to do what she needed to do, to initiate him into honest play.

"Place your wrists above your head, hands toward the posters." She'd already found her rope, playing with the length in her hand. Kash moved his arms to form a *V* from his body. Such strong arms. She slid the rope along his right arm, letting him feel the fabric and how heavy it was. She snaked the jute around his wrist, watching him shiver. She tied one end around his wrist and the other to the heavy post that held up the canopy of the bed. "Let everything else go. I want you to concentrate only on what I'm doing to you. How do you feel? Concentrate on your body and the responses to my stimuli. How did you like it when I touched you with the crop?"

His eyes closed and he breathed out, his body relaxing again. "I liked it. I liked the way it felt. I liked how unsure I was whether you would caress me with it or if you would slap that tip against my skin. And then when you struck, the pain flared, but it was good. It felt like my skin was alive."

She worked the rope over and around his wrists. "Did your cock respond?"

"Yes. It got harder. I wanted more."

She secured his right wrist and moved on to the left. "How does being tied down make you feel?"

"Oddly safe." He pulled gently at his right wrist, as though to check to make sure he couldn't go anywhere. "I feel like I'm laid out for a feast. You're going to eat me alive, aren't you, Your Majesty?"

Then he'd already figured out what her game was. Though he might not know all her moves. She tightened the left wrist, not so much he would lose circulation. Just enough so he could feel it, know he was caught and he wasn't getting away.

"I'm going to take what's mine. I'm going to feast on everything you have." She tied his left wrist down and was ready to begin.

* * * *

She was going to kill him. He was going to die and Kash was

perfectly fine with it. This was everything he needed. He needed her dirty and dominant, needed to feel like every bit of that glorious brain and stunning body was focused on one thing and one thing only—him.

Dayita wasn't thinking about what he could do for her, what his position could buy her. She craved his body, his private soul, and he suddenly realized that he'd only felt this wanted once before in his life.

That day by the river when she'd told him to hold still so she could kiss him. She'd been dominant then, too. It had been the exact quality that had drawn him to her. Day had known her mind and believed in herself. She hadn't needed a man, but she'd chosen him anyway.

He pulled at the bindings, not to try to get away, but because he liked the sensation of being so vulnerable. There was something dark and forbidden.

A king is never weak.

He forced his father's words out of his head. His father hadn't meant them as anything but a mantra, and he understood that now. His father hadn't seen him as weak. That had been Kash's own insecurities, and they had no place here. He wasn't a king in this place. He was a servant. He was Hers.

It was a good place to be.

She had the crop in her hand again. His whole body tightened at the sight of her. She was sex on two legs, pure feminine willpower. The blouse she was wearing had come open, showing the tops of her golden breasts, and he longed to see her nipples, for her to offer them to him so he could suck and lave them with his affection. The black silk of her shirt looked perfect against the golden tone of her skin. For all the tough trappings of her persona, her face was still soft and feminine even when she barked orders his way.

"Bring your knees up."

He moved them up so his feet were flat on the bed.

"Feet further apart. As far as they can go." She snapped the crop against his inner thigh, showing him what she wanted.

The pain flared and then sank into his skin. He was certain if he hadn't been so aroused, the damn crop would hurt, but now his dick threatened to explode every time she swiped it against his flesh.

He didn't think about it. He simply moved his feet until the crop came off his thigh. Wide. She'd spread him so wide. His cock was there, open and vulnerable to her. To his queen.

He gritted his teeth as she ran the crop along his inner thigh again, brushing over the little red spot where she'd flicked him. The leather tip ran along his sensitive flesh and then found his cock.

He was not going to come. He was not going to come. He was going to last.

"Stay right where you are." She put the crop down and he watched as she unbuttoned her skirt and let it drop to the floor. She slowly undid the buttons on her blouse until all he could see was the lovely green bra and lacy panties she wore underneath. And all that gorgeous skin of hers. "You're so beautiful, Kashmir. I love how hard you are. Your cock is lovely and look, it's offering me a gift."

Day reached out and swiped her finger over his cockhead, gathering the drop of pre-come that had pulsed out.

He watched as she sucked her finger into her mouth, eyes closing as though she was concentrating on her treat, as though she loved the taste of him.

He stared down his body, unable to take his eyes off her. When he was in charge, he simply fucked his partner until she came and then he would have his pleasure. Never had he spent such decadent amounts of time on the sensations of touching each other, of being vulnerable to another human being. She could call it play all she liked, but this was something more. This felt sacred to him, something he could only ever do with her because she was the right woman, the only woman for him.

The only woman who could conquer the king and let him be a man.

"You taste so good, my servant." Her nipples were hard points outlined by the silky cup of her bra.

"There's much more where that came from, my Queen. All for you." Only for her. From this moment and forever more. Only for her.

He loved the arrogant smirk that hit her lips. "I can only imagine. I think I'll have to take you up on that. I find I'm very hungry."

She ran her hands up either leg, brushing the flesh there as though inspecting every inch of her possession.

"Then the queen must have her feast. Is this what you would have done? Would you have placed me naked in your web with nothing but my cock exposed for your pleasure?" The vision tightened his gut, arousal pulsing through him. He wasn't a man who had to wait for pleasure, but now the anticipation was a form of joy. He didn't have to worry that Day would leave him like this. She wouldn't ever leave him at all.

She climbed onto the bed, her limbs moving with the sensuous grace of a cat. "Yes. I would have lowered you so I was able to easily torture your cock. A lick here. A caress there. And when you thought I would walk away and leave you wanting, all trussed up and desperate, that's when I would suck you into my mouth. That's when I would work you to the back of my throat and milk you dry."

He was not going to come. He was going to think about baseball or a sport he actually knew something about, and then he would survive her torture. "Now I wish I'd been a bit more brave."

Her nails scored lightly down his torso as she loomed over him. "Bravery has nothing to do with it. This is all about finding what works for the two of us. Privacy works for you. I'll be honest; I'm not much of an exhibitionist when it comes to sex either. I'm happy to have you to myself, happy to keep you from the lustful gazes of all those other women. And men. Many of the men were looking at you, too. They should know better than to look at the queen's property. Don't they know what happens to those who even think to take what belongs to the queen?"

Something bad because his queen was a badass. Yes. She wasn't some delicate flower who sat in the sun all day, waiting for someone to bring life to her. She fought. She worked. She protected.

She was precious.

"No one would dare and you should understand that if anyone tries to hurt my queen, I will be her warrior."

She leaned forward, her body brushing against his. "And what a warrior you are. So strong. Let's see how long my warrior can hold out on his queen."

Her mouth hovered over his, the cups of her bra sliding on his skin. He could feel the intoxicating mix of silk and warm, soft flesh. Then all that mattered was her tongue against his bottom lip. She dragged it over him and he felt the sizzle down his spine. She deepened the kiss, urging his mouth open. This he could do. He might be totally under her control, but his tongue could match hers, sliding in an intimate glide that had them both panting. Over and over she kissed him, her body pressed to his. She'd made a place for herself between his legs, and her pelvis rubbed against his dick, threatening to push him over the edge.

No. He wasn't going to give in. He wasn't going to give up. Not until she'd had her pleasure, not until she'd taken him deep inside her body and ridden him like a racing stallion.

She kissed her way down his body and he bit back a groan. She was determined to make him insane. He was sure of it. It was there in the way she kissed along his jawline, ran her tongue over the flesh of his neck. Those dainty fingers of hers found his nipples, rolling them at first, and then giving him a hard tweak.

He held on to the ropes, his only lifeline in a sea of pleasure. He had to stay focused or he would let his queen down. She was the important one, her pleasure the goal.

And that was why it worked, he realized. Day was thinking the same thing. How many times had he heard Taggart and his friends talk about the "exchange"? BDSM, he'd been told, was an exchange, and it only worked when it was one of equality, when each partner brought his or her unique gifts to the relationship, offering them up with generous hearts. Kash had laughed inside because he'd seen it as an exchange of orgasms, and wasn't that really the point of all sex?

This was more. While he was concentrating on pleasing Day, she was focused on pleasing him. While her happiness was the goal, his was also her goal.

When both partners put aside all selfishness and concentrated on the needs of the other, that was when the exchange worked.

God, he'd thought Taggart had been talking about sex. He'd been talking about love. He'd been talking about how to build a marriage.

The king and queen would always have to think about their

country, but he was more than a king. He was Kash and she was Day, and they could find their own path, their own rule, their own ways to love each other.

His father's way had been to keep all his precious memories in a lockbox and try to show everyone how strong he was. Kash could find a different way.

Day's mouth hovered over his cock, the heat nearly frying his brain. He wanted to shove his pelvis up, forcing his cock inside those luscious lips, but he held still. This was her time and he was her prize. He wasn't going to take that from her. Instead, he stared down the length of his body as she leaned over and her tongue darted out, swiping across his cockhead.

His hands tightened on the ropes, holding himself in place under the sweet lash of her tongue.

"Don't you come, my servant." The words hummed against his sensitive flesh and he could feel her lips there, smiling as she tortured his cock. Her nails brushed against his heavy balls right before she cupped him. "You won't like what happens if you displease me. We'll see how my servant feels about a cock ring."

She squeezed his balls to brush along the right side of pain.

His eyes rolled to the back of his head, and he bit his lip to stop himself from blowing then and there.

"Do you know how beautiful you are right now?" She sucked the head of his cock into her mouth, heating his body until he was sure he would burst into flames. She whirled her tongue over and around and then gave him the barest hint of her teeth. "I love watching you dance on the edge. I love watching you control yourself so you don't go over too fast and ruin the pleasure."

He shook his head. "Not about the pleasure. Want it to last because of you. Want to stay here with you. That's why I fight. I don't want this to ever end."

He wanted the moment to stay suspended, forever right here with her. It couldn't. He knew that, but he could draw it out. He could make it last so the memory would feel like days instead of hours.

"I don't either. It doesn't have to. This place where we can be whoever we want to be, it never goes away, it's merely hidden for a while. But each and every time we're alone, you'll have all of me,

Kashmir. And when we're not alone, know I'm waiting for you. Even when we're not alone, know that I will be your queen, your wife, your love. However you need me, that's what I'll be for you."

He didn't need her to be anyone but exactly who she was—his perfect match, the one who could bring out the other side of him, the only woman who could make him whole.

"Be mine. That's all I need."

The smile that crossed her face was glorious. "Only yours. I only need one servant."

"And I only need one queen."

She unhooked her bra and her breasts bounced free. She palmed them, teasing him with the sight and the fact that his hands were still tied down. They twitched to hold her, but she merely gave him a show, rolling her nipples and rubbing the satin of that patch of underwear over his cock. He could feel how wet she was, the fabric damp and slick with her arousal.

It was torture, but the best kind.

"Kash, are you sure you want this?"

"Yes, I'm sure I want this orgasm. I will take it over my next breath. If you don't hurry, it might be my last breath ever, my Queen."

She laughed, the sound magical to his ears. "That wasn't what I was talking about. I was talking about our marriage. Are you sure? Because I was thinking maybe my servant would like to help me out. My kingdom is in desperate need of a prince or a princess."

He groaned again, having to bite back the harsh shot of arousal her words sent through him.

He was going to have a family with her. He was going to have children who ran through the palace, children who laughed and played. Children who he could teach to be the one thing they needed to be—happy.

"There is nothing I could want more than to serve my Queen in this way." He stared up at her, needing her to know there was nothing playful about this. "I love you, Dayita. I'm sure. There's no one else for me from now on. It's you and me and our family."

"Just us." She leaned over and brushed her lips against his. "And the world, but mostly us."

She shifted her hips and he felt the thin crotch of her undies slide to the side as his cock finally found her pussy. Day got to her knees above him, taking him with the bold, aggressive nature he'd come to crave from her. She lowered herself onto his cock.

Kash couldn't stand it a moment longer. He tilted his pelvis up, feeling her sink onto his cock.

"I should punish you for that, my naughty servant." She moved above him, rolling her hips and taking him as deep as he would go. "But I can't help myself either. I need you. I love you."

"I love you, too, my Queen. He needed her more than he could possibly say. He worked with her, letting her ride him. Her body moved over his, taking what she needed and giving him back everything she had.

It couldn't last. When Day's head fell back and he felt her clench around him, he gave up.

The orgasm was a flash fire, running through his system and leaving him scorched. Day fell forward, her head finding his chest.

He could still feel the pulse of the aftermath when she looked up at him.

"Don't think we're done yet, my servant."

He wasn't done serving her. Not even close. He was ready to spend the rest of his life doing exactly that.

Epilogue

Ten months later

Kash stood looking out over the site that would shortly be his new world. It was nothing but a few acres of ground right now, but once the plans were finished and his contractors had brought to life his vision, this place would be filled with all the world's greatest scientists. It was a place for them to gather, to work, to research and share their ideas. It was a place he hoped could change the world.

"I thought I would find you here."

He turned, a smile on his face because there was nothing he loved more than the sound of that voice. Well, he'd also become partial to the sound of his soon-to-be-born daughter's heart. The hummingbird thud they heard when the doctor came to visit always made his heart clench. "Two more days and we break ground. I've already got meetings with some researchers who are interested in my challenges."

She joined him, her hand slipping into his. It felt natural to be connected to her. "Medical or tech?"

"A couple of doctors who don't want to work with big pharma. They're interested in my drive to cure Parkinson's." He'd put out the call. He and a few other billionaires had pooled some of their resources and offered the world's great minds money and labs and housing in order to solve the problems humanity faced.

He was going to change the world. And if anyone thought they could stop him, they would have to think again. This time he would fight. He wouldn't stop because soon he would give this world to his children, and he never wanted them to think he didn't care.

"Excellent. I heard we also recently received a hundred million dollar grant from Milo Jaye to study pollution solutions," she said with a smile. "You can thank me for that. I gave his wife all the plans and specifications for my suspension tools. They're all about suspension play right now."

"As long as you didn't give them any of our toys." He pulled her close. It was so much easier to be himself now. Something had settled inside him and the world seemed like a different place. A softer, more welcoming place.

His wife still argued with the parliament, but he'd noticed lately that the women of his country seemed to be louder than before, more sure of themselves. They showed up regularly, standing behind their queen, standing up for their daughters.

"I never would. How else would I take care of my favorite servant?" Her voice had gone dark and deliciously deep.

He felt that tug in his groin. Somehow, even though she was almost ready to give birth to their child, she was still the sexiest thing on the planet. She could still make him want to drop to his knees and beg to worship her. "I think I'll be the one taking care of you for a while, my Queen. You have another monarch to give birth to."

He'd successfully argued and won his battle to abolish the antiquated rule of succession that preferred sons over daughters. His daughter, the one who slept inside her mother now, would never worry that she wasn't enough. She would be queen unless she decided she did not want to be. As his firstborn, the choice would be hers to make.

She squeezed his hand. "I think that is going to happen sooner than we think."

"Is she kicking a lot?"

"I'm pretty sure I've been in labor all day," she said, as though talking about the weather. "We should probably go back to the palace and call the doctor. I think your mother will get to meet her namesake tonight."

Yasmine. Their daughter. Oh, god. He was about to become a father.

He was a father. He was a father and a son and a husband. He was a submissive and a king.

He could be all of those things because he was also Hers.

But first, he needed to get her home so their first child wasn't born on his construction site. He wanted his mother there. She'd defied all the doctors and was still holding on. Though the queen mother moved more slowly these days, she seemed happier than ever, ready to welcome her granddaughter into the world.

"Rai! What are you doing allowing your queen to wander around when she's about to give birth?" Kash asked.

His guard, his best friend, smiled as he stepped from behind the tree where he'd been discreetly waiting. Kash knew the man would never leave him alone. He would always be there, even when he acted like an ass. "Have you tried to tell the queen what to do?"

Day was shaking her head. "Walking is good for the labor. Stop being so overprotective."

He took her hand and started for the Jeep. When she winced, he scooped her up. "There is no such thing. I am exactly the proper amount of protective."

"Really?" she said with a grin, her arms going around his neck. "Who says that?"

"I do. And I'm the king."

After all, the king was never wrong. Kash carried his wife back to the palace and into their future.

* * * *

Also from 1001 Dark Nights and Lexi Blake, discover Dungeon Games, Adored, Devoted, and Protected.

About Lexi Blake

Lexi Blake lives in North Texas with her husband, three kids, and the laziest rescue dog in the world. She began writing at a young age, concentrating on plays and journalism. It wasn't until she started writing romance that she found success. She likes to find humor in the strangest places. Lexi believes in happy endings no matter how odd the couple, threesome or foursome may seem. She also writes contemporary Western ménage as Sophie Oak.

Connect with Lexi online:

Facebook: AuthorLexi Blake
Twitter: twitter.com/authorlexiblake
Website: www.LexiBlake.net

Also from Lexi Blake

Masters And Mercenaries
The Dom Who Loved Me
The Men With The Golden Cuffs
A Dom Is Forever
On Her Master's Secret Service
Sanctum: A Masters and Mercenaries Novella
Love and Let Die
Unconditional: A Masters and Mercenaries Novella
Dungeon Royale
Dungeon Games: A Masters and Mercenaries Novella
A View to a Thrill
Cherished: A Masters and Mercenaries Novella
You Only Love Twice
Luscious: Masters and Mercenaries~Topped
Adored: A Masters and Mercenaries Novella
Master No
Just One Taste: Masters and Mercenaries~Topped 2
From Sanctum with Love
Devoted: A Masters and Mercenaries Novella
Dominance Never Dies
Submission is Not Enough
Master Bits & Mercenary Bites: The Secret Recipes of Top
Perfectly Paired: Masters and Mercenaries~Topped 3
For His Eyes Only
Arranged
Love Another Day, Coming August 22, 2017

Lawless
Ruthless
Satisfaction
Revenge, Coming June 20, 2017

Masters Of Ménage (by Shayla Black and Lexi Blake)
Their Virgin Captive
Their Virgin's Secret

Their Virgin Concubine
Their Virgin Princess
Their Virgin Hostage
Their Virgin Secretary
Their Virgin Mistress

The Perfect Gentlemen (by Shayla Black and Lexi Blake
Scandal Never Sleeps
Seduction in Session
Big Easy Temptation
Smoke and Sin, Coming Soon

URBAN FANTASY

Thieves
Steal the Light
Steal the Day
Steal the Moon
Steal the Sun
Steal the Night
Ripper
Addict
Sleeper, Coming Soon

Discover More Lexi Blake

Protected: A Masters and Mercenaries Novella by Lexi Blake, Coming July 31, 2017

A second chance at first love
Years before, Wade Rycroft fell in love with Geneva Harris, the smartest girl in his class. The rodeo star and the shy academic made for an odd pair but their chemistry was undeniable. They made plans to get married after high school but when Genny left him standing in the rain, he joined the Army and vowed to leave that life behind. Genny married the town's golden boy, and Wade knew that he couldn't go home again.

Could become the promise of a lifetime
Fifteen years later, Wade returns to his Texas hometown for his brother's wedding and walks into a storm of scandal. Genny's marriage has dissolved and the town has turned against her. But when someone tries to kill his old love, Wade can't refuse to help her. In his years after the Army, he's found his place in the world. His job at McKay-Taggart keeps him happy and busy but something is missing. When he takes the job watching over Genny, he realizes what it is.

As danger presses in, Wade must decide if he can forgive past sins or let the woman of his dreams walk into a nightmare….

* * * *

Dungeon Games: A Masters and Mercenaries Novella by Lexi Blake, Now Available

Obsessed
Derek Brighton has become one of Dallas's finest detectives through a combination of discipline and obsession. Once he has a target in his sights, nothing can stop him. When he isn't solving homicides, he applies the same intensity to his playtime at Sanctum, a secretive BDSM club. Unfortunately, no amount of beautiful

submissives can fill the hole that one woman left in his heart.

Unhinged
Karina Mills has a reputation for being reckless, and her clients appreciate her results. As a private investigator, she pursues her cases with nothing holding her back. In her personal life, Karina yearns for something different. Playing at Sanctum has been a safe way to find peace, but the one Dom who could truly master her heart is out of reach.

Enflamed
On the hunt for a killer, Derek enters a shadowy underworld only to find the woman he aches for is working the same case. Karina is searching for a missing girl and won't stop until she finds her. To get close to their prime suspect, they need to pose as a couple. But as their operation goes under the covers, unlikely partners become passionate lovers while the killer prepares to strike.

* * * *

Adored: A Masters and Mercenaries Novella by Lexi Blake, Now Available

A man who gave up on love
Mitch Bradford is an intimidating man. In his professional life, he has a reputation for demolishing his opponents in the courtroom. At the exclusive BDSM club Sanctum, he prefers disciplining pretty submissives with no strings attached. In his line of work, there's no time for a healthy relationship. After a few failed attempts, he knows he's not good for any woman—especially not his best friend's sister.

A woman who always gets what she wants
Laurel Daley knows what she wants, and her sights are set on Mitch. He's smart and sexy, and it doesn't matter that he's a few years older and has a couple of bitter ex-wives. Watching him in action at work and at play, she knows he just needs a little polish to make some woman the perfect lover. She intends to be that woman,

but first she has to show him how good it could be.

A killer lurking in the shadows

When an unexpected turn of events throws the two together, Mitch and Laurel are confronted with the perfect opportunity to explore their mutual desire. Night after night of being close breaks down Mitch's defenses. The more he sees of Laurel, the more he knows he wants her. Unfortunately, someone else has their eyes on Laurel and they have murder in mind.

* * * *

Devoted: A Masters and Mercenaries Novella by Lexi Blake, Now Available

A woman's work

Amy Slaten has devoted her life to Slaten Industries. After ousting her corrupt father and taking over the CEO role, she thought she could relax and enjoy taking her company to the next level. But an old business rivalry rears its ugly head. The only thing that can possibly take her mind off business is the training class at Sanctum…and her training partner, the gorgeous and funny Flynn Adler. If she can just manage to best her mysterious business rival, life might be perfect.

A man's commitment

Flynn Adler never thought he would fall for the enemy. Business is war, or so his father always claimed. He was raised to be ruthless when it came to the family company, and now he's raising his brother to one day work with him. The first order of business? The hostile takeover of Slaten Industries. It's a stressful job so when his brother offers him a spot in Sanctum's training program, Flynn jumps at the chance.

A lifetime of devotion….

When Flynn realizes the woman he's falling for is none other than the CEO of the firm he needs to take down, he has to make a choice. Does he take care of the woman he's falling in love with or the business he's worked a lifetime to build? And when Amy finally understands the man she's come to trust is none other than the enemy, will she walk away from him or fight for the love she's come to depend on?

Love Another Day
Masters and Mercenaries 14
By Lexi Blake

A man born to protect

After a major loss, Brody Carter found a home with the London office of McKay-Taggart. A former soldier, he believes his job is to take the bullets and follow orders. He's happy to take on the job of protecting Dr. Stephanie Gibson while the team uses her clinic in Sierra Leone to bring down an international criminal. What he never expected was that the young doctor would prove to be the woman of his dreams. She's beautiful, smart, and reckless. Over and over he watches her risk her life to save others. One night of pure passion leads him to realize that he can't risk his heart again. When the mission ends, Brody walks away, unwilling to lose another person he loves.

A woman driven to heal

Stephanie's tragic past taught her to live for today. Everything she's done in the last fifteen years has been to make up for her mistakes. Offering medical care in war-torn regions gives her the purpose she needs to carry on. When she meets her gorgeous Aussie protector, she knows she's in too deep, but nothing can stop her from falling head over heels in love. But after one amazing night together, Brody walks away and never looks back. Stephanie is left behind…but not alone.

A secret that will change both their lives

A year later, Stephanie runs afoul of an evil mercenary who vows to kill her for failing to save his son. She runs to the only people she trusts, Liam and Avery O'Donnell. She hasn't come alone and her secret will bring her former lover across the world to protect her. From Liberia to Dallas to Australia's outback, Brody will do whatever it takes to protect Stephanie from the man who wants to kill her, but it might be her own personal demons that could destroy them both.

Tangled
A Dark Protectors—Reese Family Novella
By Rebecca Zanetti

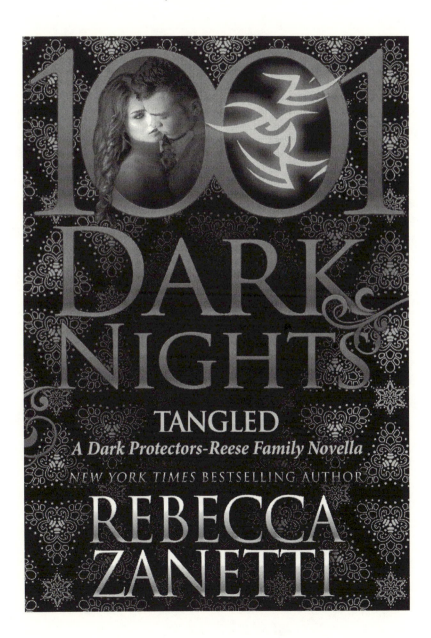

1001 DARK NIGHTS

TANGLED
A Dark Protectors-Reese Family Novella
NEW YORK TIMES BESTSELLING AUTHOR
REBECCA ZANETTI

Acknowledgments from the Author

The 1001DN project started as an exciting marketing plan for authors that has turned into so very much more. All of the people involved, from the creators to the consultants to the authors are truly amazing, and I'm honored to be included.

For many of us, this group has turned into a soft place to land in a wild industry.

We've become friends and confidants, and it's difficult to describe how much that means to me.

Elizabeth Berry, you've taken a love of reading and a brilliant marketing mind and created something really special. Thank you for including me in your world. I hope you never need to bury a body, but if you do, I'm there for you.

MJ Rose, you're a marketing genius with a truly creative mind, and you've done a marvelous job along with Liz. I don't think you'd need help burying a body, but if you ever need a buddy for a lengthy shopping trip, I'm your gal.

Jillian Stein, you've saved whatever sanity I might have retained throughout the years. I trust you with everything, and I can't thank you enough for all that you do. If we had to bury a body, I have no doubt you'd color-code and calendar the plan with a cool trailer to go with it. It'd be a well-organized adventure for us that would end with a Twilight marathon.

Steve Berry, thank you for your generosity with sharing your insights and experience in the book industry. Thank you also for your tremendous sense of humor in dealing with, well, all of us. I know I'm a peach, but that Lexi Blake is a loveable scamp.

Thank you to Kimberly Guidroz, Pam Jamison, Fedora Chen,

and Kasi Alexander for their dedication and awesome insights.

Thanks also to Asha Hossain, who creates absolutely fantastic book covers.

As always, a lot of love and a huge thank you goes to Big Tone, Gabe and Karly, my amazing family who is so supportive.

Finally, thank you to Rebecca's Rebels, my street team, who have been so generous with their time and friendship. Thank you to Minga Portillo for her excellent leadership of the team. And last, but not least, thank you to all of my readers who spend time with my characters.

The Dark Protectors are coming back with new stories in 2018, and I hope you like them!

~ RAZ

Chapter 1

Two weeks on the hunt, and now Theo Reese was dressed like a wanker from one of those popular spy movies. He tugged on the black bow tie and fully committed himself to killing the woman who'd forced him to wear a tuxedo. After chasing her through New York, London, Edinburgh, and now back to New York, he was more than ready to grip her slim neck in both his hands.

Then he'd squeeze until her stunning blue eyes bugged.

Maybe. Okay. He wouldn't kill her. Even as pissed as he was, he'd never harm a woman. Well, probably. This one had taken subterfuge to a whole new level, so he would like to scare her a little. Plus, the woman was a witch, so it wasn't like she couldn't defend herself. Creating fire out of air was like breathing for her people.

Chatter and the clinking of glasses filled the opulent ballroom of New York's most exclusive hotel. Women in long sparkling dresses and men in tuxedos milled around, drinking champagne and laughing. Christmas lights blinked green and red from trees placed in every corner.

Discreet waiters refilled glasses and offered canapés.

Theo sighed. He wanted a steak, damn it. Little mushrooms filled with green stuff would just make him hungrier.

Where the hell was she?

His contacts had said she'd be attending the fundraiser to save some otter in some forest somewhere, and he'd had to pretty much give up a kidney to get a ticket. A gold-encrusted ticket. He didn't get it. Why not just save the money on tickets, clothes, food, and drink…and give it to the damn otters? Buy them all a new river and forest somewhere.

He caught a scent. Through the heavy perfumes and fragrant appetizers, a scent he knew well beckoned him. Woman, intrigue, and Irish bluebells from her native home.

Lifting his head, he followed his nose. Even for a vampire, he had enhanced senses.

Her laugh, tinkling and surprisingly deep, had him turning left.

Ah. There she was. He'd finally found the witch. His entire body tightened, and the blood rushed from his head right to his cock. From one little sighting of her. Fuck. Taking several deep breaths, he calmed his body and cleared his mind.

Ginny O'Toole wore a sapphire colored gown that matched her eyes perfectly. The bodice was old fashioned, glimmering with sparkles, and narrowed to an impossibly small waist. Her breasts were full, her hair naturally white-blonde, her skin flawless, and her stature petite. Three hundred years ago, she'd been too thin for popularity. Fifty years ago, she'd been the ideal woman. Now, in the day and age of curves and diversity, she stood out as almost unreal. As more of a doll than a real woman.

An air of fragility clung to her, in direct opposition to strong and fierce modern woman.

Yet men flocked to her, quick to give protection, just as much today as in the past. The morons didn't realize that her pretty face masked a predator. One who used wiles and weakness to get what she wanted. False weakness. Oh, physically she lacked strength. But mentally, she was a manipulative bitch.

She was talking to a tall man who had his back to Theo. Short blond hair, wide shoulders, strong energy. Was that a shifter? Yeah. Feline. Probably lion.

Theo launched into motion, easily winding through the human throng, and reached them in seconds.

Ginny's eyes widened and then her mask dropped back into place. "Theo." She smiled, and if he couldn't hear her hammering heartbeat, he would've been fooled into believing she was actually pleased to see him. Since she'd been running from him for weeks after hacking into the main computer at one of his family's estates, he knew that to be a lie. "Theo Reese, please meet Jack Jacobson," she said.

Jacobson turned and held out a hand. "It's a pleasure."

Theo shook his hand, lowering his chin. The shifter shaking his hand was an information broker by the name of Jackson McIntosh. They'd never done business, but Theo had seen dossiers on the guy. "Jack Jacobson?" he murmured, barely flashing his canines. "That's a nice pseudonym."

Jack nodded. "I like it."

"Your business here is concluded," Theo said, releasing Jacobson and grasping Ginny by the elbow. Her bones felt fragile beneath his hand, so he loosened his hold automatically.

She didn't struggle, as if she could. Instead, her smile widened. "Actually, it is. Please get back to me with your answer soon, Jack."

Heat rushed down Theo's back. The woman thought he was so daft he wouldn't figure out what she was trying to sell? He had an idea of what information she was looking to get rid of, and that ended right now. "There's a chance your deal might be dead in the water," he said evenly.

Jack's green eyes twinkled. "Perhaps." Then he sobered, his gaze moving to Theo's hand. "Let her go."

Jesus. The woman brought out the defender in everybody. Even criminal middlemen who were well known to broker anything—legal or illegal. "No," Theo returned.

"You are so very sweet to worry about me." Ginny patted Jack's arm with her free hand. "Theo and I are old friends. No need for concern."

Old friends, his ass. Theo didn't bother to smile. If she wanted to play the polite game, she could damn well do it by herself. He didn't play games. Ever.

Jack's eyes narrowed. "You certain?"

"I am," Ginny said softly. "Theo and I have some business to conduct as well. It was lovely to see you, Jack."

Theo might just throw up. "Bye, Jack."

The shifter nodded, gave him one hard look, and turned on his polished loafers. Seconds later, he'd disappeared into the throng.

Ginny sighed. "Kindly remove your hand."

"Not a chance in hell," Theo returned, drawing her nearer. "And I'm warning you. You try to create a scene, you cause any problem, and I'll not care about collateral damage for once. You're coming with me, and we're retrieving the Benjamin file. Right now."

Her eyes widened fully, and she planted a small hand against her bare upper chest. "The Benjamin file? What in the world is that?"

He barked out a laugh. Truly, he couldn't help it. "Ginny, from day one, your act hasn't worked on me, and you know it." That was why she'd chosen his older brother to manipulate and use a century ago. Jared had fallen for her helpless act, thought he was in love, and had had his heart broken when she'd mated another male instead of him. Well, he'd thought it had been broken. Now that he'd found his true mate, he knew the difference. "So knock it off," Theo finished.

"Theo," Ginny whispered. "I truly do not know anything about a Benjamin file. What in the world is that?"

It was the computer file that detailed all of Theo's family's holdings and dealings…even the illegal ones. It could bring down and bankrupt his entire family, and most importantly, his Uncle Benjamin. Benny was a crazy thousand-year-old vampire who would easily cut off Theo's head for losing the file. "I don't have time for games. Where's the flash drive?" he asked quietly.

She shrugged creamy shoulders. "You know I don't understand computers."

The woman could lie. Well. But Theo knew better. "You firebombed our entire system, and now that flash drive is the only record we have. It proves ownership of everything we have." It also held files they'd used to blackmail others during the years, which was an acceptable way of doing business in the immortal world. He leaned down until his nose nearly touched hers. "I'm losing patience."

Pink bloomed across her high cheekbones. "Really, Theo. Ownership records are easy to find these days. Obtain the title deeds in every place you own property. Stocks and businesses have records."

He breathed out, his lungs heating. Many records had no paper trail, and she knew it. The blackmail info, and the family history, were both hidden on purpose. And even so, he didn't have time to traverse the world looking for what legitimate documentation he could find. "Where's the data?" Hopefully she'd been too busy running from him and trying to sell the files that she hadn't had time to really go through them.

He had to get the Green Rock file before anybody else read it. The damn thing might result in his entire family being killed by their current allies. It'd also break his brother Chalton's heart if he learned the truth. The Realm, his adopted family, would turn on him. "Tell me, Ginny. Now."

The witch sighed. "I'm getting a headache. Would you please just stop stalking me?"

He barely kept from glaring at her. This close, he could see dark circles beneath her eyes. Beneath his hand, her arm trembled. Running from him had taken a toll on her. He tried to steel his heart against that fact, because she'd use it against him. "Let's go to my hotel and have a nice meal." Maybe if he got some food into her, the color would return to her pretty face. "We can talk about the file there."

"No." Her pink lips turned down in a pout.

"Does that look actually work on people?" he asked, truly curious.

Fire flashed in her intriguing eyes.

Ah, he'd gotten to her. "I guess it does." He faulted his gender for being easy marks. Not once had he ever understood why she played at being so helpless. Why not be straight up? Hell, if he didn't need to get that file back, *he'd* probably be an easy mark for her if she was honest with him for two whole seconds. "You don't need games with beauty like yours, Ginny."

Surprise, the genuine kind, tilted her lips. "I thought you hated the way I look."

Right. Vampires always hated beauty. "No. I dislike the way you pretend to be something you're not. The way you look is...good." Unbelievably stunning, to be honest. But he couldn't give her an inch, or he'd be letting his entire family down. And probably signing their death sentence. "So drop the act, would you?"

She shook her head as if she was in on a joke he couldn't fathom. Regret darkened those blue eyes for just a second, enhancing the tired circles beneath them. "You only see what you want to see, Theo."

What the hell did that mean? He leaned in. "Explain."

Her slim shoulders went back. "I can't. But you're right. We do need to talk. Let's go discuss this somewhere else."

Good. She was finally going to work with him. He looked toward the nearest exit. "I agree. Let's get out of here. Why are you caring about otters, anyway?"

She blinked. "Otters?"

He gestured around.

She laughed, the sound spontaneous and so sexy it hurt. "Oh, Theo. This is a fundraiser for Other Tracks. An international nonprofit that fights the sex trafficking of children across the globe? I donate every year."

He straightened. Was she lying? "Oh." That did seem a lot more important than otters. He studied her, fighting the urge to believe her. She was so damn good at tricking men. Right now, he had other worries. "Let's go."

She sighed, her shoulders hunching. "Very well." Pivoting, she stumbled into him.

Pain flared through his arm. Heat rushed through his veins, and his head grew heavy. Gravity claimed him, and he started to fall.

"Sorry," she whispered, helping him down to the floor and setting his back to the wall.

He blinked, his tongue thickening as he saw the small syringe in her hand. The last thought he had before passing completely out was to wonder where such a curve-hugging dress had pockets.

Then he was out.

Chapter 2

Ginny rushed into the suite in her ancient hotel, running for the bedroom to quickly pack. She'd been waylaid too many times on her way out of the ball, but she'd had appearances to keep up. This identity was one she cherished, and she'd fight to keep it. She considered it her good one. The one that did honorable things like help organizations like Other Tracks.

Oh, Theo would only be out for a short time. The sedative she'd brought had been created for shifters, just in case Jack had tried something. It would take a vampire like Theo down, but not for long.

She threw clothing into her suitcase, trying to keep her energy up. After working the ball for two hours, she was spent and needed rest. Grabbing her sparkly flats, she quickly exchanged them for her three-inch heels, packing those in the bag. Where the heck should she run? She had to stay close in case Jack was able to broker a deal. Her final deal. Then she was out.

The hotel was in the seedier side of town, so no way would Theo look for her there.

Theo Reese couldn't be allowed to screw this up for her.

Damn that vampire. He was far too smart and sexy for her peace of mind. Not once, *not once*, had he ever fallen for the character she most often played in life. While that intrigued her, totally against her will, she didn't have time to explore it. Not now. Not when she was so close.

She grabbed her suitcase and the laptop bag, running into the living area.

The door crashed open and banged against the wall. Twice.

She halted, her lungs seizing.

Theo Reese stood in the doorway, his tux askew, fury across his hard face. All vampires had hard faces. Yet Theo's was a rock-like formation chiseled into rugged planes and fierce angles that had haunted her dreams more than once through the years. His body was muscled and tight, yet he moved with the grace of a panther shifter. Deadly and sure. His thick brown hair was several shades lighter than his midnight black eyes, which right now swirled with an anger that stole her breath.

She swallowed, looking for an escape.

"In that dress, you'll never make it down the fire escape." He stepped inside and shut the door behind himself. Well, he shut what was left of the door. "Your sedative didn't last long."

The bastard probably had the metabolism of a demon. Damn vampire. "I said I was sorry." She dropped her bags and let her voice go breathy. "But...but I had no choice, Theo." Yes. Good tremble on the last.

"Bullshit." He crossed his arms over his broad chest, staring down from at least an additional foot of height.

She coughed. Nobody swore at her. Ever.

He lowered his chin. "I swear, Ginny. If you don't drop the fucking act, I'm going to lose my temper. You don't want that."

No. She truly did not want that. Why hadn't she taken time to change out of the ball gown? It was nearly impossible to fight in the darn thing. No wonder it had taken so long for women to reach equality in this new world. Their very clothing had held them back. "Theo, there's no need to get nasty," she said, her mind spinning for a plan.

"You haven't seen nasty. Yet." He cocked his head to the side and focused on her laptop bag. "Is my flash drive in there?"

"No," she said honestly. "I have no idea what flash drive you're talking about." Aye, she lied that time.

His focus slashed back to her face. "Ah, baby. That's the first time we've had this type of conversation. I have a baseline for you now. You have a tell when you lie."

"I do not," she burst out before she could stop herself.

His smile was slow and somehow dangerous. "You do."

"I'm a natural redhead," she spat, forgetting all about how tired she was.

"Lie."

She breathed out. "I once climbed Mt. Rainier."

He blinked. "Truth."

Damn it. "I was very much in love with your brother."

Red flared across Theo's face, and he took a minute before responding this time. "Lie," he said thoughtfully.

"I love garlic," she said, her heart speeding up.

"Lie," he said instantly.

God. How was he doing that? "I am nearly addicted to Irish whiskey," she said quietly.

He glanced down her dress. "Truth, but that's hard to believe."

Was he guessing? So far, he'd been correct every time. "I want to sleep with you," she whispered.

He grinned, making him look almost boyish. "Truth."

Her breath relaxed. "Wrong."

"No." He moved toward her. "Feel free to lie to yourself, lady. But that was the truth."

She couldn't help but take a step back. Sure, she'd thought about him. More than she should have. But she did not want to have sex with the damn vampire. "You're such a bastard."

"True sentiment but a lie overall. My parents were married and mated," he returned, continuing slowly toward her as if he had all the time in the world.

She stumbled back and held up a hand. "Stop."

"Why?" he asked, not stopping.

"You're scaring me, Theo," she said, trying for simpering.

He stopped cold. "The wimpy tone is bullshit, but I *am* scaring you." His lip quirked as if he wasn't quite sure what to do with that information. "If scaring you gets me what I want, then I'll do it. I'm prepared to do almost anything, Ginny. Don't make me."

Now he was telling the full truth. Just how far would he go to get back the Benjamin file? For the first time, she actually doubted her ability to get a job done. "I really don't know what flash drive you're talking about." She kept her voice level this time and looked him right in the eye.

"Lie," he whispered, slowly shaking his head but somehow managing to keep eye contact. "Oh, you're good. But that was a lie."

She breathed in and settled her stance beneath the long gown without giving her intent away. "Why don't we call Jared?" Maybe big brother could talk some sense into Theo.

"He's on his honeymoon," Theo said.

She tried to drum up some sense of hurt, but truth be told, she was happy for the vampire. Jared was a good guy, and he deserved happiness. The vamp in front of her was not a good guy, and he had a hell of an ego. Anger pushed through her fear. "I'm not dealing with Reese junior here." If she could get him angry enough, maybe he'd make a mistake. "Send in the older boys, would you?"

Theo's smile was predatory, plain and simple. "Sorry. My brothers are busy. You'll have to deal with me."

His dark tone licked right across her skin. For years, she'd tried to avoid Theo Reese. He was too smart, too strong...too male. The born soldier in the family. Her damsel act had never worked on him, and that was damn unfortunate. Men were usually idiots, which suited her purposes just fine. Normally. This male...did not suit. "You're unreasonable, and you won't listen," she said softly, breathing in to push out her breasts over the top of the bustier.

His eyes flared, and satisfaction heated through her. Her breath sped up along with her heart rate. When was the last time a man had provided a challenge for her? He might read lies, but she read people, and this male wanted her. She could use that. As much as she might not want to do so, she had a job to do. A critical one. This time, she stepped toward him. "Listen to me, Theo."

His head lifted, while a veil drew down over his eyes. "I'm listening." His voice lowered to a hoarse growl.

Her abdomen heated, and her breasts grew heavy. "I—"

He wrapped a warm hand around her neck, stopping her words.

She stilled. How had he moved so quickly? Her gaze snapped up to meet his.

"No more lying," he said softly. Way too softly.

A tremble shook her that had nothing to do with fear. Her nerves flashed to fully alive, and her skin sensitized. What the hell was happening to her? Her clothes were suddenly too restrictive. She licked her lips.

His gaze tracked her tongue. Tension exploded around them,

rolling through the room.

She wanted to retreat a step, but her legs wouldn't cooperate. "Theo—"

Pressing his thumb and forefinger beneath where her jaw met her neck, he drew her toward him. "You don't speak unless it's the truth. Got it?"

Fury speared through her. "Think you can stop me?" She lost any hint of helplessness.

"Yes." His gaze dropped to her mouth. "Try me."

God. Was he saying what she thought he was saying? Her mind fuzzed. No. This couldn't happen. She knew. She *just knew* that being kissed by Theo Reese would change her world. Considering her world was full of intrigue, pain, and lies right now...that might not be so bad. But getting involved with him would be a disaster. Especially right now. "Release me because this is a very bad idea," she whispered.

A muscle ticked in his jaw. "That wasn't a lie."

"No." It wasn't.

"Where's the Benjamin file?" His gaze traveled up from her lips to her eyes.

All Saints, she could get lost in those midnight black eyes. This close, she could see different shades. Were there different shades of black? She hadn't thought so before. Now, she could see them. Ah. Vampire eyes. Wait a minute. The vamps had tertiary eye colors that came out in times of stress or great emotion or supposedly during sex. Jared's were just a darker black, which she'd seen once when he'd been in a fight as a kid. Chalton, the middle brother, had a deep blue that was almost black and didn't look much different from his normal color. She only knew that because of a background file she'd read on him. There was no such background file on Theo. Unfortunately.

Theo leaned closer. "Ginny?"

"What other color are your eyes?" she blurted.

He blinked. Once and then twice. "The only way you'll ever know that is if you're naked."

Naked. He said *naked*. She gulped down a swallow. Images of Theo sans clothing, over her, slid through her mind, down her body, and landed hard between her legs. Was it possible to faint from desire? Oh, she was a master at pretending to faint. But now, her knees actually wobbled. "How improper," she said, fighting her hardest to keep her voice mild.

"The last thing in the world you need is proper." His voice was even milder.

He wanted to play? Fine. She could play. "What do I need, Theo?" she asked in her flirtiest voice, trying to toss her head at the same time. His firm hand made it difficult, but she gave it a good effort, sending her thick hair tumbling down her back.

A growl rumbled up his chest and heated the air between them. "Not something you'd enjoy," he said, his hold tightening just enough to give warning. "Why the hell aren't you burning me? Are you that desperate to appear weak?"

The words slapped her in the face. Only training kept her from reacting. "You're not worth the effort."

His head tilted just slightly, in a curiously dangerous way. "That hurt you. What I said. Why?"

Was he a damn mind reader? Bollocks. Witches used quantum physics, among other sciences, to create plasma fire out of the air around them. It was an excellent weapon, and if she had the ability to use it, she would've already burned off every hair on his head. "You didn't hurt me."

"Lie." He said the last softly—thoughtfully. His brows drew down. "I'm not releasing you until you give me an answer."

"To which question?" she snapped.

He drew her even closer. "Both. Where's my file, and why can't you create fire?"

"I don't have your file, and I can create fire," she said.

He breathed out. "Kind of true and kind of false. Interesting. So you don't have the file right now, which makes sense. A smart thief would've hidden it elsewhere. And you can create fire, but you're unable to do so right now. Why is that?"

"You're crazy."

"Maybe. But we're not moving until you give me the truth."

She had no choice. Shoving both arms up, she broke his hold, and then just as quickly punched him in the eye.

He reared back, grabbing his eye and snarling.

Lifting her skirts, she jumped and kicked him beneath the jaw.

He flew back and hit the sofa.

She turned to run just as the front door blew open again, this time with fire. Heat flashed toward her and she screamed, ducking to avoid being burned.

Flames flashed right over her head.

Chapter 3

Theo reacted instantly, shoving off the sofa and covering Ginny with his body. He rolled them until she was behind the sofa, and then he jumped up to lunge for the door.

Plasma sailed into his chest. He ignored the pain, tackling two males into the hallway. Witches. Damn fucking fire-throwing witches. Both dressed in combat gear, already hurtling fire at him. He punched one guy right under the jaw, shattering it into pieces he could feel with his knuckles. The male went limp, knocked out. Theo back-flipped onto his feet, bounced once, and kicked the other guy in the temple.

The guy went down and just as quickly leaped up, head into Theo's gut. The force threw them both into the wall, denting the hard wood.

Two more men ran by them and into the dingy room.

Damn it. Ginny wasn't covered. Theo slammed his elbows down on his attacker's shoulders, dropping the guy to the ground. Then he punched with an uppercut, and the witch fell back onto his shoulders. Blue flames poured down his arms. He threw fire.

Shit.

Theo jumped to the side. The plasma ball hit the wall with a loud thud, and flames licked up the wood. Fire burned his arm, but he skidded on his knees, already punching for the witch's face. Blood arced, but he kept punching, ignoring the return hits, until the guy finally stopped moving.

"Asshole." Theo shoved to his feet and turned for the crappy room. The fire was spreading, and smoke filled the hallway. The alarms started blaring, and the sprinkler system ignited. Water streamed down, making the flames hiss. The smoke clogged his way. He shoved through it to see Ginny struggling between two men as they dragged her toward the door.

"Throw some fire, woman," Theo roared, pissed beyond belief.

The three paused, mouths agape. It would've been comical if he hadn't been so furious.

Ginny yanked free of one male and pivoted to punch the other in the eye. The guy reared back and slapped her across the face. Hard. The sound echoed even through the fire, alarm, and spraying water. Her head flew to the side with water matting her hair.

Theo lost his fucking mind.

With a roar that would've done a demon proud, he lunged for the guy, grabbing him around the neck and lifting. Fury and adrenaline giving him strength, Theo swung around and threw the bastard toward the wide window. The witch hit dead center and crashed through. He shrieked as he began pummeling toward the ground eight floors below.

Ginny turned toward Theo, her eyes wide with shock. "Oh my God. That was thick glass."

The other witch moved fast and grabbed her, yanking her against his chest with his arm banded around her throat. She clawed at his forearm, her eyes filling with tears.

"Let her go." Theo advanced through the smoke and spraying water toward the two.

"No." The witch tried to pull her toward the door. "I have a job to do."

"Why her?" Theo took another step, brushing soot out of his eyes.

The guy kept moving. "Don't know. Don't care."

So the men were just hired guns. It figured Ginny had more than one enemy out there, considering she was a thief. Theo couldn't have been her first mark. "I've already killed your buddy and knocked out the other two."

"Wasn't my buddy, and he's probably not dead," the guy returned, his eyes wild.

True. The witch had certainly hit the ground by now. He might not be dead, but he wouldn't be attempting any kidnappings for quite some time. Theo jerked his head toward Ginny, noting how pale she'd become. "What's she worth, anyway?"

"Twenty-five million." The guy studied him. "Considering you've taken out my team, want to split it?" Soot and water mangled through the guy's long blond hair, but his dark eyes were clear. Smart and calculating.

Ginny struggled against him, making little choking noises.

Theo paused and concentrated on her. "You can't create fire." She should've burned the shit out of the guy by now. Wait a minute. He focused back on the blond guy. "Did you know that? That she couldn't create fire?"

"No. I figured if she started to burn me, I'd just choke her out," the guy said congenially, as if chatting with a friend. "So. Do we have a deal or not?"

Theo paused, as if considering.

Ginny gasped. "Seriously? You're honestly thinking of making a deal?" Her voice came out a little squeaky. Soot marred her forehead, and a bruise was already forming on her left cheekbone where the asshole had hit her. "Theo?"

"Where's the file you stole from me?" he asked, stopping three feet away from the duo.

Her eyes bugged. "Are you jesting?"

He lifted a shoulder.

Sirens sounded in the distance.

The guy blanched. "Hey, we have to get out of here. Fast."

Theo nodded. "Seriously, Ginny. Can't you fight at all?"

"I hit you in the eye," she said, a little color filling her face. "It's been a long day." Her lips trembled, and she renewed her struggles, pushing back and obviously trying to toss the guy over her head. It wasn't even close as a contest. Strength-wise, she appeared tapped.

"What's wrong with you?" Theo murmured. Even though the guy was much larger, she was a witch and should at least have some moves. But she appeared as helpless as a human female. Would she really push her charade of helplessness in a situation like this? His gut churned. Either she was that dishonest...or there was something wrong with her. "Fight him."

"I'm trying." Tears filled her eyes, and damn if they didn't look real.

Men's shouts echoed up from the stairwell.

"They're coming. We have to go and meet my secondary team on floor two." The guy started dragging her toward the door. "I have two more men waiting for us, and they'll head this way if we don't hurry. Let's get out of here."

Theo nodded. "Okay. I'll take point." He ignored Ginny's gasp and started for the door, turning at the last second and punching the guy in the temple.

The guy fell back, and Theo followed him, nailing him directly in the throat.

Ginny sagged against the wall.

Theo grabbed her hand and her suitcase. "I hope you're as good in that dress as you act. We're taking the fire escape." All but dragging her, he hustled through the disaster of the hotel room for the far windows.

She grasped her laptop bag on the way, stumbling next to him. One of her sparkly shoes fell off, and she kept going, kicking off the other one. They looked slippery, so it was probably a good call. "We're eight floors up," she gasped through the smoke and streaming water.

"I know," he said grimly. "You can explain what the fuck is going on with you on the way down." If the humans or the other witches didn't catch them first.

* * * *

Ginny gathered her skirts the best she could and followed Theo down the hard metal fire escape. Snow and ice covered the metal, and a cold December wind blew hard against them. He'd gone first, no doubt preparing to catch her if she fell. The man had no clue how close she was to actually fainting. *Really* fainting. Her ears rang, and her entire body ached from her attempts to fight.

Tears gathered in her eyes from the damn unfairness of it all, and she angrily batted them away.

"Hurry, honey," Theo said from below her, gracefully going backward down the zillion steps.

Honey. He'd called her honey. And he'd kicked some serious witch butt when defending her. The idea warmed her entire chest, and she tried to ignore the feeling. They were enemies, and she had to remember that fact. If he won, she lost. So she'd have to figure a way out of this mess.

Once they were on the ground.

She swallowed and looked straight ahead at the worn brick. Staying at old and seedy hotels had advantages…mainly outdoor fire escapes. Her foot missed a rung, and she slipped. "Theo," she gasped, just as she fell.

He caught her around the waist on a landing. "Damn it." Grabbing her skirt, he ripped it across the bottom, leaving her legs bare from the knees down. "There. That should—" He paused and looked down at her ankle. "What the hell?"

"No time." She grabbed a rung and started heading down, ignoring the diamond and gold spiked ankle bracelet. The sirens sounded closer, and blue and red swirling lights cut through the darkness of the night. A firetruck rolled by the main street, and shouting voices echoed from up above.

Adrenaline gave her strength, and without the skirt hampering her, she quickly made it to the litter-covered street.

Theo jumped next to her and swung her up in his arms, turning and hurrying away from the emergency vehicles. Somehow he kept hold of her suitcase.

She jostled against his chest, clutching her laptop bag. "What are you doing?"

"Your feet are bare. There's glass and who knows what else on the ground." He wasn't even breathing heavily.

She tried to remain stiff in his arms, but her body relaxed right into his warmth. Theo was all muscled male strength around her, and for the first time in far too long, she felt safe. For the moment. Wrapping her arm around his neck to help him keep his balance, she gave in to temptation and rested her face against his neck.

They were both soaking wet and covered in soot, but somehow, he smelled good. Wild and masculine, with a hint of something spicy. His heart beat steadily against her chest, and she shut her eyes. Just for the second. Pretending that she was safe and belonged with him. For years, she'd fought her own battles, even while pretending to be helpless. While she was more than capable of taking care of herself, under normal circumstances, she had no problem being saved by somebody who cared for her.

It was too late to save her.

More importantly, Theo Reese didn't care for her. He saw her as the manipulative bitch who'd broken his brother's heart, and as a thief who could harm his family. "I didn't really hurt Jared, you know," she said softly, her lips moving against his warm skin.

Theo stiffened but kept moving through darkened alleys. "Yes, you did."

Her stomach ached. "He didn't love me. Not really. He loved the idea of how strong I made him feel back a million years ago."

"Maybe," Theo allowed.

She sighed. "If he'd really loved me, no way would he have let me mate somebody else. You know that." In fact, Jared had used his hurt ego to become a pirate on the open seas, which he'd truly loved. "Right?"

"There's truth to that," Theo said, his mouth next to her temple. "He's happy now, and that's all that matters. He found the right mate for him, without question."

"So stop being mad at me." She hated how needy she sounded, but fighting just took too much out of her. "Please."

"Give me the file back and we'll talk about it," he said, making another turn in the dark night. The sirens and sounds of the crowd slowly disappeared. Snow started falling, mixing with the soot covering them both.

"Where are we going?" she asked, her body beginning to shut down.

He slipped on the ice and quickly regained his footing, not slowing in the slightest. "I have a car around the next block."

She couldn't get into a vehicle with him, but her body was done. "I can't get you what you want, Theo. I'm so very sorry," she mumbled into his neck, finally giving in and relaxing completely against him.

"Then you're about to have a pretty rough night, sweetheart." His tone was all determination with more than a hint of threat.

Chapter 4

The woman wasn't faking exhaustion. Theo carried her through his apartment to the master bedroom after driving more than an hour to get through the city. She'd fallen asleep before he'd even put her in his car.

She slept soundly against him, her small body curled against his chest. The witch brought out feelings in him he really didn't like, and he couldn't exactly blame her since all she was doing was sleeping. It was the one true time he knew she wasn't trying to manipulate him, and yet, he wanted nothing more than to protect her and keep her safe. How did she do that?

More importantly, what the hell was wrong with her? Why couldn't she create fire?

He laid her down on the bed and then sighed, looking at her sopping wet clothing while switching on the bedside lamp. "Ginny? Wake up."

She didn't even stir. Surprisingly long lashes swept down her pale cheeks, and in sleep, her pink lips were relaxed and tipped up. Even out cold, she somehow smiled as if she knew a secret.

Why he liked that, he'd never know.

All right. If he left her in the wet dress, she'd freeze all night. But he couldn't just take off her clothes. Damn it. He ran a hand through his hair, scattering soot.

He'd been with more women than he could count, but this one was one of a kind. He didn't like that. Lifting her too easily with one arm, he drew back the covers and set her on her butt, her head leaning into his stomach. His dick instantly hardened to rock. Damn it. Forcing himself to relax, he deftly untied the corset and drew it off before laying her back down and quickly covering her with the bedclothes. Her thin panties could remain on. No way was he removing those.

She murmured something and turned toward him.

He pushed her hair away from her face, noting the silky softness, even with soot in it. But the mass had dried into tumbling curls. Figured she'd have naturally curly hair. "God was kind to you, darlin'," he murmured, running a knuckle down her smooth cheek. "Way too kind."

Yet what was going on?

Her pulse beat steadily in her neck, so she was unharmed at least. She sniffed and turned the other way, revealing the darkening bruise along the other side of her face.

Anger caught him in the chest. Hard. He should've ripped the head off the witch who'd hit her. An eight-story fall wasn't bad enough. He rubbed his finger across the heated bruise. Why hadn't she healed it earlier? There had been plenty of time before she'd fallen asleep. "What aren't you telling me?" He dropped to his haunches, smoothing her hair back again.

Then he examined her neck, making sure he hadn't hurt her when he'd grabbed her. Apparently she bruised easily. His chest loosened at seeing there were no bruises on her neck.

He paused. Wait a minute. He looked closer. There were no markings on her neck. Not a one. The woman had been mated, or so he thought. There would still be a bite, even from a witch. Matings were forever...until recently. A virus had been discovered that could negate the mating bond—at least when one of the mates had passed on, as Ginny's had. She had said she'd taken the virus and could be mated again. But he'd thought... Maybe he'd been wrong.

Thinking of oddities... He moved down the bed, not far, and reached for her ankle, pulling it out of the bed while making sure to keep the rest of her covered.

A anklet of diamonds and gold spikes encircled her left ankle tightly. Leather held it together, and there didn't seem to be a clasp. How did she get it off? He rubbed her ankle, and she moaned. He paused. What in the world? Looking closer, he could see a slight green ring around her skin.

Was she so vain she'd let her skin turn green to keep diamonds on? Or did the piece have sentimental value? Perhaps it had been from her mate.

Why that made Theo's chest hurt, he had no clue. He set her ankle back beneath the covers and turned to head for the master bathroom. After a very quick and hot shower, he was feeling more in control. Oh, he'd let her sleep tonight, but in the morning she was going to tell him everything.

He strode naked into his bedroom and drew on some sweats. She didn't stir, her breathing even and deep as she slept. He shook his head, heading into his living room and double-checking his security measures.

There was no way he could just go to sleep right now. It was nearly three in the morning, which made it midnight in northern Idaho. Hoping he wasn't making a colossal mistake, he booted up his television set, put in a series of codes, and sent out a call to the Realm Headquarters. The Realm was a coalition of witches, vampires, demons, and shifters. Its leader, vampire king Dage Kayrs, slowly took shape. "What the hell, Reese?" the king asked, his dark hair mussed and his silver eyes irritated. He stood bare to the waist with a rock-type wall behind him.

Theo winced. "Sorry. Thought you might be up."

"Are you being attacked or do you need immediate assistance?" Dage's eyes cleared.

"Ah, no." Theo dropped into a chair and rubbed his scruffy chin. He should've shaved in the shower. "I was hoping the queen was up and working." The queen was a brilliant geneticist who worked around the clock trying to cure human diseases. Of course, she was at least four or five months pregnant, so she probably needed her sleep.

"I'm up." Emma Kayrs passed near the camera and slid an arm around Dage's waist. The queen's dark hair was piled on her head, and she wore what looked like Star Trek pajamas. Her belly protruded, and she rubbed it. "How are you, Theo?"

"I'm a jerk," he said. "I shouldn't have called so late."

Dage ran a hand down Emma's arm. "I see you got out of the hotel fire safely. How is Ginny O'Toole?"

Theo's mouth gaped open. He shook his head. "How did you know?" Surely news of his night hadn't already reached Idaho.

Dage rolled his eyes.

Emma grinned. "He's the king. Don't make him say it. The. King."

Theo bit back a smile. "Oh, yeah. Well, since I have you, does a mating mark disappear when a former mate takes the virus?"

Emma's startling blue eyes brightened like they did every time anybody wanted to talk science with her. "No. Never. The bite mark stays in place." She leaned into Dage more. "But the mating brand, the ones from the Kayrs family, demons, and witches… That does disappear."

"Are you sure?" Theo asked, his mind spinning.

"Definitely." The queen nodded her head vigorously. "Why?"

Theo cleared his throat. "Because Ginny doesn't have a mark on her neck." He frowned. "Though witches don't—"

"Witches do," the queen interrupted. "All male immortals have fangs, even witches, and they bite during the mating process. If Ginny doesn't still have bite marks…"

"Then she was never mated," Theo finished, shocked he could find more anger in him than before. "I can't believe it."

Dage's eyes twinkled. "Things are about to get interesting now, aren't they?"

* * * *

Somebody was chasing her. Ginny ducked low and ran, her feet flying over the invisible ground. They were coming. After all this time, she was going to lose. God. She couldn't lose.

Theo. He would help her. He had to.

She turned a corner, suddenly surrounded by trees. Dark and high, they loomed over her, providing warning. No shelter or protection. No. She didn't get those. But warning. That was a nice change.

Something crashed into the brush behind her.

She yelped and ran harder, but the grass grew into weeds. They held her fast, not letting her move. Oh, no. It was too late. She opened her mouth and screamed.

"Whoa." Warmth and strength encircled her. "Wake up, lady. You're having a bad dream."

She jerked awake, her head hitting something hard. Pain

flashed through her skull.

"Damn it," Theo said, wrapping a hand in her hair and pulling her away.

Oh. She'd hit his chin with her head. "Sorry." She reached up to rub her forehead.

"You okay?" He loosened his hold, his eyes glowing in the dim light.

She blinked. Bed. She was in bed with Theo Reese. He smelled fresh and clean and male. A shadow covered his hard jaw, and his hard cut chest was bare. Oh, goodness. Did he have any clothing on? She stilled. Did she? She looked down. Nope. "You, ah, you took my clothes off." Her heart started to race.

"They were wet and dirty." He released her hair and smoothed his hand down her arm. "I didn't look." His teeth sparkled with his grin.

She blinked. Her brain went fuzzy. The bed was soft and the sheets luxurious. The world smelled strong and good…like him. "Why, I mean how, is there a light on?"

He slowly nodded. "Bathroom light. I thought you might be confused when you awoke, so I left the light on."

Now wasn't that sweet? Her body went all mushy, and she was too relaxed to stop it. "Thank you."

"That was quite the nightmare you were having," he rumbled.

She snorted. "That was nothing, believe me."

His gaze narrowed. "Really. Do you often have horrific dreams?"

Was that a weakness? She couldn't let him get that close. "No."

His lips thinned. "I thought we already discussed lying versus telling the truth. Stop lying to me."

Her chest felt heavy. The vampire had saved her from an attack squad, and he'd brought her to his home to keep safe. Then he'd left the light on for her so she wouldn't be scared. Liars really ticked him off, apparently. "Fine, Theo. I won't lie to you again." She meant every word.

His head lifted just slightly. "Do you have nightmares often?"

That was the question he'd wanted to start with? She should move away from him, but the male was all heat, and she was still cold. "Yes."

"About what?" he murmured, his gaze searching deep.

She breathed out. "Somebody chasing me. Torturing me. Killing me." It was difficult, but she forced a smile. "Normal scary dreams, you know?"

He studied her. "Who's chasing you?"

"Everybody bad," she said softly. "In the dream, I was looking for you." Heat rose to her face, making her cheeks hurt. "I mean, after last night, when you saved me, I guess that makes sense." Could she sound any more like a wimp? The idea caught her up short. When had she wanted to look strong to him? That wasn't her skill, darn it. "Thank you for saving me last night."

"You're welcome." He rubbed a gentle finger across her aching cheekbone. "Who was after you?"

"I don't know." She lifted a shoulder and then caught the sheet before it fell off her chest. "Could be anybody." Oh, she had an idea, but with her past, it really could be anybody. When was the last time she'd been in bed with a sexy, tousled male? It had been a while. And she'd bet her last pair of high heels that she'd never been this close to anybody this masculine. "I had a crush on you. Way back when," she confessed.

His eyes flared. "Then why seduce my brother?"

She winced. "I didn't seduce your brother. We were friends, and he was halfway to the high seas when we briefly dated. We shared one kiss, and it was like kissing...*my* brother. If I had one." Memories flooded her, and she smiled. "We were so young. So silly."

"Was it a cover?" Theo asked, once again threading his fingers through her hair.

Warmth tingled over her scalp. Her breath caught. "Yes. I was in Ireland to steal the McDougall emeralds."

Theo stiffened. "That was you?"

"Aye," she said, missing her homeland all of a sudden. "McDougall had stolen them first, which you probably already knew. I just stole them back for the original owners." A sweet little couple from way up north. They had them hidden to this day. "My da and I were a good team." Lord, she missed him. So very much. She had to succeed in this mission. No matter what.

"I'm sorry about your father. I heard he passed during the last war," Theo said quietly, caressing through her hair.

Sadness tried to take her, and she banished it, considering she wasn't telling the whole truth. "Yes. We were moving guns for the demons, and he ran afoul of some Kurjan soldiers." Then her life had taken a decidedly bad turn. "It's been ten years, and I still think he's going to call me up with a job." Of course, he wasn't really dead. But Theo didn't know that.

"What about your so-called mate?" Theo leaned in, his nose near to hers. "I know you never mated."

She brightened. "That was the only way I could get Jared to go follow his dream and be a pirate. He was so honorable. One kiss, and he thought I needed protection for life." She cleared her throat. "At first, I had a lifetime of debts to repay because of my dad's gambling. But he stopped gambling and we worked together. So breaking and entering, robbing and bribing, became, well, fun."

"Fun?" Theo growled.

"Yes." If Theo got any closer, his mouth would be on hers. Her thighs moved restlessly. Aye, she'd wondered through the years about him. Now he was so damn close. Did she have the courage to take a nip? "Let's not talk about your brother when we're in bed, Theo."

"Why not?" he asked, his voice hoarse.

"Because of this." Finally, she moved forward and kissed him.

Chapter 5

Theo's entire body jolted. His mind spun from her revelations of being a thief, a famous one, but right now his body ruled. Her soft lips worked his mouth, tentatively at first, and then with passion. Her small hands spread across his chest and over his shoulders, and she pressed into him with only the thin sheet and his old sweats as barriers.

He'd had more dreams about her than he could count. It had killed him when she'd chosen his brother to dick over instead of him. Yet he tightened his hold in her thick hair and tugged her back.

She gave a small sound of protest and then met his gaze. Passion had darkened her eyes to deep sapphire. "Theo?" she breathed.

His cock pounded with her so near. A part of him, one he didn't like, whispered to shut the hell up and take what she was offering. But she was a master with men, and he'd actually had a crush on her eons ago. "I like this new honesty thing you have going on, but I don't trust you."

Her eyes widened and then she laughed. Humor spilled from her. "Oh, that makes sense." She hummed and spread her fingers out over his shoulders. "I've never, not once, seduced a man like this."

He lifted an eyebrow.

She grinned and bit her lip. "I mean naked in bed. I've never slept with a mark or used sex." She ducked her head. "I've used wiles and promises, but never actual sex. I'm not that bad, Theo."

God, she was cute. Every nerve he owned wanted to believe her, and his gut said she was telling the truth. His body was already hers... He just had to protect his brain. But it was difficult with her soft skin and sweet scent so close. Finally. He wanted inside her and now. "Where's my file, Ginny?" he asked.

Her straight teeth played with her lip. "You can't have it. Sorry." She sighed and released him.

Damn it. He wanted those hands back on his skin. Now. "So you at least admit you stole it."

"Yep."

He blinked. "What game are you playing now?"

She tugged the sheet up more and wiggled around a little, as if trying to get comfortable. Good to know he wasn't the only one hurting. "You saved me, so no more lies. I'm not lying to you ever again. So the truth is that I stole the file, I'm keeping it, and you can't have it back."

Now he laughed. "Ginny, you're not the only one who's led an interesting life."

"I know all about you, Theo." She reached out and ran a finger down his jugular, sending shock waves through his body. "I know what you did in the last war. Your reputation as a soldier and a sniper. Things your brothers probably don't even know."

He frowned and leaned back. She knew about him? "Bullshit."

"They call you the Phantom. Because you can get the job done without leaving a trace. You can also get answers." She hummed. "The demons call you the Interrogator. Such a boring name."

Yet he'd earned both names. "Those are both stupid and don't come close to describing actions in war." The woman wasn't the only one with nightmares. "Apparently you've kept track of me." He wasn't sure he liked her knowing so much about him. His secrets were his own, damn it.

"I have," she said. "Call it curiosity."

His ego wanted to swell, and he batted it down. Hard. "If you know about me, then you know I'll get my file back. No matter what I have to do." He didn't want to hurt her.

She laughed again, the sound sexy and throaty. "Oh, Theo. You couldn't torture me. Not in a million years."

He smiled. "You're right."

She paused. "Okay." Now she sounded a mite worried.

He tried not to take too much pleasure in that fact. "You're obviously on a job—probably more than one. While I won't harm you, I'm also going to prevent you from finishing any job you might be undertaking. Whoever hired you is going to be pissed because you're going to fail. Repeatedly. Until I get my file back."

Her head snapped back. "You wouldn't."

Adorable. She really was. When her temper showed, she was glorious. "I would and I will." Now he leaned in, feathering his mouth across hers. "We both know you can't throw fire, and for some reason, your strength is depleted. You can't fight me and win." He kissed her softly, taking his time, enjoying the taste of woman and the thrill of the challenge in getting his file back. "You're probably out of sedatives, baby."

Her lips pursed. "This isn't an old Hepburn and Tracy movie. I can't give your file back."

"Okay." He never lost a challenge, and she'd have to learn that the hard way. Truth be told, he liked battling her. Entirely too much. The temptation of her was too much to resist, though. So he drew her close and stopped playing, taking her mouth hard.

She moaned and moved into him, kissing him back, her tongue dueling with his. Soft and sweet, her scent surrounded him. Hot spikes of lust pierced him. He took her deeper, pulling her on top of him. The second her skin met his, he groaned. Her thighs dropped to either side of his, her sex cradling his erection.

He slid a hand down her back, pressing her closer. God. White hot lights flashed behind his eyes. He could have his sweats and her panties off in seconds.

She tunneled her hands in his hair, kissing him back, her body flush on him, her nipples tight against his chest.

He should halt this. Give it a second. Make sure it was real. But his body wouldn't stop. His mouth kissed her harder, taking control.

She gave as good as she got, as if she too knew their time together wouldn't last. They were on opposite sides.

At the thought, he pulled away.

She was spread over him, her lips rosy, a stunning flush across her face. "We should stop," she mused.

"Yes." He ran his hand down her bare back, halting at the dip at her waist. God, she felt fucking amazing. "Or we go into this with our eyes wide open."

Interest and need glimmered in her stunning eyes. "Meaning?"

He was backwoods crazy to even suggest it, but who the hell cared? "This is just this. You and me satisfying curiosity from years ago and taking the edge off. The second we're dressed and out of bed, we're on opposite sides of this thing. I'll do what I have to in order to get my file back." It was only fair to warn her.

"That's crazy," she murmured, rubbing against him.

"I know," he admitted, the blood rushing through his head to ring in his ears. "But I want you and have for centuries. You're almost naked on top of me, and it's taking every ounce of self-control I have not to roll you over and fuck you so hard you forget about the file. Until you forget about everything but me."

She swallowed and sat up on him, her full breasts bouncing. "I, ah, don't want you to think I'm easy."

His heart turned over. Hard. Damn, she was sweet when she lost the act. "We moved out of the last century a while ago, sweetheart. I don't think you're easy." He flattened his hand over her upper chest and caressed down, tweaking both her nipples. "But I might not let you go."

She gasped and leaned into him, her panties becoming wet right over his cock. "I want this, too. But you have to know that I'll fight dirty afterward." Her voice was throaty and devastatingly sexy.

"I wouldn't have it any other way." He grasped her nipples and pulled her down.

She opened her mouth on a gasp, and he took full advantage, grasping the back of her head and holding her in place. He kissed her deep, his hand tangled in her hair, his other hand kneading her nipple. Yeah. His Ginny liked a little bite with her pleasure. He'd known she'd be like this.

Sexy, hot, and responsive.

She gyrated against him, her core moving along his shaft. With a moan into his mouth, she reached down and shoved his sweats off his hips.

He helped her, using his legs to completely kick them off.

The second she settled back over him, her wet core right against his dick, he almost lost his mind. Growling, he rolled over, pressing her into the bed. Her legs spread, and her soft thighs rubbed the outside of his.

"Now, Theo," she whispered, her nails scraping down his back.

Oh, she didn't get to call the shots here. He kissed along her jawline and down, taking his time with her breasts. God, she was perfect. Whether he wanted her to be or not, she was everything he'd ever wanted. Even the thieving. The damn intrigue with her went way beyond the physical.

He was in trouble, and he didn't give a shit.

Reaching down, he snapped her panties in two. Then he kissed his way down her abdomen, noting how small her ribs really were. God, he'd have to be careful with her. Reaching her core, he licked her slit.

All woman and spice. She gasped and stiffened. He grinned, going at her, showing no mercy. Her G-spot was an easy find inside her, and he used two figures to torture her. Then he licked her clit, giving just enough pressure to have her gasping for relief. Her skin was beyond soft, and her body incredibly responsive.

"Theo," she moaned, her nails raking down his scalp.

He loved the pain. But if he didn't get inside her soon, he was going to explode. So he nipped her clit and twisted his fingers inside her wet heat. She arched into his mouth, crying out, her entire body shuddering with her release. He kept her going until she settled back with a whimper.

Then he moved up her body, kissing and licking, finally reaching her mouth. "You are so sweet," he murmured.

She grinned and shoved him over, rolling on top of him again. "Remember that when I kick your ass later." Aroused, having fun, her brogue emerged.

Just one more sexy thing about the woman.

"I'll keep that in mind." He could feel her pulsing clit along his dick. "You sure about this?"

"Definitely." She leaned over and then paused. Her eyes widened. She stiffened and pulled back.

He blinked. "Ginny?"

"Oh." She scrambled back, her face losing all color. "What time is it?" She looked around, her gaze frantic.

He grabbed her biceps to keep her from falling onto the floor. "It's only about six in the morning." He tried to slow his heart rate, but her bare breasts were right in front of his face. Pretty pink nipples and full globes that already carried whisker burn from him. "What's wrong?"

She shoved off him, standing and weaving, pale in her nudity. "Oh, God. It's after five." She looked around. "Where's my laptop bag?"

"In the other room." He sat up, confusion mixing with anger. She was too pale. Way too pale. "What's going on?"

"I need my phone," she hissed, suddenly crying out. "Damn it." She hopped on one foot, panic cascading from her. "In my bag. Get my phone."

He looked down at her lifted ankle with the band around it. "What the hell is that thing?"

She cried out again, grabbing the anklet and falling to the ground. "Please, Theo. Get me the phone." Purple striations rose from her ankle up to her knee.

He launched into the other room, finding her cell phone in her laptop bag and hurrying back with it.

She held it, tears streaming down her face as she made a quick text. Then she cried out again, clutched her ankle to her body, and passed out cold.

Chapter 6

Ginny came to surrounded by softness and the scent of…Theo. Her eyelids flashed open to see his dark eyes filling her world.

"You alive?" he asked, his hair tousled as he leaned over her, his big hand on her forehead. "I admit I give a hell of an orgasm."

"Aye." She glanced around. Apparently Theo had pulled a big T-shirt over her head before setting her back in the bed. She pushed herself up to sit, shoving her hair away from her face. "So."

He sat on the bed, wearing worn sweats and a frown. His big and broad chest beckoned her to take a bite, but warning all but rolled from him. "You have three minutes to explain what's happening, or I take off that anklet." He jerked his head toward a knife he'd placed on the bedside table. "I'm assuming it's made of phanekite."

"Planekite," she corrected. "Well, it depends who you talk to in what you call it. But yes. It's made of the one mineral in the world that can harm witches." The damn stuff could kill them, and at the moment, enemies had made darts full of the stuff. But her anklet was old school.

He reached for the knife. Determination and what appeared to be fury pounded a muscle beneath his jaw. "I don't even want to know why you're continuing to wear that. Let's take it off, and then you're going to tell me all about who put it there."

She held up a hand. "It's rigged. You cut it, and spikes slash into my skin, filling me with planekite. A lethal dose."

He paused, his eyes somehow darkening even more. "Let me get this straight. The thing is made of planekite, which obviously weakens you until you can't throw fire. It can be remotely controlled to jolt you with doses, which is what I just saw happen."

He grasped her hand, his gentle touch completely opposed to the rage glittering in those eyes. "And if you try to remove it, the thing is booby trapped to kill you."

"Yes," she breathed, her shoulders relaxing. It felt so damn good to talk about the anklet. She'd had to keep it secret for so long.

"Who?" Theo asked, his jaw looking harder than a boulder.

She shouldn't say. But the heaviness of keeping the burden to herself was overwhelming. It was too much. "Saul Libscombe," she whispered.

"Goddamn motherfucker." Theo pushed away from her, standing and facing the doorway, fury vibrating the muscles in his back. "This is *our* fault?"

"No." Ginny spread her hands out on the bedclothes. "It's my fault. I'm a thief, and that life catches up to you."

He pivoted so quickly to face her that she lost her breath. "My family has been at odds with the Libscombes for years. We killed them, they killed us, and now Saul is the only one left standing. He did this to you so you'd get to us."

"Aye." Things had gotten a lot worse the last month when Jared Reese had killed Petey Libscombe, who was Saul's brother. But the Reese family had probably thought things were over, since Saul appeared to be the one good shifter in his family. The guy had a good front but was more evil than the rest put together. Ginny plucked at a loose string. "Saul has been playing the long game, while Petey kept you off balance the last few years. Saul wanted the Benjamin file, and I'm the only one who could get close enough to steal it. I'm so sorry, Theo."

"Long game?" Everything around Theo stilled, as if gathering for an explosion. "How long have you worn that fucking thing?"

She bit her lip.

"Ginny?" His voice went dangerously low.

"Ten years," she whispered, preparing for him to detonate.

He didn't move. Didn't even twitch. "Ten. Years."

She nodded, her heart beating too fast for her to ease. He was scaring the hell out of her, and that wasn't easy to do. "This has been a campaign full of movements, including stealing a lot of gold. He's been setting it up for a decade, and now he's made his move.

I'm sorry."

"Why didn't you come to me?" Theo whispered, lines cutting edges into the side of his mouth.

Her heart took a hit. He would've helped her. She could see that now. "You didn't like me." She cleared her throat, going full in. "And he has my father somewhere. Da is still alive."

Theo rocked back. "He has your dad."

She nodded. "Even if I could get the anklet off, the second I do, my dad is dead."

Theo moved for her and dropped to his haunches, gingerly taking her ankle in his hands. His broad hands could easily snap the anklet in two, but he just examined it. "There must be sensors here somewhere."

"Aye." While there was no good way out of this mess, her shoulders finally relaxed from around her ears. She wasn't alone. Finally. No matter what happened, she had Theo with her for this moment. Actually on her side. She smiled. "If I give Saul the file, the anklet comes off and my dad goes free."

Theo cocked his head to the side, and his gaze traveled to meet hers. "Ah, sweetheart. You don't believe that, do you?"

She pressed her lips together. "About the anklet? No. But I won't hand over the file until my dad is free. That's my only goal."

"I'm gonna kill your dad when this is over." Theo lifted her leg until the anklet was at eye level. He studied it for several moments. "I can't believe he made you a thief."

"I'm a great thief," she said, giving in to temptation and feeling along his jawline. Firm and solid. Yeah. That was Theo. "Da and I only stole from bad people or from people who didn't need what they had. We've financed some wonderful charities throughout the ages, and we've done some good."

"You enjoy it." Theo set her leg down and rocked back, studying her. "The thieving."

"Sometimes." Why lie about it? "I've helped a lot of people."

"You're a thief." He shook his head and stood, withdrawing.

Oh, yeah. She'd forgotten that side of Theo Reese. The honorable, law-abiding, honest guy. What he'd done as a soldier, he'd done during war. Some people didn't realize that wars always went on...just not publicly. "I am." She wouldn't lie to him again.

"Don't get me wrong. I'd love to work full time for a nonprofit like Other Tracks. Do real work and get some good done." She gestured toward the anklet. "But that's not going to be my path, and we both know it."

"You're giving up?"

"No. Just being realistic." She slid to the edge of the bed. "Now I need a shower, and then I have to meet Saul."

Theo crossed his arms, his gaze implacable. "Oh, lady. Your entire life just changed. Accept that now."

Her head snapped up, and she stood. In her bare feet, looking up at least a foot to his hard gaze, she barely held back a telltale shiver. "Excuse me?"

"You've been tagged like an animal to get to me and my family." His arms uncrossed. "You stole a file that could ruin us." He moved toward her and took both arms in his, lifting her up on her toes. "You just became my responsibility, whether you like it or not. Get on board and now."

* * * *

Theo kept his gaze stoic when all he wanted to do was punch a wall. To think she'd lived with this pain for an entire decade without anybody to help her. That ended and right now.

Her gaze softened. "You can't save me, Theo."

The fuck he couldn't. "Take a shower. We'll talk after you're feeling better." His doorbell rang, and he released her.

She jerked. "Who's here?"

"Reinforcements. I called my brothers the second I recognized the planekite. Shower. Now." He turned her and patted her ass to get her going. She slapped his hand. Good. Her spunk was coming back. "You have five minutes and I'm dragging you out of there."

She paused at the doorway and flipped him off.

He grinned and grabbed her suitcase to drop outside the bathroom. Then he headed for his front door, bypassing his sprawling living room with the quiet brick fireplace. Reaching the front door, he opened it just as Jared was about to bust through. "Geez. Give me a minute."

His brothers both stomped inside, brushing snow off their

leather jackets. Jared had black hair and even blacker eyes, while Chalton had blond hair and black eyes and much more angular features. They were both about Theo's height at six-foot-five, and right now wore matching frowns.

"She has a planekite band on her ankle?" Jared snarled, slamming the door behind himself.

"Yes. She's worn it for a decade and is now being blackmailed to hurt us," Theo said, jerking his head at the computer bag over Chalton's shoulder. "Did you bring anything that will help?"

Chalton shrugged. "I don't know. Let's take a look at the anklet." As the computer genius for the entire Realm, Chalton had the best equipment. "Though aren't you the one who hacked me last month?"

"I am." Theo grinned, unable to help himself, warming that his brothers had come immediately to help. It was good to be back in each other's lives after too long of a time. "But I don't have the hardware the Realm is using. You have it."

Chalton nodded. "Fair enough."

Jared ran a hand through his shaggy hair, taking note of Theo's bare chest. "Anything you want to tell us?"

"No." Theo gestured them into the living room, with its dark sofas, before pressing a button on the wall. The blinds lifted to reveal the New York skyline just coming awake.

"I can smell her on you," Chalton muttered, sitting and unpacking his bag. He looked toward Jared. "Is this going to be weird?"

Jared dropped into a leather chair. "Theo is always weird." He scrubbed both hands down his face. "I wasn't in love with her, and now I know that fact since I've mated Veronica. But I do like Ginny, and I hate that she's been used against us like this."

"Me too." Theo rolled his neck and remained standing. "Saul is coming after us." God. He had to keep the Green Rock file away from Chalton. Jared had known about the file way back when, but Chalton needed to be protected. "Has anybody heard from Uncle Benny?"

Jared exhaled loudly. "Yes. He's coming home from Russia to kill us. If we go quietly, he'll leave Mom alone."

Chalton winced. "All we did was blow up two of his homes

and get his private data stolen. Does that require death?"

"Yes," Theo and Jared said in unison. They weren't kidding, either. Theo looked around his high-end place. "Is there anything we could offer Benny?"

"Just our heads," Jared said grimly.

Damn it. Spare him from thousand-year-old vampires who just couldn't relax and find humor in a good explosion. "One thing at a time," Theo said. "When Saul attacked Ginny through the anklet earlier, she texted him that she'd meet him at rendezvous point *B* tomorrow at midnight. So I'm guessing it's somewhere she has to travel to reach."

"Guessing?" Jared sat back, his gaze narrowing. "She hasn't told you?"

Theo crossed his arms. "She's not going to trust us completely, especially with her dad's life, until we show we can help. She's been on her own a long time, Jar."

Jared coughed. "Her dad is alive?"

"Yes, and he's imprisoned by Saul." Theo's hands clenched into fists. "I can't believe she's dealt with this by herself for a fucking decade."

Jared and Chalton exchanged a look.

"What?" Theo asked, his instincts humming.

Chalton shrugged, typing rapidly on his computer. "You've always had a thing for her. I remember centuries ago... And you liked her."

"So?" Theo asked.

Jared grinned. "It's fun to see you be the one dangling after the last several months. You had many a smart-ass comment when Chalton and I were, ah..."

"Turning into mated wussies?" Theo asked, matching his grin.

Jared rolled his eyes. "Yeah. That."

"Listen." Theo had never lied to his brothers, and he wasn't going to start now. "I like her, but this is just temporary and to scratch a quick itch. The woman is a thief, and she'll be gone when we're done here."

Charlton snorted.

Jared coughed into his hand.

Theo rolled his eyes. "Whatever. Just because you guys got all domesticated doesn't mean I will. Come on." Even as he said the words, they sounded hollow to him. He was spared whatever retort his brothers wanted to make by Ginny moving into the room.

With her wet hair curling down her back, sans the makeup, she looked about eighteen. Pure and innocent except for the sparkle in those dangerously blue eyes. Unlike her usual fitted dress, she'd pulled on faded jeans with a soft robin's egg blue sweater. The bruise from the night before marred her right cheek with an odd purple, making her look both beautiful and tragic.

She smiled. "The Reese boys all in one place." With an exaggerated movement, she winked at Theo. "I hope your apartment is insured."

Chapter 7

Ginny moved into the room, feeling like a doe surrounded by hungry panthers. The Reese boys en masse managed to take over the very atmosphere with a sense of male power. Even among vampires, they had presence. Their closeness was obvious, and she clasped her hands together as she sat in a leather seat. "Rumor has it Uncle Benny is heading home."

"Yes," Jared said, his gaze on her bruise. "Who hurt you?" His brows drew down.

She touched the still aching cheekbone. "An idiot Theo threw out a window afterward." She smiled.

"You can't heal yourself?" Chalton asked gently.

She shook her head. "The anklet keeps my powers at bay, unfortunately." Could this be any more awkward? She'd dated Jared, kind of played him a little, had stolen from their family, and now had orgasmed from Theo's very talented mouth. Heat flushed into her cheeks, and she couldn't stop the blush.

Theo swore under his breath and moved for her, plucking her out of the chair and sitting back down with her in his lap. "Relax, lady. Jared forgives you for the past, Chalton isn't mad about the Benjamin file, and you and I are working together until we're not. Same rules as before."

Humor filled Jared's eyes. "He's given you rules?"

She snorted and rolled her eyes. "He likes rules, you know?"

Chalton nodded, his gaze on his screen as he typed. "Always has been a tightass."

That easily, she relaxed into Theo's heat. They were friends again. At least for now. "I'm sorry I can't give you the file back," she said, her chest starting to hurt.

"We'll get it back," Theo said easily. "Let's worry about one thing at a time."

She nodded. "Jared, I'm sorry in general."

The eldest Reese brother gave her a grin. "It's all good, Gin. Though my Veronica feels terrible you two got into a fistfight while you were hampered by the anklet. She would've never hit you had she known."

Ginny laughed. "That's a 'nice to meet you' among my people. I like your mate. Very much."

He smiled. "I'll let her know. Just so you know, you and I are friends and always will be. Even when you toss Theo out on his ass."

She could read people, and if she was reading Jared right, he was greatly amused by something. Was it Theo and her? That was silly. They were temporary and would soon be on opposing sides again. "Um, okay."

Chalton stopped typing. "Can I see the anklet?"

She nodded and stretched out her bare foot, planting it on the coffee table and pulling up her jeans leg.

Chalton leaned forward, took a look, and then started typing. "Since it can be activated remotely, it sends out waves. Let me see what I can find out."

Ginny nodded, allowing Theo to pull her back into his heat. She settled against him, trying not to dream about what it'd feel like to have somebody all the time. To be with Theo all the time. He made her feel safe and protected, and that couldn't last. Yet she snuggled into him anyway, letting him hold her. If she let her heart be broken by him, it was her own fault. And the ride might just be worth it.

Chalton sat back, his gaze on the screen.

"Well?" Theo asked, his breath brushing Ginny's ear.

She shivered and cuddled closer. "It can't be deactivated, right?"

Chalton nodded, his full mouth turning down. He always had been the quiet one in the family.

She turned to face Theo's dark eyes, her stomach churning. "I appreciate your trying to help, but I researched this thing extensively when it was first forced on me. It can't be removed, and the only way to deactivate it is at its source. Where Saul has it."

"She's correct," Chalton said. "The technology is as good as anything we have. Saul must've spent decades perfecting it."

Theo's face remained calm, but anger poured from him to surround her. She patted his bare chest. "It's okay. It really is."

"It's not okay," he gritted out. "Where is Saul? Let's take him out now."

"I don't know," she sighed. "Believe me, if I knew where he was and where he has my da, I would've hired an attack force years ago. But he's remained under the radar."

Realization dawned in Theo's eyes. "Until you actually stole the file. Now he has to meet you to get it."

She nodded, her gaze dropping to his mouth. "Yes. I can't wait much longer. The anklet is taking too much of a toll, and I don't know when it'll be too late for me to move against him."

"What was your real plan?" Theo pushed her curling hair away from her face, his touch infinitely gentle even with the anger glowing so brightly in his dark eyes.

"Steal the file, get my dad released, kill Saul." She was enjoying Theo's touch entirely too much.

Jared sighed. "It's not a bad plan except for the last part. Saul will be expecting an attack."

Theo nodded. "Yeah, but he won't be expecting us to be part of it."

Hope flared inside her. Hot and bright. "You'll help me take out Saul?"

"Yes, but not with the file," Theo said. "We have to find another way."

Of course. His family had to come first with him. She understood that. Forcing a smile, she made herself nod. "Okay. That makes sense."

His gaze narrowed. "Don't try to play me."

She had no choice. "I'm not." Why the hell was he so tough to fool? Her eyelids fluttered. "I need some protein to combat the planekite. Maybe some Vitamin C?" She'd found that oranges and turkey bacon had actually helped somewhat on more than one occasion. Almonds as well.

"Where's the file, Ginny?" Theo asked.

She dropped the pretense. "I'm sorry." Her phone rang in her back pocket, and she jumped.

Theo pulled it out before she could and read the face. His face went blank, and he pressed the speaker button. "Answer," he mouthed.

She glared and then shoved him in the gut. "Hello?"

Theo put the phone down on the coffee table.

"So glad to hear you survived the reminder this morning," Saul said, his voice nasally over the line. "You know what happens when you don't check in."

"Where's my da?" she returned, trying desperately to ignore the tension suddenly choking the room.

Saul chuckled. "You'll see him soon. But I needed to see what you're up to now. Your GPS puts you at Theo Reese's apartment in New York. I knew you'd do anything for a job, but Theo Reese?"

Theo's body somehow hardened around her. Only her training kept her voice from shaking. "Did you send the attack squad last night?" What was she dealing with here?

Saul sighed. "Yes. You've been so difficult to work with about the Benjamin file, so I thought we'd just take it."

"I don't have it with me, you moron." She shook her head. Saul really was an idiot. "More than that, you created the situation I'm in right now. Theo was angry I took the file you wanted, he defended me from your goons, and now he's threatening to keep me under lock and key until he gets it back. I told you he'd be a problem." She gave the man in question a hard look.

He merely lifted an eyebrow.

The line crackled. "Where is Theo now?" Saul asked.

"In the shower, Saul," she answered, forcing boredom into her voice.

"Well now, I knew you were a loose bitch," Saul snapped.

Theo growled low, and she shoved him in the stomach. The man had to be quiet, damn it. "Just because I turned you down, Saul, doesn't mean I like to go to bed lonely." She couldn't help get the dig in.

Pain flared along her ankle, and she cried out.

Theo vibrated, reaching for the anklet, determination hardening his jaw.

She quietly slapped him away. The poison entered her bloodstream, just a small dose, and her limbs went numb. Her head lolled. "That the best you've got?"

Saul laughed. "Oh, you and I are going to have some fun together once you give me that file. I'll let your father go, but you and I aren't finished. Got it?"

"You and I never got started, remember?" She wasn't going to let the asshole have any illusions. "I said no."

"That was before you'd worn a planekite anklet for years," he said slowly. "If you want that off, you'll do whatever I tell you to do, or we both know it's going to kill you. The long-term effects can't be healthy. My guess? You'll need to mate to regain your strength."

What a complete bastard. She was going to kill him, and she was going to enjoy seeing him bleed first. "Planekite is preferable to you, asshole." She waited for the blast to her ankle, but one didn't come.

"I'm offering to mate you and take off the ankle bracelet," he said easily. "I'm a shifter, you're a witch, and we would make powerful offspring. It might be your only chance at survival."

Bile rose in her throat. "One of us is going to die before that happens. I hope it's you." She meant every word. In fact, if she was going to die, so was he. For ten years she'd practiced fighting with a knife, just in case.

"Keep up your strength. You need to be free of Reese by tomorrow night to make it to our meeting spot," Saul snapped.

She eyed Theo. "Not a problem. He's strong but not the sharpest tool in the shed."

He lifted his chin, his lip quirking.

The phone went dead.

She breathed out, her body aching from the planekite.

"Where's the meet?" Theo asked.

She leaned her cheek against his chest. Just for the moment to regain her strength.

Theo tucked her close, his chin rubbing her forehead. "How did he get the band on you, darlin'?"

Sleepy. She was so damn sleepy. The planekite worked against her organs, making them fight hard just to do their jobs. "Attack squad of twelve. I gave a good fight, but…" She'd ended up with the ankle bracelet from hell.

Theo kissed her forehead. "I'll gut him for you, Gin. Naval to neck, I'll slice him open, yank out his guts, and stomp all over them."

Now wasn't that sweet? She actually loved the predatory vampire Theo kept carefully banked way down deep. "Are you courting me?" she whispered, trying to hide her grin.

"Maybe." Theo's breath stirred her hair, smelling like peppermint. "If I am, whatever you're planning just became my plan. Only one of us is fighting Saul hand-to-hand, and it's not the one of us hampered by a planekite anklet."

Just when he was sounding reasonable, he turned all male on her. She sighed. "Maybe it's better we didn't—"

"Don't finish that thought," he warned, his mouth next to her ear. "We are nowhere near done with what we started earlier. Once you're healthy, we're taking some time. Some serious time."

What the heck did that mean? She opened her mouth to ask, but she couldn't find the right words. Just what did Theo want from her? Other than the Benjamin file, of course.

"I've got Saul," Chalton said, his gaze on the computer. "Traced the call."

Her head snapped up. Man. She'd forgotten there were other Reese men in the room. Wait a minute. They couldn't trace Saul. She had to meet him. "What did you do?" she whispered.

Chapter 8

After supper, Theo kept an eye on the pacing woman, noting the blazing anger in her eyes. Man, she was gorgeous when riled. The New York skyline behind her didn't do her justice. He kicked back on the sofa, his feet extended onto the coffee table. He had finally gotten some food into her, and the protein had seemed to help. "I wish you'd relax," he said. Again. It had been a long damn day.

She whirled on him. "If you go after Saul, he'll have my father killed."

"No, he won't," Theo returned. Again. "We'll take him, torture him a little, and tell him that if he doesn't let your dad go, he dies. After he releases you from that damn anklet."

She shook her hair, and curls tumbled down her entire back. "He's not that dumb, Theo. Listen to me. This won't work."

He tried for patience. Truly, he did. The woman had been terrorized by this asshole, and she had a right to be frightened. His brothers were out preparing for the raid, and he'd spent the morning and afternoon gaining intel on Saul, his land holdings, and planekite. "We have confirmation that Saul is staying across town. He's *here*, Ginny. But you already knew that, didn't you?"

She had the grace to blush.

He nodded toward his laptop. "The king sent me all the Realm documentation on Saul. I know everything about the bastard now, including the fact that he owns a home two hours out of the city—where we traced his call. But still, I don't understand. Since your meet is set for somewhere in the city, or at least in this state, why wait?"

"Because Saul is supposed to bring my da from wherever he's being kept," she said. "I don't release the flash drive until I see my father get in a car and drive away." She swallowed. "Apparently Saul needed time to bring Dad here." Her chin lifted. "It's a good plan."

Theo narrowed his gaze. "Yeah. It's a great plan if we're all on board with you sacrificing yourself. I'm not, and I'm sure your father isn't, either."

Her shoulders slumped. "That's our only option, *T.*"

T. He'd wondered if she remembered how she used to call him that. A lifetime ago, when they'd been friends. Man, he'd missed her. To think of the years he'd spent being angry with her while not even truly knowing her. "You're not a lamb, baby." He wasn't going to sacrifice her. Ever.

"I'm sick." She looked down at her ankle. "The planekite has infected me. There's no going back." She shrugged, her jaw firming with the stubborn tilt he somehow knew well. "This is my last chance to save my father, and I'm taking it. You have to step down."

"I think you're right about the planekite poisoning," Theo said, gesturing toward the laptop he'd pushed to the side. "The queen sent me all the research data she has on the mineral, and long-term exposure seems to be fatal. It also explains why you can't create fire or even heal the bruise on your face." Every time he looked at the dark mark, he got pissed off.

She cut him a look. "Don't sugarcoat it."

"Not going to." He leaned back and clasped his hands behind his neck, stretching his torso. "I said no lying between us, remember?"

She shoved curls out of her face. "You surely did. So yes. I'm dying. Yay for the truth."

Wasn't she cute when she was dramatic? If he told her that, she'd no doubt punch him in the face. So he went for more truth. "So we need to get mated, then."

She reared up to argue more, stopping suddenly. Her pink lips opened in an O. She closed them, her mouth moved again, and nothing came out.

He bit back a grin. So much for the woman leaping into his arms with gratitude. "Gin?"

Her lids half-lowered, and she pressed her hands against her hips. "You are not funny."

"I am not kidding." He wanted her more than he'd ever wanted another woman in his long life. He liked her. Hell. He wanted to be with her. It made sense on so many levels. A voice in the back of his head laughed wildly, and he banished it.

She shook her head in an odd convulsion of denial. "You've lost your damn mind, then."

"Probably," he agreed.

She swung her arms out. "We can't get mated. That's crazy. We can barely get along."

"We get along just fine," he countered. "At least we will after you give me back the information that could destroy my entire family."

"I'm a thief," she snapped, very nice color filling her face.

He nodded. "I'd very much like for you to find another profession after we mate. Definitely after we procreate." There were plenty of legal ways to help other people.

"Procreate?" she asked, her voice trembling. "Theo, you're an old-fashioned guy."

"Exactly. Arranged matings are very old fashioned," he said easily. "I spoke with the queen after she sent me the information. She agrees. The only way for you to survive this is to mate an immortal, and not another witch. You'd poison him, most likely." He sat up. "Did you know that Brenna Dunne mated Jase Kayrs, the queen's brother-in-law, for the very same reason? Because of planekite poisoning? A long time ago." He lowered his chin. "Mating a vampire saved Brenna. It will save you, too."

* * * *

Ginny couldn't breathe. Not from the planekite, but from the vampire watching her so intently. He'd dressed in casual jeans and a dark T-shirt for the day, but there was nothing casual about him. Oh, his feet were on the coffee table, and his body was stretched on the sofa, but he was all predator, ready to lunge. She could *feel* the animal in him. "Theo, you really need to stop and think about this." Her voice shook, but she couldn't help it. The mere idea of mating Theo Reese stole her breath and slid heat through her entire body.

"This is your only option for survival. I like the idea of an arranged mating spelled out with a contract," he said evenly.

Her head jerked up. "I'm sure one of your terms is the damn flash drive."

"That's a different deal. If I get your father back, you give me the flash drive." Theo's head lifted in an oddly threatening way. "Fair?"

That did sound fair through the buzzing between her ears. What was happening? Theo wanted to mate her? He was the one guy in the universe she hadn't been able to manipulate. What kind of a mating would that lead to? "You want honesty," she whispered.

"I demand it." He cocked his head to the side, studying her. "You need it."

Oh, he did not get to tell her what she needed. "You don't trust me."

"Sure, I do. You tell the truth when you agree to do so." He leaned forward, his hands clasped between his knees. "And when you lie, I can tell."

"I don't like that about you," she burst out.

He chuckled and stretched to his feet. "I'm sure. But would you really want a mate you could easily manipulate?"

Well, no. She had to admit, she respected the guy. He was smart, strong, and sexy... And he definitely knew how to kiss. But he kept her so damn off-kilter. That couldn't be good, could it? She shook her head. "Theo, mating might save me. What do you get out of it? We both know you hadn't planned on mating for a very long time."

"I've already been alive for a very long time," he countered. "I'm not a heart and flowers type of guy, Gin. Never have been. Both of my brothers are mated, and they're happy. We're a family again. A mate fits quite well into my plans."

Well then. Undying love and all of that. She breathed out. "I-I just don't know about this."

He nodded. "I understand, but it's happening, so get on board."

Wh-What? She coughed. "Theo."

"I'm not gonna let you die, sweetheart. It's that simple." He pressed a button on the computer, and something sounded from the office next to his massive kitchen. "The king said he'd be happy to negotiate on your behalf. I've just printed out my initial offer. Please take a look at it and let me know what you think."

Fire swept her. "I don't need anybody to negotiate for me. You want to negotiate? Fine. Let's do so right now." The very nerve of the males. Hell. She'd negotiated land deals that had transferred power through dynasties before.

"Okay. My offer is mating and marriage, if you want marriage. No more stealing. We live here for a couple months a year so I can see my family, and anywhere else you might want the rest of the year. I'm a soldier in contract with the Realm, so I might need to leave for work once in a while. My other business interests can be handled from anywhere." He rolled his neck, his gaze not leaving hers. "I do the fights to the death, and you can do everything else you want. Oh, and I'd like children. Someday."

There was something almost sweet about his logical approach. Which was why there was only one answer. "No."

His gaze narrowed. "That wasn't one of your options."

She sighed. "I'm not mating for convenience, and I like you way too much to see you do that. There's too much to life. To passion and maybe love. I'll take my chances when I get the anklet off." Her smile came naturally this time. "But thank you for the offer. It means the world to me." But she needed more. Especially from Theo Reese. That realization hit her so hard she nearly stumbled.

His phone buzzed, and he lifted it from his back pocket to read the face. "We're going at midnight. There's no sign of your father at Saul's New York location, but I promise I'll get the information from that bastard. You're going to have to trust me."

She glanced at the antique clock on the mantel. They had three hours before he put himself in danger. There were so many words she wanted to say, but none of them really mattered. So she moved around the sofa and stepped into his arms. "I do, Theo. But don't underestimate Saul. He's been planning this for a while."

"I won't." Theo clasped his hands at the back of her waist, pulling her tight against what felt like steel. "We are getting mated, Gin. I'll give you a couple of days to come to terms, but I'm only negotiating on the small stuff. The bigger decision has been made."

"No," she said softly.

"I'll just have to change your mind." Without giving her warning, his mouth took hers. He lifted her, turning and walking toward the bedroom.

She wrapped her arms around his neck, holding tight, her thighs hugging his hips. Liquid lava poured through her veins, catching her off guard. Hunger shook her, shooting through her. How did he do that? She kissed him back, and suddenly cold air brushed her bare skin as he removed her shirt.

He managed to toss her bra wherever her shirt had landed, and she didn't care. "God, you're beautiful," he murmured, kissing along her neck. "That's not why, Gin."

She bit his jaw. "Not why what?"

He leaned back, desire glittering in his eyes. "Your beauty. I do like it, but it's your spirit that calls to me. Your attitude and your brains. Those turn me on even more than your unbelievably stunning eyes."

Everything in her softened.

He released her, letting her slide down his body. "I'm not good with the mushy words, but I want this. I want you. Forever."

She blinked. Those were great mushy words. "We're rushing this."

"Your survival is more important than time," he said, running his hands down her sides. "Say yes. Please let me save you."

It hit her then. Harder than any punch ever had. She wanted him. Had for centuries. When she saw her heart, when she daydreamed, it had always been him. But he hadn't mentioned love. Didn't even consider it. What better way to fall in love than to be mated? She could be what he wanted. They could find love.

She lifted her chin and met his gaze. The challenge of Theo Reese was hers to accept. "Yes."

Chapter 9

Everything inside Theo settled. Right then and there. She said yes. "You won't regret it." He'd spend a lifetime making sure of it— after he saved her life. He slid his hand up her back to capture her nape, leaning down to kiss her.

His damn phone buzzed again. Swearing, he reached for it, reading the face. "Shit. Saul ordered a car at eleven." He stepped back, his mind going into battle mode. "We have to go now." Somebody banged on his door. "Coming." He set Ginny to the side. "Get dressed, Gin." He hustled out, shutting the door and jogging through the living room to the front door. At this point, he was never going to get inside the woman.

He yanked open his front door.

Jared and Chalton moved in, already shrugging into bulletproof vests. "Where the hell would he be going tonight?" Jared muttered, handing over a vest.

"Who knows?" Theo fastened the Velcro and then moved over to remove a long painting of an island that no longer existed in the Arctic. He planted his hand flat against the wall, and it slid open to reveal a small room holding a multitude of weapons. He stepped inside and started handing out guns and knives, already knowing his brothers' preferences.

Ginny poked her head around the corner. "That's a nice Fremt."

He nodded and slid the green laser gun into the back of his waist. Lasers turned to solid bullets when impacting immortal flesh. "I don't plan to use it. I'm better with a knife." He didn't want her to see this side of him, but maybe it was necessary. When they mated, they'd need to let each other in to their hidden worlds. "I've called for Realm soldiers to guard the door and exits to the building here," he said, partly for her comfort and partly to warn her. "You're to stay safe."

She rolled her eyes. "I have the flash drive, which keeps me safe from Saul. You're the one running into danger."

"I'm glad we already have our roles straight," he said, enjoying the instant swirling temper in her eyes.

Jared cut him a curious look, but he didn't respond. So Jared finished suiting up and headed back out. "I'll make sure the guards are at post out here." He disappeared with Chalton on his heels.

Theo inserted a couple more knives along his right leg. "I'm sorry about earlier." They kept getting interrupted.

She smiled. "That's all right. We were both carried away. This is probably better."

He stood to his full height. "It's a done deal, Gin. There's no other alternative for you, and you know that deep down. Don't worry. We'll make it work." He grasped her and kissed her hard. "Stay here." Without waiting for an answer, he moved into the hallway to follow his brothers down to transport.

He fully intended to end Saul Libscombe for good.

* * * *

Ginny's mind spun, but she had to focus. The second Theo had departed, she moved toward his computer and read all the data from the queen. Her stomach turned queasy, but she forced herself to read the Realm notes. They were in line with what she'd already learned by research and by living with the damn anklet for the past ten years.

It had already killed her.

Well, if she didn't mate. She'd meant it when she'd said yes to Theo.

Could they make it work? Maybe if they ever actually made it to bed, they had a chance. She grinned and closed the computer file. Another one caught her eye, and she didn't hesitate to click on it.

Oh, she'd been studying Saul Libscombe for a decade, so she didn't expect to find many revelations in Theo's compilation. And yet, there was some new information there. "Look at that," she breathed, taking note of a safety deposit box right there in the city, as well as some land holdings he had in Russia. Of course, Theo's contacts in Russia were far better than hers. But how in the world had he found a safety deposit box she'd missed?

Squinting, she leaned forward and read the name of the bank. Oh. It was a Realm bank here in the city. No wonder she hadn't found it. The Realm was notoriously secretive. And yet, vampires helped vampires. The king had obviously sent this file to Theo. The land didn't interest her.

But the deposit box. Now that held promise.

Of course, she'd already known of several places Saul had stashed information and funds throughout the world, but she hadn't been able to make a move because of the GPS in the anklet.

Saul would be busy with the Reese brothers tonight. If she was ever going to make a move against him, it would have to be tonight before everything went to hell. If Theo's plan didn't work, Saul would set off her anklet. Now was her one chance to get him. To maybe find leverage to use.

She chewed her thumbnail, thinking. It wasn't like she'd vowed to stay in the apartment. No. Theo had just ordered her to stay, and he'd assumed she would. She'd never been a soldier, but she knew how to broker information. Breaking into a Realm bank was colossally crazy, and yet... Whatever Saul had secured there had to be good. He was a shifter, not a vampire. For a shifter to use a Realm bank, he must really want to keep something under wraps.

Reaching for her phone, she dialed up one of her many contacts.

"Phil's Brewery," said a chipper female voice.

"Hey, Sally. It's Ginny," she said evenly.

A series of clicks came over the line. Then, "Hey, girlfriend! It's been so long since I've heard from you. What's up?" Sally asked.

Ginny grinned. "So much I don't have time to tell you right now, but we'll catch up soon." The thousand-year-old witch was one of her favorite people in life. Plus, she had skills. "I need the schematics for the Realm Bank in New York City."

Sally tsked her tongue. "Are you crazy? Even you aren't insane enough to rob Dage Kayrs."

Ginny bit her lip. That was a damn good point. "I didn't say I was robbing him. I just want the bank schematics." It wasn't like the king owned the box she was going to break into. "Besides, Dage is a friend." Okay. Not her friend. But he was obviously close to Chalton.

"Then why not just ask him to let you into his bank?" Sally asked reasonably.

Ginny shut her eyes. "Because he might say no." The guy probably had contracts with people who used the safety deposit boxes, right? "I don't want to put him in a tough position."

Sally laughed high and loud. "You are still so full of blarney. I have the schematics, but they're going to cost you. A lot."

Ginny sighed. "I'm sure. Email them to me, and I'll send secured payment immediately."

"Triple my usual price," Sally said, her voice deepening with the pleasure of a good deal.

Ginny winced. "Fair enough. And if I get caught, I know the drill." She had no clue where the schematics came from.

"All right, doll. Watch your email." Sally clicked off.

Ginny waited for the beep and then sent almost her entire savings account across the world. If this worked, it'd be worth it. She stood and stretched. If Theo had the doors covered, she'd have to figure another way out of the building.

She couldn't help but smile as she got to work. If she did this right, she'd take down Saul, and she'd be home before Theo walked through the door.

What could possibly go wrong?

* * * *

Theo crouched down in the snow after taking out the guard nearest the back door. The drive to Saul's had taken more than two hours because of the damn weather. A snowstorm barreled around Theo, turning the world white and hard to see. He stepped over the unconscious shifter guard and moved silently for the window to the east. Libscombe's New York home was on two acres in the middle of a high-end subdivision complete with gate, guardhouse, and patrolling security teams.

Human teams.

Theo lifted a shoulder toward Jared, who was silently waiting in the snow for the human duo to pass by the house. Immortals would be able to sense them, but apparently Saul felt safe enough with humans around. That was odd. There had only been four shifter guards near the house. Shouldn't there be more? Theo closed his eyes and tuned in to the world around him.

Nothing. Just the billowing wind and piercing cold.

He stilled and held up his hand for his brothers to stop. Why weren't there immortal signatures around? He moved closer to the white clapboard two-story. Shifters could mask their signatures, but there should still be some sort of hint. A blur of the atmosphere.

He was getting nothing.

The human guards finally passed, good-naturedly arguing about some movie.

Theo was just about to call his brothers over when he spotted movement inside the home. Ducking low, he moved to the window to see Saul Libscombe inside a rec room complete with wall-wide television, pool table, and dartboards. Last year's Superbowl was playing across the screen in vivid color.

The bastard had a glass of amber-colored whiskey in one hand and the remote control in the other. Apparently torturing Ginny earlier that day hadn't fazed him any. Oh, he was going to bleed.

Theo gave the hand signal, and his brothers disappeared around the corners.

He brushed snow from his eyes and angled back around toward the door. Chalton had already cut the feed for the alarm, so unless there were sensors Chalton hadn't found, which was pretty much impossible, Theo could walk right in. Taking a deep breath, he slid the wide door open and crossed into warmth, just as quietly closing the door.

The sound of the game in the other room was the only noise. He couldn't sense Saul, which was intriguing. The guy certainly had a way with electronics. Once Theo sliced him open, he'd have to search the place to see what all Saul had invented. After he turned off that damn ankle bracelet.

The ability to mask immortal signatures would be very much sought after. How had Saul done it?

Theo moved silently through the house, easily reaching the rec room just as Chalton and Jared entered from the other doors, their weapons already in their hands. Theo wanted to use his knife this time.

Saul turned. "Evening."

Theo stilled. Something wasn't right. He moved directly into the room. Holy fuck. The entire room was one massive screen. A modern-day hologram that looked fucking real from outside. "Retreat," he yelled, turning and rushing for the door. He'd almost reached the back when the ground rumbled and the air bunched.

The home exploded, throwing him high and far into the wild storm. Pain pierced through his skull. His last thought was of Ginny and her pretty blue eyes. Then blackness caught him before he hit the ground.

Chapter 10

Ginny stood outside the double protected bank vault. The Realm had gone with massive cast iron, concrete, and steel rods for reinforcement. It figured the king would use modern designs. Human designs, actually. Getting into the bank had been fairly easy, even though her command of the elements wasn't up to par.

Good thing she didn't need fire for this.

Oh, she still swirled around the oxygen and created a bit of ice, but that was much easier than fire to make. Apparently the king of the Realm wasn't too afraid of witches breaching his security.

He should know better.

The lock had a dual control mechanism with a time delay that was damn impressive. The biometric requirements were daunting as well. Of course, she'd helped to design this one as a side job more than a year ago.

One should never hire a thief to create security.

Humming softly, she drew out her key card and bypassed the design elements she'd installed. A backdoor was an absolute necessity, now wasn't it? The thrill of the hunt raced through her.

Could she truly give this up? Unlikely. Though she wouldn't steal from the king again. This was a one-time deal, and only because Saul had been torturing her for a decade. If he'd hurt her father, she'd destroy him. Three clicks echoed and then three more. The massive vault swung her way.

It was almost too easy.

She paused. It shouldn't be so easy. Wait a minute. She glanced up and then to the left. Aha. So the king had made a few adjustments. Nice laser and heat sensors. Good thing she was a witch. It would cost her, but she could reduce her heat signature to nothing. Drawing in air, she did so and then eyed the floor, which consisted of a series of square cement tiles. Interesting. A pattern.

Drawing out a device she'd invented nearly twenty years ago, she ran a laser with a gas medium over the floor. Two to the left, one right, two forward on the squares. She hopped, truly enjoying herself. Then she had to perform a cartwheel that made her almost giddy. Before she knew it, she was in front of Saul's safety deposit box. A wave of her hand, and any cameras went dark. Of course, when she waved, she blew high-pollinated PT dust, which she'd also invented. It would ruin the cameras for good.

She should probably figure out a way to send money anonymously to the Realm.

The actual box needed two keys. She withdrew the two masters from around her neck and inserted them, easily pulling out the drawer. One white envelope took up the entire thing.

She grasped it and shoved it into her back pocket before returning the drawer to rights. A quick glance around showed so many lovely boxes just waiting for her to explore. She sighed. No time. Maybe she could return if she didn't leave any evidence.

After retracing her steps from the vault and through the bank, she found herself outside in the wild snowstorm. Humming to herself, she turned to hustle back to Theo's place. The ductwork in his building was superior and had created an easy way in and out where she wouldn't be detected.

Lights flashed on outside the alley. An SUV started barreling toward her.

She paused, her body going still. Bloody Hell. Lights from above shone down, illuminating Saul in the passenger's seat. How the hell did he get free of Theo? Damn it. She turned to run, and pain licked up from her ankle. Crying out, she stumbled into the side of the building.

That asshole.

If he caught her, he could torture her until she gave up the location of the flash drive. Until she did that, he wouldn't kill her. So she ducked her head and ran, drawing on strength she hadn't known she possessed. Another prick to her ankle from the bracelet, and her leg went numb.

She fell into the snowy street, head first. Pain pummeled into her forehead.

"Hey." Three college-aged boys ran toward her. "Lady, you okay?" The first one, a tall dark-skinned kid wearing a letterman's jacket, gingerly lifted her up.

She sagged against him. "Sorry. Forgot my insulin earlier." That sounded okay, right?

The second kid, one wearing a similar jacket but with blond hair and a multitude of freckles, instantly grabbed a granola bar from his pocket. "Eat this."

She took it and forced a smile, glancing quickly around. The neighborhood held several bars with boisterous sounds emerging. A lot of young people strolled around in the snow, barhopping and being rather loud. She eyed the quiet SUV that had reached the end of the alley. Saul wouldn't want to cause a scene with so many security cameras around. She smiled at the young men, noting a stairwell down into the subway system. "I really need to head home, and I think that SUV is following me."

The boys instantly turned, their chests puffing out.

"We'll take care of it," the freckled kid said, starting to move.

"Thank you," she said, starting for the subway. If she could get on a car before she passed out, she might survive the night. "You're all kind, gentlemen." Oh, Saul wouldn't hurt humans with cameras around. But this was her only chance.

She barely made it down to the platform to buy a ticket and then limped onto the first train. Going to the back, she took a seat, having no idea where she'd end up. She pressed her head against the freezing window. Where was Theo? Was he all right? The fact that Saul had tracked her GPS to the bank wasn't good. Damn it. The GPS. She had to get back to safety before Saul tracked her.

Those boys wouldn't stop him for long.

She eyed the snowy darkness outside just as her vision began to fuzz from the planekite. Oh, this so wasn't good.

* * * *

Theo came to seconds after landing, his head ringing, snow up his nose. Groaning, he rolled over to see the entire house in flames. Fuck. He shoved to his feet, weaving, and tried to push through the snow. Chalton came barreling around the east side of the fire, burn marks across his head, his arm at an odd angle and blood flowing from his temple.

Relief caught Theo. "Jared?" he yelled.

Chalton looked frantically around, his clothes in tatters. Another explosion rocked the house, and he dropped to his knees. Theo ran forward and hauled him up, ignoring the pain as his broken ribs clattered together. He grunted and helped Chalton toward the other side of the house. Where the hell was Jared? Had he made it out of the house?

Sirens trilled in the distance, and people started coming out of homes to see the catastrophe. Fuck. They had to get out of there.

Theo tripped over a snow-laden bush, and Chalton stumbled, keeping them both going.

They found Jared free of the house, facedown in the snow. Flames licked across his vest, having burned through his jacket. Theo grabbed a handful of snow and slammed it down on the fire until the flames hissed into steam. "Jared?" He turned his brother over.

Jared's nose was broken along with what looked like his cheekbone. Blood flowed freely from a cut across his cheek. His breaths were shallow, but he was breathing and his heart seemed steady.

Theo shook him, but he didn't awaken. "We have to go." Grunting, he lifted his brother, and with Chalton's help, got him over Theo's shoulder. "Jesus. He weighs a ton." Staggering under the weight, bleeding, and with more bruises on his brain than he could count, Theo followed a limping Chalton through the backyard and toward the SUV they'd stashed down the private street.

They reached the vehicle, and Theo shoved Jared inside, following him into the backseat.

Chalton dodged around the front and ignited the engine, heading for the back exit to the subdivision. The sirens got louder, and the fire crackled merrily, even with the storm. "Fucking setup," Chalton muttered, swinging around a group of people in pajamas, boots, and heavy coats who were heading toward the fire. "How did he set us up?"

Theo shrugged, removing Jared's vest and lifting his shirt to see a myriad of bruises and obviously broken ribs. "Whoa." He patted Jared's hard cheek—the good one. "Wake up, bro."

Jared didn't move but tingles cascaded from him, so at least his system was repairing the damage. Good.

Theo shoved his tattered jacket off and gingerly felt along his own ribcage. Pain drew inward and spiraled out. Yep. Broken. He kept his eyes open but started sending healing cells first to his brain and then his body. "We need to figure this out."

"The trace on his call was good," Chalton said grimly, whipping the vehicle out onto a main road. "Saul did call for the car, but he must've realized we were ready to make a move. How? How could he possibly know we were working with Ginny and not against her?"

"She didn't tell him," Theo said wearily, leaning back.

"You sure?"

Theo studied his brother. "I'm sure." Even to get her father back, she wouldn't send Theo to his possible death. "I should tell you that we decided to mate. To save her life."

Chalton eyed him through the rearview mirror. "To save her life."

Jared snorted. "I'm half unconscious and even I know that's bullshit. To save her life. God, you're clueless."

Theo cut him a look. "Why don't you fix your face and not worry about me right now?"

Jared groaned and stronger tingles cascaded around him. "Veronica likes my face. I should heal it." He shifted on the seat. "You know what this means, right? The fact that we didn't find Saul?"

Theo nodded, grimness clutching his heart. "Yeah. Ginny has to go forward with the meet."

"If she hasn't already," Chalton said quietly.

"She hasn't," Theo snapped. "There's no way she turned us in to Saul." The woman might be a thief and a manipulator, but she wouldn't purposefully cause harm. He just knew it.

"Say you're right and your future mate didn't call Saul and give him our information." Chalton sped up, moving quickly toward the city. "What if she didn't mean to tell him, but he still heard it from her?"

Theo rubbed his aching ribcage. "What do you mean?"

"What if—"

"Oh, shit." Theo smacked his head and then winced at the instant pain. "The anklet with GPS."

Chalton nodded, spraying snow and ice. "Yeah. It broadcasts location, but what if it also broadcasts sounds? What if he's been listening in the entire time?"

Theo's breath caught, and he fumbled for his phone, quickly dialing Ginny. "If he knows we left her…"

Chalton shook his head. "We left the place well guarded. If there had been any sort of problem, the guards would've called in."

Good point. But Theo's heart started beating faster as she didn't answer. "Ginny. Call me. Now." He left a message.

"She's probably asleep," Jared mumbled, keeping his eyes closed.

Theo looked at his brother. "Fix your face, would you?" That was true. Ginny could be asleep. But wouldn't she answer, considering he was on a mission to take out Saul? She would. He dialed the guards. "Check my apartment. Now."

"Affirmative," came across the line.

He held his breath. Heavy footsteps sounded, and then nothing. "Hello?" he said, his voice clipped.

The guard cleared his throat. "The apartment is empty. She didn't get by us, and there's no sign of a struggle."

"Secure the location," Theo said tersely, clicking off. "I'm going to fucking kill her."

Chapter 11

Ginny climbed through the vents before dawn, her hands freezing and her nose numb. After riding subway cars for hours and then maneuvering through the cold city, she'd finally arrived back at Theo's building. It wasn't dawn yet, so perhaps he hadn't made it home. She had to believe he'd lived through whatever Saul had planned for him.

Saul had almost caught her several times during the last few hours, but she was a master at getting in and out of tight spots.

The planekite had left her system, so she was feeling marginally better. Whatever she had in her pocket had kept Saul from killing her or even dosing her again, so she desperately needed to open that envelope.

But first, she had to get safely back into Theo's place.

Hopefully, he hadn't made it home yet.

She slid the vent in front of the kitchen open, dropped to the counter, and then back-flipped to the floor. Then she turned around and let out a small shriek.

Theo sat in a kitchen chair, bruises across his face, fury burning hot and bright in his dark eyes.

She clasped her hand to her chest and felt her thundering heart. "You scared the hell out of me."

He cocked his head slowly, the movement predatory. His dark shirt emphasized solid muscles, as did his faded jeans. Although his feet were bare, even they looked capable of great danger.

She swallowed, taking in his bruises. "I'm glad you're all right. I was worried."

He arched one dark eyebrow.

Okay. So he was a little angry. "I didn't know that Saul was setting you up," she said, trying to keep her voice calm.

Theo didn't move, but somehow more tension poured off him. "How do you know we were set up?"

She winced. "I may have seen him earlier tonight."

Both eyebrows arched.

"I, ah, saw him and ended up running all over the city trying to get back here," she said in a rush. Why couldn't she breathe? It wasn't like she was afraid of Theo. Not really. Sure, he looked like he could kill somebody right that moment, but why would he want to kill her?

"Are you all right?" Theo rumbled.

She nodded. "Yes. He engaged the anklet, but I got away. It was hours ago." Though she was starving all of a sudden. "What happened with you?"

"It was a trap that blew up. We're all fine," he said shortly, not losing any of his hard look.

She fought the very real urge to run out of the kitchen. By the look of him, she wouldn't make it. "I didn't promise to stay here."

Oops. He moved from the chair, walking for her fast, with a determined clip.

She backed up and hit the countertop. "What's—"

Then his hand was suddenly tangling in her hair and twisting. He moved her head to the side and pulled back until she faced him. Her brain just plain and simple stopped working. Vulnerability and an intriguing breathlessness caught her and held as tightly as he did.

He lowered his head until his eyes were right above hers. All of those interesting shades of black. As she watched, the sparkle turned to a deep metallic green. Stunning. His vampire colors. "I told you to stay here," he gritted out.

"I know." Wow. Those eyes were amazing. The myriad shades of both green and black was fascinating. "I, ah, am not really a sit around and wait type of lass." Her brogue emerged with her breathiness.

If anything, more anger poured from him. "In direct opposition to your sweet and helpless act."

She frowned. "Well, yes. I thought you knew that." Her brain was still fuzzy. He was too close. Lord, she still couldn't breathe.

His phone rang a bizarre tune that sounded somehow frantic.

An emergency tune, without question. Without releasing her, he reached for it on the counter and pressed a button. "What?" he barked.

"Tell me Ginny didn't rob a Realm bank tonight," Chalton said urgently. "Please."

She blanched.

"Damn it," Theo muttered. "Give me the status."

"Dage called and has me tracking down who robbed the bank." Chalton's voice was both panicked and weary.

She barely kept back a smile. "He won't find me."

"Don't speak," Theo snarled, tightening his hold in her hair. "Not a fucking word."

Chalton sighed over the line. "I'll have her in about an hour. The surrounding buildings have devices I invented with heat, video, and even sound. The devices are compiling a recording right now of the person who broke into the bank, and she'll be recognizable by morning."

Her stomach dropped, even while her mind finally engaged. "I would love to see that technology. Fascinating. The surrounding buildings—what a remarkable idea."

Theo growled. A true, furious, masculine vampiric growl.

She shivered. Her nipples went hard as rocks. Even her knees weakened.

"How long can you hold off on telling the king?" Theo ground out, his breath warm on her face.

"As long as you need," Chalton said. "Want me to blow the evidence?"

Theo closed his eyes and quickly reopened them. "No. The king is almost a brother to you. I appreciate the offer, but do your job. Just do it slowly."

"Copy that. And good luck." Chalton clicked off.

She twisted her lip. "So. I may have broken into a Realm bank tonight." Would the king call for her head? She'd heard he was a reasonable guy, but he was still a vampire. "Is there a Realm prison somewhere?" She'd escaped a human prison back in the seventies, and it'd be nice to test those skills again.

"You're not going to prison," Theo said. "We'll figure something out. What did you find?"

She took out the envelope and ripped it open, dropping a flash drive in her hand. "To think we can now take each other down with these."

Theo grasped it and plugged it into a tablet on the counter, the tension still pouring from him. "It's encrypted. I'll set a program on it while we conclude matters." He typed on the small attached keyboard and then turned her way.

She wanted to back away again, but there was nowhere to go. "I can handle prison."

Theo shook his head. "I don't think the king would send his best friend's brother's mate to prison. Dage is all about family and connections."

Her mouth opened. "You still want to mate me?"

"Yes. Right now, actually." He didn't offer any other explanation, and the green in his eyes completely overtook the black. "You need it to survive, and I need it to have a hold on you. Forever." Then he kissed her. Holding her in place, he plundered deep.

Electricity jolted through her body. The kisses from him before... Those were different. Sweet and exploring. This was firm, deep, and hot. A claiming. Whatever she'd sensed in Theo, that predator he banked low with humor and watchfulness...was unleashed. He treated her like she was a strong woman. One who could take what he wanted to give.

That alone made her want to mate him. She was a gambler, and this would be the biggest gamble of her long life.

Then he gentled the kiss, starting to back her across the kitchen. Oh, hell no. If this was going to happen, and she wanted it to happen, he didn't get to treat her like the fragile thing she'd pretended to be for so long. She jerked her mouth free. "What are you doing?"

"Going to the bedroom." His hold lightened, even as his body was a long tense line of contained power. "I won't hurt you, Gin. You can trust me."

Ah, the sweet vampire. If she'd wanted to be coddled, she would've accepted one of the many offers to basically sit on a mated pedestal through the years. So she shot a punch into his gut, giving her just enough room to slip out of his grasp.

His chin lifted in warning, and those stark eyes glittered. "What are you doing?"

She edged around the counter and toward the door. "I don't want gentle or sweet. In fact, I don't want a wimp of a mate. I need pure strength and power."

Now his chin lowered. "You think I can't protect you?"

Sure, he could protect her when she needed it. But she wanted all of him—not just the protector. "I'm fairly capable, Theo." She moved backward, keeping him in her sights, into the living area. Pain flashed along her palm. Real pain, like a deep burn. Oh God. She glanced down. The marking. The Celtic knot, winding and beautiful, that presented itself when a witch found her mate. She couldn't breathe.

He stalked her, his steps slow and measured. "What game are you playing now?"

She swallowed, focusing back on him. This was really happening. "No game. I don't want a mate I can lead around by the nose. You want me?" she whispered, stepping toward the sofas.

"You know I do." He kept coming, his movement fluid. "Stop playing."

"Make me." With a quick move, she made it around the sofa, putting it between them. Her heart thundered, and her body had sprung fully alive. Pushing him was a bad idea, horrible, really, yet she knew what she wanted. Theo unleashed. "I used to watch you, *T*."

"Did you, now?" He stopped on the other side of the sofa, in complete control of the room. "And?"

"You're uncontrollable." The idea thrilled her to the point of being too dangerous. "That's why I didn't choose you back then."

At the reminder of her messing with his brother, he changed. Nothing obvious. She noticed it because she'd watched him secretly for years. She'd wanted him so badly for eons. His eyes glittered, focusing on her with a preternatural stillness. Here was the deadly soldier she'd heard whispered about from immortals who actually feared him.

The predator he hid down deep. Brutal, primal, and terrifying.

She wanted to make him hers. "Your calm façade is disappearing, Reese. You're looking a bit deadly," she breathed, her abdomen quivering.

"I am deadly. You might want to keep that in mind." His voice had lowered, turning gravelly hoarse.

The tone bit across her skin, heading down to the pulse between her legs.

He lifted his face, his nostrils flaring. "You're aroused, baby."

"That's impolite," she returned, moving slightly to the left.

"We left politeness a long time ago." He matched her movement. "I'm going to give you one more chance. Get your ass into the bedroom. Now."

"That's not what I want," she whispered, eyeing him, preparing to run. "Not even close. The question is: What do you want?"

"You." He was up and over the sofa in a wisp of sound.

She'd been waiting. She somersaulted in the air over the nearest chair, landing by the window. "You're fast."

"So are you." He stalked her around the chair, his hungry eyes unblinking and focused like any predator on prey. Her challenge had stripped him down to the dark and primitive beast at his core.

At that look, alarm trembled through her along with anticipation. She'd wanted him unleashed. Now could she handle him? The need to run was real this time. She feinted left and went right, rushing for the bedroom and the door that hopefully had a lock.

He caught her by the nape and the waistband, ripping her off her feet and flinging her over his shoulder. Not missing a beat, he strode toward the bedroom and kicked the door shut with enough strength to crack the door frame. One hand planted on her ass, and he flipped her over, tossing her on the bed.

Her shoulders hit first, and the wind whooshed out of her lungs. Before she could strike out, he'd ripped her jeans free of her body. She rolled to the side and tried to lever off the bed, a shocked laugh escaping her when he planted one hand across her entire lower back and somehow ripped off her shirt. She squirmed on the bed like a wriggling kitten, fighting to get free, wanting him to keep her close but unwilling to give in so easily.

She couldn't dislodge his hand.

He waited, the patient hunter, with her wearing nothing but her thin bra and panty set.

The bra released. "You ever been tied up?" he asked, no exertion in his voice.

"No," she gasped. A slow burn rolled through her body. He held her down with one hand, her face in the bedclothes, her feet kicking uselessly. The man had been bruised and burned. How was he fighting so well and easily? Adrenaline was flooding her body, giving her strength, but she couldn't match him.

Her thighs rubbed together, and she bit back a groan. "If I had my fire, I'd burn you to a crisp."

"This is for leaving the apartment." The smack to her ass shocked the heck out of her. She arched, gasping. Fire shot through her skin, followed by a chill that made her tremble.

He slapped her butt again, making her skin come alive with brutal tingles. "This is for robbing a bank. A Realm bank." Three very hard smacks followed in rapid succession.

She cried out and arched again, every nerve sparking. Nobody had dared treat her so, and yet she was primed and ready for him. Her breasts felt heavy and needy, while her sex contracted several times, needing something. Needing Theo Reese. She clenched her jaw to keep from begging for him.

He held his hand against her smarting rear, holding in the heat. She panted, her eyes wide, wondering what he'd do next. After the count of two heartbeats, he flipped her over.

Then he was on her.

Finally.

Chapter 12

Theo had waited too many damn long years to wait any longer. He kissed Ginny, and the taste of woman exploded on his tongue. Honey and spice and all intrigue. She tunneled her hands through his hair, kissing him back, her body softening for him. Her thighs rose on either side of his hips, and his jeans suddenly felt way too tight.

He leaned to the side, and she helped him tug his shirt over his head. Then he kicked his jeans to the ground. Wait. He had to make sure. "Ginny."

She grabbed his head and pulled him back down, her mouth seeking his.

"Wait," he said, grasping her hands and pressing them on either side of her head. "I have to know. You need to say it."

She blinked, her blue eyes dark pools of need. "Yes, Theo. To the mating. Not just to live, either. I want you."

He'd wanted her for centuries, and he'd never thought he'd hear those words from her. Not really. There were so many words and promises he wanted to give to her, but she widened her legs, and he could feel her heat. "You like being spanked."

Fire flashed in those eyes. "I most certainly do not."

That brogue in such a classy voice nearly made him come right then and there. He kissed her hard, forcing his body to relax as he brushed the bra off her arms. "You're lying to yourself if you believe that. Regardless, you should probably behave from now on," he said, his mouth against the pounding pulse in her neck.

"Not a chance," she breathed, arching into his body. Then she paused. "Wait a minute."

Hell, no. But he levered up, letting his bare chest rub against her hardened nipples. God, she was fucking amazing. "What?"

She writhed against him, somehow frowning. "I may be a fugitive. I don't want you in trouble with the Realm just because of me."

The woman was worried about him? His heart did a long roll, and his cock pulsed against her core. She was so warm and wet. "I won't let you go to jail, sweetheart."

Her light eyebrows arched. "Oh, I can get out of any jail. I was just worried you'd go to war or something."

Get out of jail? She looked intrigued...not frightened. His gaze narrowed. "You are not going to jail or breaking out of jail." It'd take a millennium to figure her out. Three of them to tame her. Good damn thing he was immortal. "Get that out of your head right now."

Her pout was cute and sexy at the same time. God, he wanted to bind her to him forever. He'd figure out why and what to do with her later. Right now, his fangs ached with the need to take a bite. He let them slide down.

Her eyes widened, and she stilled beneath him. "I've never been bitten before. By anybody." She swallowed.

"Get used to it." He scraped along her jugular, adding pressure but not harming her. Grinning, he licked across her neck and kissed her collarbone, heading down to her amazing breasts.

She hitched her breath.

He licked her, nipping and sucking, careful to keep his fangs from harming her. The threat was there, and she held still. He flicked a nipple, enjoying her startled gasp. "I've waited so long to touch you." To think he'd almost lost her. What if Saul had pressed the button? Theo kept kissing his way down her torso, wanting nothing more than to taste her again. He had to get the mating process going to protect her in case Saul did give her too much planekite. No matter what.

Her legs trembled when he reached her core, and he slid his fangs in one inner thigh.

She cried out, the sound surprised and full of pleasure. "Shouldn't that hurt more?" she gasped, her nails raking the bedclothes.

He pulled them out, licking the wound closed. "They're too

sharp for you to feel the pain." Unless he wanted to cause pain. That was a different matter. Then he licked along her slit, kissing her clit. He could spend all fucking year doing this. Licking her, making her squirm, listening to the sounds of pleasure she made.

His chest felt full, and the beast inside him, the one deep down, reared awake. Ready to possess and claim. But he needed her ready, because he was past being gentle. So he slid two fingers into her heat, twisting them, enjoying the arch of her against him. He sucked her clit into his mouth, not making her wait. She detonated, his name tumbling from her lips as she rode out the waves he tried to prolong.

Now that was sweet. His name from her. He'd waited a lifetime to hear that.

Maneuvering up, he kissed and licked, his body on fire for her. His cock throbbed like he'd been punched, and he needed to be inside her now.

He kissed her, and she ran her hands down his sides, pausing at the contusions still there. "Theo."

"Broken ribs," he confirmed. "House blew up."

She pushed his hair back, her eyes satisfied. "I'm so sorry. I wonder how he knew."

"Your anklet," Theo whispered right against her ear and then moved to pepper her jawline with kisses. "We think it broadcasts. He could hear us talking earlier." He kept his voice quiet enough that Saul couldn't hear.

"Oh." She kissed his forehead and then paused. Her body went wooden board stiff. "Wait a minute."

Fuck. He shouldn't have said anything.

She pushed him hard enough that he rolled off her, and then she bounded to stand. Her breasts bobbed, and panic filled her face. "He can *hear* us? Right now?" she mouthed silently, gesturing wildly.

Damn it. Theo stood, facing her down. "Yes," he mouthed just as silently. It didn't matter. This was going to happen, and right now, in order to protect her. It was the only way he could possibly keep her safe before the next mission. One they both had to go on. "Come here, Ginny."

* * * *

Oh, bloody to the hell and no. Ginny backed away, the offensive anklet feeling like it weighed a hundred pounds. Her body was flush with desire, even now, but this could *so* not happen. She held up a hand to ward off Theo.

Naked and fully aroused, he looked like an avenging god standing between her and the door. "Ginny."

The way he said her name—patience and determination and possession all rolled into two syllables. "No," she whispered, not willing to speak any louder, although if the damn thing could hear her, it probably could make out the slightest of sounds. God. She'd just orgasmed. *Loudly.*

As if reading her mind, Theo smiled, his fangs still showing. "You can scream my name as loud as you like for the world to hear," he mouthed, very clearly.

Heat flared into her face. She wanted to shush him, but he'd probably start talking louder so Saul could hear. Her clothes were on the floor, and she edged toward them.

"No," Theo said softly.

Why did that low voice send butterflies winging through her abdomen? The brand on her palm ached with the need to mark him, and her entire wrist was starting to hurt. She'd have to take the pain until she could get the anklet off. She pantomimed that they needed to get it off by pointing to it.

"After," he mouthed clearly.

She gulped.

"Ginny." He let his voice raise this time.

She panicked and waved her arms to shut him up. Saul wouldn't know what they were talking about. Well, he'd probably know, but he didn't know that they knew that he could hear. She shook her head. This was crazy.

Theo watched her, his gaze nearly physical. "Get back on the bed, Ginny."

Her sex clenched. Why in the thunder of the gods did that order, said in the gruff voice, turn her insides into lava? She went with her strengths and batted her eyes, fanning her face. "Theo? I need a moment. Please."

"No."

She coughed. No? He'd said *no*? She fanned harder, letting her body sway.

"Oh, knock it off. Get your ass on the bed or I'm going to put it there," he said, his gaze implacable.

She lost the act and glared. Why the hell couldn't she fool him? And now Saul knew full on that they were arguing about sex. She put her hands on her hips.

"That's better," Theo said, his chin lifting. His torso was wide and muscled, and his cock... Well, now. Hard, thick, and full. Apparently he had no problem standing there in the nude. Why would he? "Now, Ginny."

She only had one chance. Bunching her legs, she leaped for the door. He caught her around the waist, spinning her around and over the edge of the bed. She tried to stand, but he held her in place, her face to the bedspread, her feet on the plush carpet, her butt vulnerable to the vampire. Then he reached between her legs, his thumbnail scraping her clit.

Nerves fired, sending electricity through her. She was so primed and ready. Her body moved against him, shutting out her brain. He rubbed her, his talented fingers knowing just where to touch. How hard and how fast.

She bit her lip, pressing her mouth to the bed. No way would she make a sound. The hard slap of his other hand to her butt echoed through the room. Fire rushed through her, and she cried out. Another slap. This one she arched into. He lifted her all the way onto her hands and knees on the bed, his hand still working her, his body covering hers.

She rode his fingers, unable to stop. He kissed the back of her neck and reached around to pluck her nipples. Lord and saints, it was too much. He was everywhere, his mouth and fingers, his thighs and the hard press of his cock at her entrance.

He paused, and the world seemed to stop. "Ginny." It wasn't a question, but he still didn't move.

"Aye," she said, pushing back against him. Her body ruled. She wanted this, and she wanted him. All of him. "If you can catch me." She lunged forward.

He instantly banded an arm around her waist, yanking her back toward him. Then he gently guided himself inside her, his arm solid as steel, taking his time as he took her completely. Pain accompanied his movements, followed by a pleasure so intense she had to shut her eyes. He was so big, he filled everything she'd ever be.

Yet he went slow, letting her body get accustomed to him. Or maybe making sure she understood this was a claiming of the most primitive type. There was nothing she could do but accept him.

On his terms.

The fingers on her breasts tapped up until his hand settled on the front of her neck, holding firmly and lifting her head. She swallowed, her body open to him. Her heart flooded as he finally pushed all the way inside her.

Theo Reese. Completely inside her. Tears filled her eyes. *This.* This is what she'd waited for all these years. He touched every nerve she had, inside and outside, his body bracketing hers and holding her in place. He was all male, and she'd never, not ever, felt so much the female. Oh, she'd played. But she'd never felt this feminine. "Theo," she whispered.

"Yes." He pulled out and pushed back in, his movements slow and controlled. Then again. And again. Holding her in place, taking his time, taking her.

A quivering started deep inside her in a place she hadn't known existed. It spiraled out, circling.

She closed her eyes again just to feel, her body softening. The second she did, he increased the speed and depth of his thrusts, pulling her back each time so he could go deeper. He hammered into her, hard and fast, his breath turning ragged in her ear. The quivers turned to shakes and finally sparks of live electricity.

She broke first, screaming his name, the entire world exploding and then narrowing to right this second. His fangs flashed into her neck, going deep and striking bone. Pain detonated and then pleasure overwhelmed her, shooting throughout her entire body. She came hard, nearly sobbing with her orgasm.

His fangs retracted and he licked her shoulder before pulling out and rolling her onto her back. A second later, and he plunged inside her again, lifting one of her thighs to go deeper.

His eyes had turned a startling green. Crimson covered his high cheekbones, and his nostrils flared like a predator catching prey. He pounded inside her, his gaze intent.

She clasped her ankles around his big back and tilted her pelvis to take more of him.

He growled, and his fangs dropped again.

Instinctively, she turned her neck to grant him access. The second he slid the fangs back in, she planted her palm right over his heart. The marking flowed through her, from her core, and branded on his flesh with a heat that sparked white and fierce.

His fangs retracted, and he buried his head in her neck, shuddering as he came.

She gasped out air, her chest panting, and rubbed his back. Holy saints alive. She'd just mated Theo Reese. She could sleep for a year.

He lifted his head, a lock of hair falling across his forehead. "Now we get serious."

Chapter 13

Theo spent all day trying to decipher the damn flash drive, even inventing new computer programs on the spot. Chalton checked in on the phone several times, also working the problem from his place.

Ginny worked on her own laptop across the small table, blushing several times throughout the day.

Theo let her work through her feelings, finally settling back in his chair at the kitchen table, his gaze on her. She was squirming a little in her seat, and he bit back a grin. "Sore?"

She rolled her eyes. "No. By the way, what was up with the spanking?"

It was fun listening to modern slang in her old-fashioned brogue. "Don't put yourself in danger by robbing Realm banks, darlin'." Plus, she'd liked it.

She snorted. "This isn't a Lexi Blake novel, damn it. Keep your hands to yourself."

"You don't mean that," he said, letting the smile loose. They'd mated. They should probably talk about that, but it was more important they lived until the next day. He sobered. It was time to get serious. "The meet is tonight at midnight."

"I know," she said, glancing down at the ankle monitor, her jaw tightening.

Theo grabbed her phone off the counter, scrolled through the contacts, and dialed one. "Saul?" he asked, his voice a low rumble. "I've mated Ginny, which means you have no chance. Now tell me where to meet you, and I'll give you the flash drive in exchange for you removing the anklet and letting her father go." He pressed the speaker button and put the phone on the table.

She opened her mouth to argue, and Theo held up a hand. "Trust me," he mouthed. They couldn't let Saul know they'd figured out he could hear them.

Her frown didn't hold a hell of a lot of trust. More irritation, really.

"Theo, how lovely to hear your voice," Saul said, his tone even more nasally than before. "I have to say, I think Ginny could've done a lot better."

Ginny's face blazed a bright red.

Theo bit back irritation. "I think my mate is going to insist I gut you for that. Here I thought we'd reach an agreement like reasonable men." There was nothing reasonable about the way he was feeling. His hand itched to go for his knife. "Saul, where shall I meet you with the flash drive my mate stole from you yesterday?" Yeah. He'd said *my mate* twice.

"What flash drive?" Saul said. "Oh, the one planted in the Realm bank? There's nothing on it but a new encryption program I'm developing."

Theo arched an eyebrow at Ginny, who shrugged. "I'm not buying it. I bet I'll have it cracked by tonight," he said.

"Irrelevant," Saul said. "Here's the deal. I want Ginny and the Benjamin file at the meet. Not you. Not your brothers—assuming Jared survived last night. He wasn't moving after the explosion, now was he?"

The bastard had had cameras watching them. Theo forced a bored tone into his voice. "Dude, it's Jared. He's fine and now thirsting for your blood. You know. It's a normal Tuesday for him."

"If she's not alone, I kill her father," Saul said, his voice rising imperceptibly.

Theo moved to stop her from speaking, or to comfort her, but she stared at him calmly. Oh, sometimes even he forgot what a badass she could be. "It goes without saying, and yet I'm saying it anyway. If you hurt Elroy in any way, I'll hunt you to the end of my days. For sport." He tapped his fingers on the table. "Rumor has it I have a knack for hunting."

Saul audibly swallowed. "I want the file, Theo."

"Why?" Theo eyed the program running rapidly across his screen. "It's just family information. Some land ownings, other stocks, some secrets but nothing all that interesting."

"Oh, Theo." Saul chuckled, low and loud. "I know what's in there. The Green Rock file."

Fuck on motherfucker. Theo tensed but kept his voice level. "I have no clue what you're talking about." How had word gotten out, especially to a fucking shifter like Saul? Shit. Even if Theo somehow kept the file under wraps, he'd have to tell Chalton. Just so his brother had a heads-up. "You're inventing rumors."

"You know I'm not. I know about the file, and I want it. In addition to the rest of the information on Benny and the family. I'm actually surprised he hasn't come for your head yet," Saul said.

Oh, Benny was on his way, probably with his knife already sharpened. Or sword. Benny did love his swords. "Ben is family. That trumps everything." Theo shook his head at Ginny's inquisitive look. Benny would easily slice off Theo's head if given the opportunity. The guy really did see things in black and white, and sometimes family became too much of a pain in the ass for him.

"Tell Ginny I want her at midnight. I'm tired of dicking around here, Theo. Either she brings the flash drive or I'm letting the anklet finally do its job. Your mating is too new to protect her from the planekite, so I have to strike now before she can survive it. Tell the bitch she should've mated me." Saul clicked off.

"He is such a complete dick," Ginny said, glaring at the anklet.

Theo tensed for Saul to push whatever button he used, but nothing happened. Maybe the guy wanted Ginny at full strength for the night? Or maybe he didn't want to tip his hand that he could hear them. Sick asshole.

Theo's phone rang, and he glanced at it, seeing the queen's face on the screen. "Hello, Emma," he said by way of greeting, walking out of the room so Saul couldn't hear whatever was said. He gave Ginny a calm smile as he left, but she didn't look much reassured.

"Hello. Why is Saul Libscombe going through back channels to reach me about Virus-27?" Emma said, her voice short. "I asked Dage, and he told me to give you a call."

Damn it. Theo's chest filled. "I assume Saul wants to try and negate the mating bond I just formed with Ginny O'Toole last night." The virus could negate a mating bond if one's mate was dead, but it hadn't been attempted in a living mate yet. So Saul still had plans for Ginny. Yeah. Theo was going to have to kill him. "Hey, how did Dage know about the mating?"

"He's the king," Emma said simply, her voice already distracted. "I'll make sure Saul doesn't get his hands on the virus. Say hi to Ginny for me." She ended the call.

Theo lifted his shirt to look at the perfect swirls of a Celtic knot right over his heart. Ginny had marked him but good. He smiled and turned to head back into the kitchen, where he arched an eyebrow. "You know the queen?"

A small smile played along Ginny's mouth. "I may have done a job or two for her through the years. Stealing proprietary information she could use in her work. Maybe."

Jesus. Sometimes the woman really caught him off guard. He grinned. Yeah, he liked that.

The front door opened, followed by footsteps as his brothers moved into the living room. Theo winked at Ginny and grabbed his laptop, motioning for her to stay in the kitchen. They had to keep Saul out of this plan. She blew a kiss at him as he left, warming his entire body.

He could feel the goofy smile on his face as he approached his brothers, but there was nothing he could do to stop it.

"Jesus. You mated. I can smell her on you." Jared clapped him on the back, a smile creasing his wide face. "Congrats."

"Thanks." Theo glanced at Chalton, who was grinning. "What?"

"Nothing. Just congrats." Chalton unpacked computer equipment and sat on the sofa. "I've figured out and have hacked into the anklet. The only way we can get it off her is to deactivate Saul's controller. Otherwise, the thing will explode and release enough planekite in her blood to kill her."

Theo sat on the leather chair and motioned for Jared to take the other one. "So, I didn't want to tell you this, but included in the Benjamin file is a series of data called the Green Rock file."

Jared groaned. "I thought we destroyed all of that information."

Chalton stiffened. "What's the Green Rock file?"

Theo searched for the right words. "Benny couldn't destroy the information because parties on the other side have it. It's a mutual opportunity for everyone to be protected from extortion and blackmail." He'd agreed with Benny. "But here's the deal. Ah, during the war, Benny might have, well he did, ah—"

"Jesus. What?" Chalton snapped, his angled face losing his normal calm expression.

"Benny collaborated with the demons. Before they became allies with the Realm. When they were, ah, killing vampires and kidnapping members of the Kayrs ruling family." Theo leaned back and waited for Chalton to lose his mind. He was close with the Kayrs family. Very.

Chalton paled. "Are you telling me that Benny helped facilitate the kidnapping of Jase Kayrs? My friend and the king's brother? The one who was tortured nearly to death and took forever to return to any normal life?" Chalton's voice darkened dangerously.

Maybe Theo should worry about Benny and not Chalton right now. "No. Benny had nothing to do with kidnapping Jase. But he did procure and deliver weapons to demon contacts during the war, some which may have been used against the Realm and to, ah, kidnap Jase."

"Damn it," Chalton said.

"We'll get the flash drive back," Theo said, determination filling his chest. "It can be our secret."

"Secrets get out." Chalton took his phone from his pocket and placed it on the coffee table next to the laptop.

Jared shook his head, his dark gaze on the phone like it might blow up. "Bro, I don't know Dage Kayrs like you do, considering you've worked with him for a century and I basically just met the guy. But I have heard all about him. Family is what he cares about. He'll kill all of us for even being associated with anybody who'd harmed his younger brother. Think about this."

Theo swallowed. "Agreed."

"I don't lie to my friends," Chalton said, watching his phone. "It's not who I am." He punched a couple of buttons on his phone and then turned toward the large flat screen over the fireplace, hacking it instantly to bring up a call to the king of the Realm.

Dage took shape, wearing a long black shirt with dark pants, his dark hair ruffled and his silver eyes curious. "Chalton? What's up?"

Chalton stood.

Theo faltered for a moment and then moved to stand next to his brother. Jared took point on the other side.

Dage lifted an eyebrow. "This is interesting."

Chalton nodded. "Not really. Information has come into my possession regarding my family's businesses, and more specifically, something called the Green Rock file."

"Oh, that." Dage waved a hand. "Benny and Ivan, you know the guy who owns Igor's, that bar downtown?"

Theo swallowed. "Yes. Ivan named the bar after his deceased brother."

"Yep. Benny and Ivan had a small business running weapons. Worked with the demons, the shifters, and sometimes even with us. I found out about it and gave Benny a deal he couldn't refuse." Dage's canines glinted. "He's a fun guy."

Chalton's shoulders visibly relaxed. "You knew about the Green Rock file?"

"Don't make me say it." Dage grinned. "The king, here. Besides, why didn't you just ask Ginny about the Green Rock file?"

Theo stilled. The blood rushed through his ears, ringing loudly. "Ginny?" he croaked.

Dage's forehead wrinkled, and delight darkened the silver in his eyes. "Oh. Well. Hmmm." He glanced to the side. "Coming," he called out loudly.

"Nobody just yelled for you," Theo countered. "Tell me—"

"Nope," the king said cheerfully. "My regards to your mate." The screen went black.

Theo lifted his head. "Ginny?" he bellowed.

Before she could respond, the front door crashed open, and a fully armed vampire dressed in combat gear stomped inside, fury on his face, his size eighteen boots cracking the tiles as he stomped.

Ah, shit. Theo sighed. "Hi, Uncle Benny."

"Goddamn it. Don't *uncle* me. I'm going to kill you motherfuckers." Benny, his eyes a swirling mass of different metallic colors, lifted a green gun and pointed it at them.

Ginny moved in from the kitchen, and Theo leaped to cover her.

Her face brightened in a smile. "Benjamin!" Taking a leap, she rushed him, jumping for a hug.

The massive vampire dropped his gun and caught her, swinging her around. "Ginny, girl. You sweetheart. What are you doing here?" He seemed to forget all about Theo and his brothers.

Theo moved forward, his mind spinning and his chest heating. His woman had some serious explaining to do. "Put my mate down, Benny."

Benny gently set Ginny on her feet as if handling fine china, his face falling. "You mated him?"

She nodded, her dimple twinkling. "You disappointed?"

"Yes," Benny said, his body relaxing and his full lips turning down. "Now I probably can't kill him." He paused, his eyebrows lifting. "Right?"

Chapter 14

Ginny tried to plaster an innocent expression on her face, but from the glowering coming from her new mate, she wasn't successful. "I'd really appreciate it if we kept the killing to a minimum." Including her. Theo kind of looked like he wanted to strangle her. Or Benny. Or perhaps both of them. He did have two hands. "Please?"

Benny shuffled his humongous feet. "Oh, all right."

"Thank you." She gifted him with a genuine smile.

Benny was over a thousand years old. He had metallic eyes, long dark hair, a broad jaw, and a barrel of a chest. Standing at about six-foot-seven, he was a huge, sweet, deadly teddy bear, and she'd considered him one of her uncles for eons, even though he truly was shockingly handsome in a totally wounded and fallen angel way. "So you stole my file," he murmured, losing his smile.

"Aye," she said, sighing. "I'm sorry, but Saul has my da."

"Why didn't you call me?" Benny asked, hurt in his eyes.

She widened her eyes. "I tried. You've been in Russia, totally out of communication, Ben. I couldn't find you."

Now he blanched. "Ah, darling. I'm sorry. I needed a couple of decades of alone time." He turned a harsh glare on his nephews, seemingly uncaring that they were three of the most dangerous vampires in the world. "And you three jackasses got two of my places blown up. Destroyed. Completely turned to ash." His voice lowered to a growl that sounded more bear than wolf.

Theo stepped forward. "We've had a rough month, but we'll pay you back."

"Pay me back?" Benny boomed. "Oh, hell no. You'll overpay me until you work your fool fingers to the bone."

Theo's pupils narrowed as if his temper was stretching wide awake. "For fuck's sake, Ben. It was a penthouse and a house. Surely you had insurance." Theo looked like he'd be just fine if Benny punched him in the face. Oh, man. Theo wanted a good fight and right now. "Would you just get over it?" He tensed, apparently ready for the blow.

Benny looked at him. Then at Ginny. Then once again at Theo. A smile twitched on his lips. Then he threw back his head and laughed, the boisterous sound echoing in every direction. His eyes watered, and he wiped them off, finally sobering with a couple of coughs. "Oh, boy. You just have no clue what you've gotten into."

Theo cut a hard look toward Ginny. "I'm getting the idea that may be true."

She fought the very real urge to stick her tongue out at him. Sometimes a vampire ended up pushed to his limit, and if she had to guess, Theo had reached that point more than a few hours earlier. "I've never pretended to be anything but who I am."

Theo snorted. "Are you fucking kidding me?"

Heat filled her face. "All right. I haven't pretended since I promised you I wouldn't." All saints. What did he want, anyway?

Theo turned suddenly more toward Benny. "Why the hell didn't you tell me the king knew about the Green Rock file?"

Benny's broad forehead wrinkled. "Huh. Thought I had. Why do you care, anyway?"

Red flushed across Theo's handsome face, even reaching his ears.

Ginny stepped in, patting Theo's wide chest. "Um, I think perhaps Theo was concerned that the king would be angry. Considering Chalton works with the Realm, surely you can understand that concern, Benny." She smiled at him again as if he should most certainly understand.

He stared at her a moment. "Well, uh, yeah. I guess I do understand that now." He cleared his throat and looked at Theo. "I, ah, I'm sorry I didn't tell you about that." His brows drew down and he looked at Ginny for confirmation. When she nodded with encouragement, his face cleared. "Yeah. Shoulda told you."

Theo looked down at her as if the world had started spinning backward all of a sudden. "Have you two, ah, worked together a lot?"

Benny chuckled. "Oh, yeah. Remember that cadre of wolf shifters we—"

Ginny held up a hand. "Oh, my." Panic cut through her with a large swath. Theo didn't need to know about some of the scrapes she, Benny, and her father had gotten into through the years. "We don't want to bother Theo with *that* story." Glancing to the side, she caught both of Theo's brothers staring at her, their mouths open and their brows furrowed. Amusement glittered in Jared's eyes, while Chalton just looked bemused.

Theo looked like he'd been hit in the head with a concrete block. Twice. "Cadre of wolves?"

"Wasn't nearly as interesting as when we infiltrated the dragon island. When was that? About thirty years ago?" Benny rubbed his broad jaw, his lips quirking.

Oh, man. Benny couldn't catch a hint. She pressed her lips together and shook her head at him.

"You don't remember the dragons?" Benny asked, his brow furrowing.

Theo swallowed. "We've just recently discovered that there are dragons and that they live on an invisible island. You two, ah, knew three decades ago that dragons existed?" He looked almost dazed.

Benny laughed again, his rock-hard belly visibly clenching beneath his black shirt. "Obviously. How else would we have stolen the rubies?"

"Rubies." Theo wavered. "You stole rubies from *dragons*."

"To be fair, they stole them first," Ginny rushed to say. This was going south and way too quickly. "So, Benny. In town for long?"

Benny chewed on his lip. "Nope. Just came to get my flash drive back."

She cleared her throat, her stomach churning. "I can't give it to you, Ben. I'm so sorry. But I made a deal with Saul."

Benny sighed loudly. Very loudly. "I understand. A deal's a deal." He spread his arms out and looked at the three Reese men. "Well? I can't torture her for information. We've been friends for too long. Which one of you is up to the task?"

"Nobody is torturing my mate." Theo tucked her close into his side. His computer dinged, and he glanced over at it.

Ginny partially turned, not even remotely worried that any of the four males would try to torture her. Please. Theo had to see through his uncle. Benny wouldn't hurt a woman. Code flashed across the screen. Her breath caught. Theo had cracked the code on Saul's flash drive.

Good. Now they could finally find something to trade. She moved for it.

Theo held her still. "While nobody is going to torture my mate, I am going to get the information from her." He pointed toward the laptop, and Chalton nodded, hustling toward it. "Excuse us," Theo said, drawing her toward the bedroom.

"There you go, Theo," Benny said agreeably. "I'll make some sandwiches while you get the info from her. You'd better have roast beef." He started moving toward the kitchen. "Boys, start plying me with plans to repay me for your destructive last month. I came here to slice off somebody's head, and I'm not thrilled I don't get to play today."

Theo tugged her toward the bedroom.

She stumbled, looking back at the computer. Was he serious? "I'm not going to tell you," she said, figuring it was only fair to warn him.

"The hell you're not," he said grimly, drawing her inside and shutting the door. Hard.

* * * *

Ginny stumbled and then drew free, backing toward the bed. Ice pricked down her back. "Listen, Theo."

"No. You listen." He leaned against the door, his arms crossed. His brown hair was mussed, and a fine shadow covered his angled jaw. He looked big and broad and unbeatable. "I'm finished with this bullshit. Tell me where the flash drive is, and I'll take it to Saul to get your father back."

Just looking at him made her mouth water. Why was he saying these things? "I can't. He's serious." Her voice trembled. Theo seemed to have lost his mind.

"I'm serious." He looked implacable, as impenetrable as rock.

"I'll trade what you stole for the flash drive. But I'm done negotiating with you." Moving for her, he manacled her hair, bringing her up on her toes.

She gasped, panic and anger coursing through her. "Theo, you're hurting me."

He blinked and loosened his hold, his voice remaining cold and rough. "I'll hurt you a lot more if you don't give in." Gently, he rubbed her head. Then he winked.

What? Oh. Of course. This was for Saul's benefit.

She lowered her chin. Well, then. She sniffed and let the tears fall. "Oh, Theo, I just…" She coughed several times, giving it all she had. "I'm so tired and sore. Last night we mated, and I—" Her voice rose in one of her best performances. "I'm just not strong like you."

He rolled his eyes and drew her close. "Oh, Ginny. I'm so sorry. For a moment, with all the stories, I forgot how delicate you are." Leaning back, he shook his head, his lip quirking. "You should be protected and cosseted, and that's my job now." His eyes rolled so far back, it was a wonder he couldn't see his brain.

She grinned but forced a couple of hiccups. "I, I just need rest. Just an hour, please? We can talk after that."

"Okay. I'll go eat with my brothers." He kissed her loudly on the cheek. "Just rest, babykins."

Babykins? Seriously? Talk about overplaying the role. The vampire sucked at acting. She shook her head and shoved him in the gut. "Thank you so much, Theo. I do trust you to protect me." Her voice went breathy and weak.

"Jesus," he mouthed. "Stay here. I'll be back with a plan." Turning her, he smacked her ass. She whirled back around, but he was already out the door.

She sat down, kicking her heels. After about five minutes, she started creating escape plans from the room. Those vents were truly a gift for somebody like her. Keeping as quiet as she could, trying to make Saul think she was taking a nap or crying or something, she lifted the bedside table toward the door and the vent.

Theo walked in. He took one look at her and spread his arms out in a "what the hell?" movement.

She bit back a grin and pointed to the vents and obvious

escape route.

He sighed, shaking his head. Then he handed over a piece of paper.

SAUL'S FLASH DRIVE HELD PLANS TO INFILTRATE REALM HEADQUARTERS AND TAKE BRENNA DUNNE-KAYRS. SHE'S A WITCH, AND HE PLANNED TO PUT AN ANKLET ON HER. SINCE SHE'S ON THE RULING BODY OF WITCHES, HE HAD BIG PLANS TO TAKE OVER. THE WITCHES ARE IN FLUX RIGHT NOW, AS YOU KNOW.

Ginny read, her mind spinning. Wasn't Brenna pregnant? What would an anklet like that do to a pregnant witch? Ginny's stomach rolled, and bile rose in her throat. She swallowed rapidly.

Theo handed her another piece of paper, and she read, trying not to crinkle it or make any noise.

THE PLAN TONIGHT AT MIDNIGHT:

YOU AND I GET THE BENJAMIN FILE

WE TAKE IT AND THE FLASH DRIVE YOU STOLE TO THE MEET WITH SAUL. WE'LL PRETEND WE COULDN'T GET INTO HIS DOCUMENTS.

Ginny read the last line and shook her head, pointing at the script. Saul wouldn't believe them. He couldn't afford to. Theo calmly pointed at the next paragraph.

SAUL CAN'T AFFORD TO BELIEVE US. SO WE MOVE IN AND TAKE HIM, FORCING HIM TO GIVE UP THE CONTROLLER FOR THE ANKLET.

Ginny sighed. It was a nice plan and she hated to disagree. But it wouldn't work. She motioned for a pen, and Theo handed one over, and she started to write:

THE MEET IS SET FOR OUTSIDE MARIO PIZZA'S BACK ENTRANCE. A CAR IS PICKING ME UP. I DON'T ACTUALLY KNOW WHERE THE MEET IS. I HAVE TO GO ALONE, BUT YOU CAN PUT A TRACKER ON ME. IT'S THE ONLY WAY.

It truly was the only way. Saul wouldn't let his guard down if she had a vampire soldier with her. He'd already proven he was smarter than she'd feared.

She started writing again:

YOU'RE GOING TO HAVE TO TRUST ME THIS TIME.

Theo studied her, his eyes veiled. "I'll be back in a few," he mouthed, turning and shutting the door so he could probably speak with his brothers without being overheard by Saul.

She waited two minutes, looking at the closed door. Everything she'd ever wanted was on the other side, but she had to save her father. The flash drive she'd stolen had been cracked, and Saul would assume it had, so there really was no reason for her to return it. What he wanted she had stashed across town.

Glancing at the bed that had changed her life, she stood on the table and opened the vent. There was only one path to take here. God, she hoped Theo forgave her.

If she lived.

Chapter 15

A town car pulled up next to Ginny outside the pizza restaurant at exactly midnight. She opened the door and slid inside, grateful to be out of the snow. They drove through town, and the merry Christmas lights and decorations covered most surfaces in sparkle and spirit. She swallowed, her mind on Theo.

There had been so many things she'd wanted to say to him, but there hadn't been time. And a stupid anklet broadcast her every sound. She really tried not to think about that.

The partition was up between her and the driver, so she settled back in the seat and watched the Christmas lights fly by. The car smelled like new leather.

They finally pulled up in front of a closed jewelry store. She stepped outside, noting the door was open. Glancing around, she couldn't see anybody on the street. Was this some sort of odd trap? Steeling her shoulders, she moved gingerly through the heavy snow and strode inside the shop.

The lights came on, and the door shut behind her. "Saul," she murmured.

Saul Libscombe sat across the room and behind a low counter of what looked like opals. "I commend you for coming alone."

"You didn't give me a choice." She jumped when a man stepped out from the shadows behind her, slapping him when he tried to frisk her. "I'm not stupid enough to bring either flash drive." The goon gave up, and after Saul nodded, he walked around the counter and went through a door to the back room.

Saul stood about six feet tall, with light brown hair and stark blue eyes. He was fit and strong at about five centuries old, and he dressed like he enjoyed luxury in designer pants and a perfectly pressed silk shirt. His watch was a Rolex that wouldn't be released to humans for at least a year. "Where's the Benjamin file?" he asked, his gaze sharp.

"Where's my father?" she returned, holding her ground. There were counters of jewels all around her, but all she wanted was her da.

Saul let out a low whistle, and the goon from earlier shoved out her father.

"Da!" she cried out, rushing for him.

He enfolded her in a huge hug, smelling like peppermint and bourbon. His normal smell. "Ah, my girl. How I've missed you."

She leaned back. At nine centuries old, Elroy O'Toole was one handsome man. Blue eyes, blond hair, and sharp features. Like her. She checked him over, noting a scarf over his neck. Oh God. She grabbed for it, revealing a planekite collar. No wonder he hadn't been able to escape. She'd thought about it, but she hadn't wanted to really consider the possibility. "Oh, Da."

He hugged her again. "Hasn't been so bad. Only a decade, really. I've been worried about you." He smoothed back her hair.

She forced a smile. "I've been fine."

He paused, studying her. "Something's different." His eyes widened. "Oh, my."

"Aye," she murmured, knowing he could sense the mating. "You always did like Theo, remember?"

Her da slowly nodded. "'Tis true. I did."

That was good, at least. "Where have you been? I've looked everywhere."

"Moving around quite a bit," her da said wearily. "Ready to get this collar off."

Saul lifted a remote control in his hand. "Last chance, Ginny. Give me the location of the Benjamin file or I press the button. You both die."

She turned to face him, wanting nothing more than to be able to throw fire again. Wait a minute. She'd mated. Truth be told, she did feel stronger. A little. There was only one chance, but she'd take it. "I have it." Stepping away from her father, she made her way toward Saul. "The second you release these collars, I'll hand it over."

"No," Saul said. "Collars stay on, but I won't kill you. That's a good bargain. Take it."

She stood a foot away from him. The room had an odd lemon minty smell. Probably something Christmas related. "You've kept me enslaved for a decade. Do you really think you'll ever be safe from me?"

He smiled, revealing a crooked front tooth as he lifted the controller. "Aye. I truly do."

She drew deep, going for power, thinking of Theo. His strength, his humor, his passion. That lived in her now. She only needed a little. Just a little. "All right." Her shoulders slumping, she batted her eyelashes and looked fragile. Beaten. Weak.

Saul lowered his hand.

She shuddered hard and reached inside her coat. Theo. Power. Love. "I can throw fire now." Power flushed through her on the thought, and she drew out her hand, throwing her hand toward him.

Nothing happened, but the bluff worked. He yelped and jumped out of the way, not realizing there was no fire until he was already in motion. In one smooth movement, she planted her hands on the counter and flipped over, catching the controller with her ankles. Then she swung around, hit the ground, and kept rolling, coming up in front of her dad.

Saul bellowed and quickly lifted a green gun to point at her. The kind that shot lasers that turned to lead in immortals. Shit.

Her dad held out his hands. "Enough, Saul. Enough."

Saul fired, and the impact hit Elroy in the chest, throwing him back into the wall. He pushed Ginny out of the way as he fell. She glanced frantically at the controller. It had three green buttons. What the hell?

Saul laughed and moved toward her.

Her father struggled to a seated position, blood pouring from a wound near his neck.

"Heal that," she hissed. Oh, she was going to fight. She lifted her hand and nothing happened. Fire sputtered for just a second. Wow. But that was it. No more fire. Damn it. That was all she had for the moment. She backed away, holding the controller. Saul came nearer, and she leaped up, kicking him beneath the chin. His jaw cracked. He stumbled back, his arms windmilling, fury in his holler.

His chin lowered. He turned and pointed the gun at her.

The front window crashed in, two bodies dropped from the ceiling, and the goon from before crashed through from the back, smashing into one of the counters and sending glass flying through the room.

And then all hell broke loose.

* * * *

Theo zeroed in on the threat to his mate immediately as he sprang through the glass window and kept going, straight into Saul Libscombe. Lasers impacted Theo's vest and pummeled his still healing ribs, but he didn't care. His knife was out, and he slashed across Saul's arms until the shifter dropped the gun.

Then he punched the bastard in the face. Once, twice, and then enough times he lost count.

Saul fought back, kicking and changing his nails into claws to rip into Theo's flesh.

Three shifter soldiers poured in from the back, and Theo caught Jared, Chalton, and Benny engaging in battles involving guns, knives, and some serious fang slashing.

Saul kept slashing at Theo, even while he took hit after hit after hit.

Theo didn't feel a thing. A raw possessiveness overtook him, destroying his ability to think rationally. He didn't give a shit. Ginny had been in danger, and now that threat was bleeding all over Theo. His neck was bleeding from deep gouges, and he kept swinging, carving pieces until Saul was one open wound.

A body flew over Theo's head, and he ducked after making sure it wasn't one of his team. Nope. Saul sliced a claw beneath his chin, and Theo bellowed. He saw red.

Shoving the shifter down onto his back on the floor, Theo followed him, straddling the bastard and punching all the way through to the cement. Bones shattered. More bloody claws, more temper. Damn it. Theo struck hard beneath the jaw and could hear Saul's skull crack.

Finally, the shifter stopped moving.

Theo panted, straddling the enemy, waiting for him to strike. Nothing.

"He's out, dude," Jared said, leaning down, his upper lip split wide open. "Totally."

Chalton wiped glass off his shirt, leaving a trail of blood from his bleeding knuckles. "You could kill him, but I think the Realm would really like to discuss his future kidnapping plans first. After going through the plans, it doesn't appear he was working alone. He has allies."

It was no fun to kill a guy he'd knocked out, anyway. Theo shoved to his feet, immediately turning. Shifter soldiers were unconscious in the corner, Benny was talking to Elroy O'Toole, who was already healing the bullet holes along his upper chest.

Ginny was watching him, her eyes wide, her face pale, and a black box held tightly in her hand.

Theo moved toward her. "You okay?"

"I kind of made fire," she said slowly, peering around him at Saul's body beaten to a bloody pulp. "He's gonna feel that for a long time."

"Good." Theo gingerly took the box from her. "Chalton?"

Chalton hustled over, yanking a tablet from his back pocket. "Yeah. Give me a sec." He started pushing buttons.

Theo brushed Ginny's hair away from her face, his heart finally settling. "You scared the hell out of me."

"I'm sorry." She leaned into his touch, her eyes darkening. "There wasn't a choice."

"I know." He pressed a soft kiss to her nose.

"You did?" She stiffened and then leaned back, studying him. "Wait a minute. How are you here right now?"

He was still too keyed up and pissed to grin, but it was nice catching her off balance for once. "Remember we hacked into the anklet? We followed you, lady. The entire time."

Her eyes lit up. "You knew I'd leave?"

"Yeah." He knew. It had been the hardest thing he'd ever done to let her go, but she'd been right. It had been the only good plan. And he'd covered her as soon as he could, although it had nearly eaten him up throughout. He'd discovered, right there and then, where his heart belonged. "I love you. Should've told you before.

I've loved you for centuries."

She gasped, delight brushing even more beauty across her face. "I love you, too. Ever since we were kids so many years ago. It has always been you—only you."

He kissed her, going deep. A trio of clearing voices caught him, and he reluctantly released her mouth. For now. "Chalton?"

Chalton handed over the tablet. "Here's the frequency. You were right. It's the same one we hacked. Simple but efficient."

Theo took the tablet, read the code, and then quickly started typing. Then he hit ENTER.

Ginny gasped and kicked out her leg. The anklet went flying across the room to hit a counter and fall hard.

She breathed out several times.

Saul groaned and tried to roll over.

"Hell no." She stomped over and kicked him with the foot that had had to balance that anklet for so long. Then she kicked him again in the ribs. Hard. Then again.

"Should we stop her?" Chalton asked mildly.

Theo shrugged. "No. Let her play."

She kicked Saul in the temple, and the shifter fell into unconsciousness again. Her chest heaving, Ginny looked up and grinned.

God, she was beautiful.

Then she slowly looked around at all the jewelry on the ground.

"No," Theo said automatically.

She bit her lip. "Well? Who owns this place?"

"Saul does," Benny said quietly. "Always has."

Ginny did something that looked like a cross between a happy hop and a charge for the nearest emeralds lying all over the demolished floor. "If Saul owns these, they're coming home with me." Then she looked up, delight in her eyes. "Right, Theo?"

He couldn't help it. The woman was definitely a thief because she'd stolen his heart and it had taken him this long to realize it. If she wanted to steal, especially from a jerk who'd hurt her, Theo would make it happen. "Right, sweetheart. Let me find you a big bag."

Yeah. This was definitely love. The forever kind.

Epilogue

Helen Reese kicked her feet atop the coffee table and sipped on heavily laced eggnog in her comfortable living room. The lights on the tree twinkled in tune with the festive music from the hidden speakers. Contentment filled her along with the warmth. Her three boys were mated and in love, all gathered around the Christmas tree with strong and modern women.

"You did good." Benny sat next to her on the couch after having spiked the eggnog, his gaze on the younger generation. He flattened his boots on the coffee table, loudly breaking it in two.

She sighed and let her feet fall to the floor as the coffee table did the same. "Benjamin," she murmured. Centuries ago, she'd mated his brother, and Benny had become *her* brother. Even now that she'd been widowed for so long, she loved him as a brother. A pain-in-the-behind brother, but family nonetheless.

He snorted, his boots smashing the fallen magazines. "Sorry."

She shrugged. "It's just furniture." Then she smiled. "I did do good." Sure, she'd committed treason and possibly espionage when she'd maneuvered Chalton and Olivia together, but just look how happy they were.

Chalton leaned against the wall, his legs extended, his arm around his pretty Olivia. She rested against him, so much smaller than the vampire. She talked animatedly with Ronnie, who sat on Jared's lap on the settee, idly playing with his dark hair. Even after all these years, Jared still looked like a pirate. Helen grinned at her eldest son.

Benny patted his flat belly. "Yep. A journalist, a police psychologist, and a thief. All good mates for the boys."

"Yes," Helen murmured. She'd done it. Now that Theo had

mated Ginny, they were all happily mated and would hopefully soon give her grandchildren. "You're next, Ben."

He snorted and drank his eggnog in one gulp. "Nope. Not me."

Helen turned toward him. He was huge, even for a vampire soldier. Solid barrel of a chest, long legs, dangerous hands. With his black hair and greenish-black eyes, he looked like a compilation of her sons. But bigger. "Why haven't you ever mated?"

He lifted a shoulder the size of a small mountain. "Why would I?"

Hmm. Maybe she'd just found her next project.

"Don't even think it." A small smile played on his lips as he watched his nephews. "Glad I didn't have to cut off anybody's head. It's a good holiday."

She rolled her eyes. Benny was a big talker, but he'd die for family. "It was kind of you to spare them." She could play along as his Christmas gift.

He nodded sagely. "Aye. It was." His sigh reminded her of a slumbering bear in the sun.

Ginny laughed at something Ronnie said, the sound tinkly and fun. She cuddled with Theo in the ottoman, pretty much lying in his lap.

Helen smiled. "They're happy." That made her happy.

"Good." Benny reached over his head for the pitcher on the sofa table and refilled their glasses. "Because peace ain't gonna last. Something's coming."

"I know," she said softly, as always attuned to the winds. "But not yet."

Benny shook his head. "Disagree, sister. The atmosphere is heavy. With change."

She sighed and watched him from the corner of her eye. Benny was older than even she knew, and he had a sense of the world she'd never understood. "What do you know?"

"Nothing. Yet." His solid block of a face remained calm, but a thread of caution rode his words.

"Benny," she said softly, to remind him they went way back. So many people thought Benny was crazy or just a big brute. But she knew him. There was more to Benjamin Reese than most people could see, and he enjoyed it like that. "Tell me."

"Helen, if I knew, I'd tell you." He set his glass down. "Whatever is coming will make an appearance soon enough."

She ignored the chill dancing down her back. Destiny always seemed cold. "What now?"

"Now?" He grinned and raised his voice. "Now my nephews are going to ply me with presents for being so damn fucking understanding when they blew up not one but two of my very nice homes."

The three boys groaned, already reaching for a myriad of wrapped presents.

"There had better be a pony in there," Benny rumbled.

Helen couldn't help but chuckle. For now.

Keep an eye out for more Dark Protector books in 2018. We're going back to the originals. (

XO

Rebecca

* * * *

Also from 1001 Dark Nights and Rebecca Zanetti, discover Teased, Tricked, and Blaze Erupting.

About Rebecca Zanetti

Rebecca Zanetti is the author of over thirty romantic suspense and dark paranormal novels, and her books have appeared multiple times on the New York Times, USA Today, BnN, iTunes, and Amazon bestseller lists. She has received a Publisher's Weekly Starred Review for Wicked Edge, Romantic Times Reviewer Choice Nominations for Forgotten Sins and Sweet Revenge, and RT Top Picks for several of her novels. Amazon labeled Mercury Striking as one of the best romances of 2016 and Deadly Silence as one of the best romances in October. The Washington Post called Deadly Silence, "sexy and emotional." She believes strongly in luck, karma, and working her butt off…and she thinks one of the best things about being an author, unlike the lawyer she used to be, is that she can let the crazy out. Find Rebecca at: www.rebeccazanetti.com

Also from Rebecca Zanetti

SCORPIUS SYNDROME SERIES
Scorpius Rising
Mercury Striking
Shadow Falling
Justice Ascending
Storm Gathering (September 19, 2017)

DARK PROTECTORS
Fated
Claimed
Tempted
Hunted
Consumed
Provoked
Twisted
Shadowed
Tamed
Marked
Teased
Tricked
Tangled
Talen (June 6, 2017)

REALM ENFORCERS
Wicked Ride
Wicked Edge
Wicked Burn
Wicked Kiss (July 4, 2017)
Wicked Bite (August 1, 2017)

SIN BROTHERS
Forgotten Sins
Sweet Revenge
Blind Faith
Total Surrender

BLOOD BROTHERS
Deadly Silence
Lethal Lies
Twisted Truths

MAVERICK MONTANA
Against the Wall
Under the Covers
Rising Assets
Over the Top

Discover More Rebecca Zanetti

BLAZE ERUPTING: Scorpius Syndrome/A Brigade Novella
by Rebecca Zanetti

Hugh Johnson is nobody's hero, and the idea of being in the limelight makes him want to growl. He takes care of his brothers, does his job, and enjoys a mellow evening hanging with his hound dog and watching the sports channel. So when sweet and sexy Ellie Smithers from his college chemistry class asks him to save millions of people from a nuclear meltdown, he doggedly steps forward while telling himself that the world hasn't changed and he can go back to his relaxing life. One look at Ellie and excitement doesn't seem so bad.

Eleanor Smithers knows that the Scorpius bacteria has and will change life as we know it, but that's a concern for another day. She's been hand-picked as the computer guru for The Brigade, which is the USA's first line of defense against all things Scorpius, including homegrown terrorists who've just been waiting for a chance to strike. Their target is a nuclear power plant in the east, and the only person who can help her is Hugh, the sexy, laconic, dangerous man she had a crush on so long ago.

* * * *

TEASED: A Dark Protectors—Reece Family Novella by Rebecca Zanetti

The Hunter

For almost a century, the Realm's most deadly assassin, Chalton Reese, has left war and death in the past, turning instead to strategy, reason, and technology. His fingers, still stained with blood, now protect with a keyboard instead of a weapon. Until the vampire king sends him on one more mission; to hunt down a human female with the knowledge to destroy the Realm. A woman with eyes like emeralds, a brain to match his own, and a passion that might destroy them both—if the enemy on their heels doesn't do so first.

The Hunted

Olivia Roberts has foregone relationships with wimpy metrosexuals in favor of pursuing a good story, bound and determined to uncover the truth, any truth. When her instincts start humming about missing proprietary information, she has no idea her search for a story will lead her to a ripped, sexy, and dangerous male beyond any human man. Setting aside the unbelievable fact that he's a vampire and she's his prey, she discovers that trusting him is the only chance they have to survive the danger stalking them both.

* * * *

TRICKED: A Dark Protectors—Reese Family Novella by Rebecca Zanetti

He Might Save Her

Former police psychologist Ronni Alexander had it all before a poison attacked her heart and gave her a death sentence. Now, on her last leg, she has an opportunity to live if she mates a vampire. A real vampire. One night of sex and a good bite, and she'd live forever with no more weaknesses. Well, except for the vampire whose dominance is over the top, and who has no clue how to deal with a modern woman who can take care of herself.

She Might Kill Him

Jared Reese, who has no intention of ever mating for anything other than convenience, agrees to help out his new sister in law by saving her friend's life with a quick tussle in bed. The plan seems so simple. They'd mate, and he move on with his life and take risks as a modern pirate should. Except after one night with Ronni, one moment of her sighing his name, and he wants more than a mating of convenience. Now all he has to do is convince Ronni she wants the same thing. Good thing he's up for a good battle.

Deadly Silence
Blood Brothers Book 1
Now Available

Have you had a chance to read the Blood Brothers series? Here's an excerpt from Deadly Silence, the first book in the series. Enjoy!

The first book in a breathtaking new romantic suspense series that will appeal to fans of *New York Times* bestsellers Maya Banks, Lisa Gardner, and Lisa Jackson.

DON'T LOOK BACK

Under siege. That's how Ryker Jones feels. The Lost Bastards Investigative Agency he opened up with his blood brothers has lost a client in a brutal way. The past he can't outrun is resurfacing, threatening to drag him down in the undertow. And the beautiful woman he's been trying to keep at arm's length is in danger...and he'll destroy anything *and* anyone to keep her safe.

Paralegal Zara Remington is in over her head. She's making risky moves at work by day and indulging in an affair with a darkly dangerous PI by night. There's a lot Ryker isn't telling her and the more she uncovers, the less she wants to know. But when all hell breaks loose, Ryker may be the only one to save her. If his past doesn't catch up to them first...

Full of twists and turns you won't see coming, DEADLY SILENCE is *New York Times* bestselling author Rebecca Zanetti at her suspenseful best.

* * * *

Zara Remington brushed a stray tendril of her thick hair back from her face before checking on the lasagna. The cheese bubbled up through the noodles, while the scent of the garlic bread in the oven warmer filled the country-style kitchen. Perfect. She shut the oven door and glanced at the clock. Five minutes.

He'd be there in *five minutes.*

It had been weeks since she'd seen him, and her body was ready and primed for a tussle. *Just a tussle.* Shaking herself, she repeated the mantra she'd coined since meeting him two months ago. Temporary. They were temporary and just for fun. This was her reward for working so hard...a walk on the wild side. Even if she was the type to settle down and devote herself to one man, it wouldn't be this one.

Ryker Jones kept one foot out the door, even while naked in her bed doing things to her that were illegal in the southern states. Good damn thing she lived in Cisco. Wyoming didn't care what folks did behind closed doors. Thank God.

She hummed and eyed the red high heels waiting by the entry to the living room. They probably wouldn't last on her feet for long, but she'd greet him wearing them. While she still wore the black pencil skirt and gray silk shirt she'd donned for work, upon reading his text that he was back in town, she'd rushed to change into a scarlet bra and G-string set that matched the shoes before putting her clothes back into place.

If she was living out a fantasy, he should get one, too. The guy didn't have to know she'd worn granny-style spanx panties and a thin cotton bra all day.

A roar of motorcycle pipes echoed down her quiet street. Tingles exploded in her abdomen. Hurrying for the shoes, she bit back a wince upon slipping her feet in. The little kitten heels she'd really worn had been much more comfortable.

A minute passed and the pipes silenced.

She drew air in through her nose, counted to five, and exhaled. Calm down. Geez. She really needed to relax. The sharp rap on her front door sent her system into overdrive again.

Straightening her shoulders, she tried to balance in the heels past her comfortable sofa set, clicking on the polished hard-wood floors. She had to wipe her hands down her skirt before twisting the nob and opening the door. "Ryker," she breathed.

He didn't smile. Instead, his bluish-green eyes darkened as his gaze raked her head to toe...and back up. "I've missed you." The low rumble of his voice, just as dangerous as the motorcycle pipes, licked right where his gaze had been.

She nodded, her throat closing. He was every vision of a badass bad boy that she'd ever dreamed about. His thick black hair curled over the collar of a battered leather jacket that covered a broad and well-muscled chest. Long legs, encased in faded jeans, led to motorcycle boots. His face had been shaped with long lines and powerful strokes, and a shadow lined his cut jaw. But those eyes. Greenish-gold and fierce, they changed shades with his mood.

As she watched, those odd eyes narrowed. "What the fuck?"

She self-consciously fingered the slash of a bruise across her right cheekbone. Cover-up had concealed it well enough all day, but leave it to Ryker to notice. He didn't miss anything. God, that intrigued her. His vision was oddly sharp, and once he'd mentioned hearing an argument several doors down. She hadn't heard a thing. "It's nothing." She stepped back to allow him entrance. "I have a lasagna cooking."

He moved into her, heat and his scent of forest and leather brushing across her skin. One knuckle gently ran across the bruise. "Who hit you?" The tone held an edge of something dark.

She shut the door and moved away from his touch. "What? Who says somebody hit me?" Turning on the heel and barely keeping from landing on her butt, she walked toward the kitchen, remembering to sway her hips before making it past the couch. "I have to get dinner out or it'll burn." She kept several frozen dishes ready to go, not knowing when he'd be back in town. The domestication worked well for them both, and she liked cooking for him. Enjoyed taking care of him like that…for this brief affair, or whatever it was. "I hope you haven't eaten."

"You know I haven't." He stopped inside the kitchen. "Zara."

She gave an involuntary shiver from his low tone and drew the lasagna from the oven and bread from the warmer before turning around to see him lounging against the door jam. "Isn't this when you pour wine?" Her heart fluttered at seeing the contrast between her pretty butter-yellow cabinets and the deadly rebel calmly watching her. "I have the beer you like."

"You always have the beer I like." He didn't move a muscle, and this time, a warning thread through his words in a tone like gravel crumbling in a crusher. "I asked you a question."

She forced a smile and carried the dishes to the breakfast nook, which she'd already set with her favorite Apple patterned dinnerware and bright aqua linens. "And I asked you one." Trying to ignore the tension vibrating from him, she grasped a lighter for the candles.

A hand on her arm spun her around. She hadn't heard him move. How did he do that?

He leaned in. "Then I'll answer yours. I know what a woman looks like who's been hit. I know by the color and slant of that bruise how much force was used, how tall the guy was, and which hand he used. What I don't know…is the name of the fucker. Yet."

"How do you know all of that?" she whispered.

He lifted his head, withdrawing. "I just do."

There it was. He'd share his body and nothing else with her. She didn't even know where he lived when he wasn't on a case. From day one he'd been clear that this wasn't forever, that he wasn't interested in a future. Neither was she. He was her walk on the wild side, her first purely physical affair, and that's why he could mind his own business.

Hold Me
A Stark Ever After Novella
By J. Kenner

1001 DARK NIGHTS

HOLD ME
A Stark Ever After Novella

J. KENNER

NEW YORK TIMES BESTSELLING AUTHOR

Chapter 1

"See?" I say, balancing on the edge of my daughter's bed as I close her favorite book, *Goodnight, Sleep Tight, Little Bunnies*. "All the animals are asleep, and now it's time for Lara to go to sleep, too."

"Kitty sleep?" She holds up her stuffed cat, its once plush fur now matted and dull, a reflection of its status as the best-loved animal in her menagerie.

"Kitty and Lara can both go night-night, okay?"

She wraps her arms around Kitty and nods, her thumb going into her mouth.

"I love you, Lara Ashley Stark," I say as her eyes start to flutter closed. Honestly, mine are a little fluttery, too. Who would have thought that taking care of an infant and a two-year-old could be so exhausting?

"Love Mama," she murmurs around her thumb as I bend over to give her another kiss, breathing in the scent of baby shampoo and powder.

Her eyes open again, and she blinks at me. "*Baba?*" she asks, still using the Chinese word for Daddy that she's used since the day we adopted her. She was twenty months old then. And although it's been only eight months since we came home from China, it's already hard to remember what it was like not having this precious girl in our lives.

"Daddy loves you so much," I say, stroking her hair and speaking softly so that she'll drift off. "Close your eyes, baby girl. Daddy will come kiss you night-night later. When you're already in dreamland."

I have to fight a melancholy frown. Although Damien tries hard to be home for both our daughters' bedtimes, his work as a master of the known universe sometimes keeps him away.

In contrast, I've been a permanent fixture in our Malibu home ever since we brought Lara home. Except, of course, for the hospital stay when our second daughter, Anne, was born almost four months ago.

At first, I'd stayed home to bond with Lara. And for that first month, both Damien and I had concentrated one hundred percent on our family. Then he'd returned to the office, and I'd started to handle a few work tasks from home.

I had intended to take a typical three-month maternity leave with Lara, then spend the last month of my pregnancy working in my office in order to make sure all of my clients were happy and every project on track before Anne came along.

But I ended up on bedrest for the last month, which turned out to be only two weeks, as Anne came early. And as soon as she made her appearance, I dove immediately into another three months of leave.

Now I'm on the last weekend before I return to my office and a full-time work schedule. And even though I'm starting to go a little stir-crazy during my maternity leave, I also know that I'm wildly lucky. I have two beautiful, healthy daughters, and I'm married to a man who not only adores me and our children, but who makes my heart flutter with nothing more than a glance or the whisper of my name.

Even more, he's a man whose talent and resources have ensured that we have an amazing home, that our children will never want for anything, and that even if neither one of us ever works another day, we have the means to keep our family not just afloat, but living in comfort and privilege.

I've known about Damien's wealth as long as I've known him. Longer, really, since as a former professional tennis star turned billionaire entrepreneur, Damien's reputation is both deep and wide. And goodness knows I've experienced firsthand the luxury and convenience that his dollars can buy. Everything from private jets to personal drivers to penthouse suites in hotels all over the world.

But it wasn't until after we had our girls that I started to truly *feel* the impact of his wealth. How it will protect their future. How it's a cushion against all the scary stuff that life can throw at you.

Except that's bullshit. And as I look down at my daughter—at her sweet, innocent face—I have to sigh. Because the truth is, there's no protection. Not ever. Not really.

No one knows that better than Damien and me.

I grew up in Dallas with the kind of money and privilege that oil and gas interests can buy. Not Stark-level money, but not shabby. And yet those dollars didn't shield me from pain. Didn't keep me from trying to escape from the dark corners of my life by taking a blade to my own skin.

And the empire that Damien built didn't erase the abuse he suffered as a child or eradicate all the challenges that have been tossed at him—at us—over the years. Everything from physical assault to blackmail to professional sabotage.

But not my kids, I think fiercely. Maybe I can't protect them from everything out there in the world, but I can damn sure try. And at least they have me and Damien as parents, and not Elizabeth Fairchild or Jeremiah Stark.

The very idea makes me shudder, and I stroke a soft hand over Lara's hair. "I love you, baby," I whisper. "And I will *always* be there for you."

Always.

The word seems to expand in my mind, reaching out and poking me with guilt-stained fingers. For the last three months, I've mostly left my still-nascent business in the hands of Eric and Abby, my two employees, both of whom have been with me almost two years now.

But Monday, our nanny starts working full time—and I'm going back to work. And the truth is that I can't wait. Even though I adore my girls—and even though we don't need the money—I'm eager to dive back into my business and get dirty. I started with just a love of coding and designing apps, and from that meager start, I built Fairchild Development from the ground up. I'm incredibly proud of not only the business, but its products and services, its growing client base, and, most important, its excellent reputation.

And while I can do some of the work from home, it's not the same as being in the office in much the same way as Damien. Sitting behind my desk and running my empire—albeit a much smaller one.

So, yes, I'm excited about Monday. But as I gently stroke Lara's warm cheek and watch the rise and fall of her chest as she breathes through parted lips, I have to admit that I'm also dreading it. Because my girls will be here in Malibu while I'm about an hour away in Studio City. I'm going to miss something wonderful, just like Damien so often misses dinner or bedtime. A word or a reaction. A silly face or a boisterous giggle.

And even though that hasn't even happened to me yet, the inevitable certainty feels like a knife in my heart.

With a heavy sigh, I stand slowly, careful not to move the bed too much. But apparently not careful enough, because as I rise, Lara's eyes flutter open, and her mouth moves in a silent *Mama*.

"Mama's here, precious," I say softly. I raise my hand to cover a yawn—it's been an exhausting day. "Go back to sleep, sweetie."

"*Baba*," she says sleepily, extending her hand.

"I know. Mommy wants *Baba* here, too."

"*Baba*," she repeats, and this time a sweet smile touches her lips before she breaks into a wide grin. "*Baba* kiss."

Damien.

I don't see him, but I know he's there. And not just from Lara's reaction. It's his presence. His heat. The way he fills the room like a force of nature, so that everything in it shifts just a little, making it impossible to not be aware of him.

I turn slowly, my own smile blooming wider as I see him in the doorway. He's leaning against the frame, those incredible dual-colored eyes reflecting so much love it makes my heart swell.

"How about a kiss for both my girls?" he says, his smile aimed at Lara, but his gaze going to me.

I nod, then sigh happily as he moves to Lara's bedside, then bends to kiss her. "Look at you in your big girl bed." She moved from her crib to the toddler bed only a week ago, and it's still a source of endless fascination.

"Big!" she says, her expression and her tone making clear that her daddy's presence is enough to tease her away from dreamland. She thrusts out her arms. "Up!"

"Oh, no," Damien says, easing her back, then handing her Kitty before pulling up her little blanket. "It's late. And big girls with big girl beds have to get their sleep. Right, Snuggles?"

"Lara!" she says. "Lara Ashley Stark!"

"Oh, that's right." He taps the end of her nose. "This big girl is Lara. Give Daddy a kiss, then time for sleep."

"Buf-eye," she insists, and Damien obliges, leaning in to use his eyelashes to give her a butterfly kiss on her cheek.

"And now night-night, okay?"

She nods, her thumb going back to her mouth. "Da*ba*," she says, and I press my hand over my mouth to stifle a laugh. "Nye nye."

He tucks her in, then stands up slowly before turning to me, a delicious grin tugging at the corner of his mouth. "Mama, kiss?" he asks, making me laugh.

I hold out a hand, then lead him into the hall. "Kiss," I demand, then melt as he pins me against the wall, his mouth closing over mine, hard and demanding, as if we'd been apart for weeks instead of just hours.

"I missed my girls today," he says as we break apart, leaving me breathless. "All of them. But I missed you the most."

I sigh happily. "I didn't think you'd be back so soon. You said you were trapped in San Diego." Even though it's Saturday, he'd been summoned to one of Stark International's satellite offices just after lunchtime, and he'd told me that the nature of the crisis was such that he probably wouldn't be done before midnight.

"For a while there, I thought I might have to fly from San Diego to Pittsburg," he says. "But we managed to get things back on track around six. I came home in the chopper," he adds. "You didn't hear it land?"

Damien installed a landing pad at the same time he built the house, and it's come in handy on more than one occasion. Usually, I hear him coming and going, but this time, I shake my head. "I guess because Lara's room is on the other side of the house."

"Good," he says. "If I take it home more often, I don't have to worry about waking the girls."

"Good point," I say, then press my hand over my smile, fighting the urge to laugh.

"Helicopters are funny? Because I know waking the kids isn't funny. That way leads to crankiness."

"Now you're being funny," I say. "No, I was just thinking a few minutes ago that we have more resources than other parents. Your arrival illustrates my point."

He chuckles, his eyes crinkling with amusement. "Always happy to help."

I ease up closer, hooking my arms around his waist. Then I lift myself up on my tiptoes and murmur, "I can think of a few other things you can help me with."

His hands slide down so that he's cupping my rear, and when he draws me closer, I feel the press of his erection and release a soft moan of anticipation.

He says nothing else, just takes my hand and leads me toward our bedroom.

The master bedroom is on the third floor of this house that Damien was building when we met in Los Angeles. Technically, we'd met six years earlier, but that brief encounter when he was a celebrity judge and I was a beauty pageant contestant is little more than a prologue to the life we now have together.

In a somewhat unique design, the third floor serves as the heart of this house and features a massive area for entertaining that opens onto a balcony with a stunning view of the Pacific. A small but well-designed kitchen dominates the opposite side of the floor. Originally planned as a workstation for caterers, it's turned out to be our primary kitchen, as it's much more user-friendly than the commercial monstrosity on the first floor.

The master bedroom is behind the open area, and in fact it shares a wall. And though we rarely used it before adopting Lara, there is another room on the floor that was designed as a guest room. It's tucked in behind the master bedroom, shares a wall with the master closet, and boasts windows that open onto both the back and the side of the house.

It's Lara's room now, done up in a cheery yellow, which is fitting since our cat, Sunshine, spends so much time in there, watching over the little girl that Sunshine has decided is her responsibility. As Damien leads me through the double doors that mark the entrance to our bedroom, Sunshine passes us going the opposite direction, her tail high as she trots toward Lara's room, ready to curl up in the armchair she's claimed and guard her charge for the night.

"She's been checking on Anne," I say, nodding toward the master sitting area, which we've converted to a nursery. Sunshine adores Anne, too, but she knows that she isn't allowed in the crib, which makes the baby much less interesting to her. Still, our cat has a nightly ritual, and it involves circling the bassinet two full times, as if searching for any possible dangers. Only when she's certain that Anne is secure does Sunshine head to her nighttime post in Lara's room.

"I think the cat has the right idea," Damien says, still holding my hand as he steers us toward our youngest daughter.

I put her down over an hour ago, and now she's sleeping peacefully, her little hands curled around the edge of the striped blanket that came home with us from the hospital. A truckload of toys and blankets and other loveys from our friends, but her favorite thing in the world is a thin blanket from the maternity ward.

I lean my head on Damien's shoulder and his arm goes around me as we watch our little miracle sleep. I have a somewhat rare uterine condition, and the odds of me carrying to term were pretty crappy. So Anne is our miracle baby, although every day that I watch her I realize how miraculous every child is.

"What did she do today?" he asks, though I know what he's really asking is, *Did I miss something spectacular?*

It's the hardest part of not being here. Of going away to a job. And as I tell him that our little princess rolled from her tummy to her back for the very first time, I can't help but wonder what milestone I'm going to miss when I go back to work.

"Did you get it on video?"

"I didn't have my phone handy," I admit. "I'm sorry."

"Maybe she'll show me herself in the morning." He leads me out of the sitting area and to our bed. "Right now, I'm thinking of a different kind of rolling."

I laugh. "Is that right, Mr. Stark? Maybe you better show me what you have in mind."

Chapter 2

Damien, of course, is happy to oblige.

He takes both my hands and tugs me toward him. He catches me, then falls onto the bed in one motion, my body held tight against his. I laugh and protest, though it's really only for show. But he shuts me up—first with a kiss, and then by literally rolling us over to the far side of the bed.

"Damien!" I squeal when he pins me beneath him. But my squeal quickly turns into a moan as he slides my T-shirt up over my head, then twines it around my wrists, holding them together.

"I like that," he says, eyeing me hungrily. He unbuttons his shirt and pulls it off, giving me a lovely view of the tight muscles of his athlete's body. Then he runs his hands down my arms and cups my now-bare, very sensitive breasts. I rarely go braless these days, what with breastfeeding the little one. But I'd been planning to relax in the bath once Lara was down and had changed into nothing more than a shirt and loose yoga pants.

"And I like this, too." He kisses the swell of my right breast, and a hot, tight cord of need extends like a fuse from my nipple all the way to my core, making me ache with an insatiable hunger. I writhe beneath him, overwhelmed by the flood of desire that's racing through me.

I grab one of the vertical iron posts that make up the headboard of our old-fashioned iron bed frame. At the same time, I arch up, silently demanding more of his mouth, his touch.

He doesn't disappoint, and as his mouth closes over my nipple and his tongue teases me mercilessly, his free hand slides down my belly, lower and lower until he reaches the waistband of my yoga pants. He tugs the cord to untie them, then slips his fingers inside, moving down until he strokes my clit with a feather-soft motion that acts like a flame, igniting a wild passion that rips through me, from my clit to my breasts to every cell in my body.

I gasp and squirm, but I don't let go of my grip on the bed. On the contrary, I hold on tighter, fighting an explosion that I know is coming as Damien's fingers so expertly play me.

Except the explosion never comes. Just as I'm on the verge, Damien pulls his hand away, leaving me teetering on the edge, frustrated and needy. "Damien," I beg. "Please."

He raises his head so that our eyes meet, and his lips brush my nipple as he speaks. "Hush, baby. Let me take care of you."

I whimper, knowing that begging will do me no good whatsoever—and also knowing that even though he's left me hanging, the ultimate explosion will be that much more intense. After all, he knows my body intimately, and he knows how to play me to perfection.

Slowly, he starts to kiss his way down, his tongue tracing the curve of my breast, his lips brushing my ribs.

He trails delicate kisses down my midline. And with each touch of his lips against my overheated skin, I feel a corresponding ache in my core, my body clenching with an urgent desire to have my husband inside me.

As his mouth moves lower, so do his hands, until he's peeled my pants down below my knees, leaving me bare. Slowly, he eases his hand up, his fingers moving slowly over the most violent of the scars that mar my inner thighs even as his lips trace the surgical scar from Anne's birth.

I'm a cutter. It started when I was a teen, trying to escape from a life that had me trapped, the blade acting as an outlet, the pain centering me. I don't cut anymore—not now that I have Damien. But I know that it's still inside me and that it will always be a part of me.

Now, I bite my lower lip, feeling strangely self-conscious as he traces those two very different scars. Damien knows I used to cut, of course. But my self-inflicted scars feel shamefully shallow and weak compared to the one that brought our daughter into this world. "It's nice to finally have a scar that's a reminder of joy," I say softly. "Not pain."

Damien tilts his head up, and I see nothing but fervent support and love. "You know how I feel, baby. Every one of your scars reflects strength. But yes," he adds, brushing his lips over the C-section scar. "This one is definitely my favorite."

I smile, his heartfelt answer erasing my lingering discomfort. "That's because you claim part ownership."

"Do I?" He chuckles, his mouth dipping lower until his tongue flicks over my clit and a flurry of sparks ripple through me, a promise of fireworks to come. "Of what? The scar? The baby?"

"All of that," I say. "And all of me." I shift my hips in a silent demand. "Damien, please."

He brushes his lips lightly over my pubic bone as his hands move to my inner thighs, stroking up—but not far enough. I'm burning with anticipation. Craving his hands, his mouth, his cock. I want all of him. I want everything. I want—

"Mama? *Baba?*"

The little voice makes me yelp, and Damien slides down the bed as I draw the covers up over me. He's shirtless but still wearing his jeans, and now he fastens the top button before holding out his hand to call her over. "Hey, Snuggles. You can't sleep?"

We have the third floor thoroughly baby-proofed, which is a good thing as Lara has taken to wandering now that she's in her toddler bed instead of a crib. Usually we hear her through the baby monitor. Tonight, she was apparently using stealth tactics.

"Come on, then," Damien says, lifting her up. "Let's get you tucked back in."

He glances at me and I grin, loving the way he looks holding his little girl in his arms. "Back soon," he whispers. "Don't go away."

"Yes, sir," I say, then stretch out as soon as they've left the room, imagining he's still beside me. The brush of his breath. The heat of his touch.

A moment later, I hear them through the monitor. Soft footsteps. The low timbre of Damien's voice as he urges Lara back to bed. Then gentle, rhythmic words as he reads her a Sandra Boynton bedtime story.

I close my eyes, letting the words drift over me, the sweet sound of Damien reading to our daughter. The soothing tone of his voice.

And the last thing I remember thinking is how much I love that man, and what an incredible father he's proven to be.

The next time I open my eyes, the room is bright with sunshine. For a moment, I'm confused. Then I get it, and I sit bolt upright.

It's tomorrow.

And although I feel pretty damn well-rested, I don't feel well-fucked. And since I know that Damien is in his home office this morning on an international video conference, that situation isn't going to be remedied anytime soon.

I sigh.

Because right then, I really, really want a do-over.

Chapter 3

My morning is spent feeding Anne, settling in for some quick emails while she goes back to sleep, and then taking a quick shower.

When I get out, I pull on my robe and head to her bassinet. She's not there, though, and I know that she must be with Bree.

I head for the kitchen to get the scoop on my family and hear Bree's voice urging Lara to eat her yogurt and Cheerios. "How do you expect to grow up to be strong and smart if you throw your food on the floor instead of eating it?"

As I round the corner, I see her standing with her hands on her hips, her head cocked as she stares my daughter down. According to Bree, her mother is a full-blooded Cherokee and her father grew up in Brooklyn, where his Jewish parents landed after escaping from the Warsaw Ghetto.

"I'm not sure what that makes me," she told me during her first day on the job, when we'd sat together drinking coffee and watching Lara.

I don't know either, other than that it makes her stunning, with sharply cut cheekbones, deep-set eyes, and long dark hair that gives her an air of both sophistication and ethereal sweetness.

She's in her early twenties and is taking a year off from college, and she decided that being a nanny made the most sense while she figured out what she wanted to do next. We hired her when I was on bedrest, but after Anne was born, I took over, wanting to be the girls' full-time mommy. At least as much as I could.

Whenever I had phone meetings or had to run to my office, Bree would come over from the guest house and take over. These last few days, though, she's been working full time since we want the kids to be used to having her around all day once I go back to work.

"Come on, Lara," she urges now, taking the spoon herself and dabbing a bit on Lara's lower lip. "Just a little taste."

Lara, however, is having none of it.

Bree's about to try again when Anne starts to fuss.

"I'll get her," I say, and poor Bree actually jumps.

"I didn't see you there, Mrs. Stark."

"I just came in, and you can call me Nikki. Remember?"

"Sure, Mrs. Stark," she says, and grins. We've had this conversation already, so I just roll my eyes and move on.

"Oh, good girl," she says a few moments later, then claps when Lara takes a full bite.

Then she looks over her shoulder to where I'm holding Anne against my shoulder. "You must be excited about tomorrow," she says. "And today. A party to send you back to work with a smile on. I just love that."

I shift Anne so that I can see her precious little face. "Well, it's not really a party, is it?" I coo to her. "But Auntie Sylvia and Uncle Jackson are coming, and so are Aunt Jamie and Uncle Ryan." Jamie and Ryan aren't technically related, but since Jamie's my absolute BFF, I figure they deserve the title.

"See-vee?" Lara says, waving her spoon and flinging Cheerios. "Jay Me?"

"Yup," I say, moving to give her a kiss on the head. "And as soon as you finish eating, Miss Bree's going to put you in one of your pretty dresses."

My oldest daughter is a born Fashionista, and this is apparently serious incentive, as the cereal and yogurt start actually making it past her lips.

Bree catches my eye, and I wink. "And to answer your question, yes. I really am excited. But it's bittersweet, too."

"Bittersweet?"

I only shrug. How do I explain the flurry of conflicting emotions that are raging inside me, determined to pull me in opposing directions?

Because the truth is that I love my work, and I've genuinely missed it. But I also love my girls, and know I'll miss them, too.

I feel like I'm split down the middle, and it's not a feeling I like.

On top of that, my emotional turmoil is underscored by a legitimate ache in my breasts, which have started to leak simply from being near my baby, who isn't the least bit hungry at the moment.

"I should go pump," I say, returning Anne to the bassinet, then heading to the bedroom to do that. I've been stockpiling breast milk in anticipation of this coming Monday for weeks, and usually the act makes me happy, knowing that what I'm doing will mean that my daughter won't have to drink formula when I'm out in the world.

This time, though, I feel sad. And a little lost.

I know it's just the emotional pangs from fully going back to work for the first time since either of our daughters came home, but that doesn't make it easier. And when I return to the kitchen after pumping and see Lara smiling at Bree, a wave of resentment and envy almost knocks me over, followed by a wash of guilt and stupidity. Because, dammit, this is my choice. So what the hell exactly am I resenting?

"It must be exciting going back to work," Bree says. "Can you clap for Mommy, Lara? Say, *Yay, Mommy!*"

Lara bangs her spoon and says, "Mama! Mama!" and I have to swallow to keep the tears that are now lodged in my throat from escaping.

"Do you know if Damien is still on his call?" I ask, fighting to sound normal. But right now I need Damien almost more than I need to breathe.

"He came up to see the girls and said he was going to get in a quick workout before everyone comes."

I nod, then kiss both my girls before making my way to the first floor. He's not in the weight room, and I'm about to check the pool when I decide to go into the downstairs bath. Usually he showers upstairs in the master, but sometimes when he's squeezing in a workout, he'll clean up and change down here.

Sure enough, I hear the pounding of the water as I step inside the large, luxurious bathroom. I can't see him yet, though. The shower is the walk-in kind, and it's on the other side of the wall from where I stand.

I head that way now, then simply stand there, breathing in the incredible sight of this perfect man and reveling in the fact that he's mine.

He's facing the back wall, his head tilted so that the spray from one of the six shower heads hits him right in the face. I know from experience that his eyes are closed, and he runs the fingers of both hands through his jet black hair, rinsing out the shampoo.

Remnants of lather cascade down his body, slick bubbles that move over the rippling muscles of his arms and shoulders and back. Damien may not play professional tennis anymore, but he's never let himself get out of shape. And I lean against the tiled wall and watch him, this man who is so much more than physical beauty. He's strength and intelligence, commanding and tender. He's honorable and strong, fierce and loyal.

And he loves me.

Loves me so much, in fact, that a tiny part of me wonders how there could be enough left in him to give to our kids. But there is. There's more than enough, and I have no idea what I ever did to deserve him, but I wouldn't change a thing. He's a miracle.

More than that, he's mine.

I watch, mesmerized, as he presses his palms to the wall in front of him and lets the water pound on him. The position tightens the muscles in his thighs and his ass, and though I'm enjoying the view, I really can't take it anymore. My body is still thrumming from last night, and now I'm about to shift into overdrive.

I untie my robe and drop it on the floor, not even bothering with the hook. Then I walk slowly toward him, trying to stay quiet. I press against his back, then slide my hands over his hips, then along the line of his pelvic bone until my hand finds his cock. He's wet and slick, and I circle him, then stroke in slow, rhythmic motions, my own body reacting when I feel him harden in response to my touch.

"Careful," he murmurs. "My wife could walk in at any time."

"She's a lucky woman," I say. "How did you know I was behind you?" He did, of course. Other than his hardening cock, he didn't react at all when I touched him. On the contrary, he seemed to be expecting it.

"Sweetheart, haven't you learned by now?" He turns in my arms so that his erection is pressing against my belly. "You're part of me. How could I ever lose sight of you?"

His words melt me, and I slide my hands in his hair and tug his head down for a kiss. Sweet at first, and then wilder. Because I need him. His hands on me, his cock inside me. Every bit of desire from last night rushes back to me, adding another layer of desperate need to the way my body is currently firing from his kisses and the feel of his naked body against mine.

In other words, I'm a wild, desperate, horny mess.

"Damien," I murmur when we break the kiss.

"Good morning," he says with a grin. "You look refreshed."

I grimace. "I'm sorry I ruined last night. I didn't realize how tired I was. You left, and it just snuck up on me."

"Baby, how could you ruin anything? And if you're tired, it's because you're a mom now. Mother to my daughters." He trails a finger down my body, from my neck all the way to my clit, so that I'm practically melting when he speaks again. "Do you have any idea how sexy that is?"

I look up at him through my lashes and keep my voice low. "Maybe you should show me."

The corner of his mouth twitches. "That's a challenge I'm happy to take on." His hands slide over me, while at the same time he urges me to turn around. So that ultimately, he's under the shower head again and I'm facing the wall, my back to Damien, his rock hard erection teasing my ass.

Steam surrounds us, and our bodies are wet and slick, and when he tells me to bend over and press my hands against the wall, I do. I spread my legs for him when his hand strokes the curve of my ass, then dips between my legs to find me hot and wet and ready.

"That's my girl," he murmurs, thrusting his fingers inside me as I grind against him, suddenly overwhelmed with the need to be filled by him.

"Please," I beg.

"Please what?" he teases.

"Fuck me, Damien. I need to feel you inside me."

One of his hands moves to cup my breasts as he bends over me, then whispers in my ear. "Baby, it will be my pleasure."

His words are still echoing in my mind when his other hand slides around so that he's stroking my clit, his fingers taking me right to the edge even as he takes his hand off my breast, then teases me mercilessly by spreading my ass cheeks and stroking his cock along my perineum.

I whimper and bend over more, widening my stance in what I hope is a very obvious demand that he just, please, fuck me already.

And then—thank God—he's right there, the tip of his cock easing barely inside me, and I have to actually bite my lower lip to keep from crying out with frustration. Because as much as I want to feel him inside me—as much as my body is clenching with longing—I can't deny that this slow torment is oh, so sweet.

Finally, though, I can't stand it any longer, and I push back from the wall, essentially impaling myself on him. "Yes, Nikki, God, yes," he cries as he uses both hands to hold my hips, pulling me harder to him. Tighter. And thrusting deep inside. Slowly. Rhythmically. Then building speed until I swear the steam in that shower isn't from the water but from our rising passion, getting hotter and hotter until we have no choice but to explode, and I cry out as my knees go weak, and I ease to the floor in Damien's arms.

He holds me close against the wall, the spray from the shower's nozzles shooting a curtain of water just beyond us, enclosing us in a warm, steamy cocoon of heat and skin and each other's arms.

"Wow," I say, snuggling close. "I could stay here all day."

"So could I," he murmurs, then kisses me again before he stands and shuts off the water. "But our guests will be expecting us on the pool deck."

"True. And we'd turn all pruney," I add, making him laugh.

He steps outside of the stall and grabs a fluffy white towel from the heated drawer. He hooks it around his hips in a way I find absolutely, mind-blowingly sexy. Then he grabs another towel, returns to me, and enfolds me in its warmth.

I sigh and let him dry me. "What time is it, anyway?"

"Time for us to get dressed. Unless you had a different kind of party in mind."

"I don't think so. I share you with no one, Mr. Stark. Best you remember that."

He grins. "Sweetheart, I wouldn't have it any other way."

Chapter 4

"He's such a little man," I say to Sylvia as we watch Jeffery splashing in the shallow end of the pool with his younger cousin Lara, inflatable yellow rings encircling both kids' arms. "And Ronnie's a fish."

"I know," she says, beaming. "Ronnie's convinced she's all grown up. And Jeffery's into everything, now. I missed most of this with Ronnie, so it's an adventure."

I glance toward her husband, Jackson Steele, who's sitting on the edge of the pool, keeping watch over the little ones. Like his half-brother Damien, he's got the chiseled good looks of a corporate warrior. But instead of Damien's hypnotic dual-colored eyes, one amber and the other black, Jackson's are an icy blue. His daughter Ronnie, now a precocious first grader, takes after him—fearless and confident—as evidenced by the way she's currently cannonballing into the pool off the diving board, over and over and over.

"You'll have some of the same experience," she says. "You're getting to do with Anne the time you missed with Lara."

"I know," I agree. "But it's weird, because it doesn't feel like I missed a thing with her, even though twenty months went by without me and Damien in her life."

Syl casts a warm smile toward the diving board. "I know exactly what you mean."

"Mommy!" Ronnie yells, waving wildly. "Watch me! Watch me!" She holds her nose, bounces once, and leaps into the deep end.

"I swear the kid's going to be a marine biologist. She'd live in the pool if we'd let her."

Right before we adopted Lara, Jackson and Syl built a pool in their Pacific Palisades backyard. Like ours, it has an infinity edge, so that you have the illusion of swimming off into the void. Or at least into the Pacific. And I'm pretty sure that every single time we've gone to visit, Ronnie's spent at least a little time in that pool.

Damien waves to us from the bar, where he's talking with his best friend and Stark International Security Chief Ryan Hunter. "No, don't get up," he says as I start to rise. "Just tell me banana or strawberry."

"Strawberry," I say, and like magic only moments later I'm sipping on a virgin daiquiri while Sylvia enjoys a red wine.

Jamie comes running up just in time to take her own glass of Cabernet and get a kiss from her husband, Ryan. "Sorry," she says as she passes me a small package wrapped in pink paper. "I left this in the car."

"For me?"

"For Lara," she says.

I lift the package, which weighs almost nothing, up to my ear and shake it, but I don't hear a sound. "Okay, I give up. What did you get her? Air?"

"Fuzzy slippers," she says. "Sheepskin lined baby moccasins, actually."

"Oh, how cool," Sylvia says. "They'll be a great transition to actual shoes."

"That's what I was thinking," Jamie says.

My heart squeezes a little. "That's wonderful." Despite all our resources, baby slippers in the months following surgery hadn't occurred to me.

Lara was one of the "waiting kids" in the Chinese adoption system that have special needs. Hers was polydactylism, which basically means having extra fingers or toes. In her case, she had an extra toe that grew sort of sideways just past her pinky toe on each of her feet. Not a big deal, except that it makes wearing shoes almost impossible.

She had the surgery to fix it about two months ago. She's all healed up now, but we haven't transitioned to regular shoes yet. And Jamie's right. A moccasin-style shoe will make a wonderful interim pair.

I glance toward Lara, prepared to call her over so she can open her present, but Jamie shakes her head.

"We're here all day—I'm *not* missing out on watching Damien and Ryan work the grill tonight. So she can slather Aunt Jamie with love and affection later. Right now, I want this," she adds, then lifts her glass in a toast. "To Nikki. Off to enter the wild world of working moms with nannies."

I clink glasses and smile and dutifully take a sip, but it's a melancholy one. For the last few months, I've been bringing Lara and Anne outside almost daily. I'd set up the portable crib for Anne in the shade and then get in the pool with Lara. And sometimes Anne would even join us, her little face showing priceless expressions every time she splashed in what she surely considered a very big bath.

I have a zillion pictures on my phone documenting almost every second of every minute of every hour of every day. And starting tomorrow, there will be whole chunks of time that I'm not recording.

I'll see it, sure. Bree will take pictures and we have video monitors in the kids' rooms. But that's not the same. Not by a long shot.

I sigh, and Syl puts her hand on my knee, smiling softly. She doesn't say anything, but I'm certain she knows where my mind has gone. She's a mom, too.

Jamie, on the other hand, is pulling off her T-shirt and stretching out on one of the chaises in her shorts and bikini top.

"Comfy?" I say, laughing.

"I asked Ryan if we could just live here with you guys, but for some reason he doesn't like the idea." She pushes her sunglasses down so that she can look at me over the rims. "So I'm doing what you always say and making myself at home."

"Love you, James," I say affectionately, using her long-time nickname.

"Back at you, Nicholas."

"As for me," I add, standing, "I'm going to join the kids. Syl?"

"Absolutely."

I head for the shallow end to relieve Jackson. And as soon as Sylvia has a kiss from him, she moves to the deep end so that she can dive for plastic sticks with Ronnie.

All in all, it's a wonderful, relaxing day, that ends with the kids asleep and the grown-ups coupled up around the fire pit. By the time everyone leaves and I crawl into bed next to Damien, I'm exhausted, but happy.

Of course, morning comes far too quickly. Even though I didn't drink, I'm drained from spending the day in the sun, and even a scalding shower and two cups of coffee has barely brought me back to life.

"What time is it?" I ask as I lean against the counter, wondering if some genius in one of Damien's research labs can invent an intravenous coffee-supply system for me.

"Just past eight," he says, and I curse softly.

"I need to rush," I say. "I told Eric and Abby I'd be there at nine-thirty."

I hurry back to the bedroom to dress and do my makeup in record time. My hair is still damp from my shower, but I decide to let it air dry to give me a few more minutes with the kids while I brew a coffee for the road. I snuggle with Anne, then crouch down and call Lara into my arms.

"Mama, bye-bye?"

"Just for a little bit," I tell her, forcing a jolly tone. "I have to go to work. Miss Bree's staying with you today."

"Mama, stay!" she demands, her words like an arrow right to my heart. "Stay with Lara!"

My throat thickens, and I pull her close. "I'll be back, sweetie," I promise. And though she doesn't cry, her thumb goes to her mouth and her dark eyes blink as she holds Bree's hand.

It takes a heroic effort on my part to actually leave the house, and even after driving all the way to Studio City, the image lingers in my mind as I arrive at my office—fifteen minutes late because of traffic.

"I'm sorry, I'm sorry!" I say as I slam through the door that opens onto my suite of three offices and a small reception area. I'd moved from my old one-man office to this new space on the same floor a few weeks after Damien and I decided to adopt. I needed the extra space for Eric and Abby. Plus, the move fit with my plan to take over the entire floor and hire five employees by the end of the year.

I've had a plan for my business ever since I designed my first smartphone app. Hell, even before that. My mother is a straight-up bitch who tried to convince me that all I was good for was beauty pageants and being a wife. She didn't care that I loved science. She sniffed at my double major in computer programming and electrical engineering.

And when my self-inflicted scars finally ended a hated pageant career, she swore that I was a spoiled, selfish girl who would never amount to a damn thing.

I think I've done a fine job of proving her wrong, even if I only have three employees and a corner of the floor to show for it. Considering I was busy with building a family, I figure I'm still on track.

"They're in Abby's office," Marge—my third employee—says from her desk in the reception area. She used to be the receptionist for the building's entire floor. Then I hired her to work as my part-time assistant. And when I moved offices, I asked her to come with me. So now she's all mine, and she's been instrumental in saving my sanity over the last eight months.

"Traffic was horrible," I say, thrusting my purse into her outstretched hand. Then I take a deep breath, tighten my grip on the folio that has my electronic tablet and paper notes, and step into Abby's office.

She's tall and thin, with shoulder-length blond hair that resembles my own, but with more curl. It bounces when she walks, and with her youthful face and perpetually eager expression, she makes me think of Nancy Drew.

Right now, she's perched on the edge of her desk while Eric sits in front of her in one of the guest chairs, flipping through a trade magazine. They both look up as I come in, Abby with a bright smile and Eric with a quirk of his lips and a small wave.

"I have everything ready," Abby says, passing me a folder. "Status updates on all the accounts. Notes on the latest update for the Greystone-Branch interface, and, oh, just everything."

She glances at Eric, as if passing the mic, and he fidgets a bit, not at all his usual, eager self. Eric's solid on the tech, but his real skill lies in business development, whereas Abby's happy just sitting in front of her computer all day. So she's become my right hand on the tech side, whereas Eric is my go-to guy for client relations and business development.

My stomach twists a little, since I'm certain that his current malaise must mean that we've lost a client.

Turns out, though, that I'm wrong. It's worse. And when Eric says, "Yeah, I know this is sudden, but I'm afraid I'm giving notice," I drop into Abby's other guest chair and turn to meet her eyes, which look as surprised as I feel.

"But," I begin, then have to take a breath. "But I thought you liked working here." My operation is small but busy, and both he and Abby are getting tons of exposure and experience. Working for someone like me would have been my dream job when I was just starting out. So to say this comes as a shock is an understatement.

A shock—and a problem. Because this isn't a business I can run with just Abby at my side, not and build it the way I planned.

Not and still be a mom to my daughters the way I want to be.

Something like panic wells up in me, and I turn back to him, knowing I must sound like a needy beggar, but at this point I don't care. "Are you sure? Eric, why? I thought you loved it here."

"I do," he says, and I see real frustration and sorrow on his face as he runs his fingers through his short blond hair. "I swear I wasn't looking to move, but a buddy of mine—well, he told his boss about me, and I got a call, and, well, it's a really great opportunity.

"And I know the timing sucks," he says, rushing on, "but I have to be in New York by Monday. I'm really sorry, Nikki. But today has to be my last day."

Chapter 5

"Promise me you're not going to leave," I say to Abby, once we're alone in my office. We spent the last four hours with Eric, going over every single action item on his plate and making sure all of his client files are in order. Now he's in his office packing his personal things, and Abby and I are trying to figure out where to go from here.

Or, more accurately, I'm trying to figure out where to go from here. Mostly, I'm just trying to get through the day and take it all in stride. Fortunately, there are no current client crises, and if we can just maintain that status quo for the next week or two, then maybe I can find a replacement for Eric, get myself back into a work groove, and get the business moving forward again.

"Are you kidding?" Abby says. "I'm not going anywhere. I mean, it sucks that Eric dumped this on us, but you gotta admit, it makes for a pretty good opportunity for me." She grins as she lifts one shoulder, looking impish.

I smile. "You think?"

"Hell, yeah," she says. "Talk about an opportunity to make myself indispensable. I mean, I pick up the slack, and you realize that you can't live without me. I figure I'll get a raise, a promotion, and probably a Ferrari as my Christmas bonus."

I laugh out loud. "And that, Abby, is why you are my favorite employee in my tech department."

She snickers. Of course we both know that she's the only employee now in my tech department.

"Seriously," I say. "Thanks."

She shrugs. "Don't worry, Nikki," she says. "You got this."

While she's there in my office cheering me on, I actually

believe she's right. But as soon as she leaves, my confidence fades. How the hell am I going to pull this off? Especially since Abby—although eager and bright—doesn't have the skill set to be indispensable. Not on the client development side of the equation, anyway.

Which means that falls on me. The phone calls. The travel. The inevitable chats over cocktails and dinner. All those things Eric was so good at. Things that I can certainly handle, but when? After Anne's evening feeding? Before Lara's bedtime story?

And what about all the little fires that have to be put out on a daily basis? I mean, hell. It's not even been a day yet and Eric has already left me with a list. Not to mention all the calls I need to make to clients to tell them that I'll be taking over their account personally until I'm certain that someone even more competent than Eric can take the reins.

The whole thing makes my stomach hurt.

I love my business, but I got into it for the tech. Because I was designing kick-ass phone and web-based apps, and had even paid for much of my college education with the income from sales across the various platforms. I wanted to keep doing that—only on a much larger scale—and I wanted the freedom to run the business the way I wanted to. So I focused on learning the business side of things, and when I was ready, I launched my small company, relying on Damien's expertise, but not his money.

Only after the company was solidly on its feet did I license my web-based note-taking app to Stark International. The product is pretty brilliant, if I do say so myself, and since it's utilized across all Stark International offices, affiliates, and subsidiaries, it brings in a nice income. It also requires a significant amount of time on the backend, implementing upgrades and troubleshooting.

I'd already intended to hire more people, I just hadn't planned on it quite so soon. But with Eric's departure, I don't really have a choice. Between the two of us, Abby and I can service Stark International and handle any crisis that pops up with any of the apps and products I've designed for other clients. But we can't take on new business.

And without new business, Fairchild Development can't grow.

I put my elbows on my desk, then bury my face in my hands.

Well, fuck.

I'm deep into my own little pity party when the alarm on my phone rings, reminding me that I'm supposed to meet Jamie for a quick drink—virgin for me—at five so that I can give her the scoop on my day. I glance at the phone and see that it's already four-thirty.

Double fuck.

I'm sure she's already on her way, but I snatch up the phone to call her and cancel. I hate doing that so last minute, but I plan to make a bold gesture of apology. Like giving her and Ryan access to our Lake Arrowhead house—and the wine cellar—on the weekend of their choosing.

The moment I pick it up, the phone starts ringing, and I answer without checking the screen, certain that it's Jamie. But it's not. It's Sylvia.

"I wanted to check in," she says. "How's the first day back?"

"Not so great," I admit, then tell her about Eric leaving.

"Well, that sucks," Syl says, cutting straight to the chase. "Anything I can do to help?"

"Can you hire me a rock-solid team and train them?"

"Ah, yeah, no. I was thinking more along the lines of delivering chocolate."

"Well, that's good, too," I say, and we both laugh. "Honestly, I don't know how you do it. Especially back when Jeffery was so little. Yesterday I thought I'd be fine, but today it feels like I've cut off a limb."

"It gets easier," she assures me. "But never easy."

I lean back in my chair, grateful that she's not sugarcoating the truth.

"I wouldn't trade it for anything, though," she continues. "Not after how I fought for this job."

She did, too. She started out as Damien's executive assistant, but she wanted a career in real estate and she kicked serious ass to get it. And even got Jackson along the way.

"And I had it a little easier than you," she adds. "I mean, Ronnie already had a nanny even before Jackson and I got married. And he does a ton of his work at home."

Jackson's an extremely sought-after architect. And while he also has a development side to his business, that branch is mostly run by his staff, freeing him to sit at a drafting table and dream up the brilliant, cutting edge designs that launched him as a "starchitect."

For that matter, Syl's pretty flexible, too. She's a project manager for Stark Real Estate Development, and though she manages a team, she also has a ton of support and flexibility. But me? I'm already feeling like I'm locked behind this desk. Because even if I hire more people, I'll have to train them. And that will eat into my time even more.

At Stark International, there's an HR Department to shoulder part of that load. Here, it's all on me.

"I get that," Syl says when I explain how I'm feeling. "But I still think it will get better. This was your first day out of the gate, Nik, and it sounds like it was a crazy one. Cut yourself some slack. I promise, you've got this."

Those words are still rattling around in my head when we end the call. *You've got this.*

That's what Abby said, too. But do I? Because despite their confidence, I'm still feeling like a surfer on stormy seas, doing everything I can just to stay upright.

I'm plowing through emails when Abby buzzes that she's about to head out, and that she's taking a pile of work home with her. Since Marge left at five, she promises to lock up. So I'm surprised when my door opens a few minutes later.

I glance up, expecting to see Abby with a question or some bit of news that she forgot.

Instead, it's Jamie.

"Oh, dammit," I blurt, and she laughs.

"Great to see you, too."

"Sorry," I say, immediately contrite. "I meant to call and cancel, but I got distracted. Do you hate me?"

"Yes," she says, in true best-friend form. "My hatred for you runs deep." She plunks herself down on the small couch in my office. "So? How'd it go?"

"Fine," I say, because I don't want to share my angst again, not even with Jamie.

"Rough, huh?" she says, and my shoulders sag with relief. Because of course she gets it. Jamie always gets me.

"Syl swears it'll get easier."

"Well, since I don't have kids—"

"Yet," I say, and Jamie rolls her eyes. She and Ryan are still pretty much in the newlywed phase, and although I know he'd be thrilled to start a family now, he's mostly happy that he finally got Jamie to the altar.

"*Since I don't have kids,*" she begins again, "I couldn't say. But I figure she knows what she's talking about."

"Yeah," I say, but I'm not convinced. I sigh. "So do you mind if we blow off happy hour?"

She nods at my desk. "Too much work?"

"Yes," I say truthfully. "But mostly I just want to get home and see the kids."

Want, however, isn't good enough, because apparently my will alone doesn't have the power to make traffic run more smoothly. And when I finally burst into the house, Bree gives me a small, sad frown.

"I wanted to keep her up, Mrs. Stark. But we had a busy day, and she just zonked out after her bath."

"That's okay." I'm frustrated, but I get it. It's only seven-thirty, but I know well that my little girl often conks out before eight. "Anne, too?"

"Yes, ma'am. She went to sleep no problem. She's been a perfect baby today. Not a problem at all."

"That's great," I say, even though a little devil inside of me wants to hear how much they'd both cried for me. And I'd really wanted to see their faces light up when I walked through the door.

I already know that Damien is running later than I am, because he'd called while I was stuck in traffic. Now I dismiss Bree for the night, then go peek in on both my girls. I want to wake them, to cuddle them close, but I let them sleep, contenting myself with watching the steady rise and fall of their little chests.

Then I take a quick shower, change into yoga pants and a T-shirt, and stretch out on our lovely iron bed, surrounded by paperwork.

That's where I am when Damien finds me—although I'm asleep instead of busily working.

"Hey," he says, brushing a kiss on my shoulder. "Long day?"

As I claw my way back to consciousness, he gathers my papers and sets them on the bedside table. There's a glass of wine, too, and he hands it to me. I try to avoid alcohol since I'm breastfeeding, but I also did the research and know that a little bit isn't a problem so long as I wait to pump or feed Anne.

"The longest," I say, then take a grateful sip. I lean sideways against him, my back supported by the pile of pillows that rest against the wall. I give him the full rundown, the highlight of which is Eric's surprising departure.

"You can handle continued growth," he says, his loyalty giving me a nice warm boost of confidence. "But you're also well-positioned to simply hold the line if that's what you want to do. Even to downsize if it works out that way."

I push away from him, frowning as my chest tightens uncomfortably. "What?"

"I'm just saying that you don't have to go back to work full-throttle."

I sit up straight. "Excuse me? Why? Because you can support us?"

"I *can* support us. But what I'm—"

"So I'm supposed to feel guilty about wanting to work just because you bring in billions?" Dammit, he *knows* how important my job is to me. How hard I've worked to build my business on my own, not relying on money that comes from Stark International.

He stares at me like someone might stare at a wild hyena. "That's not what I'm saying at all."

"Maybe, but it sure sounds that way to me," I retort. "*Well-positioned*, my ass."

"Nikki—"

"How many times have we talked about my business?" I snap. "About ramping it up? About really making a splash in the tech world? You know what I've been working for, Damien. How many conferences have you gone to with me? And didn't you hold my hand when I actually braved Dallas to land Greystone-Branch?"

I grew up in Dallas, and that trip hadn't been an easy one, though in a lot of ways, my return to Dallas is the reason we have our girls now.

"The ocean's not going anywhere," he says. "And neither is

your talent. You can make a splash in a few months or next year or five years."

I bristle. "That's not the kind of attitude that makes a business thrive, and we both know it."

"Oh, baby," he says in a soothing tone that I would normally find sweet, but right now is just pissing me off. "All I'm saying is that you don't have to do everything. If Eric left things hanging, maybe those are things you should trim."

"Is that how you built Stark International?"

He draws a deep breath. "I didn't have a family then. I'm not alone anymore."

I tilt my head. "How was San Diego on Saturday?" I ask, referencing the fact that he scurried down there on a weekend in order to perform crisis control. And, yes, I know I'm being bitchy, but the intimation that Stark International is more important than Fairchild Development grates on me. Maybe that's empirically true, but Fairchild Development is important to me. Building it. Growing it.

And right now, even with Damien right beside me, I feel terribly, horribly alone.

"Nikki..."

I hold up a hand. "It's okay. I just—it's okay." I slide out of bed and he takes my fingers, as if to pull me back.

"I want to check on the kids," I say, slipping my hand free of his. I draw a breath and walk away, feeling a bit lost as I do because Damien's not at my side right now, and yet he's always been the compass to guide me home.

Tonight, that compass is my kids, and I peer first into the bassinet at Anne's sweet, sleeping form, and then move down the hall to find Lara hugging Kitty tight. I look at her, so innocent and perfect, and swallow a lump in my throat. That's when I realize I'm crying.

Roughly, I brush the tears away, then crawl into her bed beside her, so that she's snuggled against my chest, her little body melding to mine.

I stay still, letting the rhythm of her breathing soothe me, knowing that Damien is giving me space but at the same time wishing that he'd come to me. But he doesn't, and I simply lie there, trying to let the night take me.

But then I look up and see a shadow in the doorway. Damien may not have come to me, but he is checking on me. And the steel band around my chest eases a little.

I kiss Lara's cheek and carefully slide out of her bed.

"I'm sorry," I say when I find him in our room, a magazine open on his lap. "I'm tired. I'm frustrated. And I'm bitchy."

"No." He holds out a hand and I take it, then slide onto the bed next to him. "I'm the one who should be apologizing. You're frustrated about something important to you, and rightfully so. My first response shouldn't be that you can cut back. That's not fair to you or to what you've accomplished with your work."

I close my eyes and nod, a single tear escaping to trickle down my cheek. "Thank you," I whisper.

"I want to help, Nikki," he says. "But I need you to help me too. I need you to tell me what you want."

I take a breath and open my eyes. I look around our beautiful room, then at my wonderful husband. I think about our kids and our friends and the family we've made. The life we've built together.

"I have everything I want," I say, snuggling close. And as I lie in his arms moments later, I know that I've spoken the absolute truth.

But if that's the case, why am I still unsatisfied?

Chapter 6

Better?

I smile at the text from Damien, then immediately tap out a reply.

Much. Thank you.

It's past noon, and I've spent a productive morning in my office getting all my proverbial ducks in order. Marge is making calls to all our clients to let them know about Eric's departure and to tell them I'll be calling to update them later in the week. Abby is taking point on hiring one new person who can walk the line between tech and client relations, and I'm doing everything else.

So far, there've been no crises today, and I'm feeling about eight thousand percent better than I was yesterday. It was still hard leaving the girls this morning, but I went in a bit later, and so we had breakfast and some playtime together.

Glad to hear it. Sending a car for you at five.

I frown, then tap out a reply.

I have Coop here. I drove my Mini Cooper into the office this morning and he's tucked away in the small parking garage that serves my building.

He can stay in the garage overnight. I want you relaxed. We have plans tonight.

I laugh, delighted.

Are you handling me, Mr. Stark?

His reply is swift: *Absolutely.*

Love you. (Whispers: but I want to see my babies)

I can almost picture him smiling when he sends the next reply.

No need to whisper. I want to see them, too. Then I want to see you. Alone.

I sigh and realize that I'm smiling, the stress of the last twenty-four hours fading to zero. Maybe Jamie and Abby are right. Maybe I have got this.

Sounds good to me, I reply.

His final text comes almost immediately, tugging at my heart—and at other more intimate places.

Excellent. I'll see you tonight, Ms. Fairchild. Until then, imagine me, touching you.

For the rest of the day, I spend a lot of time doing exactly that, and by the time Edward—Damien's personal driver—comes into the office to tell me that he's ready to take me home, I'm very much in the mood to see my husband.

I leave Abby in charge of the few outstanding threads of the day's work, then follow Edward out to the street. He's brought the limo, which surprises me, and I half-expect to find Damien in the back waiting for me. He's not, and a tug of disappointment washes over me. I'm not deprived of sex or cuddling—not by a long shot—but as I settle into the far back seat of the limo, I realize that it actually has been a while since we've gone out for a romantic evening. Not since we brought Lara home, in fact.

A truism of parenting, I suppose, but I feel a pang of regret nonetheless.

"Mr. Stark asked that I pour you a drink. Wine? Whiskey?"

"Bourbon," I say, since apparently it's a night for alcohol. "Straight up."

He hands me the drink and a small box wrapped in silver paper with an envelope on top, tucked in under a matching silver bow. I take it, delighted, as Edward tells me that I'm supposed to read the card first. Then he shuts the door and leaves me alone. I pull out the envelope first, then run my finger around the edge of the fancy linen stationery, with DJS embossed on the flap. I almost don't want to open it, because I'm enjoying this game so much.

But since it is a game, I realize I have to. After all, there will undoubtedly be instructions, and I carefully slide my finger under the flap, open the envelope, then pull out the card inside.

It's a simple message, and my skin prickles with anticipation when I read it:

Take off your panties before opening the box. Touch yourself—but don't come.

>*Then open the box—you'll know what to do.*
>*And for the rest of the ride, imagine me, touching you.*
>D
>*P.S. Tonight you're all mine, all ways, all night.*

My mouth is dry, and my pulse is pounding with anticipation. I glance at my phone, wondering if he's going to text. Surely he knows that I've received his message by now.

But my phone stays silent, and I decide not to text, either. After all, it's fun to let him wonder, too.

For that matter, I consider disobeying. Leaving the box for later. Keeping my panties on. Sitting here in the back of the limo as I sip my bourbon and check my emails. He'll know I've disobeyed, of course. And sometimes with Damien, the punishment can be very, very satisfying.

It's such a tempting idea that I seriously consider it for a few minutes. But what if the punishment doesn't involve touching me? That's something I don't want to risk.

I toss back the rest of the bourbon, feeling the burn in my throat and the immediate flush of heat over my skin. I pumped before I left the office, and I'm going to dump all the milk I pump later, just to be safe. So right now, I'm going to enjoy myself.

I close my eyes and lean my head back, knowing that the alcohol will hit me soon, and I'll feel pleasantly buzzed. And, with Damien's words lingering in my mind, that I'll soon feel even more pleasantly turned on.

Touch yourself, he'd ordered, and though the command had been on paper, I hear his voice in my head. A low whisper in my ear. Commanding and insistent. *Now, baby. Imagine it's me. My hand, easing up your skirt. My fingers, tugging down your panties.*

There is no voice I know more intimately. No touch as familiar as Damien's. And as my imagination conjures him, I put the box on the seat beside me, then rest my hands on my thighs. I'm wearing a stretchy knit skirt, and the material is smooth under my palms.

Slowly, I flex my fingers, easing the material up. Over my knees. Up to mid-thigh. *Good girl. All the way. I want your bare ass on the leather. I want you hot. Wet.*

I actually whimper, the fantasy of him beside me making me a little crazy—and a lot turned on. I raise my hips so that I can gather the skirt around my waist, and then slip my hands back down, taking my panties with them.

Now I'm just as he ordered, the leather warm against my bare skin. And his voice in my fantasy urging my fingers to slide between my legs. To imagine it's him. Touching me. Spreading me.

Fucking me.

I gasp as I stroke myself. I'm already so damn wet—but why that should surprise me, I don't know. Just the thought of Damien makes me melt. And the knowledge that he has something wild in store for us makes me throb in all the right places.

My fingers dance over my clit, and my body trembles. Immediately, I pull my hand back, because Damien said I couldn't finish. And as much as I want release, I don't want it without him. Not really.

Not tonight.

I squeeze my legs together, squirming a bit to fight off this rising need, then reach for the package, hoping that the simple act of opening it will distract me.

I really should know better.

I peel the paper off slowly, thinking that the extra time will calm this sensual feast. But that's just foolish. All I can think of is slowly undressing. Myself. Damien. And this package is standing in proxy for both of us.

Finally, I rip it the rest of the way open. Beneath the paper is a black cardboard box with a top that lifts off. I open it, then push back the tissue to reveal my present. And I laugh with delight even as I squirm a bit on the seat.

Because I know what this is, all shiny and silver and shaped like a small egg. I've seen it before. Hell, I've used it before.

We'd been dating—if you can call it that. I'd agreed to some rather unconventional modeling terms. A million dollars in exchange for me posing for the nude, albeit anonymous, portrait of me that now hangs on the rock wall that's visible upon climbing the stairs to the third floor. And during those days and nights when I was a model, I agreed to belong to Damien.

Completely to Damien.

When it was over, he got the painting, I got my million, and we both got each other.

It was by far the smartest deal I ever made, I think as I carefully pull the egg out and hold it in my hand. It's not vibrating now, but I can already imagine the feel of it. Not moving in my palm, of course. But inside me. Because this little egg is a remote control vibrator…and I'm already on the edge of exploding merely from the knowledge that Damien could turn it on at any moment.

Hell, for all I know, he's in the front seat with Edward. Or driving right behind us in another car.

I press my legs together in defense against a persistent, needy throbbing. But I can't stay like that, I know.

There are rules to this game. And I bite my lower lip as I slowly spread my legs.

And as I reach down to slide it inside me, all I can think is, *Oh, yeah. Tonight is going to be fun.*

Chapter 7

Damien meets me at the door with one hand in the pocket of his jeans and a fresh drink in the other. He may not have texted me during the drive, but apparently Edward contacted him to let him know my drink of choice.

He also has a twinkle in his eye that hints at all sorts of decadent possibilities. He holds out his hand. "Panties," he demands.

I tilt my head. "What makes you think I obeyed?"

His lips curve up. "Because I know you, Mrs. Stark," he says at the same time that the silver egg inside me starts to vibrate. I gasp, my already primed body begging for more, but the vibration stops as quickly as it started.

He pulls me close, making me moan as he lifts my skirt, then slips his fingers between my legs, finding me slick and ready.

"I think somebody likes her present."

I meet his eyes. "Or maybe I just like you."

I'm still in his embrace, though he's pulled his hand back and let my skirt fall. Now he cups my head, and there's so much heat in his eyes I almost fear getting burned.

He bends his head to kiss me, so deep and hard and demanding that I want him to just swoop me up, carry me to the bedroom, and take me fast and hard. For a moment, I even wonder if that's his plan because I would be just fine with that. But he breaks the kiss, eases back, and flashes a lopsided grin.

"Panties," he asks again, and this time I hand them to him. He tucks them in his pocket, then slides an arm around me. "I asked Bree to get the kids ready for bed, and then babysit until we get back. But I told her we want to tuck them in."

"And then?" I ask, walking with him up the stairs.

"I guess you'll find out."

I glance at him sideways and see that he's already looking at me. "I like this game," I admit, and he laughs, then tells me he likes it, too.

We check on Anne first, and I hold her while Damien reads her *Goodnight, Gorilla* and she smiles and blows bubbles and grabs at the cardboard pages.

Lara is next, and she sits on Damien's lap as I read *Goodnight, Sleep Tight, Little Bunnies,* a book she apparently never tires of. When I shut the book, her eyes are drooping, and Damien tucks her into bed, the covers pulled up and Kitty snuggled close.

"What now?" I whisper once we're back in the hallway.

He raises a finger to his lips, then leads me to the kitchen. There's a clay bowl there, and in it, I can see a dozen or so bits of folded paper. "Pick one," he orders.

I do, and when I unfold it, I see that it says *beach* in neatly typed letters. I look up at him. "And now?"

"Now you grab your purse and come with me."

Normally, I'd expect *beach* to mean our beach, at the end of the path that meanders across our property. But since he has me bring my bag, I'm not surprised when we go out the front door and get back into the limo. But I *am* surprised when Edward only winds the limo down the service road to the beach bungalow that Damien had built for me just over a year ago.

"What's going on?" I ask when Edward opens the door to let us out. But Damien doesn't answer. Instead, he puts a finger over my lip and leads me inside.

Damien built the bungalow as a surprise for me because I'd once told him that as much as I adore our Malibu house and its amazing view, I'd love to be able to simply walk outside and then stroll along the beach. And because Damien spoils me mercilessly, soon enough, a small bungalow appeared on our property... And it was nestled right on the beach.

It's a charming little two-bedroom property, the best feature of which is its patio, which boasts two levels. A traditional patio off the back door runs the length of the house and curves around to the front door. It offers an amazing view of the beach and the

Pacific, and also has a set of stairs leading down to the sand, as well as a small, free-standing shower and footbath so that the beach doesn't have to come into the house with us.

But it's the second level that is truly exceptional, because it's a rooftop patio. It's superbly designed, with areas for both shade and sun, but what I like best is that if you're stretched out on one of the oversized chaise lounges, you can't see the beach at all. Just an infinity of wide-open ocean. It's like being on a magic carpet and escaping from everything, even if only for a little while.

There's where Damien takes me now, forgoing entering the house at all. Instead, we walk along the lower patio to the stairs leading up to the roof. There, I'm greeted by a bottle of champagne chilling on ice and a bowl of strawberries.

I tug him to a stop and slide into his arms. "When did you pull this together?"

"I just snapped my fingers," he says. "I have magic powers, you know."

I laugh, mostly because sometimes it seems like that's true.

"But I think you're trying to get me drunk. Bourbon. Champagne. You know I—"

He shuts me up with a kiss so intense that my knees go weak, and he scoops me up and carries me to the chaise. "Yes, wife of mine, I intend to get you a little drunk. Or maybe a lot drunk. The baby will do just fine on the milk you've stored."

I grin. "In that case, I think I'd like some champagne."

He pours me some, and as I'm sipping it, I feel the slightest of rumbles in my core. I close my eyes and tilt my head back against the cushion as Damien slowly ramps up the vibrations of that delightful little bullet inside me.

My skirt has no zipper. Just a wide, stretchy band at the waist. Now I feel the cushion shift as Damien sits next to me. His fingers hook under the band as he tugs the skirt down over my hips, then tosses it onto a nearby chair.

The patio is somewhat shielded from the wind by a glass barrier that surrounds the area, but I can still feel the chill, and it feels exceptional against my overheated skin. Slowly, he trails the fingers of one hand up my inner thighs, barely stroking my sex as I tremble and gasp at the flurry of sensations threatening to sweep me away.

His hand continues upward, and he pulls my top off, leaving me in a lacy bra. Then he kisses his way back down my abdomen, slowly decreasing the vibe inside me until it's completely turned off by the time his tongue flicks lightly over my clit.

I make a soft noise of protest and he chuckles, then lifts his head, stands, and holds out a hand to urge me to my feet.

I hesitate, because I'm honestly not sure my legs have the strength to stand, but then I let him pull me up, and I walk with him to the glass barrier that faces the ocean. He stands behind me, unfastens my bra, then lets it drop to the floor.

"Close your eyes," he says, and although I'm standing at the edge of my roof, completely naked, the wind caressing me and the sound of the waves crashing in my ears, I do exactly as he says.

"Someone could see," I murmur as he pulls me close so that my bare ass brushes his clothes.

"Then they're lucky, because you're beautiful. But no one will."

I know he's right. The beach is technically public, but it's also very secluded, and the property is such that we're a long way from our neighbors. And maybe I'd be uncomfortable if it was more likely that we'd be seen, but right now, I can't deny that it feels exciting and wonderful to be standing naked under the sky with Damien like this.

"Touch me," I beg. "Please, Damien. Please, fuck me."

"Is that what you want?" he murmurs, his hands roaming over me. My breasts, my hips, my thighs. "Are you sure?"

"Yes," I whisper. "Please."

"Mmm." One hand slides up until he is cupping my neck, right under my chin. The other slides down until his palm cups my sex, his fingers slipping inside me, pushing the egg even deeper. My knees go weak, and as I start to sag, the pressure on my throat increases. I'm not scared—how could I be with Damien?—but there's an aspect of danger to this that we've never played with before. And when his mouth brushes my ear and he whispers, "Mine," I feel a flood of desire run through me that almost knocks me over.

And when he slides his fingers out long enough to find the switch that triggers the egg, I really do start to fall. Damien, however, is right there to hold me up. "I've got you," he says, one hand still tight around my neck and the other steadying me at the waist. "Watch the water, baby," he says as the vibrator ramps up again, sending waves through my body that seem to come in time with the movement of the Pacific.

His lips brush my bare shoulder, and his hand returns to cup me. With the tip of his forefinger, he circles my clit, coming close, but never quite taking me all the way. And all the while he's holding my throat, just tight enough that I feel the pressure as I gasp with pleasure.

"Do you trust me, baby?" he asks as he strokes and teases me, taking me right to the edge.

"Of course." I have to fight to get the words out. Talking really isn't on my agenda right now. Besides, it's not like he needs to ask. I may not know what he has in mind, but I trust Damien with my life, my body, my heart.

He doesn't answer, but I hear a low noise of approval. At the same time, I feel a tug between my legs and then the slick sensation of the egg sliding out of me. As it does, Damien tightens his grip on my throat as he arches my body back, so that I'm the most vulnerable at the same time the vibrating egg leaves my body.

The sensation is amazing, all the more so because of the way Damien is holding me. But when he tightens his grip at the same time he skims the egg over my clit, I break completely apart. A wave of ecstasy crashes over me, seeming to last forever as my body struggles to come back together even while I try to draw a cohesive breath.

When the last vibrations of the orgasm pass, Damien scoops me up. He has no choice, really, because my legs are essentially nonfunctional at this point. He carries me back to the chaise and lays me down as I keep my arms hooked around his neck.

"Please," I murmur. "Don't make me beg."

He kisses my nose. "I like it when you beg. But right now, I can't wait any longer." Gently, he pulls back, forcing me to either rise with him or to release him. I choose the latter, letting my fingers graze his face, tracing over the light scruff of his evening beard as he straightens and I sink back into the cushion.

I watch as he strips off his clothes. His shirt falling to the ground. His jeans sliding over his hips. His gray boxer briefs easing down to free his cock, which is hard and huge and ready.

For a moment he just stands there, and I gaze greedily at him, this man who belongs to me. The sun is sinking low in the sky, casting an orange glow over the patio and illuminating Damien's skin. I can imagine him as a sculptor's model, his image carved in marble forever.

But it's not his beauty that I crave, it's what's inside him. I want the man who loves me. Who makes me laugh and makes me feel safe. The man who is the father of my children, and who will always—*always*—watch over us.

I hold out my hands in a silent demand, and he comes to me, easing up the chaise between my now-spread legs. "Make love to me," I whisper, then melt a little when he says "Nikki" with such tenderness that his voice feels like a caress.

He kisses me, feather-light at first, but then harder and more demanding, and I cling to him, my hands tight on his shoulders. I want him inside me, to feel the connection, so deep that I don't know where I end and he begins. And I hook my legs over his, easing them higher until I'm gripping him with my thighs, and his cock is right at my center, and I'm open and wet and so completely ready.

"Damien," I demand, squirming against him as I close my eyes and soak in the feel of him. "Now. Please, please, now."

"Look at me," he says, and I open my eyes, only to see so much heat and longing and intensity reflected back at me that I would swear he was already inside me. I feel my core tighten, clenching and unclenching in a silent demand. And when he shifts just enough so that he barely slips inside me, I gasp from the sensation of being entered—and in anticipation of being filled.

"Now," he says, his eyes still on mine. And in time with the word, he pistons his hips, thrusting inside of me, and then going deeper and deeper with each slow, mesmerizing thrust.

Gradually, he speeds up, our combined passion fueling a need. Until finally, he's pounding inside me, thrusting me back against the chaise as I cling even tighter, certain that somehow he's going to fuck me so hard that we're going to actually meld into one person.

"Touch yourself, baby. I want to feel you explode."

I'm so close, and I do as he says, taking one hand off his back and sliding it between our bodies so that I can stroke my clit as he thrusts inside me, until the melding of the sensations is too much to bear and I feel an electrical prickling on my inner thighs, a signal of a coming orgasm.

"Damien," I beg as I stroke myself, desperate now to go over that edge. "Please," I add, though I'm not even sure what I'm asking.

But as my body starts to shake—as I arch up and cry out as millions of electric sparks race over my body—I know that I was demanding that he come with me. And now my body is milking him, clenching tight around his cock again and again, in the throes of a massive orgasm.

Above me, I see the storm on Damien's face, a raw, wild pleasure that fades into an expression of pure adoration when the orgasm passes and his body relaxes.

"Hi," he says when we can both breathe again. He slowly lowers himself, then settles next to me, using a nearby napkin to gently clean me up.

"Hi, yourself." I curl up next to him, wanting both his touch and his warmth. After a moment, he eases off the chaise, then returns with one of the blankets we keep in a waterproof trunk by the door. He carefully covers me, making sure I'm all tucked in, then joins me again, pulling me close so that I'm snuggled against his chest.

"Warm?" he asks.

"Mmm-hmm."

"I thought we could lie here for just a little bit, relaxing and watching the stars."

I prop myself up enough to see him. "I think you're pampering me, Mr. Stark."

"You could call it that," he says.

"What would you call it?"

"Being."

I shift, confused, and pull myself all the way upright, the blanket falling off in the process. "What are you talking about?"

"You," he says simply as his hands roam my naked skin, making it hard to concentrate on his words.

"You're going to have to give me more to go on."

He chuckles, then sits up, pulling the lever on the chaise so that we have a back rest. He draws me toward him again, then pulls the blanket back to cover us. "You've spent months being a mom," he says. "And a wife. And a business owner. All of which are wonderful and important."

"But?" I ask, because he's clearly going somewhere with this.

"But it's been a long time since you've had the chance to just *be*. So that's what tonight is for, baby. To simply enjoy the night and each other. To just be Nikki and Damien."

"Thank you," I say, my heart swelling from the sweetness of the sentiment, and from the knowledge that he's arranged all of this to take care of me.

We stay like that for a while—our fingers twined, our bodies touching—until Damien gets up, telling me to wait while he goes inside to get something.

He's back in less than five minutes, a paper bag in his hand. "Pick one," he says as I sit up, already smiling.

"Again?"

He shakes the bag at me in silent demand, and I laugh but comply. When I unfold it, I read it to Damien. "Dinner. Hmmm," I add.

"What?"

"Just thinking," I say.

"Always dangerous. What were you thinking?"

"About those slips of paper." I make a fast grab for the bag, but he pulls it away from me and sets it out of reach on a table behind us. "I'm thinking that if I draw another note, it'll say dinner, too." And then, just to prove my point, I make another lunge toward the sack.

This time, Damien grabs my wrists and pulls me up for a gentle kiss, topped off with a sharp bite to my lip and an equally sharp smack on my rear. "Don't even think about it."

But I know I'm right, and I grin happily as I hold him close. "Thank you for planning a wonderful date."

"You're welcome," he says. "But it's not over yet."

"I know. I'm just telling my husband—" I cut myself off with a frown because my phone is chiming an incoming call, using the ringtone I designated for Abby.

I meet Damien's eyes, hating the fact that I need to grab it. I see the disappointment in his eyes, too, but he nods, and I leave his arms to go find my phone in my small handbag.

I miss the call, but before I can check to see if she left a voicemail, a text comes through: *SOS. Crisis with Greystone-Branch. Can you come to the office?*

Damien is standing behind me, and when I turn to meet his eyes, I see the heat fading to an all-business demeanor. A cold wave of regret washes over me. But what can I do? Greystone-Branch is my biggest client next to Stark International, and having them on my roster upped the prestige of Fairchild Development considerably.

So I do the only thing I can do—I text back, *On my way.*

Chapter 8

I yawn and lean back in my desk chair. Behind me, the sky in Studio City is already bright, morning having come and gone while Abby and I have been holed up here in my office.

We've spent the night hunched over our computers, trying frantically to clean up a mess of malicious code left by a disgruntled ex-Greystone employee, and to plug all possible holes so nothing like this could happen again.

But we've managed. And as I take a long sip of my coffee, I give myself a few moments to bask. This particular crisis couldn't have been foreseen, and only a limited number of people have the skill set to pull off that type of sabotage. So Abby and I had faced something unexpected and rare, and we've come out victorious.

More than victorious, really, since we've prevented further attacks of that nature.

And that, I think, is pretty damn cool.

"You did great," I tell her, as she returns from the break room with her own mug of coffee. "Let's lock this place up, get out of here, and call it a day."

"You sure?"

"Absolutely." I glance at the clock. "If I hurry, I can get home before Bree takes the girls to Lara's very first Gymboree class. And after that, I can take the world's longest nap. You should do the same. The nap," I clarify. "Not Gymboree."

She laughs, but then turns serious. "I'm sorry I couldn't handle it on my own. I know you were having a night out."

"Don't be ridiculous," I say. "You never have to feel bad about bothering me during a crisis. Especially a crisis involving my business. But," I add, "for the record, I think you could have handled it just fine if I hadn't been around."

"Yeah?"

"Absolutely. You did great. You held the client's hand. You worked the problem. You were ferocious in writing the new code and getting it uploaded. I was a hundred percent impressed."

Her cheeks turn pink as she smiles. "Thank you."

"You're welcome," I say. "Now go home."

She scurries out, as if afraid I might change my mind. No chance of that—I want too badly to see my kids.

After Edward dropped me off in the limo last night, Damien had offered to stay with me and help, but I'd sent him home. I don't go with him for a crisis at Stark International. And besides, if we weren't getting to enjoy our date, at least one of us should be enjoying our kids.

Which means that Coop is still in the garage where I left him yesterday, and I hurry to him, sending a text to Damien as I walk to let him know that I'm done and heading home.

Then I climb into Coop, whip out of the garage, and push that Mini to the max as I race from Studio City back home to Malibu. I check the clock obsessively as I drive, and I have to remind myself not to be reckless and jump lights or zip back and forth between lanes. Maybe it would buy me a minute or two, but the idea is to get home to my kids, not to end up with a mangled car. Or worse.

Still, I'm anxious for the entire drive, and it's only when I turn onto our street with five minutes to spare that I relax. *I made it.*

I race through the gate, waving to our guard as I pass, then avoid the garage, instead skidding to a stop on the circular drive, right in front of the entrance.

I hurry inside, calling out, "Mommy's home!" But I'm greeted only with silence.

I frown, then trot up the stairs to the third floor, calling for Bree as I do.

It's only when I reach the kitchen and see that the kids' snack bag is gone that I allow myself to believe what I've already figured out—that Bree took the kids early. That no one is home.

Like Damien, I've now missed one of the "firsts" for our kids. Just a children's class, sure. But I wanted to hold Lara's hand. To stand beside her when they make balls bounce on the parachute and walk in a circle in time to music, or all the other stuff that the director told me about when I signed up for the class.

I'll take her next time. And the time after that. But even if I take her to every class from here on out—even if I take Anne to her very first one when she's two—I've missed *this* first. And I can't ever get that back.

I sigh, then drop into one of the chairs at the small kitchen table. For a moment, I consider following them, but I'd end up arriving late, and I don't want to be *that* mom. The one who interrupts class and disrupts all the kids.

So instead, I just sit here in the quiet, empty house. No kids. No Damien. No Bree. Even Gregory is gone, the valet who's been with Damien for years and now serves as a butler and everything kind of guy. His sister in Connecticut is ill, and he flew out a week ago.

"Just me and you," I say to Sunshine, who's wandered in for kibble. But even she's not interested in me. She comes for one single pat on the head, then trots away, presumably to find a sunny spot in which to curl up and sleep.

I feel much the same way.

I'm still in my clothes from last night, and I feel grungy and achy. I want sleep, but I want a shower more, and so I head to the master bath, stripping off my clothes as I go. I turn the shower on full blast, the heat cranked up almost to scalding, and I let the room fill with steam.

I adjust the temperature back to tolerable, then step in, tilting my face up toward the spray as I lean against the tile wall and let the water sluice over me, washing away the day, my troubles, my mistakes, my disappointments.

Except even the hottest shower can't do that, and as I stand there—the water pounding down on me—the hard, cold truth hits me. It just flat out hits me.

It's not the firsts that matter, it's the moments. Little moments that make up a life. And I missed countless moments in the last twenty-four hours alone. And not only moments with my kids, but with my husband.

I missed a night out with Damien.

I missed an afternoon with my kids.

How many smiles have there been? New toys? New discoveries.

That impish grin when Lara crawls sneakily up to attack Sunshine.

Anne's expression of wide-eyed wonder when the light makes a rainbow through the window. Or her gurgle of delight when she strokes the cat's fluffy tail.

So many moments I want to witness. So many that I'm going to miss.

I've known it, of course. But now the weight of that reality seems too heavy to bear, and I sink down and drop my face to my knees and let my tears flow as the water beats down on me.

That's where I am when Damien finds me, his urgent voice pulling me back to the moment.

"Did you cut? Dammit, Nikki—did you cut?"

He's holding my hands, crouched in the shower beside me as the water soaks his clothes.

"No," I say. "Damien, you're drenched."

"What's going on? Goddammit, Nikki, talk to me."

The fear in his voice breaks my heart, and I squeeze his hands as I look deep into his eyes. "I didn't cut. I swear. Honestly, it didn't even occur to me."

His gaze skims over me, hunched up on the floor of the shower, and I can see the disbelief in his eyes.

"I promise. Please, turn off the water. I'm fine. I love you, and I'm fine."

He hesitates but does as I ask, then gets two warm, fluffy towels from the drawer. He wraps one around me, then peels off his clothes, leaving them in a wet pile on the floor of the stall.

When he's dry and the towel is twisted around his hips, he holds out his hand to help me up. I take it, then let him lead the way into the bedroom, trading my towel for my snuggly robe along the way.

"All right," he says once we're both in robes and sitting on the bed. "What happened?"

I give him the rundown of the crisis at Greystone-Branch. "Abby was amazing," I say. "Smart and focused. I couldn't have been more impressed."

"You hired good people."

I shrug. "Eric left."

"That's the risk you take with good people."

I nod but brush it off. We've gotten too far off topic. "The point is that I came home exhausted. But even on no sleep and completely drained, I wanted to make it in time for Gymboree."

"Lara's first class." There's a wistful note to his voice, and I realize that he's gone this same road, too.

I take his hand, then nod. "I wanted to be there. But I missed it. Bree left earlier than I expected. And I just missed it."

I press my lips together, determined not to cry again. When I'm certain I'm in the clear, I say, "That's it. Just sadness. And exhaustion. But no cutting. Not even an inkling of a smidgeon of a thought about a blade. I promise."

The relief on his face is palpable, and I know that I've finally convinced him. "I need to sleep now," I say. "But why are you here? The house was empty when I got home."

"I got your text," he says. "And since I have a meeting soon in Santa Monica, I thought I'd come home and see my wife. But I need to go now." He strokes my cheek. "Are you sure you're okay? Do I need to reschedule my meeting?"

"No—no, seriously, I'm fine." I take a deep breath, then smile. "Honestly, right now I'm feeling steadier than I have in days."

And it's true. Unexpected, maybe. But true.

Damien's brow furrows, and I can tell he's uncertain. "You're thinking about something," he finally says.

"I am," I agree. "I'm thinking I desperately need a nap."

What I don't say is that I think I've made a decision, but I have to figure it out for myself before I can tell him. And right now, it's all still a blur in my head, everything mixed up together. Work. Damien. The kids. Even the fact that I didn't want to cut. That I didn't even think about it.

The tangle of thoughts reminds me of the code that Abby and I attacked. All the bad stuff had been twined together with the good, so we had to hack carefully to get to the core. But when we finally got that one essential thread, the rest was easy.

That's what I need, I think.

Right now, I need to find the core thread inside of me.

Chapter 9

The sun is low in the sky when I wake from my nap to the sound of Lara giggling outside. Damien's left the doors to the balcony open, and her sweet laughter is floating in with the ocean breeze.

I'd changed into sweats and a T-shirt before lying down, and now I pad barefoot to the balcony, which has a view of a portion of the pool deck and a grassy area that had been wild with ground cover before the kids, but which we'd had landscaped during the months that we were waiting for our travel authorization to go to China.

Now, it has a neatly manicured lawn, a sandbox, and a toddler-friendly playscape.

Right now, Damien is wearing Anne in a baby sling as he pushes Lara on the rocking horse swing.

She's holding on tight and alternating between squeals and cries of "Geep!", which I'm assuming means *giddy-up.*

Now she turns toward me, and I wave, then blow her a kiss.

"Mama! Mama! Come here, Mama!"

Since I can hardly turn down an invitation like that, I wave again, then yell that I'll be down soon. That I just have a couple of things to take care of first.

Since it's cool outside now, I head first to the closet for some canvas flats and a light hoodie, then go back toward the door, planning to take the outdoor stairs down to the first level.

I don't make it back that quickly, though. Instead, I'm waylaid by one of the framed photographs on the bureau. Tears prick my eyes as I pick it up, a silver-framed picture of me and a dark-haired girl, six years older, with mischievous eyes and a quick smile. *My sister, Ashley Anne Fairchild Price.*

"I miss you," I whisper to the girl who'd also been my best friend. I'd thought she was so lucky when my mother had given her a pass on the pageant circuit because she simply didn't win. I'd been so envious—hating every crown I earned and wanting nothing more than to have time and food and my mother's love that didn't come with strings. Especially since those strings were the threads of pageant gowns.

I'd thought that Ashley had escaped my mother and her belief that everything—and everyone—had to be perfect. Ashley had been my rock, sneaking me food when my mother kept me on an eight-hundred calorie, no-carb diet. And talking to me so I wouldn't be scared or stir-crazy when Mother locked me in a completely black room so that I'd be forced to get my beauty sleep.

I'd thought she was together, and I'd drawn part of my strength from her. But when her husband left her and she killed herself because she'd believed she wasn't the person she should be, I knew that Mother had gotten in her head, too.

"I'm sorry," I whisper to her now. "I'm so sorry she screwed you up—hell, I'm sorry she screwed both of us up." I draw in a breath. "But I'm doing better. I think you'd be proud of me. I love you," I say. "And I miss you."

I wipe the tears from my eyes as I return the picture to the bureau. I meant what I said. I *am* doing better. I've been doing better ever since I moved out of my mother's house. But it wasn't until I met Damien that I truly felt like I was wriggling free of the quicksand in which my mother had buried me.

But now—with the laughter of my daughter echoing just outside the window—I know that I can be better still. And, I think, I finally know what I need to do.

It takes a few minutes for me to get all my ducks in order, but once I've thought it all through and made a couple of phone calls, I know that I'm on the right path. The knot in my stomach has disappeared, along with the band around my chest. I feel light and giddy, and as I hurry down the steps, I feel Damien's eyes on me and wave happily.

Lara is in the sandbox now, building something that I think is supposed to be a castle, but might be a horse, her current favorite animal.

I pause to give her a kiss and come away with my lips a little gritty. "Let me talk with Daddy," I say. "And I'll come back in a little bit, okay?"

"Okay, Mama," she says, then shoves her hands deep into a mountain of sand. I take a quick detour to peek at Anne, napping in the shade in her portable crib, then I head toward Damien.

"Feeling better?" Damien asks, moving over so that I can sit beside him on the edge of the hot tub and dangle my feet in the water.

"Yeah," I say, taking his hand. "Thanks."

"For what?"

I laugh. "Well, we could start with everything. But mostly for putting up with me lately."

He lifts our joined hands and kisses my knuckles. "It's hard. We've gone from two to four. Plus, there are diapers in the mix."

"True, that," I say, then kick my feet, splashing us both a little. "Ashley killed herself because she felt like she wasn't perfect."

My voice is low, barely a whisper, but I know from the way Damien stiffens beside me that he's heard every word.

"I know." His eyes move as he examines my face. "Is that how you feel?"

"Yes. No." I draw a breath. "Not anymore. I—"

I pull my hand free and run it through my hair, trying to organize in words the feelings—and the decision—that are so clear in my heart. "So here's the thing. I love designing my apps. The small challenges. And the large ones. Working out tricky code. Thinking up clever or funny or useful programs that will grab people's attention and give them a break or help them with productivity."

"And you're good at it."

"I am," I agree, because my talent and skill in my job is something I've never questioned. "And when I first wanted to go into business for myself, it was so that I could do what I wanted. Not what my boss said, or a client I didn't sign personally asked for."

"Control," he says dryly. "I get that."

I lean over and bump him with my shoulder. "Yeah, I'm sure you do."

I start to sit up straight again, but he hooks an arm around me. "And now you're overwhelmed because you've taken on something that's even bigger than the work—the business. You've got the coding that you love, and all the other bullshit that you don't."

"Payroll taxes and accounting and client development and all of it. Yes," I say, not at all surprised that he understands. Damien knows me well, after all. "But I don't want to give it up. I just want—"

"The core," he finishes for me.

I look at him, surprised by his choice of word. "Exactly. And I'm not sure whether I felt like I had to compete with you or if I was trying to prove what a success I was to my mother, or if I just didn't want to feel like I failed. But the truth is, I know I didn't. I have a great business, and I don't have to go at it a million miles an hour. Not when I can slow down and enjoy everything else I have." I take his hand again and squeeze as I look toward Lara and Anne.

"You've been doing a lot of thinking."

"Mostly in the back of my mind. It's been churning, I think, without me even really being aware. But it was when you asked me if I'd cut that everything clicked into place."

Again, he tenses beside me, and I press my hand onto his thigh. "It clicked in a good way," I explain. "With the cutting…well, I think I needed the blade when I was lost. When I couldn't see any other way around the pain or the fear and the mess of everything that overwhelmed me."

"But this time you didn't want to cut," he says softly.

"Didn't even think about it," I confirm. "Not even a tiny bit." I smile up at him. "Do you get it? It's because I already knew what to do. I just hadn't let myself think about it yet."

"And what are you going to do?"

"Step back," I say, firmly. "I want my business, but I don't want or need to be Stark International." I flash a grin toward my husband. "You have that covered pretty well."

"I appreciate your vote of confidence," he says, and I laugh.

"And I'm going to sell the office in Studio City," I say. That one's harder. Because Damien bought my original unit as a present one magical Christmas, but I know it's the right thing to do. "I'll reinvest, but in something closer. Santa Monica, maybe. Or even

Malibu. And in the meantime…"

I trail off, looking toward the beach. "Actually, I was thinking I could use the bungalow as a temporary office."

"It's your beach house, baby. If that's what you want, I say go for it."

"It is. I can have the kids with me, or if they're in the main house with Bree, I can be home in two minutes." I draw in a breath. "I think I was hearing my mother's voice in my head. That I had to be perfect—and somehow I confused perfect with doing it all. And the truth is, I don't have to be either."

"No," he agrees, "you don't. But never forget that you're perfect for me."

"Ditto," I say, then sigh, feeling relieved and centered and happy.

"What about Abby and Marge?"

"I'll keep them on. We'll use the living room as office space, and they can both work from home part time. But about Abby—there's more I haven't told you. Because, well, I want time here. With you and the kids. And it's a lot to shoulder, running even a scaled-back business. Don't laugh," I say when he starts to smile. "I'm not you, and you have about a billion people working for you. And entrepreneurism doesn't flow in my veins. That's your shtick."

"It is," he agrees.

"And you're exceptional at it. But I want someone helping me shoulder the load. A different kind of help than I get from my husband," I add with a grin. "So I asked Abby if she wanted to be a partner," I continue. "Starting at ten percent, but working her way up to fifty." I hesitate a little as I look at him because usually I run my business decisions by Damien before I float them in the world. But this time, I'd called Abby before even coming down the stairs.

"I think that's a great idea. And Abby will be an asset. It gives her a stake and takes some of the pressure off you. And," he adds, with a definite edge of humor, "you still have Stark International as a client. And I hear that company is always growing. So that's got to be good for your bottom line."

"It is," I agree, grateful he understands. "I want to keep my business. I'm proud of it, and I love what I do. But not if it means I miss all of this." I glance toward Anne's bassinet, then smile at Lara, who's now toddling toward us, covered in sand.

"I don't need to be Stark International. I just want my work. Mostly," I add, leaning in close, "I just want you."

"You have me. Don't ever doubt it."

"I don't," I say. "And I have something for you."

I stand, then leave wet footprints as I pad across the pool deck to where I'd left a small paper bag on a table at the foot of the stairs. When I come back, I hold it out to Damien, who looks up at me, confused.

"Pick one," I say, shaking the bag and making the tiny squares of folded paper rustle.

He laughs, but complies and then opens it. "Road trip," he reads. He glances up at me. "Want to clarify that?"

"Nope." I grin. "But you'll find out what it means tomorrow."

Chapter 10

"You're not going to tell me where we're going?" Damien asks. It's just past eight in the morning, and Edward is driving us eastward on Interstate 10 in the limousine.

"Not a chance," I say, taking his now-empty champagne glass and making him a fresh mimosa from the OJ and champagne I had Edward stock in the limo's bar. "You're stuck with me until we get there."

"There being...?"

"Ha. Like I'd fall for that."

He chuckles. "Worth a try." He takes a sip of the mimosa, then slides it into one of the holders designed for stemware. "How about this—if you won't tell me where we're going, will you at least tell me where the girls are?"

I tilt my head as if considering. "Do you trust me?"

"Completely," he says.

"Good," I say. "And you'll find out where your daughters are soon enough."

"Soon," he repeats, sounding almost disappointed.

I frown. "What?"

He shrugs. "Just that it's hard to take advantage of all that a limo has to offer if the ride is that short."

I narrow my eyes. "You're being sneaky, aren't you?"

"Me?"

I point at him. "Don't act all innocent. You're trying to figure out where we're going by figuring out how long the ride is."

He holds up his hands. "I plead not guilty."

"Hmm." I finish refilling my own mimosa and then slide back across the seat to sit next to him. "Well, the truth is, that all of those advantages that a limo has to offer is one of the reasons we're taking it and not one of your toys." Damien owns an impressive collection of cars, and rarely turns down an opportunity to take one on the open road. This morning, however, I wanted Damien beside me, and his hands somewhere other than the wheel.

"Really?" he replies. "I'm intrigued."

"Good," I say casually, reaching over him to put my mimosa beside his. Then I climb onto his lap and kiss him lightly. "Because it occurred to me that making out like teenagers in the backseat would be a very fun way to pass the time until we get to where we're going."

I can tell he's about to answer, but I silence him with a kiss. Soft at first, then harder and deeper when his lips part and I can tease him with my tongue. Then harder still as I feel him harden between my legs. I'm straddling him, my knees on the leather car seat, and the crotch of my khaki shorts pressed against his jean-clad erection.

We kiss and fondle for miles, stroking each other, teasing each other. Letting the heat build and build until it's harder and harder to resist the lure of taking this all the way, even though resisting is exactly what I intend to do.

I'd planned this morning to be about the heat and excitement of being in each other's arms, of simply turning each other on. But like a teenager, I'm craving more. And when Damien's hand snakes up my shirt and tugs my breast free of my bra, I arch my back and moan with pleasure.

"Am I going to get to third base, Nikki?"

"Absolutely not," I say, even as I grind against him, my body on fire. "I'm not that kind of a girl."

But I know I'm going to lose that battle—and that even in the losing, I'll win. I can see the challenge all too clearly on his face. And if my game is not telling him where we're going, then his game is fucking me in the back of the limo.

The truth is, where Damien is concerned, I have little resistance. And when he slides his hand up the leg of my shorts and strokes the soft skin at the juncture of my thigh and pelvis, I just about lose my mind.

"Take them off," he demands, and though I know I should

argue, I eagerly comply, stripping off the shorts and underwear as he unfastens his jeans and frees his cock. "On me," he demands, and I'm so wet, so ready, that I don't hesitate. I straddle him, then lower myself as he guides his cock inside me. I move slowly, teasing us both, but in the end neither of us can stand it, and when he grabs my hips and slams me down on him, I cry out in both relief and passion.

"That's it, baby," he says. "I want you to ride me."

I reach up, using the roof of the limo to balance as I thrust down over and over on his cock.

At the same time, he teases my clit with his finger, while his mouth closes over my breast, his teeth grazing over my sensitive nipples.

The feeling is incredible—like a wire of passion from my breast to my core—and I find a rhythm, letting the sensation build and build. Harder and faster and wilder and deeper until I really can't take it anymore. "Damien," I cry out, exploding all around him, then collapsing forward to cling to his neck as he continues to fuck me, finally exploding inside me while his arms hold me tight, and then whispering, "Dear God, baby. I love you."

We cling to each other for a few miles, and then clean up and get dressed again, and as I snuggle close, I have to admit that I'm glad these teenagers in the backseat went all the way, because I feel wonderful.

When we reach San Bernardino and turn off the highway toward the mountains, Damien says, "Hmmm," and I turn to look at him, my eyes wide and innocent.

"Something to say, Mr. Stark?"

"Not a thing. I still have absolutely no clue where we're going."

"Uh-huh." I laugh, because of course he knows. We're heading to our house in Lake Arrowhead, and when we arrive at the Alpine-style chateau, Damien looks at me and grins.

I shrug. "It's a getaway," I say. "I cleared my calendar. And I had Rachel clear yours. We're both free until Monday. And," I add with a grin, "there are two little girls waiting inside who are going to be very glad to see their daddy."

I'm right about the latter. As soon as we go through the door, Lara comes racing toward us calling "*Baba, Mama,*" and Damien scoops her into his arms as Bree passes me Anne.

"They were good on the drive?"

"Angels," she assures me. She drove here in Damien's Range Rover and is going back in the limo.

I cuddle Anne and remind Bree that Edward already knows the limo is at her disposal until we get back. "So do something fun. Have Edward take you and some friends on a jaunt."

"I don't know," she says, but her small grin makes me think she has something—or someone—in mind.

As soon as she's out the door, I turn to Damien and Lara. "Ready to go back out?"

Damien's brows raise, but I just shrug. "It's time for breakfast. And I'm thinking I know a little girl who might like a waffle."

The shopping area has a wonderful restaurant right on the lake with the best waffles in the world, in my opinion. Certainly good enough to satisfy my waffle-loving kid.

"Waffa! Waffa!" Lara squeals and starts clapping, getting so excited and squirmy that Damien has to put her down.

"Family weekend," I say with a shrug. "I thought we could spend the morning having breakfast, then maybe take one of the boat tours on the lake. Lara would get a kick out of that. But if you'd rather, we can make waffles here."

I'm a terrible cook, but Damien's not. Which means that Damien would make the waffles. But if he wants to stay in, I'm game.

But he shakes his head and puts his arm around me, gazing down at Anne's sweet face. "Nope," he says. "A day out with my girls sounds like heaven. So long as I get a night in with my wife."

"Absolutely, Mr. Stark," I say, then kiss him lightly.

It takes a little time to load the Range Rover up with all the baby paraphernalia, but soon we're on our way and unpacking it all over again in the parking lot for the Lake Arrowhead Village shops.

Damien pushes the double stroller, but only Anne is in it. Lara is skipping along, holding my hand and chattering on about everything.

When we reach the restaurant, the owner greets us warmly. "So good to see you again," he says, then adds. "I haven't yet met the children." He smiles at Lara, who boldly holds her hand out to shake, then clucks over Anne.

Finally, he aims a wide smile at me before turning to Damien. "You have a lovely family, Mr. Stark."

Damien squeezes my hand as he looks down at our girls. "Yes," he agrees. "I do."

THE END

* * * *

Also from 1001 Dark Nights and J. Kenner, discover Tame Me, Tempt Me, Caress of Darkness, Caress of Pleasure, and Please Me.

About J. Kenner

J. Kenner (aka Julie Kenner) is the *New York Times, USA Today, Publishers Weekly, Wall Street Journal* and #1 International bestselling author of over eighty novels, novellas and short stories in a variety of genres.

JK has been praised by *Publishers Weekly* as an author with a "flair for dialogue and eccentric characterizations" and by *RT Bookclub* for having "cornered the market on sinfully attractive, dominant antiheroes and the women who swoon for them." A five-time finalist for Romance Writers of America's prestigious RITA award, JK took home the first RITA trophy awarded in the category of erotic romance in 2014 for her novel, *Claim Me* (book 2 of her Stark Trilogy).

In her previous career as an attorney, JK worked as a lawyer in Southern California and Texas. She currently lives in Central Texas, with her husband, two daughters, and two rather spastic cats.

Visit JK online at www.jkenner.com
Subscribe to JK's Newsletter
Text JKenner to 21000 to subscribe to JK's text alerts

Also By J. Kenner

The Stark Trilogy:
Release Me
Claim Me
Complete Me
Anchor Me

Stark Ever After:
Take Me
Have Me
Play My Game
Seduce Me
Unwrap Me
Deepest Kiss
Entice Me
Hold Me

**Stark International
Steele Trilogy:**
Say My Name
On My Knees
Under My Skin
Take My Dare (novella, includes bonus short story: Steal My Heart)

Jamie & Ryan Novellas:
Tame Me
Tempt Me

Dallas & Jane (S.I.N. Trilogy):
Dirtiest Secret
Hottest Mess
Sweetest Taboo

Most Wanted:
Wanted
Heated
Ignited

Also by Julie Kenner

The Protector (Superhero) Series:
The Cat's Fancy (prequel)
Aphrodite's Kiss
Aphrodite's Passion
Aphrodite's Secret
Aphrodite's Flame
Aphrodite's Embrace
Aphrodite's Delight (free download)

Demon Hunting Soccer Mom Series:
Carpe Demon
California Demon
Demons Are Forever
Deja Demon
The Demon You Know
Demon Ex Machina
Pax Demonica

The Dark Pleasures Series:
Caress of Darkness
Find Me in Darkness
Find Me in Pleasure
Find Me in Passion
Caress of Pleasure

The Blood Lily Chronicles:
Tainted
Torn
Turned

Rising Storm:
Tempest Rising
Quiet Storm

Discover More J. Kenner/Julie Kenner

Please Me: A Stark Ever After Novella by Julie Kenner, Coming August 28, 2018

From New York Times and USA Today bestselling author J. Kenner comes a new story in her Stark Ever After series…

Each day with Damien is a miracle, each moment with our children a gift. And yet I cannot escape the growing sense that a storm is gathering, threatening to pull me away, to rip us apart. To drag me down, once again, into a darkness to which I swore never to return.

I have to fight it—I know that. And I am waging the battle with of all my heart. But it is Damien who is my strength, and we both know that the only way to push away the darkness is for him to fold me in his arms and claim me completely. And for me to surrender myself, once again, to the fire that burns between us.

* * * *

Tempt Me: A Stark International Novella by J. Kenner, Now Available

Sometimes passion has a price…

When sexy Stark Security Chief Ryan Hunter whisks his girlfriend Jamie Archer away for a passionate, romance-filled weekend so he can finally pop the question, he's certain that the answer will be an enthusiastic yes. So when Jamie tries to avoid the conversation, hiding her fears of commitment and change under a blanket of wild sensuality and decadent playtime in bed, Ryan is more determined than ever to convince Jamie that they belong together.

Knowing there's no halfway with this woman, Ryan gives her an ultimatum – marry him or walk away. Now Jamie is forced to face her deepest insecurities or risk destroying the best thing in her life. And it will take all of her strength, and all of Ryan's love, to keep her right where she belongs…

* * * *

Tame Me: A Stark International Novella by J. Kenner, Now Available

Aspiring actress Jamie Archer is on the run. From herself. From her wild child ways. From the screwed up life that she left behind in Los Angeles. And, most of all, from Ryan Hunter—the first man who has the potential to break through her defenses to see the dark fears and secrets she hides.

Stark International Security Chief Ryan Hunter knows only one thing for sure—he wants Jamie. Wants to hold her, make love to her, possess her, and claim her. Wants to do whatever it takes to make her his.

But after one night of bliss, Jamie bolts. And now it's up to Ryan to not only bring her back, but to convince her that she's running away from the best thing that ever happened to her--him.

* * * *

Caress of Darkness: A Dark Pleasures Novella by Julie Kenner, Now Available

From the first moment I saw him, I knew that Rainer Engel was like no other man. Dangerously sexy and darkly mysterious, he both enticed me and terrified me.

I wanted to run–to fight against the heat that was building between us–but there was nowhere to go. I needed his help as much as I needed his touch. And so help me, I knew that I would do anything he asked in order to have both.

But even as our passion burned hot, the secrets in Raine's past reached out to destroy us ... and we would both have to make the greatest sacrifice to find a love that would last forever.

Don't miss the next novellas in the Dark Pleasures series!

Find Me in Darkness, Find Me in Pleasure, Find Me in Passion, Caress of Pleasure...

* * * *

Storm, Texas.

Where passion runs hot, desire runs deep, and secrets have the power to destroy...

Nestled among rolling hills and painted with vibrant wildflowers, the bucolic town of Storm, Texas, seems like nothing short of perfection.

But there are secrets beneath the facade. Dark secrets. Powerful secrets. The kind that can destroy lives and tear families apart. The kind that can cut through a town like a tempest, leaving jealousy and destruction in its wake, along with shattered hopes and broken dreams. All it takes is one little thing to shatter that polish.

Rising Storm is a series conceived by Julie Kenner and Dee Davis to read like an on-going drama. Set in a small Texas town, Rising Storm is full of scandal, deceit, romance, passion, and secrets. Lots of secrets.

Wicked Grind
Stark World Novels, Book 1
By J. Kenner

Sometimes it feels so damn good to be bad

Photographer Wyatt Royce's career is on the verge of exploding. All he needs is one perfect model to be the centerpiece of his sexy, controversial show. Find her, and Wyatt is sure to have a winner.

Then Kelsey Draper walks in. Stunning. Vibrant. And far too fragile for a project like this. Wyatt should know—after all, he remembers only too well how their relationship ended all those years ago.

Desperate for cash and frustrated with her good girl persona, Kelsey sets her sights on Wyatt's show. But only the show. Because she knows too well that Wyatt Royce is a danger to her heart.

But when Wyatt agrees to give her the job only if he has complete control—on camera and in his bed—Kelsey can't help but wonder if she's in too deep. Because how can a good girl like her ever be enough for a man like Wyatt?

All Wicked novels stand alone.

* * * *

Prologue

I'd thought he was out of my life forever. That all that remained of him was a memory, sharp and forbidden. Terrifying, yet tempting.

The one man who changed everything.

The one night that destroyed my world.

I told myself I was past it. That I could see him again and not feel that tug. Not remember the hurt or the shame.

That's what I believed, anyway.

Honestly, I should have known better...

Chapter 1

He was surrounded by naked women, and he was bored out of his mind.

Wyatt Royce forced himself not to frown as he lowered his camera without taking a single shot. Thoughtfully, he took a step back, his critical eye raking over the four women who stood in front of him in absolutely nothing but their birthday suits.

Gorgeous women. Confident women. With luscious curves, smooth skin, bright eyes, and the kind of strong, supple muscles that left no doubt that each and every one of them could wrap their legs around a man and hold him tight.

In other words, each one had an erotic allure. A glow. A certain *je ne sais quoi* that turned heads and left men hard.

None of them, however, had it.

"Wyatt? You ready, man?"

Jon Paul's voice pulled Wyatt from his frustrated thoughts, and he nodded at his lighting director. "Sorry. Just thinking."

JP turned his back to the girls before flashing a wolfish grin and lowering his voice. "I'll bet you were."

Wyatt chuckled. "Down, boy." Wyatt had hired the twenty-three-year-old UCLA photography grad student as a jack-of-all-trades six months ago. But when JP had proven himself to be not only an excellent photographer, but also a prodigy with lighting, the relationship had morphed from boss/assistant to mentor/protégé before finally holding steady at friend/colleague.

JP was damn good at his job, and Wyatt had come to rely on him. But JP's background was in architectural photography. And the fact that the female models he faced every day were not only gorgeous, but often flat-out, one hundred percent, provocatively nude, continued to be both a fascination to JP and, Wyatt suspected, the cause of a daily cold shower. Or three.

Not that Wyatt could criticize. After all, he was the one who'd manufactured the sensual, erotic world in which both he and JP spent their days. For months, he'd lost himself daily inside this studio, locked in with a series of stunning women, their skin warm beneath his fingers as he gently positioned them for the camera. Women eager to please. To move however he directed. To contort their bodies in enticing, tantalizing poses that were often unnatural and uncomfortable, and for no other reason than that he told them to.

As long as they were in front of his camera, Wyatt owned those women, fully and completely. And he'd be lying to himself if he didn't admit that in many ways the photo shoots were as erotically charged as the ultimate photographs.

So, yeah, he understood the allure, but he'd damn sure never succumbed to it. Not even when so many of his models had made it crystal clear that they were eager to move from his studio to his bedroom.

There was just too much riding on this project.

Too much? Hell, everything was riding on his upcoming show. His career. His life. His reputation. Not to mention his personal savings.

Eighteen months ago he'd set out to make a splash in the world of art and photography, and in just twenty-seven days, he'd find out if he'd succeeded.

What he hoped was that success would slam against him like a cannonball hitting water. So hard and fast that everybody in the vicinity ended up drenched, with him squarely at the center, the unabashed cause of all the commotion.

What he feared was that the show would be nothing more than a ripple, as if he'd done little more than stick his big toe into the deep end of the pool.

Behind him, JP coughed, the harsh sound pulling Wyatt from his thoughts. He glanced up, saw that each of the four women were staring at him with hope in their eyes, and felt like the ultimate heel.

"Sorry to keep you waiting, ladies. Just trying to decide how I want you." He spoke without any innuendo, but the petite brunette giggled anyway, then immediately pressed her lips together and dipped her gaze to the floor. Wyatt pretended not to notice. "JP, go grab my Leica from my office. I'm thinking I want to shoot black and white."

He wasn't thinking that at all, not really. He was just buying time. Talking out of his ass while he decided what—if anything—to do with the girls.

As he spoke, he moved toward the women, trying to figure out why the hell he was so damned uninterested in all of them. Were they really that inadequate? So unsuited for the role he needed to fill?

Slowly, he walked around them, studying their curves, their angles, the soft glow of their skin under the muted lighting. This one had a haughty, aquiline nose. That one a wide, sensual mouth. Another had the kind of bedroom eyes that promised to fulfill any man's fantasies. The fourth, a kind of wide-eyed innocence that practically begged to be tarnished.

Each had submitted a portfolio through her agent, and he'd spent hours poring over every photograph. He had one slot left in the show. The centerpiece. The lynchpin. A single woman that would anchor all of his carefully staged and shot photos with a series of erotic images that he could already see clearly in his mind. A confluence of lighting and staging, of body and attitude. Sensuality coupled with innocence and underscored with daring.

He knew what he wanted. More than that, somewhere in the deep recesses of his mind, he even knew who he wanted.

So far, she hadn't wandered into his studio.

But she was out there, whoever she was; he was certain of it.

Too bad he only had twenty-seven days to find her.

Which was why he'd stooped to scouring modeling agencies, even though his vision for this show had always been to use amateur models. Women whose features or attitude caught his attention on the beach, in the grocery store, wherever he might be. Women from his past. Women from his work. But always women who didn't make a living with their bodies. That had been his promise to himself from the beginning.

And yet here he was, begging agents to send their most sensual girls to him. Breaking his own damn rule because he was desperate to find her. That elusive girl who was hiding in his mind, and who maybe—just maybe—had an agent and a modeling contract.

But he knew she wouldn't. Not that girl.

No, the girl he wanted would be a virgin with the camera, and he'd be the one who would first capture that innocence. That was his vision. The plan he'd stuck to for eighteen long months of squeezing in sessions between his regular commercial photography gigs. Almost two years of all-nighters in the dark room and surviving on coffee and protein bars because there wasn't time to order take-out, much less cook.

Months of planning and worrying and slaving toward a goal. And those sweet, precious moments when he knew—really knew—that he was on the verge of creating something truly spectacular.

He was exhausted, yes. But he was almost done.

So far, he had forty-one final images chosen for the show, each and every one perfect as far as he was concerned.

He just needed the final nine. That last set of photos of his one perfect woman. Photos that would finally seal his vision—both of the girl in his mind and of what he wanted to accomplish with this solo exhibition.

He'd sacrificed so much, and he was finally close. So damn close... And yet here he was, spinning his wheels with models who weren't what he wanted or needed.

Fuck.

With a sigh of frustration, Wyatt dragged his fingers through his thick, short hair. "Actually, ladies, I think we're done here. I appreciate your time and your interest in the project, and I'll review your portfolios and be in touch with your agent if you're selected. You're free to get dressed and go."

The girls glanced at each other, bewildered. For that matter, JP looked equally puzzled as he returned to the studio with Wyatt's Leica slung over his shoulder and a tall, familiar redhead at his side.

"Siobhan," Wyatt said, ignoring the trepidation building in his gut. "I didn't realize we had a meeting scheduled."

"I thought you were going to shoot a roll of black and white," JP said at the same time, holding up the Leica in the manner of a third grader at Show-and-Tell.

In front of Wyatt, the girls paused in the act of pulling on their robes, obviously uncertain.

"We're done," Wyatt said to them before turning his attention to his assistant. "I have everything I need to make a decision."

"Right. Sure. You're the boss." But as JP spoke, he looked sideways at Siobhan, whose arms were now crossed over her chest, her brow furrowed with either confusion or annoyance. Quite probably both.

But Wyatt had to hand it to her; she held in her questions until the last model had entered the hallway that led to the dressing room, and the door had clicked shut behind her.

"You got what you needed?" she asked, cutting straight to the chase. "Does that mean one of those models is the girl you've been looking for?"

"Is that why you're here? Checking my progress?" Shit. He sounded like a guilty little boy standing in front of the principal.

Siobhan, thank God, just laughed. "One, I'm going to assume from the defensive tone that the answer is no. And two, I'm the director of your show first and foremost because we're friends. So take this in the spirit of friendship when I ask, what the hell are you doing? We have less than a month to pull all of this together. So if none of those girls is the one you need, then tell me what I can do to help. Because this is on me, too, remember? This show flops, and we both lose."

"Thanks," he said dryly. "I appreciate the uplifting and heartfelt speech."

"Screw uplifting. I want you on the cover of every art and photography magazine in the country, with your show booked out on loan to at least a dozen museums and galleries for the next five years. I couldn't care less if you're uplifted. I just want you to pull this off."

"Is that all?" he asked, fighting a smile.

"Hell no. I also want a promotion. My boss is considering moving to Manhattan. I covet her office."

"Good to have a goal," JP said, tilting his head toward Wyatt. "I covet his."

"Go," Wyatt said, waving his thumb toward the dressing room. "Escort the girls out through the gallery," he ordered. The space was divided into his two-story studio that boasted a discreet entrance off the service alley, and a newly remodeled gallery and storefront that opened onto one of Santa Monica's well-trafficked retail areas.

"So you're really done?" JP pressed. "That's it? Not even a single shot?"

"I don't need to see anything else," Wyatt said. "Go. Chat them up so they don't feel like they wasted their time. And then I'll see you tomorrow."

"That's your subtle way of getting rid of me, isn't it?"

"Don't be ridiculous," Wyatt retorted. "I wasn't being subtle at all."

JP smirked, but didn't argue. And with a wave to Siobhan, he disappeared into the back hallway.

"So how can I help?" Siobhan asked once he was gone. "Should I arrange a round of auditions? After all, I know a lot of really hot women."

That was true enough. In fact, Siobhan's girlfriend, Cassidy, featured prominently in the show. And it had been through Cass that Wyatt had originally met Siobhan, who had both a background in art and a shiny new job as the assistant director of the Stark Center for the Visual Arts in downtown Los Angeles.

Originally, Wyatt had envisioned a significantly smaller show staged in his studio. The location was good, after all, and he anticipated a lot of foot traffic since folks could walk from the Third Street Promenade. He'd asked Cass to model about eight months ago, not only because she was stunning, but because he knew the flamboyant tattoo artist well enough to know that she wouldn't balk at any pose he came up with, no matter how provocative. Cass didn't have a shy bone in her body, and she was more than happy to shock—so long as the shock was delivered on her terms.

Siobhan had come with her, and before the shoot, Wyatt had shown both of them three of the pieces he'd already finished so that Cass would have a sense of his vision. It was the first time he'd laid it out in detail, and it had been cathartic talking to Siobhan, who spoke the language, and Cass, who was an artist herself, albeit one whose canvas was skin and whose tools were ink and needles.

He'd explained how he'd originally just wanted a break from the portraits and other commercial photography jobs that paid the bills. And, yes, he was beginning to make a name for himself artistically with his landscapes and city scenes. That success was gratifying, but ultimately unsatisfying because those subjects weren't his passion. There was beauty in nature, sure, but Wyatt wanted to capture physical, feminine eroticism on film.

More than that, he wanted to make a statement, to tell a story. Beauty. Innocence. Longing. Ecstasy. He wanted to look at the world through the eyes of these women, and the women through the eyes of the world.

Ultimately, he wanted to elevate erotic art. To use it to reveal more about the models than even they were aware. Strength and sensuality. Innocence and power. Passion and gentleness. He envisioned using a series of provocative, stunning images to manipulate the audience through the story of the show, sending them on a journey from innocence to debauchery and back again, and then leaving them breathless with desire and wonder.

That afternoon, Wyatt spoke with Cass and Siobhan for over an hour. Showing them examples. Describing the emotions he wanted to evoke. Listening to their suggestions, and taking satisfaction from the fact that they obviously loved the concept. They'd ended the conversation with Cass posing for another hour as he burned through three rolls of film, certain he was capturing some of his best work yet.

Then they'd walked to Q, a Santa Monica restaurant and bar known for its martini flights. They'd toasted his project, Cass's pictures, and Siobhan's career, and by the time they ended the evening, he was feeling pretty damn good about his little pet project.

The next morning, he'd felt even better. That's when Siobhan had come to him with a formal offer from the Stark Center. He'd said yes on the spot, never once thinking that by doing so he was tying another person to his success—or, more to the point, his potential failure.

"I'm serious," she pressed now, as his silence continued to linger. "Whatever you need."

"I'll find her," Wyatt said. "I have time."

"Not much," she countered. "I need the prints ahead of time for the catalog, not to mention installation. Keisha's already getting twitchy," she added, referring to her boss. "We don't usually cut it this close."

"I know. It's going to be—"

"Twenty-seven days to the show, Wyatt." He could hear the tension in her voice, and hated himself for being the cause of it. "But about half that before you need to deliver the prints. We're running out of time. If you can't find the girl, then you need to just find a girl. I'm sorry, but—"

"I said I'll find her. You have to trust me on this."

Right then, she didn't look like she'd trust him to take care of her goldfish, but to her credit, she nodded. "Fine. In that case, all I need today is to see the latest print so I can think about the promotional image. And you'll email me a file for the catalog?"

"Sure. This is it," he added, walking to a covered canvas centered on the nearest wall. He pulled down the white drape, revealing a life-size black and white photograph of a woman getting dressed. At first glance, it wasn't the most titillating of his images, but that was because it was such a tease. The woman stood in a dressing room, and hidden among the dresses and coats were at least a dozen men, peering out to watch her.

The woman, however, was oblivious. She was bending over, one foot on a stool as she fastened a garter. The view was at an angle, so at first glance the audience saw only her skirt, a hint of garter, and the woman's silk-sheathed leg.

Then they noticed the mirror behind her. A mirror that revealed that she wasn't wearing panties under the garter belt. And even though absolutely nothing was left to the imagination, it still wasn't a particularly racy or erotic photograph. But then you noticed the reflection in the mirror of another mirror. And another. And another. Each with an image of that same woman, and each slightly more risqué, until finally, as the mirror approached infinity, the woman was nude, her head thrown back, one hand between her legs, the other at her throat. And all those men from the closet were out in the open now, their hands stroking and teasing her.

Most important, the mirror was so deep in the image that you had to stand practically nose-to-print to see it.

Wyatt couldn't wait to see how many people did exactly that at the showing.

"This is fabulous," Siobhan said with genuine awe in her voice.

"It was a hell of a photograph to set up and then develop. Lots of work on the set and in the darkroom."

"You could have set it up digitally."

He scoffed. "No. Some of the images, sure. But not this one." He turned his head, regarding it critically. "This one had to be hands-on. It's as much about the process as the product."

"Yeah. I get that." She met his eyes, and the respect in hers reminded him of why he didn't just take photos for himself. "I want to take it back with me right now and show Keisha," she added.

"Soon." Although Siobhan and Keisha had wanted him to deliver each print upon completion, Wyatt had balked, explaining that he needed the art surrounding him in order to ensure the continuity of story in the overall exhibit. And the size of the canvas and the particulars of the way he handled the image in the darkroom were such that duplicates weren't adequate.

That meant that when Siobhan needed to see a piece, she came to him. And now that she was not only putting together the official catalog, but also doing promotional pieces from the images, she was coming a lot.

Wyatt was adamant that the images not be revealed prior to the show, but Siobhan's team had promised him the rapidly expanding catalog mockup would be kept under lock and key. More important, the pre-show promotion wouldn't reveal any of the artwork—while at the same time teasing the art's sensual and daring nature.

So far, they'd not only managed to do just that, but the campaign was already a success. The gallery had been releasing one image a month—one of his photographs, yes, but only a sexy snippet shown through a virtual barrier laid over the image. Once, it was yellow caution tape. Another time, it was a keyhole in a hotel room door. Clever, yes, but also effective. Wyatt had already been interviewed and the exhibit pimped out in no less than five local papers and magazines. And he was booked on two morning shows the day the exhibit opened.

Not bad, all things considered, and he told Siobhan as much.

"If you really want to see a bump in our publicity," she replied, "we should get your grandmother on board."

"No." The word came swift and firm.

"Wyatt..."

"I said no. This exhibit is on my shoulders. I can't hide who I am, but I don't have to advertise it. If we trot my grandmother out, book her on morning shows, make her sing little Wyatt's praises, then everyone is going to come. You know that."

"Um, yeah. That's the point. To get people to your show."

"I want them to come for the show. Not because they're

hoping to get Anika Segel's autograph."

"But they'll see your art. They'll fall in love then. Who cares what brings them through the door?"

"I do," he said and was relieved to see that she didn't seem to have an argument against that.

She stood still for a moment, possibly trying to come up with something, but soon enough she shook her head and sighed. "You're the artist." She made a face. "And you have the temperament to go with it."

"See, that's how you wooed me into doing the show with you. That embarrassingly sentimental flattery."

"You're a laugh a minute, Wyatt." She hitched her purse farther onto her shoulder, then pointed a finger at him. "Don't fuck this up."

"Cross my heart."

"All right then." She leaned in for an air kiss, but caught him in a hug. "It's going to be great," she whispered, and he was surprised by how much he appreciated those simple words.

"It will," he agreed. "All I have to do is find the girl." He glanced at his watch. "An agency's sending someone over in about half an hour. Nia. Mia. Something like that. Who knows? Maybe she'll be the one."

"Fingers crossed." Her grin turned wicked. "But if she's not, just say the word and Cass and I will dive into the search."

"A few more days like today, and I'll take you up on that."

"A few days is all you have," she retorted, then tossed up her hands, self-defense style. "I know, I know. I'm leaving."

She headed for the front door, and he turned back to the print, studying it critically. A moment later he reached for the drapes that covered the prints on either side of the first image, then tugged them off, revealing the full-color photos beneath.

He took a step back as he continued his inspection, ensuring himself that there were no more refinements to be made. Slowly, he moved farther back, wanting all three in his field of vision, just like a visitor to the exhibition would see. One step, then another and another.

He stopped when he heard the door open behind him, cursing himself for not locking up as Siobhan was leaving. "Did you forget something?" he asked as he turned.

But it wasn't Siobhan.

It was her.

The girl who'd filled his mind. The girl who'd haunted his nights.

The woman he needed if he was going to pull this exhibit off the way he wanted to.

A woman with the kind of wide sensual mouth that could make a man crazy, and a strong, lithe body, with curves in all the right places. Eyes that could see all the way into a man's soul—and an innocent air that suggested she wouldn't approve of what she saw there.

All of that, topped off with a wicked little tease of a smile and a sexy swing to her hips.

She was a walking contradiction. Sensual yet demure. Sexy yet sweet.

A woman who one minute could look like a cover model, and the next like she'd never done anything more glamorous than walk the dog.

She was hotter than sin, and at the same time she was as cold as ice.

She was Kelsey Draper, and he hadn't spoken to her since the summer before his senior year, and as far as he was concerned, that was a damn good thing.

Her eyes widened as she looked at him, and her lips twitched in a tremulous smile. "Oh," was all she said.

And in that moment, Wyatt knew that he was well and truly screwed.

Sign up for the 1001 Dark Nights Newsletter
and be entered to win a Tiffany Key necklace.

There's a contest every month!

Go to www.1001DarkNights.com to subscribe.

As a bonus, all subscribers will receive a free copy of
Discovery Bundle Three
Featuring stories by
Sidney Bristol, Darcy Burke, T. Gephart
Stacey Kennedy, Adriana Locke
JB Salsbury, and Erika Wilde

Discover 1001 Dark Nights Collection Five

Go to www.1001DarkNights.com for more information

BLAZE ERUPTING by Rebecca Zanetti
Scorpius Syndrome/A Brigade Novella

ROUGH RIDE by Kristen Ashley
A Chaos Novella

HAWKYN by Larissa Ione
A Demonica Underworld Novella

RIDE DIRTY by Laura Kaye
A Raven Riders Novella

ROME'S CHANCE by Joanna Wylde
A Reapers MC Novella

THE MARRIAGE ARRANGEMENT by Jennifer Probst
A Marriage to a Billionaire Novella

SURRENDER by Elisabeth Naughton
A House of Sin Novella

INKED NIGHT by Carrie Ann Ryan
A Montgomery Ink Novella

ENVY by Rachel Van Dyken
An Eagle Elite Novella

PROTECTED by Lexi Blake
A Masters and Mercenaries Novella

THE PRINCE by Jennifer L. Armentrout
A Wicked Novella

PLEASE ME by J. Kenner
A Stark Ever After Novella

WOUND TIGHT by Lorelei James
A Rough Riders/Blacktop Cowboys Novella®

STRONG by Kylie Scott
A Stage Dive Novella

DRAGON NIGHT by Donna Grant
A Dark Kings Novella

TEMPTING BROOKE by Kristen Proby
A Big Sky Novella

HAUNTED BE THE HOLIDAYS by Heather Graham
A Krewe of Hunters Novella

CONTROL by K. Bromberg
An Everyday Heroes Novella

HUNKY HEARTBREAKER by Kendall Ryan
A Whiskey Kisses Novella

THE DARKEST CAPTIVE by Gena Showalter
A Lords of the Underworld Novella

Discover 1001 Dark Nights Collection One

Go to www.1001DarkNights.com for more information

FOREVER WICKED by Shayla Black
CRIMSON TWILIGHT by Heather Graham
CAPTURED IN SURRENDER by Liliana Hart
SILENT BITE: A SCANGUARDS WEDDING by Tina Folsom
DUNGEON GAMES by Lexi Blake
AZAGOTH by Larissa Ione
NEED YOU NOW by Lisa Renee Jones
SHOW ME, BABY by Cherise Sinclair
ROPED IN by Lorelei James
TEMPTED BY MIDNIGHT by Lara Adrian
THE FLAME by Christopher Rice
CARESS OF DARKNESS by Julie Kenner

Also from 1001 Dark Nights

TAME ME by J. Kenner

Discover 1001 Dark Nights Collection Two

Go to www.1001DarkNights.com for more information

WICKED WOLF by Carrie Ann Ryan
WHEN IRISH EYES ARE HAUNTING by Heather Graham
EASY WITH YOU by Kristen Proby
MASTER OF FREEDOM by Cherise Sinclair
CARESS OF PLEASURE by Julie Kenner
ADORED by Lexi Blake
HADES by Larissa Ione
RAVAGED by Elisabeth Naughton
DREAM OF YOU by Jennifer L. Armentrout
STRIPPED DOWN by Lorelei James
RAGE/KILLIAN by Alexandra Ivy/Laura Wright
DRAGON KING by Donna Grant
PURE WICKED by Shayla Black
HARD AS STEEL by Laura Kaye
STROKE OF MIDNIGHT by Lara Adrian
ALL HALLOWS EVE by Heather Graham
KISS THE FLAME by Christopher Rice
DARING HER LOVE by Melissa Foster
TEASED by Rebecca Zanetti
THE PROMISE OF SURRENDER by Liliana Hart

Also from 1001 Dark Nights

THE SURRENDER GATE By Christopher Rice
SERVICING THE TARGET By Cherise Sinclair

Discover 1001 Dark Nights Collection Three

Go to www.1001DarkNights.com for more information

HIDDEN INK by Carrie Ann Ryan
BLOOD ON THE BAYOU by Heather Graham
SEARCHING FOR MINE by Jennifer Probst
DANCE OF DESIRE by Christopher Rice
ROUGH RHYTHM by Tessa Bailey
DEVOTED by Lexi Blake
Z by Larissa Ione
FALLING UNDER YOU by Laurelin Paige
EASY FOR KEEPS by Kristen Proby
UNCHAINED by Elisabeth Naughton
HARD TO SERVE by Laura Kaye
DRAGON FEVER by Donna Grant
KAYDEN/SIMON by Alexandra Ivy/Laura Wright
STRUNG UP by Lorelei James
MIDNIGHT UNTAMED by Lara Adrian
TRICKED by Rebecca Zanetti
DIRTY WICKED by Shayla Black
THE ONLY ONE by Lauren Blakely
SWEET SURRENDER by Liliana Hart

Discover 1001 Dark Nights Collection Four

Go to www.1001DarkNights.com for more information

ROCK CHICK REAWAKENING by Kristen Ashley
ADORING INK by Carrie Ann Ryan
SWEET RIVALRY by K. Bromberg
SHADE'S LADY by Joanna Wylde
RAZR by Larissa Ione
ARRANGED by Lexi Blake
TANGLED by Rebecca Zanetti
HOLD ME by J. Kenner
SOMEHOW, SOME WAY by Jennifer Probst
TOO CLOSE TO CALL by Tessa Bailey
HUNTED by Elisabeth Naughton
EYES ON YOU by Laura Kaye
BLADE by Alexandra Ivy/Laura Wright
DRAGON BURN by Donna Grant
TRIPPED OUT by Lorelei James
STUD FINDER by Lauren Blakely
MIDNIGHT UNLEASHED by Lara Adrian
HALLOW BE THE HAUNT by Heather Graham
DIRTY FILTHY FIX by Laurelin Paige
THE BED MATE by Kendall Ryan
PRINCE ROMAN by CD Reiss
NO RESERVATIONS by Kristen Proby
DAWN OF SURRENDER by Liliana Hart

Also from 1001 Dark Nights

TEMPT ME by J. Kenner

On behalf of 1001 Dark Nights,

Liz Berry and M.J. Rose would like to thank ~

Steve Berry
Doug Scofield
Kim Guidroz
Jillian Stein
InkSlinger PR
Dan Slater
Asha Hossain
Chris Graham
Fedora Chen
Kasi Alexander
Jessica Johns
Dylan Stockton
Richard Blake
BookTrib After Dark
and Simon Lipskar